A
THOUSAND
STITCHES

A THOUSAND STITCHES

a novel

Constance O'Keefe

FITHIAN PRESS | MCKINLEYVILLE, CALIFORNIA, 2014

Published by Fithian Press
A division of Daniel and Daniel, Publishers, Inc.
Post Office Box 2790
McKinleyville, CA 95519
www.danielpublishing.com

Distributed by SCB Distributors (800) 729-6423

LIBRARY OF CONGRESS CATALOGING-IN-PUBLICATION DATA
O'Keefe, Constance.
A thousand stitches : a novel / by Constance O'Keefe.
pages cm
ISBN 978-1-56474-565-1 (pbk. : alk. paper)
1. Pilots and pilotage—Japan—History—Fiction.
2. Marriage—Fiction.
3. Reflections—Fiction.
4. Emotions—Political aspects—Fiction.
5. Autobiography—Fiction.
PS3615.O394T46 2014
813'.6—dc23
2014010787

To Isako Imamura

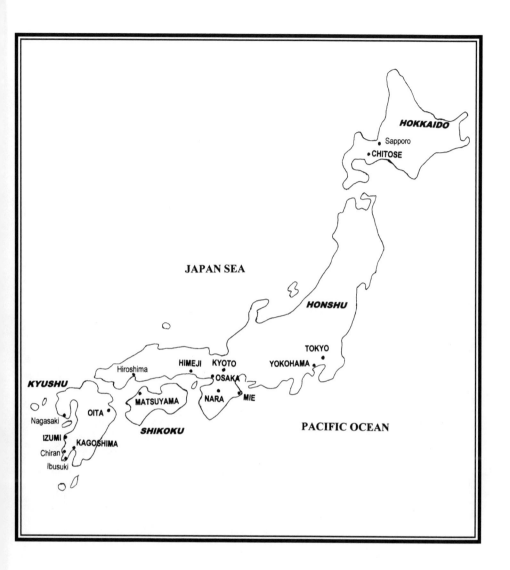

HOKKAIDO

• Sapporo
• CHITOSE

JAPAN SEA

HONSHU

TOKYO

HIMEJI   KYOTO   YOKOHAMA
Hiroshima   OSAKA

KYUSHU   MATSUYAMA   NARA   MIE

Nagasaki   OITA

SHIKOKU   PACIFIC OCEAN

IZUMI

Chiran   KAGOSHIMA

Ibusuki

Contents

Foreword

A THOUSAND STITCHES is a gift from Constance O'Keefe, the author, to Isako Imamura, the widow of Professor Shigeo Imamura (Shig). Shig and Isako had a great impact on Connie's life, beginning when she was a graduate student working with Professor Imamura at Michigan State University. After graduation, Connie obtained a teaching position in Japan thanks to Professor Imamura. Thus began her lifelong love of Japan: the country, its people, its history, its language, and its culture.

When Shig died in 1998, Isako asked Connie and two of Shig's other graduate students (Stephanie Vandrick and me) to help her see his memoir published. Isako was committed to telling Shig's story—an anti-war story of a Nisei, Japanese American, who moved with his parents from San Francisco to Japan in 1932 at the age of ten. After serving in the Imperial Japanese Navy during World War II, Shig spent his life promoting peace through international education and cultural understanding. We three quickly agreed to help Isako and began work on what we called the "Shig Project. "

In 2001, *Shig: The true story of an American Kamikaze: A memoir* by Shigeo Imamura was published. Anyone who knew Shig hears his voice in his memoir, a straightforward recollection of his experiences. About this time and with Isako's blessings, Connie began working on a fictionalized version of Shig's story—*A Thousand Stitches*. In the novel two stories are tied together by a *senninbari*, a belt of a thousand stitches made by a thousand female hands given by wives and sweethearts to Japanese men on their way to war as an amulet: one the main character's story, largely based on Shig's life, and the other a fictionalized story of his high school sweetheart who gave him a *senninbari*. Connie's work began as an extension of the Shig Project. This time, however, she was not the coordinator of the project; rather she was the sole creator.

Connie threw herself into writing the novel with the same intellect, enthusiasm, patience, and attention to detail that she gave to all her work, professional and personal. Building on her extensive knowledge of Japan and its culture and her research for the memoir, she began. A voracious reader since childhood, she read anything she could get her hands on about World War II–era Japan, about fiction writing, and topics closely and peripherally related to the content of the novel. She researched every detail, amassing books on such topics as Japanese cranes, Japanese poetry, the Zero plane, memoirs of Japanese and U.S. soldiers, stories of Japanese civilians, and World War II history books. She joined and built writing communities, in person and online.

When she was diagnosed with ovarian cancer in 2008, she had a draft of the novel and had already sent parts out to several people for comment. She continued to work on the novel as long as possible: checking details, adding and rearranging material, and polishing the prose. During times when she was feeling well, she would walk to the nearby public library several days a week to work there. She was committed to her dream of publishing the novel for Isako and telling Shig's story. She was able to complete the novel before her death on March 19, 2011. During her illness, she asked me if I would see that her novel was published. I was honored and quickly gave her my promise. We agreed that any profits from the novel would go to the Shigeo and Isako Imamura fellowships that Mrs. Imamura endowed: one at Michigan State University and the other at the University of San Francisco.

I am pleased that Connie's dream and her gift to Isako are now a reality. In her acknowledgments, Connie graciously thanks many people and notes the joy she found working on the novel and the Shig Project. I add my thanks to those who knew and supported Connie. Also I thank the many, some of whom never met Connie, who have supported and encouraged me on this journey to fulfill my promise to her. With her request asking me to see her novel published, Connie gave me a wonderful gift. I am forever grateful to her for this and much more.

Johnnie Johnson Hafernik
January 8, 2014

A
THOUSAND
STITCHES

CHAPTER 1

AKIKO

Himeji, 1999

EVERYTHING WAS READY. Tasty tidbits in small *kozara* plates covered the table. Akiko stood in the kitchen doorway, untying her apron.

Junko turned the angel around and caressed the blond hair cascading down her back. She turned her around again and touched her golden harp and sky-blue dress. She ran her finger around its hem and settled her back in place. She touched three more ornaments, a star, a basket, and a Christmas tree.

Picking the angel up again, she said, "This was always my favorite." Still fingering it, her back to Akiko, she said, "You're going to put them away after the party, aren't you?"

"Yes, after tonight," said Akiko, remembering how Sam had insisted on unpacking and arranging them in December even though he hadn't felt well. Just before the hospital. And Christmas Eve, when she left the hospital for the last time and came home to the ornaments and the emptiness.

"I'll put them away tomorrow," she said. "It's time. Time to do all the things I promised him."

Junko put the angel down and nudged it back into place, but didn't say anything more.

"Thank you for helping me start with my promises tonight," said Akiko.

WHEN the Maruyamas arrived, Akiko and Junko sat them down, mother and daughter, with Sam's colleague, Professor Inagaki, and his wife.

"Welcome to this unusual forty-ninth-day commemoration. You all know how adamant Sam was about no priests and no temple ceremonies.

Thank you for helping me do what he wanted—raising a glass in his memory. With the holiday being celebrated on Monday we'll have two full days to recover, so let's eat and drink!"

"To my brother-in-law," Junko said.

"To Imagawa-san," said Mrs. Maruyama, the professor, and his wife.

"To *Sensei*," Harumi said.

After the toast, Akiko refilled glasses. "Please try the fried chicken," she said. "His mom learned to make it in their San Francisco days, and his friend Shirley taught me when I first got to the States. He always loved it and was still asking for it in the hospital."

In response to Mrs. Maruyama's question about the cards stacked next to the ornaments, Akiko said, "The one on top arrived this morning from a former student who lives in Atlanta, where she's the president of Fullman College. Harumi, there's a typed note inside the card. Would you please read it and translate for everyone else?"

Harumi began. When she stumbled, Akiko helped.

Dear Akiko, I just learned that Sam passed away at the end of last year. He opened the world for me when I was a kid who had never before been out of Chicago. He challenged and inspired me, and gave me the courage to apply for my first job abroad. And he accepted me, as he accepted all his students, no matter who or what we were or where we were from. I only hope that someday some of my students remember me the way I know hundreds remember him— and you—because you were always there, for us as well as for him. I will never forget the first time I came to your house. I had never seen anything like your kokeshi dolls, and I had never ever eaten anything like sukiyaki. I owe him, and you, so much. Oh, I have to stop now because I'm in tears. God bless you.
Your friend, Katherine."

Mrs. Maruyama broke the silence by asking quizzically, *"kokeshi?"* Her question pulled Akiko back more than fifty years to a hot afternoon in Ukawa. The work in the fields was finished for the day. Akiko had helped her mom carry the spinach they had picked to the home of the village chief. Her mom had sent her home so she could stay and have tea and a good chat with the chief's wife.

Akiko was happy to have the house to herself. She lay on her stomach on the *tatami*, kicking her heels in the air. Her stomach wasn't full—lunch had been barley gruel and the hated grasshoppers her mom insisted she eat in order to have a bit of protein—and the work in the fields had left her hungry again. She had carefully saved a piece of the candy her dad had made for her. Her mom had sighed when Dad made the latest batch, reminding them both that they were lucky to have the local *mikan* mandarin oranges when they wanted something sweet. But Akiko still dreamed of chocolate, and indulgent Dad made her sweet potato candy whenever he could. She always made sure she saved a few pieces for special occasions. This was one.

Extravagance is the Enemy. The oft-repeated wartime motto of the radio and pompous official adults, like Principal Mochizuki, echoed in her head. She smiled at her piece of candy, set it by her right hand, and flipped the pages of the magazine. They went quickly, and she settled at her favorite page: the *kokeshi* and the pictures from the town far away in the north where the graceful, cylindrical dolls were carved. One picture of the town, two of the carver and his son, and three of the dolls. Fifteen dolls in the pictures. Each different. Each wonderful. Her favorite was the second tallest. The best. Not the most decorated. Not the most memorable face. But the best: beautiful, perfectly contained, *elegant.*

Is elegance an enemy too? She pictured herself standing in front of Principal Mochizuki. With just the right tone he would think she was stupid rather than insolent. If she could pull it off, he wouldn't be able to punish her. He would have to conclude she was a dolt rather than a disrespectful farm girl who dreamed of both extravagance *and* elegance. Akiko linked her ankles together, popped the candy into her mouth, rested her chin on her hands and gazed at the *kokeshi* in the picture as the candy began to melt.

Years later, when she first arrived in Tokyo, she found one just like that elegant favorite at an antique shop in Kanda. The *kokeshi* waited for her every night when she came home to her tiny apartment; the doll was an embodiment of her childish dreams of the exotic, and proof that she was an adult. She added another one after each month's payday, marking her time in Tokyo. The time typing and filing, smiling at the biology professors who couldn't remember her name but who were all too aware of her unfashionable country accent. The collection was warm and welcoming, the wood gleaming in the light when she threw the switch as she stepped into the *genkan*. She imagined them calling "Welcome home"; they brightened her empty room and empty nights. Until the night Sam was outside her door when she arrived home. Until the end of the week of his siege, until she said yes, until he helped her wrap and carefully position them in the new suitcases he had bought for their move to the States.

PULLING herself back together, Akiko said, "Before I went to the States, I collected them. When I was a girl, I thought those Tohoku dolls were really exotic. I got rid of them years ago. I suppose they *were* the most exotic things ever seen in our town in Ohio."

Junko proposed another toast, "To all those *gaijin* students, and to all of Sam's students here. I know my exotic sister really loves to hear from them."

"And," Akiko added, "a special toast to Harumi, Sam's last student. He would be so proud of how good her English is."

As they all raised their glasses again, Akiko remembered the last time she had seen Katherine and the other graduate students from Katherine's year at OSU. She could picture where everyone was seated in the restaurant in Japantown in San Francisco. It was already almost twenty years ago.

❀ ❀ ❀

"NO, I have no idea, tell me!" laughed Pauline.

"Have you swallowed it all?" asked Sam.

She gulped and said, "Yes, come on! I'm ready for the news."

"Did you like it?" he teased.

"Tell me!"

"Sea urchin!"

"It looks disgusting but isn't that bad," Pauline giggled.

"Did you actually taste it?" Sam asked before he went on to describe the hard work involved in harvesting sea urchins from the ocean floor and in extracting them from their spiny shells.

"Can you believe that *sushi* has become as fashionable as it has, Sam?" asked Morgan.

"Yes, it's amazing, isn't it," he responded. "That's why we have to make sure that sophisticates like Pauline are properly educated. Akiko's done her best with all those *sukiyaki* meals, but we have to make sure this generation knows more about Japan."

Everyone laughed, and Akiko looked around the large table as conversation broke into groups. Maxie and Claire were talking about whether Claire should stick with law school. Maxie's husband, Max, and Katherine were comparing their new administrative tasks, Max, the scientist, as Assistant Chair of the Biology Department at Bay Area State, and Katherine at the historically black Fullman College in the Atlanta suburbs. Pauline, Morgan, and Sam continued joking about *sushi* and Japanese cuisine.

Sam proposed another toast, "To San Francisco. Where I think my heart will always be. Akiko and I are so lucky that our visit here has coincided with Morgan's, as well as with Claire's and with Katherine's. And I'm especially happy that Pauline, Maxie, and Max have made their lives here, and that Pauline and Maxie are doing such a good job with the International English Center. It's a true pleasure to see all of you who are so dear to us from our days together at Ohio State at the same time as I get to see one of my oldest friends, Morgan, who grew up with me in Matsuyama."

Glasses were raised, and more *sake* tossed back all around. The waitress arrived to sweep the empty flasks off the table and replace them with fresh, warm ones. Sam leaned toward one, but Morgan reached it first and poured for him. "Do you think I've forgotten all my Japanese manners, my old friend?" he asked.

"No, of course not," Sam said, smiling. "I'm so glad to see you tonight. I'll think of you next week when I'm standing on the grounds of Matsuyama Castle and looking at the Inland Sea."

"Oh, Sam, I haven't been there for almost forty years. Do you remember climbing up there on my last day in Matsuyama in the summer of 1941? Everything was packed in boxes in the house, and my mother was concerned that we wouldn't get back in time to catch the train. But Dad was happy to see us go on our excursion because he had so many good memories of our hikes himself."

"Yes, I remember," said Sam, but didn't add anything before Morgan continued.

"Oh, I remember it so well. When we got back to our house, you didn't come in because you were on your way to see Michiko and didn't want to be late. That was fine, because it was sheer chaos, and Mother and Dad had said their formal goodbyes to you already."

Akiko was watching Sam and suspected that he remembered the Michiko part better than the hike with Morgan. A funny time, just before and just after the war. Memories were buried, stretched, retouched, or just crumpled up and tossed to the wind.

Sam turned and swept Katherine into his conversation with Pauline. Morgan turned to Akiko. She asked about his wife, his job as an editor in Washington, D.C., and about the trade show he was covering in San Francisco. They had moved on to talking about Sam's various job prospects in Japan and speculating what the final interviews would be like, when Morgan stopped and said, "What is that song?"

Akiko had been aware of it as she sat and chatted. She remembered the first time she had heard it, six years earlier, when she and Sam were living in San Francisco for a year, as he set up the English language program at the university where Maxie and Pauline were still teaching. She had been in Soko Hardware, just about two blocks from the restaurant where they sat now, when the song, *"Seto no Hanayome,"* had played on the store's sound system. When the proprietor had seen her stop and listen, he said, "My son just came back from three years in Japan and says that this was *the* hit of a few years ago. Very evocative, isn't it, especially if you know the Seto Inland Sea area." Akiko nodded yes and lingered a little longer to listen after she paid for her purchases.

"Isn't it something about a bride and a boat trip on the Inland Sea?" said Morgan. "My Japanese is rusty, but—"

"Yes," said Akiko, "it's the story of a young woman leaving her small island and her family, including her little brother, to travel to another island to marry."

"Ah," said Morgan.

"It's a love match," said Akiko, listening as the second verse shifted pace, the strings swelled, and the singer's voice edged toward but never quite into tremolo. It reminded Akiko of "You'll Never Walk Alone," which she had heard in a student production of *Carousel* the month before. As much as she thought it was ridiculous, she melted as Julie sang of her Billy's love beyond death and time, using the same vocal techniques

Rumiko Koyanagi was using as she sang of the small boat rounding the cape, the sunset glow, the promise of a clear day on the morrow, and the hopes of the couple for their future. The cloying sentiment was the same, the swelling of the violins the same, *"Walk on, walk on, with hope in your heart..."*—*"Don't cry, little brother, you'll be fine with Mother and Father..."*

"Sam, Sam, listen to this song," Morgan called, but by the time Sam finished what he was saying and turned to Morgan, the song was winding down: the violins faded and the sound effects—the cries of Seto sea gulls—brought it to its conclusion. "You don't know this song?" Morgan asked.

"No," said Sam. He called the waitress over. She explained that the tape would loop back to it in about an hour. When Morgan and Sam both began telling her about their childhood in Matsuyama and the many ferry trips they took across the Inland Sea, she smiled and said she'd ask the manager to reset the tape.

She was back in a few minutes and was saying, "He's agreed to reset it. He said he knows the area himself," as the tape squeaked to a stop. There was a moment of silence before "Seto Bride" began again.

Everyone listened. The manager came and stood by the big round table to listen with his customers. Morgan and Sam translated bits as the song flowed past them. Pauline asked for a complete explanation when it was over, and the two old friends did the best they could. "Akiko says it's about a love match," said Morgan.

"Claire saw the Inland Sea the year she taught in Japan," said Sam, "but for the rest of you, that treat still lies in the future. I'm so glad Akiko and I decided to go back to Japan. It's time for me to slow down. Perhaps I'll be lucky enough to end up at a university in Matsuyama again."

"It is tranquil and beautiful," said Claire. "It must have been a great area to grow up in." She looked at Akiko as Morgan and Sam nodded. Akiko caught her eye, and turned away, smiling at Morgan, and responding to his latest comment.

Please, please don't let Claire or any of the others see my panic. I think I'm keeping it off my face. Just be calm. It is time to go home. I would love to see my sisters. And he has three good possibilities for jobs. We're just as likely to end up in Tokyo or in Himeji as we are to end up back in Matsuyama.

She remembered another *sukiyaki* dinner that she had prepared when

Claire had come back from her year in Japan. Claire had described her trip to Shikoku, where she had visited Takamatsu and had climbed the steps all the way to the top of Kotohira Shrine in nearby Kotohira before traveling to Matsuyama, where she toured the city and the hot spring at Dogo.

"I'm sorry I didn't bring you anything special from Shikoku," Claire had said to Sam.

"What I want is some fresh sea bream from the Inland Sea," he replied, "and that's something you couldn't get through customs."

Claire had helped Akiko clear the dishes after that *sukiyaki* feast and had said, "Akiko, you don't seem as excited about Matsuyama as Sam does. Isn't it your hometown too?"

"Yes," she had said, "or at least sort of. I'm from a small mountain village in a remote corner of the prefecture. But I've never enjoyed the best opinion of Sam's family."

"Why, what could be the problem?" Claire had asked.

"Oh, it's a long and complicated story," said Akiko. "But I have no regrets. I was lucky enough to have a love match marriage at a time when they were virtually unknown," she said as she closed the door to the dishwasher and shook out a tea towel.

As Sam continued to talk about Matsuyama and his job prospects there and in other Japanese cities, Akiko was overwhelmed again. Sam's mother had refused to meet her on their first visit to Matsuyama as a couple on a Christmas break from Ohio. She remembered walking the short distance from the department store back to the hotel as the light faded from the afternoon sky and fat *botan yuki* peony snowflakes fell. Her packages, with presents for the children of her sisters and her friends back in Ohio, were heavy, and the snow, so unusual in Matsuyama's mild winters, stuck to sidewalks, seeped into her shoes, and soaked her coat. She sat alone in the hotel room drying out and waiting for her husband to come back. The weight of the hometown values and the social system she had defied pressed down on her.

Her proud, strong mother-in-law went to her grave having never acknowledged her second daughter-in-law. The next year, Sam's father visited Ohio. He was a pleasant elderly gentleman who enjoyed being in the States again, but was lost without his wife. Akiko had waved goodbye at the airport in Columbus. Sam went with his father to San Francisco and saw him off from there before coming back to Ohio. His father was dead before the end of the year, and Sam went alone to the funeral. When he returned to Ohio, Akiko had thought that that was the end of Matsuyama in their lives.

But Sam had grown sentimental in the past few years. He had been on a few professional visits, and Matsuyama now seemed to be number one on his list as he considered jobs in Japan.

"After I've chosen my new job and we go back to Japan at the end of the next academic year," he was saying, "we will have spent a total of eighteen years here in the States. I think that my last job in Japan will be a nice counterpart. If I'm lucky, I'll have another eighteen years—or more—to work in Japan."

Akiko smiled and thought how glad she was that she was going to stay in Tokyo with her sister while Sam went to visit Matsuyama to talk to the officials at Ehime University. *Stop fretting. You defied them—all of Matsuyama—before. You can do it again if you have to.* And right then and there she decided that if she had to go back to Matsuyama, she would do so with her head held high. Her life in the States had been a grand adventure. She could walk through any storm she had to.

❀ ❀ ❀

A MONTH later, Akiko opened the china closet and took out the parcel from the crematorium. She sat at the table and slowly untied the white *furoshiki.* The box inside had a white paper wrapper with religious symbols. She opened it, knowing that inside the drawstring bag she would see exactly what she didn't want to see, what she had seen the day she brought it home. She told herself she had to do what he wanted, had to get it done by his birthday. And she had to have this taken care of before she could deal with the manuscript.

She went to the kitchen for the extra *suribachi* and *surikogi* mortar and pestle still in their box from the pottery shop. She placed them on the dining room table, remembering the drinking party and how happy it had made her to hear Harumi read Katherine's letter. She went back to the kitchen and boiled water for *genmaicha,* her favorite tea, and told herself she had to get to work.

Her hand slipped. She applied more pressure, leaning all her weight into it, but the entire bowl slipped from her grasp. She thought she had broken it but then realized the bowl was fine; it was her finger that was hurt. The scrape bled on the chunk of bone as she picked it up from the floor and put it back in the box. When her hands stopped shaking, she went to the phone.

"*Ne-san*, I started that job I told you about when you were here. I can't do it."

"I'll take the next train. Wait at your counter," was Junko's only response before she hung up.

AT two-thirty Junko came through the ticket barrier. Looking determined as usual, she marched up to the tourist information counter where Akiko was talking with Ichikawa-san. Akiko introduced her big sister and explained that she had come to visit from Osaka.

As they walked away from the counter, Junko said, "Taxi. I'm carrying too much for the bus." Along the way, the taxi swung by the Castle, and Junko said, "Can't say that I mind seeing the White Heron when I come here. It really is beautiful and looks great in the fine weather." When they pulled into the entrance to Akiko's condo, Junko said, "Oh, little sister, I have news. I read my newspaper on the train. Shotaro Miyazawa has died. Big funeral tomorrow. I guess it's a major event for corporate Osaka."

"So Michiko's a widow now too," Akiko said.

Junko slipped out of her shoes in the *genkan* and began pulling things out of her shopping bag. "Here's the article from the Osaka paper. And here are some Kobe cakes. They sell them in the department store in Osaka Station now. It's a plot to make me even fatter. And here's a new *suribachi* and *surikogi*. I decided that's probably the best way to do our job."

"I have an extra set too. Maybe we can finish quickly."

THEY had tea and ate some of the Kobe cakes before they began. They picked big chunks of bone from the box with new chopsticks. "Don't think," Junko said, and she went first. They took turns wrapping the large chunks in the white *furoshiki* and smashing them with a hammer. Then they began grinding.

I'm making my husband dust, Akiko thought. Was this the hand I held as he lay dying? The hand he wrote me letters with? The hand that held mine as the plane landed at Narita? *So what if it's an unseemly public display of affection?* She could hear him whispering in her ear.

When Akiko stopped grinding, Junko looked up and saw tears brimming in her sister's eyes. She chose that moment to launch an old family favorite. "Remember the time Farmer Kiriyama got drunk and almost drowned in the rice paddy?" Akiko shook her head, trying to will the tears away. Junko kept grinding and continued, spinning the story out, embellishing and elaborating the saga of the Kiriyamas, as tears spilled down her sister's face.

Slowly, Akiko was drawn into the details of the misadventures of their childhood neighbors and recovered enough to join in, "No, you're not remembering it right. The father only lost *one* of the boys in the train station in Matsuyama, not both of them."

AS the afternoon light was fading, Akiko's hand slipped again and again a piece of bone landed on the floor. As they crawled about looking for it, Junko grumbled about how stubborn her brother-in-law always had been and how he was *still* being difficult. Junko found the bone under a corner of the rug. She held it up and sat back on her heels. "Now how do I get my own old bones up off this damn floor?" They laughed and helped each other up. When they were back in their chairs, Akiko's laughter turned to tears. As Akiko cried, Junko made more tea. By the time they finished the tea, Akiko had recovered and they began grinding again. They worked in silence until nine o'clock.

Junko said, "Okay, now we have ashes—or at least something more like powder than chunks. What about the *suribachi* and *surikogi?*"

"Put the ashes in here, and give it to me. And put both of the *suribachi* and *surikogi* in the box your set came in, and wrap the box in this," Akiko said, reaching for a faded indigo *furoshiki* from the drawer below the shelves of the china closet.

After Junko poured the ashes into the drawstring bag, Akiko stood, wrapped the box in the white *furoshiki* from the crematorium, and returned the ashes to the china closet. She then reached up to the top shelf and took out two crystal tumblers and Sam's single-malt scotch. "This is not a beer occasion."

As Akiko was putting the tumblers and the scotch on the table, Junko, struggling with the box said, "It won't work. The two sets are too big." Akiko took the two *suribachi* from her sister, wrapped them quickly in the indigo *furoshiki* and smashed them with two sharp slams of the hammer. She shook the pieces out of the *furoshiki* into the box and wrapped the box in the indigo cloth. "Please pour," she said to her sister.

❀ ❀ ❀

TWO DAYS later Akiko was due at her volunteer job at the tourist information office's kiosk. She left very early, carrying the indigo *furoshiki*, and got off the bus at the Castle, several stops before the train station. The cherry petals had just fallen from the trees. She walked through the pink carpet on the path from the Castle keep to the garden, enjoying the tattered scraps that were all that remained of the beauty of the blossoms. She regretted not seeing them the week before in full flower, but knew that she wouldn't have been able to bear the noisy, drunken crowds. She went slowly from the garden out to the street and decided to walk down *Otemae-dori* to the station, even though she knew it would take her twice as long as it should. She had lunch at a coffee shop a block from the station, grateful to sit and rest her tired feet and aching knees. She arrived at the kiosk by one.

ICHIKAWA-SAN was struggling with a tall blond couple who had come from the Castle and wanted to know how to get to Kyoto and climb Mt. Hiei by the end of the day. When Ichikawa-san saw Akiko, she stammered, "Ah, here is Mrs. Imagawa. She lived in America. She can help you."

The young Germans began telling her what they wanted in their almost perfect but heavily accented English. Akiko smiled and reached for a train schedule as she walked into the kiosk, where she slipped the *furoshiki* under the counter, out of sight. After she finished explaining the schedules, she and Ichikawa-san stood and waved goodbye. "I'm surprised they didn't want to see Kyoto and climb *Mt. Fuji* by the end of the day," said Akiko, with her public smile still in place.

Ichikawa-san was still giggling when a group of businessmen entered the station. They were coming from the White Heron Grand, Himeji's best hotel, across the street. The three Japanese hosts had a tall, beleaguered-looking American with them. Akiko guessed that he had been

treated to a fancy lunch of unfamiliar foods and forced to drink more than he was used to in the middle of the day. Her guesses were confirmed when one of the group urged the others towards the information counter saying, "Come on, we can't let Samueruson-san leave Himeji without seeing the most beautiful castle in Japan," repeating this in broken English.

Samuelson, thinking no one heard him, muttered, "But I already *saw* it—from the train."

"Do you have anything in English?" the youngest of the Japanese demanded.

Akiko told him she did but made sure she handed the English language pamphlet directly to the American, telling him, "It's called the White Heron Castle, and it really is considered the most beautiful castle in Japan. We Japanese like to make lists and rankings of things. This one won the most beautiful castle category. Everybody agrees."

"Oh, *thank you.* This day has been a bit much. We were on our way to Osaka, but my hosts decided we had to get off the train here for lunch."

"Where are you coming from?"

"We were visiting a fish farm site on the other side of the Inland Sea. Outside Matsu—Oh, I forget."

"Well, it was probably either Takamatsu or Matsuyama."

"The first."

"Good luck getting to Osaka."

"Thanks. I think I'll be okay if I don't have to drink any more."

"You'll be fine, and the Castle really is lovely. I bet they pile you in a taxi and give you the grand tour before you catch the train again."

"Thanks. Did you live in the States?"

"Yes, Columbus and San Francisco."

"I'm Pete Samuelson. I'm from Cleveland."

"Say hello to Ohio for me. My sister loves the Good Morning Ohio joke that I'm sure you've heard from this group."

Samuelson laughed, "*Oh, yes!* I'm so glad we met you."

Impatient with all the English, the oldest of the three Japanese businessmen asked Akiko if they had time to see the Castle and still make the three-o'clock *Shinkansen* bullet train to Osaka. When she answered affirmatively, they hauled Samuelson out into the taxi line and folded him into the front seat of a cab, the three of them climbing into the back.

When they were gone, Ichikawa-san said, "It was exhausting just watching them and trying to answer their questions. I hope that *gaijin* is okay."

Akiko laughed, "He'll have great stories to tell when he gets home."

ON her way home Akiko got off the bus at the Castle, entered the garden, and went straight to the far corner, where a bamboo screen hid equipment. She found the gardener there, as she thought she would.

"Imagawa-san, can I help you?" he asked. "Did one of your foreign tourists lose something?"

"No, Higuchi-san, I have a favor to ask." Akiko nodded in the direction of the branches and twigs stacked against the back wall of his work area. "Now that the cherry blossoms are gone, and we have fewer visitors, I know you'll be burning everything from your spring pruning. Would you please add this to the fire?"

"Of course, Imagawa-san. Is there anything else I can do?" he said, accepting the *furoshiki* with both hands.

"No, but thank you. I truly appreciate it." Akiko smiled with gratitude and turned to leave. As she walked away, she made herself think only about Higuchi-san, and how hard he worked to keep the cherry trees healthy and blossoming spectacularly far into advanced old age. She retraced her steps through the beautiful complex passages that were the result of his meticulous work, left the Castle grounds, and headed for the bus stop.

CHAPTER 2

GENTARO

Berkeley, 1999

THE SECOND DAY she brought the photograph and they sat together at lunch looking at it. The day before all he could do was look at her scars—one cut across the bottom of her chin like an upside-down scimitar and the other slashed from the forehead across her right eyebrow and past her eye to her cheekbone. It had taken him a while to hear what she was saying. Finally, he realized that she was laying claim to him, reminding him of the Peters School in Pacific Heights.

Now, relaxed on the grass, they were looking at their childhood. "See, Gen, you're standing behind me," said Lynn.

"I remember the day this was taken," he said. "My dad had been called out to the hospital before dawn, and I gave my mom a really hard time about the shirt she wanted me to wear. But now, looking at the photo, I don't know which of us won the argument. I don't know if the shirt I'm wearing is the one I loved or the one she wanted me to wear. It was so important at the time, and now I can't remember."

"And can you believe that one little girl could own as many purple and pink items of clothing? Look at how I had dressed myself. My mom was too lenient!"

As he fingered the photo, Gen remembered more. How the photographer was pleased by the sunlight that had flooded the schoolyard when the clouds unexpectedly parted. "Now," he had said, "we have our chance, even if just for a moment. Smile everyone."

The kids stood straight and smiled, and then laughed along with their teacher when the photographer added, "That means you too, Mrs. Arthurson."

Gen had been keenly aware that he had been standing behind Lynn, looking down at her blond hair spread out below him. He had even reached out quickly to touch the curls at the back of her head. Joey Trista standing beside him hadn't noticed, and Lynn hadn't felt it, but, both guilty and pleased with himself that he had been so bold, Gen had been delighted to know that her hair was as soft to the touch as it looked. His hand tingled as he looked at her now; the same soft curls shone around her, lit by the sun behind her.

They spent the rest of their time that day sketching the basics of the missing years; they filled in the details slowly in the days that followed.

Her brother Bobby had been driving on the bright, sunny winter afternoon of the accident and had escaped injury. "He says he doesn't feel guilty, and it absolutely was the other driver's fault," said Lynn. "But he decided during the summer after the accident to go to Berkeley rather than Cornell. I think he's still reassuring himself that I really am okay. He came to the hospital every day, helped Mom nurse me once I got home, and helped me get through the physio. But even with everything that happened, it really wasn't a bad year. I learned a lot about how wonderful it is to be alive and to know that you're really loved. And I don't mind being a high school senior a year late. My friends didn't know what to do with me last year."

Gen told her about the International School in Yokohama and how he had ended up there after a half year at his local school in Kamakura proved to everyone that he didn't fit in after four years in San Francisco. And he explained the idea of *ronin*—masterless *samurai*—and how he was one because he had failed his entrance exams.

"It happens all the time in Japan. And with my background it was no big surprise. The usual thing is to just postpone going to university for a year."

"Bobby says it's called a gap year in England."

"I guess," he said. "But *ronin* aren't supposed to leave a gap. They're supposed to spend the year cramming."

"Gen, do Berkeley High classes that are far too easy for you count?"

"Probably not," he laughed. "But coming back here was the best thing I've done this year."

AFTER that second day, they sat outside every day, sharing their lunches. Lynn brought salads with ingredients from her mother's garden and

Gen brought rice balls. He and Yuko, his Japanese-American host mother, made them in the morning for Yuko's husband, Dave, and for each of the three young kids, as well as for themselves. Yuko was determined to train him so he could astonish his own mother when he went home. Dave laughed the first morning he found his wife and Gen in the kitchen patting the balls into shape. "Now that I know you want to learn how to cook, Gen, I'll get my mom to teach you how to make rugguleh when she comes to visit at Christmas."

Gen and Lynn made a game of guessing about the lunches every day. He was eager for figs, kiwi, and avocado, and she wanted rice balls with black sesame seeds or *shiso* leaves. She claimed she was conducting an experiment to determine if she preferred the *shiso* fresh or dried.

One day when she teased him about his *ronin* status, he told her the story of the Forty-Seven Masterless *Samurai,* trying to explain that every school child in Japan knew the story. Lynn was lying on the grass and had started out laughing when he began the story but fell silent as he described the stalwart dedication of the *samurai* as they planned to avenge their lord and told of the snowy night, when, having waited patiently for more than a year, they were finally able to achieve their goal, and how, having finally done so, their own lives came to an end.

"But your story will have a happy ending, Gen," she said, rolling over and holding his gaze with her wide green eyes. "You will pass the exams, and after school in Japan you'll come here, just as your dad did, and work at UCSF. It's your fate. You have all of your dad's connections, and mine. Remember, I know lots of doctors at the hospital too."

Sitting in the weak autumn sun and listening to Lynn, Gen decided that he wouldn't go back to Japan at the end of the semester. He would stay the entire school year and then go back, take his time, cram as much as he had to, and take the exams again at the beginning of the year after next.

Lynn started gathering their things. As he moved to help her, he said, "Yes, that's what I'll do." She was kneeling on the grass, pushing lunch boxes into her knapsack. She turned and smiled at him, but didn't say anything.

He was surprised at how calm and confident he felt, happy that he was able, finally, to let the burden he had felt since he failed the exams just slide off him. Her smile invited a response, but he couldn't summon any words, and as he stood with dirty napkins in his hand, Gen thought they would never be sufficient for the task of describing how he felt.

Lynn started through the trees and across the school's lawn. He trailed behind her. As the dappled sun fell on her, her light hair glowed and faded, glowed and faded.

When she turned to see if he was still behind her, he shuddered. All he wanted to do was touch her. His second-grade longing for the girl with the beautiful hair was still there, but now desire was all through him, in his very marrow, and spreading up and over the surface of who he was. He wanted the young woman before him in a way he had never before wanted anyone or anything. This second revelation chilled him, sobered him, and brought him to a halt. Yes, he thought, words are far too small and shabby for this.

"We'll be late, Gen, if you don't get a move on," she said, her voice low. She turned away from him again and took a few more slow steps through the sun, the shade, the sun, the shade.

When he fell into step beside her, she was no longer smiling. She looked at him fully, inviting and accepting what he felt as he looked at her. What she had to say was just a simple statement of fact. "Yes," she said, "we do belong together."

AT the end of September, Lynn proposed the trip to Point Reyes. "It's the best time of the year. It'll be sunny, not the usual fog."

Gen thought he remembered a trip to Point Reyes years before when one of his father's colleagues from the hospital in Yokohama came for a visit, but Lynn told him they weren't going to the beach with the lighthouse and promised him the hike she had in mind would be special. They chose the day, a weekday in mid-October when they would be free, thanks to a teachers' conference.

GEN awoke very early that Tuesday morning. He went down the dark stairs and headed to the back of the house. He had discovered the early morning magic of the kitchen his first week with Dave and Yuko, when he was still jet lagged. The day Yuko found him there they had agreed that the morning light was special, and their lunch-making ritual dated from that sunny morning.

Gen didn't know if Yuko also knew how special it was to watch the room fill up with light as the dark of the night and the ambiguous shadows of the early dawn receded. Once or twice he had wondered if she had left him alone with the growing light, waiting until the room was new-day bright before she walked in. He loved being in the midst of the change; it was calm and dramatic all at once. Change that launched the day and promised the future. It began gently, with the faintest of light, and ended gleaming and glorious.

He sat at the table, witnessing it again. The first light slanted across the room from the east window, catching the faucets and making them shine. It inched up and set aglow the flowerpot, the *raku* tea bowl, and the ceramic bird on the windowsill above the sink.

By the time Yuko stepped into the kitchen, the sun had swept through the room. The light was on the edge of ordinary: the red bowl filled with shining green apples had just finished blazing and its radiance was slipping away into the unseen sheen of everyday.

"Good morning, Gen. I think something special for today. You are here to help, aren't you?"

LYNN drove, navigating I-580 with confidence. After they crossed the Richmond-San Rafael Bridge, they passed the grim bulk of San Quentin, swung along leafy Sir Francis Drake Boulevard, and swept up and over the pass to the forests and hilly grasslands of West Marin. Gen read off the names, hesitating over some of them: Tocaloma, Olema, Bolinas. Lynn explained that the Miwok Indians had lived in the area, long before the Spanish arrived. The names were just about all that was left of the Miwok, layered in with all the saint names the Spanish left behind. "Actually," Lynn said, "some of those Miwok names sound Japanese to me."

Gen rolled them around on his tongue and said, "Well, maybe Olema. It could be a Japanese name, but it would come out as O-ri-ma." As they drove on and the deserted, narrow two-lane highway crossed wide pastures, he continued, "I like the idea of the Indians walking here. Now that we're away from the city, you can begin to imagine it."

The road abruptly turned to gravel. A plume of dust trailed behind them as they arrived at the Palomarin Trail Head parking lot. Lynn chose a space in the shade at its edge. Gen got out, stretched, and breathed in the sharp, clean air and the tang of the ocean. He smiled at her across the top of the car. "I'm ready," he said. "Bring on the adventure."

They walked across the parking lot. "Alamere Falls Trail," Gen read on the sign. "Four miles. Shouldn't be bad."

"We'll see," she said, as she climbed the steps up to the trail itself. "Bobby has brought me here before, but we've never gone all the way because of the fog. It should be good today, and most of the trail is not too hard."

At the top of the stairs, they started on the trail, through a fragrant grove of eucalyptus. Just past the trees, they brushed against bushes with perfect, waxy white berries. When Gen stopped to take a picture, Lynn laughed, and said that this was just the first of many beautiful things to photograph.

In what seemed like just a few more steps, the trail emerged from the woods and they were on a ridge above cliffs; the ocean rose up to meet them.

"Gen, look at this. The sun is shining for us, and so is the ocean," she said, smiling. They stood next to each other, feeling the breeze on their faces, delighting in the sky and the ocean. The beautiful wide Pacific lay before them, its stripes of colors merging to the blue that met the horizon.

Gen gazed at the shining expanse, aware that he was a tiny thing at the edge of great power. *Vast, but not endless. Far away on its other side is the other half of my life. I will, I will make the two parts come together and stay together.*

The trail was easy going. When Gen said so, Lynn told him again, "We'll see." After about twenty minutes, two groups coming the other way passed them, everyone smiling with the shared pleasure of a perfect sunny day. Soon afterward, they reached a small, deep lake surrounded by high, forested banks, its ripples shining in the sunlight. Gen stopped and stood still. The blue waters are so inviting, he thought, drinking it in. He imagined the Miwok swimming here and wished he had brought a bathing suit.

But Lynn had no interest in dawdling. "Let's go," she said. "We have a lot more to see." They descended a bit from the dense green around the lake, and the trail again approached the coast. The day was so clear and bright that Gen could see the hook of Point Reyes extending into the ocean to the north and west, with the lighthouse at its tip. The trail slipped back into the woods. After about another half hour they came to

Pelican Lake, where the ocean was again visible beyond the quiet blue waters.

For the rest of the hike, the sound of the ocean accompanied them through the quiet of the woods. They inhaled the heady combination of the smells of the salt water and the Douglas firs. Lynn commented on the plants and flowers along the way; Gen snapped more photos. They found a perfect specimen of foxglove. Gen's picture captured the dramatic contrast of the purple markings inside the delicate white of the bell-shaped flower.

Gen put his camera away and grumbled good-naturedly as the incline of the trail increased, and Lynn once again said she thought great things were in store for them. "We're now farther along than Bobby and I were ever able to go," she said. "The best really should be ahead of us."

They found their reward for the climb when the trail turned and again emerged from the woods. They stood high on a cliff with the Pacific spread out before them and a series of falls cascading below them, the last ending on the beach far below that was dotted with tide pools. Once they caught their breath, they stood in silence and looked and looked.

"Lynn, you were right," was all Gen could manage.

"Yes, it is special, isn't it?" she replied, and stepped forward to stand beside him. She shook off the weight of the beauty before them, and laughed as she caught his eye. "And now the fun begins. We have to get ourselves down to the beach."

They began in good order, stepping carefully sideways down the steep trail. As the sandy soil gave way to loose gravel, they both began to slip. They paused when they reached the foot of the first falls and looked up at the flow of the water in the sunlight. They felt the drops blown into their faces by the ocean breeze and listened: the water fell straight and swift, and as it landed, splashed in a pool. Gathering itself for a brief, still moment, it rushed off to take the next fall.

When they started off again, descending parallel to the second of the falls, Gen slipped and lost his footing. He picked himself up and started again, slowly, crabwise, making it about twenty feet before he fell again. He gave up after a few more unsuccessful tries, and bumped along scrabbling downward with his hands, bouncing his rear end on the path. He could hear Lynn behind him, laughing as she managed to stay upright for a bit longer, and then laughing even more as she joined him.

"Gen, we may not be graceful, but we're getting there," she called.

"And at least we're closer to the falls. We're no longer creatures of the high ground, looking down on them. We're with them; we're embracing them."

When they reached the beach, they staggered to their feet, squaring their knapsacks on their backs as they looked up at the last of the falls, and taking in the spectacle of the whole series stepping their way to the beach.

"Amazing," said Gen.

"As I promised you," she said.

They moved across the beach, from wet to dry sand and then back to wet again as they skirted the tide pools. At one of the largest Lynn took his hand and walked him to the edge. She kept her hand in his even as they squatted to look more closely.

"Look," she said, "it's a chiton," and proceeded to point out the shapes of the mollusk's eight shells hidden below its outer skin. She explained how the creature moves and told Gen that the ones along the Pacific coast, like this gumboot chiton, were the largest of all the chitons. "And the Miwok probably ate them too."

When Gen said he was impressed that she knew all of these details, she said, "Well, people think Bobby is just a computer geek, but he knows a lot about nature. He's made sure I know at least a little about our flora and fauna. And you have to admit, Gen, that he was right about this hike. Even if the last bit was difficult, this is the most wonderful place. We have the beach entirely to ourselves."

"And, look," she continued, her eyes fastened again on the tide pool, "there's a little limpet just near the chiton."

As she leaned over and pointed, Gen lost his balance; their hands fell apart and he dropped to one of his knees to steady himself. When he got up, he took out his camera and snapped away, capturing the details of the intricate world in the tide pool.

They retreated up the beach to where the sand was dry, spread out a faded Mexican tablecloth Lynn pulled from her knapsack, and got out their lunches.

"What did you and Yuko come up with this morning, Gen-chan?" Lynn said, trying out the affectionate suffix she had heard Yuko use that morning when she walked Gen to the car and wished them both a good day.

"You'll have to see, but I think you'll like it."

"You too," she said. She pulled figs, carefully packed in a plastic lunch box, from her pack, and Gen unwrapped rice balls with centers of fresh chopped *shiso* and *umeboshi*, pickled plum paste.

"And," Lynn said triumphantly, "mint chocolate cookies along with oranges for desert. We'll need the energy for the climb back up to the trail."

WHEN they finally crested the slope and were within sight of the trail again, they met a group of six who were debating whether the trip to the beach could be done, and if it would be worth it. Lynn and Gen laughed as they assured them that it was worth it.

"But," she said, "you shouldn't try it if your dignity is really important to you. We promise you you'll be in awkward positions on the way down."

As Gen and Lynn tightened each other's knapsacks, they witnessed the end of the debate and then the plunge of each member of the group, one after another, down the trail. It wasn't long before the shouts and laughter from below floated back up to the trail. "We told them that dignity would go," he said, as they turned and began the hike back.

They didn't stop until they had passed Pelican Lake and were again on the shore of the first lake they had encountered that morning. "Now you'll see why I hustled you along," Lynn said. "I wanted to get back here while it was still light." She knelt down and pulled a towel out of her knapsack. She stood up quickly and had stepped out of her pants, pulled her shirt over her head, and dived into the lake before Gen had really registered that she was wearing a bathing suit under her clothes.

"Gen," she called when she surfaced a third of the way across the lake, "you didn't happen to wear a bathing suit, did you?"

"No, was I supposed to?"

"No, I did just in case. I wasn't sure it would be sunny, and I wasn't sure we'd have time. I'd suggest skinny-dipping, but it really is cold in here. Glorious, but cold."

She took a few strokes on her back. "I have to keep moving or I'll freeze. I won't be able to last much more than a few minutes longer."

As she predicted, it wasn't long before she climbed out of the lake and balanced herself on a large flat stone. He handed over her towel, noticing another long scar that snaked around the thigh of her right leg, longer and deeper than the ones on her face. After she had rubbed herself dry, she wrapped a sarong around her legs and stretched, reaching toward the sky as she laughed with sheer joy at where she was and what she had done. "The sun is so beautiful, and it feels great after being in the water."

With a few graceful steps she moved to where she had left her knapsack. She pulled her camera out and handed it over to him before moving back to the stone.

"Take my picture," she said, tilting her chin up and smiling at Gen.

He held her image in the viewfinder for a moment. He was silent, and she stood patient and content, waiting for him. As he clicked the shutter, he realized that this is how he would always remember her, fearless and beautiful. How she would fill his thoughts, steady his resolve, and rule his heart. Lynn, his Lynn.

CHAPTER 3

MICHIKO

Nara, 2000

AKIKO WAS WINDED by the walk from the bus stop. As she stood in the *genkan* catching her breath, Michiko observed the walking shoes, the characterless black pants, the turtleneck, and the long dull red vest straining over an ample middle. Akiko struggled out of her shoes, and as she stepped slowly up into the room, Michiko realized that her guest was plagued by arthritis. The much-gossiped-about hussy had bad knees. Despite the decade that separated them, she too was an old woman.

As soon as she had opened the door, Michiko regretted her dress and make-up. As Akiko presented her *omiyage*, obviously a fancy sweet, Michiko decided there would be no tea in the *tatami* room. "Let's sit in the dining room," she said as she led the way to the back of the house. "Even though it's too chilly to open the windows, the sliding screens are open in the *tatami* room, and we can see out to the garden from the dining room table."

Michiko brought tea and slices of cake to the table. The vernal equinox holiday would be in two days. The garden was wet from the morning's rain and the sky still gray, but the buds on the weeping cherry promised spring. A single branch of forsythia was arranged with pussy willow in a vase in the *tokonoma*, and the scroll hanging above it had a Soseki quote and brush strokes that suggested a cat. More yellow branches were a bright blur in the neighbor's garden.

Akiko kept a hand-quilted *furoshiki* in her lap. Whatever was wrapped in it was neither large nor heavy. Michiko wondered why Akiko had used one of the old-fashioned carrying cloths for something that could have fit in her purse. When she admired the *furoshiki*, Akiko smiled and said, "Oh, yes, my sister Junko made this. She's become quite interested in these old *sashiko* patterns in the last few years"; but as she spoke Akiko tightened her hold; the *furoshiki* remained in her lap.

Akiko picked up her tea cup, and Michiko said, "I hope you like the cake. I have to confess that I used the event of your visit to buy my favorite."

Akiko looked at her plate and smiled. "*Yuzu?*" she asked. "I love it too. The house I grew up in Ukawa was surrounded by *mikan* groves. This taste reminds me of home. I wonder if people who grew up in To-hoku or Hokkaido feel about citrus fruits the way we did in Shikoku."

"Or Kyushu," said Michiko.

The thought of Kyushu reminded Michiko of a family trip to Ka-goshima: the lava fields, Shotaro luxuriating in the warmth of the black sand baths, and Tetsutaro eating *bonton ame* and saying, "Mama, I like these funny citrus candies. It's fun to eat the wrapping. How does it disappear?" And then she was back on *Okaido*, with Sam, headed for the Castle to watch the sunset and laughing about the *bonton ame* she had found on a dusty high shelf in the storeroom behind the shop. She remembered the sensations as the candy melted in her mouth and the last of the sunlight faded from the summer sky.

"We're both Ehime girls," said Akiko. "It's embarrassing, but what I brought is a *yuzu* cake too. Actually, the exact same one. I'm sorry."

"Not at all. You now know I'll enjoy it as much as you do. I'm an-other Ehime girl."

They laughed, and as their laughter died away, the moment was gone. They were no longer Ehime girls; they were old ladies, widows. They started again, proceeding slowly, with full formality and careful po-liteness. Michiko accepted Akiko's condolences and answered questions about her son, her daughter-in-law, her grandson. After a pause, it was she who mentioned Sam's name. She offered Akiko condolences, saying she was sure there must have been a number of celebrations of the life of such a distinguished teacher. Akiko appeared eager to take up this theme and recounted stories about events in Himeji, Atsugi, and San Francisco. She talked about Sam's students and Sam's students' students. She talked about a *gaijin* speaking Japanese at the memorial in Atsugi, about the cer-emony to hang a portrait in the college in Himeji, and how she suspected her husband's colleagues had drunk themselves silly after she had been seen safely off in a taxi. And then she talked about the Japanese, Chinese,

Egyptian, Colombian, Brazilian, Saudi, German, and Swiss students all giving speeches in English in San Francisco, in a chilly room at the top of a tower with a sweeping view of the City, the Bay, and its bridges. She pulled photos from her purse. Michiko, dutifully polite, leaned forward to look. The photos showed earnest youngsters grinning out of their black, brown, tan, and deathly pale faces. Middle-aged, clumsy-looking teachers appeared at the ends of rows, all of them too fat, too tall, or none-too-well groomed.

Akiko stopped when she was about half way through the stack of photos. She reached for the envelope to put them away, but Michiko pointed to the one that was now on top—an off-center photo with a black-sleeved arm in the lower right hand corner and wilted flowers floating in choppy green water. "Wait," she said. "Tell me about this one, please."

Akiko took a deep breath, sipped her tea, and said, "I wish I still smoked."

"Good God, so do I, but there's a limit to the foolishness we're allowed now, isn't there?"

"He wanted his ashes scattered in San Francisco Bay. Do you know that American song about leaving your heart in San Francisco?" She hummed a bit before she continued, "Well, I decided to do it. We did nothing at the temple. He always said he didn't want it, didn't want any priests. So Junko, our neighbors, and some of his colleagues helped me celebrate. On the forty-ninth day commemoration, I decided to do what he wanted about San Francisco.

"Evidently, having their ashes scattered in San Francisco Bay is something many Americans want to do. So Sam's wish wasn't unique, but I quickly found that there were a lot of rules and restrictions. I was lucky because one of his former students now does environmental work and arranged all the licenses.

"Junko went with me—there she is in this picture—and my neighbor Harumi. Sam used to joke that she was his last student. She's using the English he taught her in medical school in Australia now."

Michiko examined another photo of a small group on a boat—Junko, an older, dour version of Akiko, Harumi, young, slim, and stylish, and a small group of some of the same foreigners from the other photos.

"Junko has been such a help to me. I don't think I could have gotten on a plane with my husband's ashes in a shopping bag if I hadn't had my sister with me. And without her I couldn't have let him go, have left him there, knowing I'd have to come back here to be alone."

The silence between them filled with the sounds of birds in the garden, a scolding squirrel, laughter of children on their way home from school, and the faint resonance of a temple bell. Michiko said, "I still think of *kaki kueba* almost every time I hear that bell," and the two of them recited Shiki's words aloud together: *Kaki kueba / Kane ga naru nari / Horyuji.* As I bite into a persimmon / A bell begins to ring / Horyuji.

As they finished, Ehime girls again, Akiko gathered up the photos and tucked them into her purse. "I shouldn't have been so melodramatic. I'm actually quite happy I was able to make the gesture he wanted. And I've asked his former students in San Francisco, the ones in those pictures— they're teachers themselves now—to help get his memoir published. It's just a manuscript in English at this point, but I know they'll get it done."

"He would have appreciated his wife making sure he had exactly the funeral he wanted and making sure he ended up where he thought he left his heart," Michiko said with a smile. She used the word *okusan*, giving Akiko the proper, formal, and honorific title for wife and thus fully acknowledging her status. When Michiko finished speaking, they fell silent again.

Finally, looking down at the *furoshiki* rather than at her hostess, Akiko said, "You know, Michiko, he always loved you—until the very end." She looked up and held out the *furoshiki*. "That's why I brought this for you. I found it in his bottom desk drawer. Take it. Please."

Michiko reached across the table. When she had the *furoshiki* in front of her, Akiko said, "It's not just another *omiyage*. Don't put it aside. This is why I invited myself today. This I want you to open." Michiko unfolded the *furoshiki* slowly, and the silence came again. This time it was deep and long, the silence of loss, regret, and history. Around them the ancient capital grew quiet in the deepening shadows. Without another word, Akiko rose from the table and walked back to the *genkan*. After she had put on her shoes, she stood with her back to the room and said, "I must get going. If I don't hurry, I'll miss the train back to Kyoto and then won't be able to catch the express that will get me home. Thank you so much for your hospitality."

As she put her hand on the doorknob, she turned back. Michiko was kneeling and bowing at the edge of the *genkan*, whispering her thanks. "*Samazama*," Akiko said. "*Samazama*," answered the other Ehime girl. They didn't need the rest of the words. Michiko remained kneeling in place long after the lock clicked into place, until all the light faded out of the afternoon, until her own knees ached.

ALMOST FIVE months later, Michiko again sat at the dining room table, surprised that the radio reports on the anniversary of the end of the war had so washed her in memories and melancholy that she again had the *furoshiki* in front of her. She told herself that the package that had arrived from Himeji the week before was another reason for what she was doing. The thick manuscript Akiko had mailed was nearby, on a shelf in the sideboard.

She was dressed as she preferred: a loosely cut white shirt over slim black slacks. With the veranda windows open, the obliterating heat of the day extended inside and filled the house. What wasn't occupied by the heat was filled with the swelling and ebbing cries of cicadas. Michiko had a glass of icy *mugicha* at her right hand. She moved slowly, as the heat and the noise commanded. Junko's tiny white stitches made an impressive, intricate pattern and a strong contrast with the indigo cloth of the *furoshiki*. Michiko ran her fingers over the pattern, took a sip of the cool tea, and then sat still for a full minute before she untied the *furoshiki*. She slid the contents out and put the carrying cloth aside. Then she unfolded the *senninbari* and spread it out over the table.

She smoothed the cloth to its full length, and touched the red stitches. As she thought of the lonely days in front of the train station and all those who had helped her by adding a stitch, *samazama* again came to mind. *Samazama*, she said to herself, and then recited the words of Basho's famous poem: *Samazama no / Koto omoidasu / Sakura kana*. So many things / Are brought to mind by / Cherry blossoms.
Michiko continued to finger the stitches and thought of all the years, all of her memories, and how different Akiko's must be. Falling under the spell of the cloth spread before her, she thought of all the lost cherry blossoms of the Imperial Navy. When she shook the memories away, she walked across the room to the telephone and punched in her son's number in Kamakura.

"Mariko, I hope you're well. I've been thinking of you because I know you're interested in textile arts. I have a nice *furoshiki* I think you'll like—it's white *sashiko* stitching on a piece of deep dark Matsuyama-area indigo. But I'm really calling to ask how Gen-chan is doing and tell you about an idea I have for our *ronin*."

CHAPTER 4

SAM

Matsuyama, 1932

"So, Gran, my job is just to read and translate this story?"

"It's the memoir of an elementary school classmate."

"In English?"

"He lived in San Francisco until he was ten. He wrote it in English first and intended to translate it but died before he could."

"Sorry, Gran."

"I knew him a long time ago, and I never saw him again after the war. The first chapter says 1932. That's when he—Sam, which is what the Americans made of Isamu—came back to Japan, to Matsuyama." She handed over the manuscript, and picked up her needlework.

Gen leaned back on the sofa, smiled at his grandmother, and began.

MY FIRST EXPERIENCE of the Seto Inland Sea made no impression on me. In the years to come, its beauty would seep into my bones. It has never abandoned me. In all the years since I left Matsuyama, thoughts of that beauty have been at the core of my homesickness. But that day, boarding the ferry was just one more in a series of first experiences flowing past an overwhelmed ten-year-old.

Two days earlier I had been awed by Mitsukoshi in the Ginza. Thronged with elegant shoppers, it sparkled with exotic merchandise. It was vast, much bigger than the Emporium in San Francisco, where a trip with Mother had been a special treat. And just three days before that, Father's niece Kazuko and her husband, Masaaki, a Tokyo University professor, had met us when the *Tatsuta Maru* docked in Yokohama. Mother had talked during the entire crossing about how wonderful it would be to be back home in Japan, and how nice it would be for us all to be together in Matsuyama, once Father finished the job of getting our affairs in order and was able to join us. I had found her talk as confusing as I had found all the talk at home since the New Year holiday. I kept remembering Father standing at the dock in San Francisco as the horn blew and the ship slipped from the pier. It had felt like I was going backward and leaving Father behind.

In the months before we left San Francisco, I had tried to stay awake to listen to the late-night talks. I remember certain words that floated up the dark stairs: stability, opportunity, prejudice, family status, Matsuchu. On the *Tatsuta Maru,* I wanted to ask Mother what "getting affairs in order" meant, but knew that there would be no answer I could understand.

Despite my worries, the trip was fun. There were other kids my age; we played every day and gorged ourselves at the buffet, which served both Japanese and Western food. Mother laughed when I ate *soba* and spaghetti at the same meal. I was happy when she joked; I enjoyed her teasing before I ran back to the buffet for even more.

When the ship bumped against the dock in Yokohama, Mother said, "Home again. Finally. March twenty-third, Showa Year Seven."

That means March 23, 1932. I'm arriving "home" to a place I have never been.

Kazuko and Masaaki took us to a Japanese-style inn somewhere in the huge city, which felt as big as the ocean itself. Kazuko was tremendously kind, even though she and Mother had met only once before. She had lived in Tokyo for more than a decade and was our tour guide while her husband worked. We visited Yasukuni, but my only real memory is that it was the biggest wooden building and the first real Shinto shrine I had ever seen. Mother and Kazuko talked a lot about the shrine's cherry blossoms, about the trees that were ready to bloom, and how magnificent it would be in a week.

The morning we left Tokyo was bright and chilly. Kazuko came with us to Tokyo Station. Mother and I were booked to Osaka on Japan's fastest train, the *Tsubame,* the Swallow. The sleek *Tsubame* was far beyond my experience: all I knew were the boxy cable cars that inched up and then swept down San Francisco's hills. Kazuko and Mother assured me that the highlight of the eight-hour trip to Osaka would be the view of Mt. Fuji. Kazuko helped us get settled and made sure we were seated on the right-hand side. "We want Isamu's first sight of Mt. Fuji to be front row center," she laughed. "There should be a good view on this beautiful clear day." Back on the platform, she kept chatting with Mother through the open window as we waited for the train to get under way.

The conductor called, "All aboard." As the *Tsubame* slid into motion, Kazuko bowed deeply, and then stood smiling and waving her hanky as we gathered speed.

Mt. Fuji, as promised, was about a third of the way to Osaka. I had heard about it my entire life and seen many pictures, but I wasn't prepared. It loomed in majestic isolation over a broad plain, completely out of proportion to everything around it. It was huge, powerful, and austerely beautiful. I was riveted and craned my neck until it slipped out of sight as the train moved south and west. Mt. Fuji meant Japan; that much I knew from San Francisco. And now I was in Japan—"home." I was living where each new day began when the light of the rising sun struck that magnificent mountain. I would finally become really Japanese. Yes, that was it. I was to be Japanese, truly Japanese.

Up until that moment, being Japanese was something like having red hair. Kevin O'Rourke and Suzy Meecham, two of my classmates at Raymond Weill Elementary School in San Francisco, were redheads. It was their trademark. My trademark was that I was really good at music. Of course I could speak Japanese, but that wasn't anything special at Raymond Weill, which was on the edge of San Francisco's Japantown. Although most of our immediate neighbors were Caucasians, three other Japanese families lived within two blocks of our house on Cedar Street: the Sakuyamas, with four girls, and the Wajimas and the Nishizawas, each with two sons. We all played together and developed our own *patois* of our two languages. I was often in and out of their houses, as they were mine. The Wajimas had decorated their living room with portraits of the Emperor and Empress that seemed mysterious and alien to me. My family had no such thing. Nor did we have any religious pictures or paraphernalia, like the Buddhist altar at the Sakuyamas or the crucifixes at the Kellys, our next door neighbors.

Like all the *nisei* kids, I had to go to the Japanese school, Kimmon Gakuen, "Golden Gate Institute," every day for two hours after we finished at Raymond Weill. Some of my classmates hated the extra school time, but I didn't mind. Thanks to our parents, we all spoke Japanese, so learning to read and write wasn't too difficult. The Kimmon Gakuen teachers were certified by Japan's Ministry of Education and used the textbooks students in Japan were using. The ethics class at Kimmon Gakuen was a novelty. It featured stories about historical figures famous for hard work, thrift, bravery, or some other exemplary virtue. Most of the stories were easy to understand, and hearing about Japan this way made it easier for us to understand some of the things our parents said, especially when they were trying to discipline us. I first heard the story of Kinjiro my last year at Kimmon, never imagining that a statue of Kinjiro would be a constant in my life in just a few years.

When our Kimmon classes finished, we still had time before we were expected home for dinner, and we had lots of energy to burn off after being cooped up all day. The Kimmon schoolyard was too small for ball games, so we played leap-frog, tag, and hide-and-seek. The winners of our schoolyard games always shouted *Nippon katta. Nippon katta. Rosha maketa. Japan won! Japan won! Russia lost!* I have no idea how we learned this phrase, which dated from the Russo-Japanese war of 1905. Perhaps our fathers had brought it to the States with them, and the schoolyard taunt of their generation became ours in the City by the Bay.

FROM Osaka we took an overnight ferry to Matsuyama. At dawn, Mother got me up and took me out on deck. "This is the Seto Inland Sea," she said. "Now I know we'll soon be home." At first all I registered was that the ferry was by far the largest vessel on the water. The few small fishing boats I could see were of unfamiliar design and shape. I thought they looked *oriental*.

Mother took my hand, smiled, and turned her face to the cool breeze. As I stood there with her on the empty deck, I finally saw what was before me: it was breathtakingly beautiful—scattered deep green islands floating on a calm blue sea shimmering in the soft morning light. Right then and there, the Seto Inland Sea began taking possession of me.

When we reached Takahama, the port area of Matsuyama, at sunset, we were met by the Nishiokas: Mother's oldest sister, Yoshie, and her businessman husband. They took us by trolley—another new experience—to Matsuyama City Station, and from there we walked to their home. On the ferry, Mother had explained that the Imagawa family had a large estate in Ishii village outside the city as well as a house right in the middle of the city in a neighborhood called Yanai-machi. She and I were going to live in the city house, but first we would stay with the Nishiokas while our city house was repaired and renovated. By the time we got to the Nishioka house, it was dark. Aunt Yoshie gave her husband, Mother, and me a late night snack of *ochazuke* and explained that her daughters—my cousins—were already in bed.

The next morning, Uncle left early for work and Aunt Yoshie and Mother introduced me to my cousins Yasuko, Yoshiko, Yumiko, and Yuriko. After breakfast Mother went to Bancho Elementary School to consult with the principal about my future. Aunt Yoshie went to the kitchen to wash the dishes and told her daughters to take care of me. We all sat in the family room looking at each other. I thought, well, it's four girls, just like the Sakuyamas, so I know how to deal with this. I was still having trouble sorting out who was who, but Yasuko, the oldest, was closest to my age. Little Yuriko showed me her picture book, and we went through it picture by picture—duck, frog, cat, horse, monkey. Yuriko was inching closer, and I thought I had won them all over when Yasuko startled me by interrupting.

"This is boring. We've all read Yuriko's book a thousand times. Let's do something else. What do you want to do, Cousin?" she said, turning to me. Her three sisters stopped what they were doing and stared at me.

I stammered, "I really don't know. What do you want to do? Can we go outside?"

It was only when Yasuko's face twisted and the three younger girls pulled away physically that I realized my words had come out in English.

"Oh, I'm sorry, what do you all want to do?" I said, switching to Japanese, but it was too late.

I WAS happy to see Mother when she returned. She had met with Principal Tomihisa and explained that I had finished fourth grade in the San Francisco schools. In fact, I was well into my fifth grade year when we picked up and left, and one of the reasons that my parents had decided that March was when Mother and I should return was that the Japanese school year started in April. At first the principal considered putting me in fifth grade even though I was the age of the average Japanese fourth grader, but he soon changed his mind when he learned that I had only finished the third grade materials at Kimmon Gakuen. "You'll be a Bancho fourth grader," Mother told me.

I stuck close to Mother for the next two days, wondering what all this would mean for me. Then Monday morning, and the beginning of school, arrived. The first day, Mother explained, as she walked me to Bancho, would be ceremonial. At the front gate of the school, she delivered me to the custody of a pretty young lady. "Isamu, this is Miss Tatsukawa, your teacher," she said.

"Welcome to Matsuyama, to Bancho, and to my fourth grade class," said Miss Tatsukawa. She was very kind and asked me a lot of questions about my life in San Francisco. In about five minutes a bell sounded, and Miss Tatsukawa walked me into the auditorium and showed me to my seat.

As I sat down, I felt the eyes of all nine hundred of Bancho's students on me. Everyone was looking. And at that moment, I realized how wrong, how out of place I was and understood why my cousins had treated me like a visitor from outer space. I was dressed the way an American boy would be on a formal occasion—in my nice new suit, with a necktie. My parents had bought the suit for the trip, and I had worn it when we three had our portrait taken just before Mother and I departed. *That* was the problem. The boys were all wearing uniforms—black, military style uniforms, with high stand-up collars and long rows of gold buttons. And my hair! It was combed neatly, but just the fact that my hair could be combed made me stand out. All the boys had their hair cropped very short—in fact, their heads were shaved. So there I was—a nattily attired, well-coifed little gentleman the likes of which had never been seen in Matsuyama. I did not fit in. I sat there with growing dread that I never would.

I was relieved when the assembly began. The first item on the program was the singing of *Kimigayo,* the national anthem. I knew it from Kimmon Gakuen and was glad I could sing along. Next, the principal turned his back to the assembly and stepped up on a raised platform at the front of the auditorium. He made a deep bow. It was only then that I noticed that there was a little shrine on the wall. The principal slowly folded back its wooden doors, revealing portraits of the Emperor and Empress. The head teacher, who was serving as master of ceremonies, called out an order: *"Saikeirei!"* Deepest Bow! Everyone lowered their heads and kept them down until the head teacher ordered us to look up again.

Principal Tomihisa turned back toward us, moved to the front of the platform, and placed the long oblong box he had removed from the shrine on a small table. He bowed low before the box, opened it care-

fully, and lifted out a folded piece of Japanese rice paper. As he unfolded
it, I could see that it was very large. He held it with both hands, spread
his arms wide, and began reading, slowly, deliberately, and with a highly
exaggerated intonation pattern. I really couldn't understand what he was
saying but thought it sounded old-fashioned. The first graders at the back
of the auditorium giggled, but I found it strange and mysterious. I was
deeply impressed by Principal Tomihisa's sincerity and the solemnity of
this ritual. There must be a good reason for him to be reading this docu-
ment so seriously and in such a formalized manner. The teachers were
lined up on both sides of the auditorium. They too looked serious and
bowed their heads as the principal read. It seemed to go on forever, but
probably only took about five minutes. When he finished, the principal
refolded the paper, put it back in the wooden box, put the lid back on
the box, took a step back, and made another deep bow. He then picked
up the box, turned around, walked to the back wall, returned it to its
repository, and closed the doors on the shrine. The entire room took yet
another deep bow with him. This time we didn't need the head teacher
to tell us what to do.

Returning to the front of the platform, Principal Tomihisa cleared
his throat and began a talk in his own voice. This I could understand. It
was what I had heard for years at Raymond Weill and at Kimmon: stay
healthy, study hard, obey your teachers, and respect your fellow students.
But I didn't really pay much attention to this familiar advice because I
was trying to figure out what I had just witnessed. What was that ceremony? Why all the formality? Why such seriousness? What could it all
mean?

I soon learned that what we had heard was the Imperial Rescript on
Education. It dated from 1890 and was supposedly written and promulgated by Emperor Meiji for the benefit of his subjects. It followed by
one year Japan's first Constitution, also promulgated as a gift from the
Emperor to his subjects.

With the overthrow of the Tokugawa Shoguns and the restoration
of the Emperor to power in 1868, Japan re-engaged with the rest of the
world, from which it had kept itself isolated for almost three centuries.
The Meiji Era was one of tremendous change in Japan, and compul-
sory education for all—through the sixth grade—was first introduced in
1872. The Imperial Rescript was the blueprint for Japan's national public
educational system. Its obscure language delivered a familiar message—

obedience to parents, love of country, and harmony among siblings and classmates.

It all sounds rather innocuous and charmingly archaic, but Professor Ienaga, who studied the war in great detail and delivered landmark lectures at Tokyo Educational University in the 1960s, described the Rescript as inspired by a blend of Confucianism, state-oriented authoritarian constitutionalism, and militaristic patriotism. He highlights the militaristic phrases of the Rescript, such as "Should an emergency arise, guard and maintain the prosperity of our Imperial Throne," and notes that while the Rescript has references to the Constitution, the emphasis is on the obligation of the people to obey the law; there is no acknowledgement of the rights of the people or any mention of limits on the power of the State. According to Professor Ienaga, the Emperor-centered patriotic ceremonies on the opening day of school each year—the veneration of the royal portraits and the solemn reading of the Rescript—were designed to instill an awed obedience to the Emperor and the State. I was certainly awed. The rest came later.

The next day classes began: reading, music, science, and arithmetic in the morning. Music was my favorite. Lunch was at the school, but unlike at Raymond Weill, there was no cafeteria—no spaghetti for me to pile on my plate. Mother had sent me off in the morning with a *bento* lunch box, and I ate with my classmates, all of us sitting at our desks. History was after lunch, and the last class of the day was ethics. At least I had heard of it at Kimmon, but the lessons at Bancho seemed much more serious; they had the same feel as the ceremony with the Imperial Rescript. When I reflect now, I realize how the syllabus shifted in my years at Bancho—along with the newspapers, magazines, and movies—growing more militaristic with each passing year.

But our school day didn't end with the last class. Our final task was cleaning the school. The work was allocated on a strict rotation basis—there were crews for cleaning the classrooms, the playground, and even the toilets.

My lasting impression of my first week at Bancho was that I never wanted to experience anything like that again. On the first day of classes, Miss Tatsukawa kept me with her in the classroom at recess, making sure I was familiar with the Japanese textbooks and asking me questions, most of which I felt I wasn't answering well, about my Raymond Weill texts, teachers, and classmates.

The next day, Miss Tatsukawa walked with me to the playground at recess, telling me she was sure I was happy to be able to play. I stood just outside the doorway. The boys were playing ball on the far side of the open area, and a group of the girls were playing hopscotch. My cousin Yasuko was part of the group. She was standing in line, waiting her turn and cheering on the other competitors. I couldn't catch her eye. Miss Tatsukawa, seeing my hesitation, stood with me, pointing out what was going on in the playground and chatting about Bancho's history. After a few minutes, Principal Tomihisa appeared beside her in the doorway and said he needed to talk with her in his office.

Trying not to feel abandoned, I turned my attention again to the hopscotch game and saw Yasuko hopping back toward the beginning of the grid. I caught her eye as she finished, and started to take a step forward. She whispered to one of the girls cheering her on, and without turning to look at me, ran off toward another group of girls, who were jumping rope.

I stood in the same spot until the bell rang, thinking that there were two more days until the week would end.

THE last day of that first week, Mother was waiting for me in the doorway when I got back to the Nishiokas. "Give me your book bag," she said. "Take this money and go to the barber shop. Tell him you want your hair cut like all the other schoolboys."

When I repeated Mother's instructions, the barber said, "What a shame. Your long hair is quite nice. But your mother is right. It has to go now that you're a Japanese student." When he finished, my head was prickly.

Mother was waiting for me again and laughed when she saw me scratching at my head. "Here," she said, "try this on," as she lifted a brand new Bancho uniform out of a box. It felt different from the loose weave of my San Francisco suit. It even smelled sharp and tight. I slipped my arms into the sleeves and shrugged it over my shoulders. The fit was perfect. Mother smiled as she knelt and helped me fasten the bright buttons, and then took my hand and walked me to the mirror in Aunt Yoshie's room. She stood behind me, still smiling. "Now you're just like any kid on the block," she said. "Now you're a real Matsuyama Bancho kid."

On Monday, no one seemed to notice at school; there were no comments in the classroom about my hair. At recess, however, I still had to force myself to walk toward the boys' ball game. When I was halfway across the playground, Shin, who was the liveliest student in my class, fell into step beside me. "Did you really live in America?" he asked.

As soon as I answered, he followed up with, "What was the name of the place where you lived?" Several more classmates joined us as we continued across the playground.

By the time we reached the edge of the ball game, I was surrounded, and the group was peppering me with questions. They demanded that I say things for them in English and collapsed in laughter when I obliged them.

After a few minutes of this, Shin said, "Let's go. I want to play." I was swept along into the game.

From that day forward I no longer stood out. I really was just another Bancho kid. I was convinced I was really becoming Japanese.

FOURTH grade was the first year students studied Japanese history. My second week at Bancho I learned the story of Amaterasu. I believe that my class was the first for which the old origin myths were included in the syllabus and taught as historical fact. I had only heard passing references to Amaterasu in San Francisco and was impressed, albeit mystified, by the story.

As I listened to Miss Tatsukawa, I tried to take in the story of the god and goddess, Izanagi and Izanami, high above the clouds dipping their spears into the sea, stirring the waters, and then lifting those spears and letting drops of water fall from them—drops of water that turned into the four main islands of Japan. After they created Hokkaido, Honshu, Kyushu, and Shikoku, the god and goddess became the parents of two children—Amaterasu Omikami, the Great Sun Goddess, and Prince Susano.

There were a few stories about these gods, and I got somewhat confused by the details, but tried to retain as much of the stories as I could. Amaterasu's grandson, Ninigi-no-Mikoto, descended to earth and became Japan's first ruler. His grandmother gave him the three treasures of Japan's ruling family: her mirror, her jewels, and her brother Susano's sword. Later, Amaterasu's great-great-grandson, Jimmu Tenno, became Japan's first Emperor. The Imperial Family, Ms. Tatsukawa told us with reverence, had ruled from that day until ours in an unbroken line, and still retained the three treasures.

I realize now that in teaching these myths as history the government was attempting to indoctrinate the nation's children and convince them, to the depth of their souls, that Japan was a divine nation of chosen people. For me it was so grand and so far beyond the myths we had heard at Raymond Weill—like the story of George Washington and the cherry tree—that I related all of it that I could remember to Mother as soon as I got home from school that afternoon. She laughed, correcting me and supplying details when I faltered, and promised that someday we would take a trip to Amanohashidate, the place on the Japan Sea coast where the god and goddess stood as they dipped their spears and created the Japanese islands.

WHEN Mother and I arrived in Japan, the Manchurian Incident, when the Japanese garrison in Manchuria took possession of the whole of Manchuria, was a year in the past, and huge numbers of Japanese troops were already in China. About a month after we arrived, Mother and all the Nishiokas and I went to watch a parade that marched a group of recruits to the station. I was happy to be in my school uniform, and admired the young men, who all looked brave and determined. And I loved how the instruments glinted in the sunshine and how the band music blared. The shining trumpets made a sound I found absolutely thrilling. The crowds waved flags and shouted, *"Banzai! Banzai!"* The shouts of the crowd and the music were so loud I couldn't tell if the noise was inside me or outside me. Towards the end of the parade, the shouts of the crowd swelled to a crescendo of *"Tenno Heika Banzai!"* My youngest cousin, Yuriko, slipped her hand into mine and held on. Our hands together, we flowed into and with the noise and the crowd.

Mother was flushed with excitement as we walked back. "Yoshie, things have changed so much," she said to her sister. "What an impressive parade! The young men looked so resolute and so proud."

"Well, we want to show our support and send the troops off in style," said Aunt Yoshie. "The girls like the excitement of seeing the soldiers and being part of the crowd."

"Yes," said Mother, "they looked so cute waving their flags."

It was all over by noontime, and that afternoon Mother and I moved into our city house. I was now a resident of the Yanai-machi neighborhood of Matsuyama City on Shikoku Island, in Japan. Japan, the Land of the Rising Sun. I was Japanese.

We settled in, establishing our routines. I was fitting in fine at Bancho. We went a few times to the Ishii Village house, and I loved the
wide-open spaces there. But I wouldn't be playing there in the summer
because, on the Japanese schedule, school continued through most of the
summer months.

On June 1, we switched to our summer uniforms, trading the heavy
black wool for cooler gray cotton. It was about then that a visitor arrived one day on a motor scooter. He introduced himself to Mother as
Yamamura, a teacher at Matsuchu. Everyone talked about Matsuchu all
the time: it was the city's prestigious middle school. "Middle" school for
Japanese boys of those days followed eight years of elementary school and
was the equivalent of high school in the States.

I listened to Yamamura-sensei explain to Mother that he taught English and music at Matsuchu, and that he had heard that her son spoke
perfect English. "I'm sure you're aware, Mrs. Imagawa, that young children can easily forget a second language if they don't have a chance to use
it. That would be a tremendous waste in the case of your son. I think I
could help by introducing your Isamu to the American missionary family
that has been living in the big house just across from Bancho for about
a decade."

"Well," she said, "I suppose that would be fine. Isamu's father has
always been proud that his skills in both languages are so good."

When Yamamura-sensei explained that he had already spoken to the
Graham family, and that they were willing to have me visit them every
Sunday, Mother readily agreed. She was pleased to be able to take Yamamura-sensei's advice; he was an important person in Matsuyama. Plus,
since he had made all the arrangements, she didn't have to try to deal
with the Grahams in English. Mother was, without question, completely
Japanese herself, and I know she was happy to be home in Japan where
she could communicate perfectly rather than stumbling as she always
did in San Francisco. But still, I think she missed our old life somewhat.
Maybe she thought I did too. And I think it must have been lonely for
her without Father.

The next Sunday was the first of many I would spend with the Graham family. Morgan, their oldest son, was exactly my age, and we became
great friends. Sundays were now given over to hiking with Reverend Graham, who was eager to be outdoors when morning services were finished,

to games and sports of all sorts with Morgan, to family dinners of fried chicken and apple pie, and to hymn singing in the parlor after dinner. There were no more excursions with Mother to watch the parades of new recruits marching to the station and off to war. My Sundays were now taken up with "Rock of Ages."

❀ ❀ ❀

WHEN MY second year at Bancho began, the schoolyard had a new statue of Ninomiya Kinjiro. Kinjiro was a poor Edo-era boy who had long been held up for children as a model of honesty, diligence, thrift, and moderation. His story was no longer just a lesson of how a poor boy could succeed and prosper; it was suddenly a model for the kind of behavior the government wanted to inspire in young people all around the country—the ideals of self-sacrifice and hard work were now promoted because they served to aid the nation and the war effort. I was fascinated by the statue of the earnest boy with his bare feet, his bundle of gathered firewood on his back, and his gaze fixed on a book even as he trudged through his daily chores. I was so interested that on the second day of the new school year, I got to Bancho early so I would have time to myself to inspect the statue thoroughly. As I was doing so, Principal Tomihisa came up behind me and said, "Well, Imagawa, I see you admiring our new statue. It's impressive, isn't it? And now that we're lucky enough to have our own statue of Kinjiro, I hope it'll help to remind you every day of the important goals we talked about at assembly yesterday."

"Yes, Principal Tomihisa," I said, wondering if somehow the fact that the word *oriental* had just popped into my mind for the first time in a year somehow showed on my face.

"Run along now," he said. "You don't want to be late." As I did, I resolved to pay better attention to what my teachers told me—I might look Japanese but I still had a way to go before I really fit in.

ALTHOUGH it was never spoken about, I think the real reason my parents decided to go back to Matsuyama was that the Depression was wearing on them in San Francisco. They were not advancing as Mother believed they should. Father's jobs—clerk in a book store, shipping agent at a trucking company—were never, I think, what she thought appropriate, and the salaries were far too meager. I'm sure she thought things at home would be a bit better. The Imagawa family had been prominent for generations in Matsuyama and in Ishii Village, where it owned a great deal of land. I think Mother decided to reclaim that status for herself and for me. Finishing elementary school in Japan would give me time to get acclimated and prepare for the Matsuchu entrance examination. A Matsuchu education would be the first step toward a successful life for me in Matsuyama.

FATHER arrived home the second summer we were back in Japan. Mother was displeased that he had not brought anything from our Cedar Street house with him, and even more displeased when she learned how little he had sold everything for. When he stepped off the ferry, he said, "Isamu, how you've grown. How tall and strong you've become." At first, it was strange to have him around again, even though I was happy to see him and happy that we were all together again.

Later that first week, when I was relating what we had learned at school about the advances of the Japan's Kanto Army of the East in China, Father said, "It's not just that my boy is growing tall and strong, he's also grown a whole new set of opinions." He never said anything like that again, but I think now that he must have been astonished at the changes in me. At that point, I needed no coaxing to hold forth on Japan's military prowess and the nobility of the Yamato race.

Father wanted to spend as much time as possible at Ishii Village. Our family didn't actually farm; the land was all rented out to tenant farmers. Father said he loved to be out in the open and that that was the best part of leaving San Francisco behind. He was especially fond of a creek on the edge of our Ishii property. He and I went fishing often. It was easier than our excursions from Japantown to Tiburon, where he had occasionally taken me to catch rock cod. Now, we just strolled through the fields and spent a peaceful summer afternoon. What was the same was the special time with Father.

That first summer, one morning when we were staying in Yanai-machi, Father walked me up *Okaido,* Matsuyama's shopping street, to the city's main street, where municipal and prefectural buildings flanked the broad boulevard beyond which the Castle hill rose. From there we took the trolley out to the city's far suburbs and Dogo, Japan's oldest hot spring. But the hot spring wasn't our destination that afternoon. From the trolley station we climbed the hill and hiked to Ishiteji Temple, which was having a festival. This was my first time in a Buddhist Temple. Outside we saw a large group of people dressed all in white. Each of them was wearing a large inverted-bowl-shaped straw hat.

"Father, why are there so many priests?" I asked.

"Isamu, they're pilgrims, not priests," he laughed. "You really are still an American kid, aren't you? There may be lots of priests, but not *that* many. Here in Shikoku there's a special pilgrimage tour. The pilgrims dress in white and walk all around the whole island. They visit eighty-eight temples. It usually takes months. They are following the steps of a pilgrimage circuit established by Kukai, Kobo Daishi. Do you know who he is?"

"Not exactly."

"Well, he was born in Shikoku more than a thousand years ago. He became a monk, traveled to China, and brought Buddhism to Japan. He was also a great educator. He opened schools that were open to everyone, not just aristocrats."

"Oh," I said hesitantly, trying to absorb all of this religious talk.

"And," said Father, who probably understood my confusion all too well, "one more thing to help you remember what we've seen today. Do you know that *daruma* dolls are in the image of the Indian monk Bodai-Daruma, or Bodidharma, who three centuries before Kobo Daishi, brought his version of Buddhism to China from India? He taught martial arts as well as Zen Buddhism."

"Yes," I said with relief. *Daruma* gave me some footing in the conversation.

"So the next time you get one of those roly-poly dolls with just one of its eyes painted in and make a wish with a promise that you'll paint in the other eye when it comes true, you'll think of Buddhism, the discipline of martial arts, the pilgrimage, and Ishiteji Temple. Let's go in."

The main gate and the pagoda were impressive, and the temple's many gravestones eerie. Father mentioned that the temple's architectural style was Chinese and told me that both the main gate and the pagoda dated from the fourteenth century.

An alley of stalls was set up for the festival. It was crowded, but everyone was smiling and cheerful. There were stalls with games, stalls with fortunes, stalls with second-hand goods, and stalls with all sorts of food and drink. I inhaled the sweet, pungent scent of *miso* paste on grilling seafood. It made me hungry, and the happy crowd and the rich smell filled all my senses and reminded me of an excursion in San Francisco. The Japanese fleet had come to town and opened one of its frigates to the public on the weekend. Mother, Father, and I toured the ship. I was awed by the power of the vessels and the vigor of the seamen. They were young, strong, and very handsome in their uniforms. They stayed in town for a week, and after our visit to the port, we saw them walking the length and breadth of the city, taking in all the sights. What stayed with me the longest, however, was the smell at the wharf of the paint of the frigate. That smell still filled all my senses as we stepped back on land. From then on, my idea of the Navy was positive and linked with the smell of paint.

As we walked away from the Temple, Father stopped and pointed out a large weathered stone outside the gate. "We probably should have stopped on the approach to the Temple," Father said. "This is something you should see. Take a look."

I walked closer and saw characters carved into the stone. They were worn down but I could read them, and they were all simple enough that I had no trouble understanding them: *Namu Daishi / Ishite no tera yo / ine no hana.* Praise Daishi / the temple at Ishite / rice plants in bloom.

"Nice, isn't it," said Father. "It was written by Shiki, a Matsuyama hometown hero and famous *haiku* poet. I've always liked our city's romance with poetry in general and *haiku* in particular."

Before we got on the trolley, we toured the arcades around the hot spring. Shop after shop featured Dogo souvenirs. One cake shop was crowded with tourists, who emerged back into the arcade with big grins and shopping bags with the logo of the Dogo souvenir. Father gave me a little push and said, "We can't buy any of them today, but go take a look." I wiggled to the front of the crowd. The machine making the cakes clanked and whirred in mechanical splendor. After a few minutes, Father called to me over the crowd, "Isamu, come. Let's go. We need to get on the trolley and start back."

CHAPTER 5

SAM

Matsuyama, 1935–1937

I WAS NEVER as good a student at Bancho as Mother wanted me to be. So Mother, Father, and I were all pleasantly surprised when I passed the entrance exam for Matsuchu. I started in April of 1935, or *Showa 10*. The system of referring to years in terms of the length of the reign of the Emperor, which was something I had been taught but never really understood at Kimmon Gakuen in San Francisco, was now fully familiar.

Matsuyama Chugakko—almost always shortened to "Matsuchu"—Matsuyama's most prestigious secondary school, graduated its first class in 1879, *Meiji 12*. But its real fame came in 1906, *Meiji 39*, with the publication of Natsume Soseki's *Botchan*. *Botchan* is one of Japan's most famous novels, and every Japanese knows it, or at least knows about it, the way Americans know about *Huckleberry Finn*. Soseki is so famous that in 1984 the Japanese government put his picture on the 1,000-yen bill.

As a bright Tokyo University graduate with no particular prospects, Soseki was recruited to teach in Matsuyama. He lasted only one year at Matsuchu, the school year 1895–96. Soseki was miserable away from the cosmopolitan capital. He had no talent for suffering gladly his foolish colleagues, pompous supervisors, and sluggish students. But he did have a talent for skewering all those local characters. The put-upon narrator of *Botchan*—a teacher at a higher school in a provincial backwater dissatisfied with his lot in life—spends the entire tale in a beleaguered *why me* mode. *Botchan* is endearing because some of its most hilarious scenes poke fun at the narrator himself.

For Soseki, the best thing about Matsuyama was Shiki, a young poet with whom he formed a deep friendship. And just as the Midwest survived Sinclair Lewis, Matsuyama survived Soseki and *Botchan*. In fact, by the time I arrived in Matsuyama, Soseki and Shiki were revered local heroes. They had put Matsuyama on the map, and made it famous for the whimsical characters of Soseki's novel and the tiny perfect jewels of Shiki's *haiku*.

For me, there were lots of new things about Matsuchu. First, it was a boys-only school. The girls from Bancho who continued their education past the elementary years attended either the Prefectural Girls' High School, or Saibi, a private academy. Officially, we no longer had any contact with them: there was a strict no fraternization policy, and boys and girls were completely separated. And that's why one of the other new things about Matsuchu was so good. It was twice as far from Yanai-machi as Bancho, about a twenty-five minute walk. To get to Matsuchu, I had to walk almost the entire length of *Okaido,* Matsuyama's main shopping street. I was usually in a group with my buddies. And we almost always saw the girls across the street, headed for their schools, which were in the opposite direction. I was always happy to see my old friends and classmates and at first had trouble understanding why suddenly they were supposed to be exotic. Without knowing what motivated me, or any of us, I was an enthusiastic participant in the hijinks the boys devised to get the attention of the girls. There were often times when the groups on the two sides of the road collapsed in giggles. But as time passed, the girls really did begin to seem exotic and alluring. We desperately wanted them to notice us.

Eventually, I really began to treasure the few occasions when I was by myself and saw my Bancho classmate Michiko Shizuyama. If I saw Michiko "alone" like this, it made my whole day, and I still hold those memories dear. Michiko's parents were the proprietors of a small sweets and sundries shop on *Okaido,* and on days when I didn't see her, I walked especially slowly as I passed the shop.

Matsuchu also featured a lot more regimentation. Of course we wore uniforms. They were on the same military model as the Bancho uniforms, but they had the characters for *matsu* and *chu* stamped on their bright gold buttons, and our caps sported a distinctive patch with the same characters. Mother was delighted the first day I put on my Matsuchu uniform, and I must admit that I was quite proud of it myself. Father commented on how different I looked from my San Francisco days and

I heard him say to Mother the first morning I left the house in my new uniform, "Now that he's getting bigger, it's much too easy, isn't it, to imagine the military uniform I fear the future holds for him."

I found the rigmarole about the book bags much less agreeable. But I had to obey. We were all issued a standard bag and instructions on how to use it. On the way to school, we were to carry it slung across our chests from our left side, switching to the right side on the way home. Ridiculous, but we obeyed.

The old Japanese proverb about the nail that sticks up getting hammered down may be a bit dated today, but it was absolutely true then. Uniformity and conformity were the rule. Each day began in the broad yard in front of the school. It was our playground, but also our morning assembly site. As soon as we arrived, we ran to our classrooms, left our book bags at our desks, and then hurried to the schoolyard. Each class lined up in double rows, facing east. The home room teachers stood in front of the rows of their students. The principal, standing on a raised platform at the front of the assembly, faced the students. On the barked command of the head teacher, the students, their teachers, and the principal bowed to each other and shouted *"Ohayo gozaimasu,"* Good morning! The principal then turned so he too, faced east, toward Tokyo, and he, with the rest of us, followed the next command of the head teacher, "To the Imperial Palace, deepest bow!"

Also new was military training as part of the school curriculum. This was in addition to our regular physical education classes, which included calisthenics, *judo, kendo*, other martial arts, baseball, and other team sports. Matsuchu, like every secondary school in the country, had military officers on its faculty. First-year students at Matsuchu learned to march and handle a rifle; all of our training strictly complied with army regulations. And it took place daily. When it rained, we were excused from marching and drilling but had to listen to lectures on military history and strategy. So I was only twelve when I began hauling about one of those long rifles and first learned to name the parts. We were proud that the Model 38 infantry rifle we trained with was the one actually used in the army. I'm sure I'm not the only Japanese my age with memories of running my finger over the Imperial chrysanthemum crest stamped right on the Model 38.

The culmination of all this training, in our fifth year at Matsuchu, was the day we marched to Matsuyama Regiment and fired real bullets on the shooting range. And in the summer of our last year, the officers assigned to all the schools in Matsuyama organized a huge event. Again we were marched to Matsuyama Regiment. There the officers divided us into a Red Force and White Force, gave us orders, and set the two groups at each other in a mock battle that lasted all day. When we finally finished, we were hot, dirty, and exhausted. But we had to line up in formation again. Before we marched back to our schools, the regiment Commander inspected us, and gave a talk about how important our military lessons had been and how proud our parents and our teachers were of us. He concluded by telling us that we should be proud of ourselves and the work we were doing to prepare ourselves to serve our nation. As tired as I was, I was jolted into shock when his talk turned to China and Japan's mission there. His use of the derogatory term *Chankoro* brought to mind my Raymond Weill friend and classmate Henry Fong. I thought that maybe *Chink* was the English equivalent, but no teacher at Raymond Weill would have tolerated hearing that term from any of the students, much less use it themselves—any more than they would have tolerated or used the term *Jap*.

ENGLISH language training, in those days, began in secondary school, and my experiences with English at Matsuchu were always challenging— not in terms of the language itself but in terms of everything else associated with studying English. The only good experiences with English I had while at Matsuchu were outside the classroom, with Yamamura-sensei and the Grahams. Somehow I was unlucky enough to never be assigned to Yamamura-sensei's class, but he knew about my struggles, was always supportive, and made time to speak English with me. My first bizarre experience came just a few weeks into the first semester, in algebra class. One day, Mr. Kashiwagi, the teacher, suddenly said, "Imagawa, I understand you speak perfect English. Come up to the front of the room. I think we need a demonstration."

I was scarlet with embarrassment by the time I reached the front of the room. Matsuchu was still new, and no one knew this about me. I even think that my few Bancho friends who were with me at Matsuchu had forgotten about the perfect little English-speaking gentleman from San Francisco. I'm sure I blushed even more when Mr. Kashiwagi announced what he wanted. "Tell us the fairy tale of *Momotaro* in English. I think we'll all be interested to hear something so familiar in another language."

I stumbled through as best I could, trying not to be insulted that I was being made to perform like a trained monkey and forced to recount such a childish tale to boot. When I finished, my classmates laughed and clapped, and one smart aleck in the back of the room let loose a loud whistle. Mr. Kashiwagi silenced the commotion with a stern look and then turned to me, "Well, Imagawa, I couldn't understand a single word, but it sounded good to me. You may return to your seat." I did, yearning for my lost anonymity and desperately hoping this humiliating experience wouldn't be repeated.

Mercifully, it wasn't. Mr. Kashiwagi's curiosity was satisfied, but my troubles with English were far from over. I thought the worst was when I realized I couldn't, without great effort, understand the teachers on the few occasions when they actually spoke English. I got in trouble when I pronounced words correctly rather than repeating their mistakes. But the worst really came when we studied grammar. To me it seemed like astrophysics—something extraordinarily abstract and complex with no relationship to anything connected to everyday life. I just couldn't make myself memorize and spew back all the rules, which in my view, had nothing to do with English. By the end of my time at Matsuchu, I was a C-minus English student.

Even though I was never in his class, Yamamura-sensei was my best teacher at Matsuchu. On the second day of our first year, the principal explained all the club activities, and before the end the day, Yamamura-sensei sought me out and told me that he would save me a place in the band. I loved music and took every chance I got to sing. I thought about it all week, and by the time I went to the first meeting of the music club, I had decided that I wanted to learn the trumpet. Yamamura-sensei suggested the saxophone, but I was determined—I wanted to play the trumpet. But wanting it wasn't enough; one of the seniors had the school's only trumpet. The next best thing was the cornet. As the cornet player, I was a member of the school's marching band. The first-year students didn't march in public, but we spent a lot of time practicing on our instruments, marching around the schoolyard after classes.

Our first public performance was at the opening day ceremony of

our second year. I was proud to stand with the rest of the band. During the parts of *Kimigayo* when I wasn't playing, I loved having the music flow through me, happy to be part of something so big and so beautiful. Two weeks later the school band marched to the station with a group of recruits. Mother came to watch the parade, and at dinner talked about how proud she had been to see me. "Isamu, do you remember the first parade we saw, when we had just returned and were staying with your Auntie and Uncle? And now, just four years later, you're in the band yourself. You looked great today."

We accompanied recruits to the station three more times that year, but my real initiation to the world of military bands came at the beginning of my third year, when one of the military officers assigned to Matsuchu pulled me out of class. "Imagawa, if you can play the cornet, you can play the bugle. From now on you're the bugler." And I was, starting with practice that afternoon.

I soon came to appreciate what at first I thought was nothing more than pure military caprice. As the bugler I was always at the front of the band, following right behind our leader, Yamamura-sensei, and when the Matsuchu students were on military maneuvers, I didn't have to crawl across fields, roll in trenches, shoot blanks at my friends, and charge "enemy" lines. My only task was to stand by the commanding officer and sound the bugle at his direction.

CHAPTER 6

SAM

Matsuyama, 1939–1940

MY LAST YEAR at Matsuchu was the beginning of a period of disappointment and confusion. The next step was university, one of the military academies, or a local college. Many from the class ahead of me, and even some in my own class, had already left home to follow these paths. At the start of my last year, in April 1939, it was time to start making decisions. I secretly yearned for Keio or Waseda in Tokyo. I was confident I could do the work. It was all I could do to ask Mother and Father if I could try for a private university in Tokyo. I didn't dare to mention which ones I was thinking about. They would have thought I was aiming too high. It took them several days to come back with their answer, and it was no.

"We're sorry, we can't agree to let you go," said Father. "Not with the war the way it is. And you know that your mother may be conscripted into the Nurse Reserve Corps. We can't let you go to Tokyo now." At this point, the National Mobilization Law had been in effect for a year; my parents' concerns that Mother could be called to service were completely justified. The nation was on a war-time footing.

So my options were Matsuyama Higher School or Matsuyama Commercial College, the two local colleges, since the military academies weren't really discussed in my family as an option. The school year was off to a dispiriting start. I saw my future coming, and couldn't generate much enthusiasm about my prospects.

DESPITE the disappointments, there was one somewhat auspicious occasion early that last year, one that boosted my confidence in a most unusual way. It had to do with an addition to the schoolyard. In some ways this event paralleled the appearance of the Kinjiro statue at Bancho, but it was a much more serious matter. The first day it was there, we had no idea what it could be. The new wooden structure just inside the main gate of Matsuchu was about seven feet tall and three feet wide. It had the curving roof of a Shinto shrine. At the next assembly we were told that it was a storage facility, of a very special type. The only things it housed were portraits of the Emperor and Empress. When explaining it, Principal Sato and Colonel Matsuura, our army drill master, referred to it as a *Hoanden*.

What? I thought I was past not knowing Japanese words. I finally understood everything about the ceremonies like the one that had mystified me on my first day at Bancho, but I had no idea what this new word was or what it could mean. My fellow students had the same blank looks on their faces. This was news to everyone. Actually, I don't think any of us learned the meaning of the word; we just learned what we were supposed to do. The big Kodansha Japanese-English dictionary I keep on my desk informs me that the proper translation is "Enshrinement Hall."

Now that Matsuchu had this *Hoanden,* there were new rules. Veneration of the Imperial portraits was now a full-time requirement. They might not be on display when locked in the *Hoanden,* but we still had to show our respect. Every time we passed through the school's main entrance we had to stop, take off our caps, and make the deepest bow possible before the *Hoanden.* It went without saying that the bow was to be accompanied by a prayer for long life for the Imperial couple and prosperity and victory for the nation. Even if we came through an entrance to the schoolyard that wasn't near the *Hoanden,* we were supposed to stop as soon as we were on the school grounds, face the *Hoanden,* and pay our respects. Needless to say, this ritual was honored most often in the breach. But for some reason, I was captivated and promised myself I would never fail in this new duty. I realize now that I was still working to fit in.

At the end of our morning assembly about a month after the *Hoanden* was installed, the principal stepped up on the podium and told us that Colonel Matsuura would make a few remarks before we went to our classrooms.

"Boys," the Colonel said, "I am distressed that I must remind you of your duties to the nation and the gratitude, respect, and obedience you owe to the Emperor. Some of you are shirking those duties when you enter the school grounds and fail to pay your respects to the *Hoanden*. Just because no one is looking—or you think no one is looking—doesn't mean that the rules don't apply. The heavens have eyes and I too have been observing. You should let Imagawa be your model. He obeys the rule at all times; he always shows his respect. Follow his example."

I was flabbergasted. Me, a role model? I thought I was just doing what I was supposed to. As my friends and classmates—who I thought of as truly Japanese—turned to look at me, I tried to stand up tall and look proud rather than embarrassed by the attention. I realized with a rush of pride that I had finally succeeded in my quest to be completely Japanese myself—and maybe I was even a bit more Japanese than some of my peers.

WE WERE hot and tired. As always, it was thrilling to march with the military, but this was the third time that week we had been to the station. Another group from the Matsuyama Infantry Regiment was heading for the front. It was our job to send them off in style.

A mounted officer led, and I was in the group of ten buglers behind the first column of soldiers. The rest of the troops followed behind. The instruments gleamed, the music blared. The soldiers moved forward to their futures, through the heat, through the dust.

As we neared the station, we swept past the groups of high school girls waving flags and shouting encouragement. *"Banzai! Banzai!"* And the families. The old grandparents, the parents, the little brothers and sisters. A few of the mothers and grandmothers were trying to hide their tears, but most were beaming with pride. I spotted Michiko in the crowd with her parents and realized that her second brother must be in this group, following his older brother to Manchuria, leaving Michiko alone at home with her parents. I knew she saw me and hoped she admired my uniform.

It was high summer, and my parents and I were staying at the Ishii Village house. As the parade broke up, Yamamura-sensei, on duty as music director, said, "Imagawa, I know your family is out at Ishii this week. I'll give you a ride on my scooter. Otherwise, it'll be dark by the time you get home."

When we arrived, no one was home. I was sure Father was across the fields, fishing in the local stream. Yamamura-sensei and I decided to take a walk and see if we could find Mother in the orchards behind the vegetable garden.

"How are things in Suzuki-sensei's class?" he asked.

I didn't know how to answer. Everyone in the school knew I had gotten in trouble during the last pronunciation test, by writing my true best guess—*bear* instead of *bell*. Did Yamamura-sensei know that Suzuki-sensei had no idea how to properly pronounce English words?

"Well," he continued, not waiting for an answer, "it's not easy studying systematically. You know English in your bones and your heart. But Suzuki-sensei has the job of analyzing it and teaching his students how to do the same. And you have the difficult job now of learning how to analyze."

So knowing how to speak wasn't important—at least in the classroom this year. My job was to listen and to accept the word of the teacher.

"And, besides, who knows how much longer any of us will be able to teach English." I wasn't sure what Yamamura-sensei meant, but he switched topics before I had much time to think about it. "How are the Grahams?" he asked.

"Fine."

"Still singing?"

"Yes."

"Still eating all those *gaijin* foods?"

"Yes."

"Are you and Morgan still speaking English?"

"Yes, the whole family climbed up to the Castle last Sunday. We haven't done that for years. Morgan's dad says the view of the Seto Inland Sea up there 'nourishes his soul.'"

"More poetic than the Buddhist priest," said Yamamura-sensei.

We hadn't found Mother and had tramped so far into the orchards that we sat down to rest. The heat was receding. It would be light for a bit longer, but the birds were beginning to find their way to their perches, their day winding down, as was ours. We sat down under the large oak at the end of the orchard. Yamamura-sensei began to quiz me in English, expecting the answers in Japanese.

"Listen Isamu. Ears first. Now tell me."

"*Kakko?*"

"Yes, and the other?"

"*Tsutsudori.*"

"Yes. Listen, I think I hear a *woodpeeker* too."

"Wood*pecker, Sensei.*"

"Thank you. Now tell me the name."

"*Ao-gera?*"

"Probably, and now the names of the others."

"*Oaka-gera, ko-gera,* and...and... "

"And what about our old friend Basho and the woodpeckers?"

I stumbled, but once he prompted me with the first word, it rolled out, "*Kitsutsuki mo / io wa yaburazu / natsukodachi.*'"

"Yes," he said, "yet another word for woodpecker. How can we translate this *haiku* into English, Isamu?"

"I don't know, *Sensei.* It's hard. Maybe, '*The woodpecker doesn't tear at the thatched cottage in the summer grove,*' but I don't think it sounds as good in English."

"I agree. It needs something. Maybe we could switch it around, but we still have to get the idea that the woodpecker, who usually loves to attack anything wood, is leaving the humble thatched cottage alone. How about, '*In a summer grove, the woodpecker doesn't peck, sparing the thatched cottage*'? Still isn't exactly right. Ah, how difficult speaking and thinking in another language is."

"Yes, *Sensei,*" I said.

"I think we're almost finished with the birds, but I want you to learn the words *komadori* and *meboso mushikui* too. I'll show you the pictures in my book next week. Maybe you'll know the English. They're warblers. You'll like their songs. Now it's time for my quiz. Are your ready?"

When I had first come back from San Francisco, Mother had shown Yamamura-sensei my second grade class portrait from Raymond Weill Elementary School. She apologized for the scruffy, undisciplined-looking bunch, but Yamamura-sensei had been enchanted and loved my explanation that the photo was taken on a "Show and Tell" day.

"It's Henry Fong holding the *Songs and Tales from Mother Goose* book," he said. "That I remember. Please tell me the others."

I'd lost the ability to rattle off the roll alphabetically as Mrs. Murphy had every morning, but I could still manage most of the names. My memories were fading, but Yamamura-sensei had fixed the photo in my head. "Mary Jean Wallace, Ellen Nakamura, Patricia Nolan, Suzy Meecham, Danny Eguchi, Pete Semanovich."

"I love 'Se-man-o-vich,'" Yamamura-sensei said with a smile.

"We used to think it was a difficult name, and the Japanese kids used to tease him with, '*Nihon katta, Rosha maketa,*' even though we really didn't know what it meant."

"Ah, that old playground rhyme. It's from when I was a student. Well, now, if you believe the government, we're winning everything, and we always will."

"Yes," I said, hesitantly, but he didn't give me time to continue.

"Keep going." I knew he wanted to hear his favorites and repeat some of the names.

"Esther Gimbel, Stanley Crowe, Arthur Miyamoto, Clarissa Peters, Nicholas Johannsson."

He played, as he always did with "Clarissa," trying and re-trying to get his tongue around all the slippery sounds. Again, as part of our ritual I said, "*Sensei*, that sounds like 'Chris.' We had no one named *Christopher* in our class. It's *Cla-RISS-ah.*"

"Fine. Let's hear the rest."

"Bobby Walsh, Billy Wong, Samuel Fujita, Evelyn Quinn."

"Ah, yes, Miss *Queen.*"

"*Quinn, Sensei. Quinn.* She was definitely not a *queen* or even a *princess,*" I said, enjoying our best joke.

"Susie Da Silva, Tommy Maida, Frankie Falucci, Joey MacNamara, Julie Shimamura, Kevin O'Rourke, Juan Chavez, Kathryn Kalsen, Terence Tanaka, Charles Kawabata."

"The San Francisco League of Nations. Thank you Isamu. I love to hear all those mixed-up names. But it's time to go back now."

When we stood, we saw Father on the other side of the orchard, on a path angling through the paddies. He waved and called, "Good to see you again," to Yamamura-sensei.

"My son here still making all that awful noise under your tutelage?" Father asked as we met at the edge of the orchard. Despite Father's jokes, I knew he was proud of my musical skills and happy that I retained my English. We all turned toward the house and walked together through the vegetable garden.

"Ah, Mrs. Imagawa," said Yamamura-sensei. "I'm so glad to see you." Mother was standing just outside the back door, bowing.

"*Sensei*, I'm so sorry I missed you. I was taking our neighbor Mrs. Ishizuki some cucumbers from the garden. Please come in and stay for dinner. I see that my husband had a successful afternoon by the river."

Father grinned and held up a string of fishes. It didn't look like much to me.

"Thank you, Mrs. Imagawa, but my wife is waiting for me. I know she's preparing dinner at home."

"But, oh, *Sensei*, please take some of these cucumbers. It's impossible for us to eat so many."

Yamamura-sensei walked back to his scooter, and he and Mother tied a *furoshiki* full of cucumbers on its back. As he said his farewells, he told Mother and Father, "It's really commendable that the two of you have encouraged Isamu to keep up his English. It will be so important for him. The future will be internationalism. That's the world all our young people will live in."

"Yes, and I hope that world comes soon, without too much more blood shed in vain," said Father.

Mother smiled and waved as Yamamura-sensei pulled away.

THE NEXT week—in mid July—my friend Masao, who had left to study at the Naval Academy, came home for a visit. I was happy to see him, but at the same time I was a bit intimidated. He seemed stronger, tougher, and somehow smarter. Maybe it was just that he was more confident. And he looked wonderful in his uniform. He was a cadet, which gave him semi-officer status. His uniform had a waist-length tunic top. His stand-up collar had gold bars. Their shine matched that of the gold dagger flashing at his waist. He was full of stories about his training and how much he was learning. I listened, rapt, as he speculated about which ships he might ultimately be assigned to. Oh, I thought, a career! One that would be right for me. Every day that I spent time with Masao made me more certain. I was sad to see him go, but happy that his visit had shone such a bright light on my future for me. I now had a purpose.

Mother and Father quickly squashed that dream too. When I went to them after Masao had gone back to the Naval Academy, I had all my

arguments marshaled. The Naval Academy was just across the Seto Inland Sea, only a four-hour ferry journey. My education would be at government expense. Their refusal was immediate, absolute, and shocking.
Perhaps they saw my request coming; my fascination with Masao must
have been obvious. "No," Father said.

"We're not ready to offer your life to His Majesty yet," Mother said.

The matter was closed. I kept telling myself that. It's closed. Mother
and Father had to be respected. They had the final word. Now I had to
figure out something else to do with myself. It was back to Matsuyama
Higher School or Matsuyama Commercial College. I sighed the first day
I sat down to study for the entrance exams. As the summer passed and
autumn arrived, I kept studying and kept sighing. I knew my time at
Matsuchu was coming to an end, but couldn't imagine what would come
next. Sometimes I thought of my experience coming to Matsuyama. That
too was a time of great uncertainty, but I had been a baby then, and in
the hands of my mother, my aunt and uncle, Miss Tatsukawa of Bancho,
Yamamura-sensei, and even the Grahams. Now things were different. I
was facing the great unknown of the future alone. I wasn't a little boy
in short pants anymore. I had to go meet the next part of my life, without any idea of what I wanted and no certainty that I was equal to the
task.

Late in the fall, Mother was conscripted. She was assigned to the
Naval Reserve Corps and stationed three hours away at Zentsuji. She was
still on Shikoku Island, but far away from us, closer to Takamatsu. All
the patterns of everyday life changed as Father and I adjusted to Mother's
absence.

We stumbled through the winter. Father had a new job, at a machine
tool factory outside the city. Because the factory was past Ishii Village, we
moved to our house there and rented out the Yanai-machi house. I had
a long walk to school every day, and even from Ishii Village, Father had
a long bicycle ride to the factory. We didn't do well at keeping the house
neat or clean, but Father somehow got us up and out the door every day.
In the deep winter, we were getting up, dressing, and leaving in the dark.
Father didn't work on the factory floor—he worked in the office, keeping
the accounts and tracking shipments. He had had several jobs like this
since we had returned to Matsuyama. He was recruited for this new job
because he knew the president of the company, who persuaded Father

that he needed his help. That was certainly true. Father worked long hours because production at the factory had been stepped up to meet the demands of the military. But he somehow managed to make me dinner every night and prepare my lunch for the next day before he fell into bed exhausted.

Mother came home for the New Year holiday, but only for two days. As we had our small celebration at home, she chided me, telling me that I needed to pull myself out of my doldrums. She told me that she was sure I would do well on the exams for Matsuyama Higher School, which is what we had all decided was my first choice. On New Year's morning, she brushed the lint off my jacket as we got ready to pay a call on Aunt Yoshie and her family. When she finished brushing my back, she spun me around, held me with her arms on my shoulders, looked me straight in the eye, and said, "Isamu, you will do well. This year will be a good one. You have a bright future here in Matsuyama."

I took the exam in February and failed. I regretted not trying for Matsuyama Commercial College as well. I would have nothing to do the next year. I would be a *ronin*, a student without a college to attend, adrift for at least a year. Everything before me was bleak. My days at Matsuchu came to an end. I found myself dreaming about the Navy again. One Sunday when Father and I were fishing in the river beyond the fields that stretched behind our house, I talked about the Naval Academy again. He let me talk, and over the next few weeks, I was able to persuade him to at least let me try. I'm not at all sure things would have been the same if Mother had been home, but Father on his own was a soft touch. The night he consented the light at the table was low as we sat after dinner for the few moments we had together before he had to get to sleep to be ready for the next day. "You make a good argument," he said. "It's not what I've ever wanted for you, but you're right, there are few alternatives at this point."

The Naval Academy exam was in November. I buckled down and started studying again. Now I made our simple dinners and packed Father's lunch for him. I saw him off early in the morning and sat down to study. I didn't allow myself a break until mid-afternoon. Often I would walk into town even if I didn't even have any errands to run. One day I found myself in front of Bancho. Soon, it became my routine to go there every day. I had to prepare for the Navy's physical exam too. I ran around the track and practiced jumping and climbing on the jungle gym. I wanted to be tough enough to meet the Navy's exacting standards. Then I walked back to Ishii and studied again until Father got home.

ON my way out of Bancho one day, I saw Mrs. Graham walking down the street. Her face was twisted in sadness, but when she saw me, I watched her sweep it all aside. "Isamu, my dear," she said, "how wonderful to see you. A friendly face is just what I need. Come in with me and have some tea. Morgan's out this afternoon, but Reverend Graham will be delighted to see you."

"Darling," she called as she stepped into the *genkan,* "I'm back, and I have Isamu with me."

The Reverend came to the entryway. He smiled at me, but his eyes were on his wife as he said, "Sam, great to see you. Come in."

"I need some tea," said Mrs. Graham, "and I've persuaded Isamu to have some with us."

"Excellent! Darling, I'll help you in the kitchen. Sam, why don't you go sit in the parlor?"

I went to the familiar room and sat on the piano bench, fingering the keys.

"It was absolutely beastly hot queuing today," Mrs. Graham said in response to her husband's inquiry. I could hear most of what she then went on to tell the Reverend. She had stood in the ration line for a long time as the sun beat down on the dusty road. She was talking about Abe-san, the grocer in their neighborhood. He was now the assistant rations officer. She said he sneered when he saw her and made a great show of looking up her name on his list, mispronouncing it, and then giving her a receipt with her coupons that had the word "FOREIGNER" scrawled where her name should have been. I heard her voice break. "Richard, everyone else just looked away. No one would catch my eye. These people have been our neighbors for fifteen years. They laughed and cried with us and watched our children grow. I thought they cared for us. What has all our work been for?" I thought she might be crying.

"Margaret, I simply won't let you do that again by yourself," said Reverend Graham. "And we'll talk about it more later. For now, give me that tray. You finish the tea. Take your time. Pull yourself together."

The Reverend strode back into the room with the tray. "See how clever Mrs. Graham is. She found some cookies for us to have with our tea. Tell me, Sam," he said as he sat down, "how are you?"

"I'm fine. I'm sorry to be here when I'm so sweaty and dirty."

"Nonsense, it's great to see you. It's been so long since we went hiking. You and I don't get much of a chance to talk anymore. What are you doing downtown today?"

"I'm taking a break from studying. I started taking walks in the afternoon and realized that Bancho is a great place to exercise."

"Why so much exercise? Isn't the walking enough? Don't tell me you miss the calisthenics and all those drills now that you're finished with Matsuchu."

"No, it's not that. I'm just trying to prepare for the physical exam."

"The physical?" said Mrs. Graham as she walked into the room with the teapot.

"Yes, for the Naval Academy. I'm taking the exam in November. I really want to do well."

"I see," said the Reverend. He stood up, took the teapot from his wife, added it to the tray, and took her elbow to help her onto the sofa. "Sam, when did you decide on the Academy?"

"Really last year when my friend Masao came home for a visit."

"Masao Kato?" asked Mrs. Graham. "Such a handsome boy."

"Yes, I realized what a great opportunity it would be. A career. And my duty as a Japanese. Last year Mother and Father said no, but now at least I'm taking the exam. It's a long shot, but I want to give it my best."

"Sam," said the Reverend, "you're brave and ambitious. We will always wish the best for you."

"And we'll pray for your safety, my dear," said Mrs. Graham.

I don't remember what I thought about as I walked home. Maybe about what Father and I would have for dinner. Maybe about how many chin-ups I'd be able to do the next day.

I ENTERED the Regiment Gate with anxiety and pride. The physical was first. I was pleased that I did well. Those who didn't were sent home immediately. There was no point in letting them take the written exam. After lunch at the Regiment, the candidates took the exam in one of the barracks, which had been arranged like a huge classroom. I found the math part of the exam particularly difficult and was sure I had failed as

I turned my papers in. As I left the Regiment I saw a few of my friends from Matsuchu in a group outside the Regiment Gate. I just waved and called, "Have to get home. They're waiting for me," and didn't stop. I wanted the solitude of the walk back to Ishii by myself.

The results came before the end of the year. I didn't pass. I was not surprised, and I think Father was secretly pleased. I know Mother had been displeased that he had let me take the exam. But now, with her experiences as a war nurse, I suspect she had come to accept that military life was inevitable for her only son. She heard my news about the Naval Academy on one of her rare weekend visits home. She said, "So, it's Matsuyama Commercial College for you now, my dear." That night, she and Father sat up after I went to bed. I heard her telling Father about a new patient she had at the hospital that week. He had stepped on a land mine somewhere in China and lost his right arm, his left hand and most of both legs. She described how the nurses had to do everything for him. "His mother is supposed to arrive this weekend," she said. "I'm glad I won't be there to see it."

I went back to studying, took the Matsuyama Commercial College exam, and passed. I was finally going to be a college student. My terrible, drifting *ronin* year was over.

CHAPTER 7

SAM

Matsuyama, 1941–1943

MATSUYAMA COMMERCIAL COLLEGE, "Kosho," for short, was founded in 1923. Even though it was still a new institution when I began my studies there in the spring of 1941, it was already one of Japan's leading business colleges. On our first day that prestige was brought home to us when we learned that Kosho had accepted only one of every seventeen applicants; it made me feel a little better about failing to qualify for Matsuyama Higher School, but I wondered how long it would be before I felt comfortable. I didn't know anyone sitting near me in the auditorium. I was painfully aware of having been a *ronin*. It made me think of my first day at Bancho.

I struggled with classes new to me: economics, business administration, bookkeeping, civil law, and logic. But I did well in English and chose German as my second foreign language. Kosho emphasized an international outlook: because we were preparing for careers in trade, the assumption was that languages would be essential. The physical and military education familiar from Matsuchu continued. I signed up for basketball; the military training wasn't difficult after my *ronin* efforts to get myself in shape for the Naval Academy exam.

Kosho's faculty had a full complement of academic characters. Our English teacher was Professor Takahashi. We focused on business letters and stories in English. Professor Takahashi often gave me the job of reading aloud and explaining vocabulary items he knew the other students would have trouble with. On a few occasions, I suspected that he wasn't all that sure of the words himself, but I didn't mind. He was a nice, easygoing teacher, really a bit of a dreamer. We read Mark Twain, Dickens, and eighteenth- and nineteenth-century essayists. Classes were always pleasant. And often we didn't even get to the business letters or the English stories or essays. Professor Takahashi was himself a poet. He chatted away about his hobby during class time. By the time I was at Kosho, Matsuyama's *haiku* tradition was fully familiar, and Professor Takahashi introduced us to his own ideas that built on that tradition. He loved to talk about "free style" *haiku*. Sometimes, when he was lecturing on "business English," he would interrupt himself and recite a free style *haiku*. Then he would say something like, "I came up with that one last night, just as I was about to fall asleep. What do you think?" Not being much of the poetic type, I thought it was silly, but kept my mouth shut and let someone else answer.

But one day, Professor Takahashi's poem reached out and grabbed me. In English, it goes something like: *Wherever you go, you see grass, green and growing.* I sat in the Kosho classroom with the light streaming through the tall windows, listening to Professor Takahashi's words. *Yes, exactly. How true.* A wonderfully succinct and poetic way to counter *tonari no hana wa akai*—the neighbor's flowers are red—or, in English, *the grass is always greener....* I thought of Raymond Weill for the first time in a long while. I thought of the grass in front of our Cedar Avenue house and the grass behind our Ishii Village house. Yes, grass is grass. And, I thought, kids are kids. I could feel myself running around the playground at Raymond Weill, at Kimmon, and at Bancho. I was the same kid running around in the three different places. And years later, as I traveled as an international education consultant, I thought of Professor Takahashi and recited his poem to myself, in Madrid, in Rome, in Tehran, and even one lonely night in Riyadh.

At the beginning of my second year at Kosho, we were astonished one day when Professor Kagawa, an economics professor, showed up in our German class. "Gentlemen," he announced, "I am here at the request of President Tanaka. Unfortunately, Professor Lenz, who was supposed to teach this class, has not been able to travel to Japan, due to the war situation. So, on we must struggle. And I'm afraid it will be a struggle. I haven't done anything with my German since my own student days. But let's plunge in and see what we can do." Plunge we did, and struggle he did. He often had to stop to wipe his sweaty brow and ended each class with thanks for our patience, an exhortation to do our homework, and a promise of a better time next class. I don't think we learned much

German, but we respected him for the efforts he made and had great affection for him because he was so good-natured. The next year, he left to take a job at a school in Taiwan. On his journey there, his ship was torpedoed. All onboard perished.

The last of the memorable Kosho characters was Professor Hoshino, the legal expert who taught us Jurisprudence. He was known for his liberal thinking and his sharp wit. Occasionally, as he lectured on a legal point, he would say something like, "That's what the law says now, but you never know what will happen once 'you know who' takes over." He was referring to General Tojo, who was then a member of Prime Minister Konoe's cabinet. When I think about it now, I realize that these were probably the last days that liberals like Professor Hoshino could make remarks like that in public.

The everyday deadening influence of the *kempetai* and *tokko*, the military and civilian thought police, were still in the future, at least as far as regular folks knew. I didn't think much about what he said, one way or the other. But the drumbeats of wider war grew louder my first year at Kosho. Not the familiar war, not the "incidents" and "necessary occupation" of China, but intimations of the great Pacific war to come, the war that would take Professor Kagawa's life and the lives of so many others. It was that summer that we began to hear about the "*ABCD*" line—the alliance of the Americans, British, Chinese, and Dutch. Radio reports and the newspapers detailed how these countries were working together to thwart Japan's access to petroleum, rubber, and bauxite, the natural materials we needed from Southeast Asia.

THE summer of 1941, as the radio and the newspapers blared news of this sort at us day after day, my dream of the Naval Academy returned. Masahiro Yoshimatsu, who had been two years ahead of me at Matsuchu, had also gone to Kosho, but he transferred to the Naval Academy after his first year. Once again, I ran the justifications through my head: my parents wouldn't have to pay, I'd get a quality education, and I'd be doing my duty. That seemed more important every day, as the news reports increased in seriousness and drama. I somehow got another application, but I kept it hidden. One day, when I was home alone, I started to fill it out. When I got to the box for my birth date, I finally read the associated small print at the bottom of the page. I was crushed to learn that I was two months too old. Only applicants born on or after November 1, 1922 were being considered. I ripped the form into tiny pieces and put the pieces in my book bag. I didn't want Father to see them in the trash when he came home from the factory. I didn't want to have to explain. When I think about it now, I can only assume that that form and all the others I filled out in the years to come just asked for date of birth and not place of birth. The fact that I was born in the United States and still a U.S. citizen never came up.

I was eighteen when I started Kosho and turned nineteen that summer. Even through the pre-war tensions of the summer, we enjoyed ourselves as college students. I was still a year under the official drinking age, but drinking parties were a regular event. No one thought to stop us; even the police turned a blind eye. Many of my classmates also began smoking openly. I think the only reason I didn't was because Father was such a heavy smoker, and I had always been bothered by the smell of tobacco. The hated restrictions of Matsuchu were gone. We could, and we did, go to coffee shops and movie theaters. The only reason we didn't go to bars and restaurants was that we couldn't afford them—and we were still a bit intimidated by the high life that such establishments represented.

Sometime that summer the Grahams left, evacuated first to Kobe, where the U.S. Consul was assembling groups of Americans, and then by ship to the West Coast. They were there one week, gone the next, but I don't remember doing anything special to mark their departure, other than climb, one last time, to the top of the Castle with Morgan.

WHAT I remember better is my climb the same day with Michiko. When I was finally a college student, years after our giggly walks to school on *Okaido*, I would stop in the Shizuyama's shop and chat with Michiko as I made my selection. Small change and small talk.

When I got up my courage to move beyond the small talk, I used those memories of the walk and the pleasure of seeing each other across the street. Talking about those days and laughing about them with her, I was eventually able to persuade Michiko to go walking with me one Saturday when she finished closing up the shop. Three other Saturday walks followed that year. We took sweets from the shop, ate them as we walked the length of *Okaido*, crossed the main boulevard, and climbed the hill to the Castle to watch the last light fade from the Inland Sea.

We always talked about our school days and laughed at our memories of the *Okaido* promenade. As the sun set on the day I had already climbed the Castle hill with Morgan in the midday heat to watch the old cannon from the Russo-Japanese War be shot off at noon, my muscles burned, but I didn't care. Standing with Michiko and watching the Inland Sea glow, I was perfectly content. The whole world was just me and Michiko. Although we did see each other a few times over the next two years, our excursion that day had a valedictory tone that had somehow escaped me as I dealt with the Grahams on their last days in Matsuyama. I wonder now if the anti-foreigner rhetoric of the day had infected me. Maybe. Or maybe my feelings about the Grahams were so complicated that I didn't allow myself to feel them. Or maybe my all-too-clear feelings about Michiko are the only ones strong enough to survive all the time and events since those days, some of them flowing over and past me, some of them carrying me along.

As we walked back down from the Castle, the cool breezes caressed us, the last of the light melted away, and we both knew that this time— or sometime soon—could be our last time together for a long while, if not forever. I would soon be drafted, and, as a healthy, young, unmarried woman Michiko was likely to be conscripted. By the time I walked Michiko to her front door, night had fallen. Walking home, I thought of the years ahead of us, years of service and struggle to achieve victory for our nation, knowing that I would have my memory of our time together to sustain me. That evening shimmers for me still.

EARLY the morning of December 9, I was listening to the radio with Father as we ate breakfast. Since General Tojo had become Prime Minister in mid-October, the broadcasts sounded more and more ominous every day: diplomatic rebuffs, military advances, reports on economic conditions. And that morning, the announcement, when it came, broke all the tension of the year. It was official and serious, and the language was neutral until the end of the message: *Here is a special news bulletin. This is a special news bulletin. The Imperial Navy entered into a combat situation with the United States today at dawn in the Western Pacific. This is a special news bulletin. The Imperial Navy entered into a combat situation with the United States today at dawn in the Western Pacific. Banzai!!*

"Hooray," I shouted and jumped up from the table. As I hopped about the room, I yelled at Father, "We did it! We finally did it. Hooray."

Shouting *"Banzai"* at breakfast certainly didn't please Father, but I was very excited. He half smiled at me, and sat watching until I sat back down to finish eating. All he said was "Now it's really going to be a long time before Mother comes home." When I put my rice bowl and chopsticks down, he got up slowly from the table and began to get ready to go to work. I felt then absolutely, completely, unquestionably Japanese, but was glad that Father had never seen the ripped-up pieces of the Naval Academy application. I wondered what he thought of what had happened to his son, the San Francisco kid.

MY second year at Kosho began in the spring of 1942. During the vacation before the school year started, I had decided to drop basketball club. I was at best an indifferent guard. The first day of classes, one of the military officers assigned to Kosho stopped me in the hall and asked if I would be interested in organizing a horseback riding club now that I had free time. How did he know I dropped basketball, I thought as I stood in the hall at attention and said, "Yes, of course, Sir. I'd be honored." I didn't know a thing about horses; I had never ridden and never thought about it. But I had always been impressed by the beauty of the horses in the cowboy movies I loved. Thoughts of Tom Mix, Hoot Gibson, and Johnny Mack Brown floated through my head, along with snatches of some of the cowboy songs I remembered.

It didn't take me long to get together a group of about ten. We were all complete amateurs, but our enthusiasm was high. On Sunday, the officer took us to the Matsuyama Regiment. Since the Regiment was infantry, they only had about a dozen horses. The officers rode them in parades and the few who lived in private residences off the base rode them to the Regiment. But the horses needed more exercise. That was where the Kosho Riding Club came in. The officer introduced us to Mr. Oichi, the stable master.

When Mr. Oichi realized what complete beginners we were, he started that first day showing us how to saddle and bridle the horses and how to wipe them down and groom them after exercise. The next Sunday, we were allowed to ride the horses around the Regiment compound a bit. In the following weeks, we progressed from trotting to galloping, and over the course of the year even to steeplechasing. But always confined to the Regiment's grounds. The army was getting free assistance with the exercise of the horses and doing a little indirect recruiting with us, but

Mr. Oichi couldn't be talked into letting us ride the army horses through the town. He said that his superior officers simply wouldn't allow it, but I wonder if that was really just his own judgment, because he had guessed that our real motive for wanting to take the horses out was nothing more than a desire to show off.

After our summer vacation that year, the other members of the Riding Club talked nonstop about Mr. Oichi's restriction. Eventually, as President of the Riding Club, I found myself searching for civilian horses for the club members to ride outside the Regiment. It took a long time, but I finally found one. The horse—and there was only one—belonged to Mr. Miyamoto, the owner of a transport business. More and more of the business involved truck transport, and Chestnut, a mahogany brown mare with a white blaze, was rarely called into service. Mr. Miyamoto was glad to have us exercise her. We took turns after school, and each day one of us took Chestnut out. At first we stayed close to Mr. Miyamoto's stable, but soon we were roaming all over the city. We were a great object of curiosity. College students had never before been seen horse riding in Matsuyama. As people got used to seeing us, they would wave and smile. I was always proud to be out on Chestnut, and knew I looked good in my Kosho uniform.

Riding Chestnut was one of the treats of that year. As college students who would soon be in the military, mounting tension was our constant companion—at Kosho, at the Regiment, throughout the city; it pervaded the entire nation. While I know I felt this, I was somehow also managing to drift. All of the things I heard on the radio were far away and had little to do with me, or my everyday life with Father in Matsuyama. But changes had crept into our daily lives. The coupon system was well entrenched, and it wasn't just sugar that was hard to get. Now rice too was rationed, and even clothing. Fuel was tough enough for the military; it was virtually impossible for civilians. The few cars on the road in Matsuyama were official. People were taking the trolley, riding their bicycles, or walking.

And the regime that flowed from the National Mobilization Act now touched everyone's life—a large number of civilians were conscripted into war industries. Mother, with her practical nursing skills, had been in the forefront. More and more familiar faces vanished from my life as they went off to duties in faraway places.

THE Battle of Midway in June of 1942 was obviously important to Japan's Pacific position. The news reports were quite stirring. Thoughts of dramatic sea battles filled my head for weeks, and it was comforting that the press reported that a U.S. carrier had been sunk while our warships were only slightly damaged. So I was especially excited when I got a note from Yamamura-sensei in September inviting me to a party. *Sensei* organized the party in honor of Keisuke Mori, who had been four years ahead of me at Matsuchu.

Keisuke had been in the Navy since his graduation from Matsuchu. He was serving on the aircraft carrier *Hiryu* during the Battle of Midway. He was home to finish recuperating: he had been burned on his face and his hands. Keisuke's story of the battle was heartrending. He described how the *Hiryu* was bombarded, caught fire, went up in flames, and eventually sank. I looked at Keisuke's injuries, but I couldn't believe what he was saying. And I simply couldn't process what he said about the sinking of the three other carriers: the *Akagi,* the *Kaga,* and the *Soryu.* It wasn't true. It was impossible for the Imperial Navy to be defeated and turn and run. What Keisuke said couldn't be right—it wasn't what had been reported; it wasn't what we had been told and it wasn't what I was sure, in my heart and in my soul, to be true.

AS my third year at Kosho started in April 1943, I took the physical for the draft and passed. But I was deferred so I could finish my studies. At the oral interview, when I was asked if I preferred the infantry or the cavalry, I had Chestnut in mind as I answered cavalry. And as I walked home I thought too of Mother. In the infantry, I would be drafted into Matsuyama Regiment; for the cavalry, I would go first to Zentsuji, where she was stationed.

But in just a few weeks, my old dream of the Navy came back again. The Navy announced that it was recruiting a large number of college graduates for the Naval Reserves. The test was at the end of May. The prospect of flying would be a possibility for me in the Naval Reserves. This time I asked Father. I was going into the military no matter what. I might as well take this one last chance for my dream if I could. I knew Father was still reluctant, but he wrote to Mother, and when her answer came, he told me they had agreed that I should try. Half a train car of Kosho students traveled together to Takamatsu to take the exam.

CHAPTER 8

SAM

Mie, 1943

Gen had slept late but was in the living room with a cup of coffee when Michiko returned from early morning errands.

"Gen-chan," she said, "is there anything you need?"

"No, Gran, thanks. I'm ready to start again whenever you are."

She knelt on the tatami *at the entrance to the living room and said, "Let me get these flowers arranged and then we can start."*

"Anytime, Gran, but I do want to ask you about this Sam guy. I've never heard anything about him. Are you sure you want me to read the next chapter? Is it going to get hotter?"

"Gen-chan, hot is hardly what I'd call what you've read so far."

"'That moment shimmers for me still...' seems pretty hot to me, Gran."

"I only saw him once more after he left Matsuyama to join the Navy."

"I'm interested in what will come next. And what about Gramps, Gran? What did he think about all of this?"

"Gen-chan, I didn't meet your grandfather until the last months of the war. Long after the time you were just reading about." She turned and picked up flowers that she had spread out on the newspaper she had carried them home in and started arranging them in the tokonoma. *Gen could only see her back.*

"Gran, I haven't talked to you about Gramps since his funeral last year. I miss him."

"I know. I do too, my darling." There was silence until Michiko finished. When she positioned the vase in the tokonoma *she turned back to her grandson, got up off her knees, crossed from the* tatami *room into the living room, picked up her needlework, and said, "What's next?"*

I WAS THINKING about President Tanaka as Father and I walked out of the early autumn sunlight and onto the ferry. Just five days earlier, on September 7, 1943, I had stood with six others in the office of the President of Kosho. In August, word had arrived that we were among the very few— fewer than 5,000 of the 70,000 who had taken the special exam in May— who had passed and who were to become Naval Reserve officers. Our graduation from Kosho, scheduled for the next year, had been accelerated by six months because we were headed for formal service to the nation.

The hastily arranged ceremony was unusual but no real surprise. We were military age. We were strong and healthy. Our country needed us. Glory awaited us.

"YOUR diplomas will be sent to your families a little later," the president said. One of the many details of normal life swept aside; they were just too slow to keep up with the rush of events. He looked each of us in the eye and told us that we should be proud to be Kosho graduates. "All my best wishes for a successful military career. Take care of yourselves, and come home alive."

As we filed from his office, I thought of the kindness of this gentle man, of my wonderful experiences at Kosho, and how he didn't, any more than any of us, believe what he said. Despite his best efforts to be positive, his words were suffused with resignation and melancholy. His sorrow was so close to the surface that his formal demeanor barely masked it.

Crisis was in the air. There had been news reports that Italy had surrendered to the Allies. Those reports disappeared quickly, but rumors about the war in Europe continued. Each day brought a new one more shocking than the last. The official news focused on the Pacific war, battlefield successes, and civilian efforts to support the military; the stentorian, authoritative voices poured from the radios, backed by stirring martial music. Despite all that, everyone knew that military service was essentially synonymous with certain death. Perhaps that was why it was easy for Mother to get special leave on short notice and come home just to see me off.

As we approached the benches on the lower deck, Father reached for the bags I was carrying and said, "I'll find a place for these and save us seats. Why don't you go up on deck? I'll join you in a minute."

I LEANED over the handrail and scanned the crowd on the dock, shading my eyes against the morning sun. My glance moved from Mother's solid figure to those around her—Kosho friends, as well as buddies from Matsuchu, some Bancho classmates, and neighbors from Yanai-machi. All the adults had the same look on their faces I had seen on President Tanaka's. By the time Father came to stand beside me, murmuring that he had found a good place to store my bags, the ferry was beginning to move. He raised his hand to wave at Mother, and she and I locked eyes. As the boat pulled me away, I thought that this would be my last sight of her, my last sight of all these dear and familiar friends, and my last sight of Matsuyama. The Inland Sea, which cradled and sustained our city, which was never far from our thoughts, the source of so much of the beauty in our lives, would carry me away. At its other side would be hustle, bustle, challenge, glory—and death. I hoped I looked stoic as they watched me fade from view.

The ferry was bound for Hiroshima. As Father and I settled in on the benches he had saved by stacking them with my bags, I thought about the last time I had taken this trip. In March, my entire Kosho class had spent our spring vacation in "voluntary labor service" at Kure, a Naval Arsenal outside Hiroshima. We had all traveled together to and from Hiroshima. The group of long-time friends had enjoyed being away from home, but the work—packing gunpowder destined, we believed, for the huge guns on Japan's mammoth battleships, the *Yamato* and the *Musashi*, was unfamiliar, rather difficult, and, I realize now, extremely dangerous. But it had been an adventure for us, and I remember how proud we were of our patriotic work. No one told us anything directly because so many of the details about the *Yamato* and *Musashi* were classified and closely guarded state secrets, but we were impressed that the explosives we were working with would be used in the largest guns—forty-six centimeters—in the history of battleships. And while we were at Kure we ate very well. The military provided items that had long disappeared from the civilian diet. I especially remember the sweet brown tea we had on breaks. Sugar was scarce at home. At first the tea was so sweet it was shocking, but it soon became a much-anticipated mid-morning and mid-afternoon treat.

WHEN we reached Hiroshima Port, Father and I took a streetcar to the train station. I remembered a few sights from the spring, and enjoyed the view of the mountains behind the city. The cherry blossoms were long gone, and the trees had not yet taken on their autumn colors. I added these few impressions to those I had already had—but I still had no real sense of the city. When we had all been there in the spring, we were never allowed to leave our dormitory in the evening; the threat of air raids was too great. At Hiroshima Station, Father and I boarded a train for Osaka. We changed trains there and finally reached Matsusaka in Mie Prefecture late in the afternoon.

AS we were settling in at our inn and consulting with the maid about dinner, Father rummaged in the basket he had brought with him and pulled out a bottle of *sake*. I couldn't imagine where he had gotten it. He handed it over to the maid and asked her to warm it up and serve it with our meal. My twenty-first birthday had been a few weeks earlier, in mid-August, and this was the first time Father allowed me to drink with him. Now we were the two adult men of our family, drinking together as we ate our dinner, on the eve of a war-time parting. We talked and talked that night, but the next morning I couldn't really remember what we said. To my regret, to this day, I still can't remember.

The next morning, when we got up early again, there were no words left, and really no need for them. I had to report no later than nine A.M. We walked from the inn to the train station, and took the first train to Karasu Station. Father went with me on the long walk from the station to the front gate of Mie Naval Air Station (NAS), where there was a crowd of young men, their families, and friends. We got as close to the gate as we could, and put all our bags down. Father grabbed both of my hands in his. "Stay well," he said, paused, and looked like he was going to say something else. Instead, he gave the slightest shake of his head and turned away. As he did, I saw tears in his eyes. He didn't look back, and as I watched him walk away, I thought that that would be the last I would ever see of him.

I struggled to the guardhouse with my bags, had my name checked off a long list, was directed to Division One, Barracks Five, and stepped into the base and my life in the military.

FOLLOWING instructions, I dumped my things on one of the beds arranged in the large open room of the first floor of the barracks and walked to the broad parade ground. Hundreds, if not thousands, of young men milled about. Like me, everyone was wearing his college uniform. I scanned the badges on the caps, looking, in vain, for colleagues from Kosho. Soon enough, an officer climbed the platform at the front of the parade ground and barked "Attention!" through a loud speaker. "You are all to line up. Division One at this end; Division Twelve at that end. Each Division should make three lines." Once we had scrambled into a semblance of order, the officer, who was the Vice Commander, told us to go back to our barracks and change into the work suits we would find there. We would no longer need our school uniforms. Ever again. Orientation would commence that afternoon.

THE white cotton work suits were stacked on tables on the second floor of the barracks. As we changed, I looked around—it was another vast room with tables and benches arranged on either side of a central walkway. We weren't due back at the parade ground for a while. My comrades were sitting on the benches, chatting and getting to know each other. In my stiff new clothes, I sat down and started talking to a tall handsome guy. Tetsuo Kobayashi was from Tokyo and had been a long-distance runner at Chuo University. I liked him immediately. I told him about Matsuyama, Yamamura-sensei, the band, the riding club, and my parents. I didn't mention Michiko.

WHEN we reassembled on the parade ground for orientation, the divisions were separated and introduced to our commanding officers. Lieutenant Senior Grade Yamamoto, an impressive Naval Academy graduate, introduced himself. He explained again that fewer than seven percent of those who took the test had been accepted into the special Naval Reserve program for college graduates. Half of the 4,988 who had passed, he told us, were at Mie; the others were beginning their training at Tsuchiura Naval Air Station north of Tokyo. He then went on to tell us about Mie NAS, which had opened only the previous year. He emphasized that it was an honor to be at a beautiful location on Ise Bay not far from the Grand Shrine of Ise, the most sacred of the nation's Shinto shrines—the repository of Amaterasu's sacred mirror, one of the nation's treasures. I stood a little taller in the autumn sunshine, happy that, come what may, I was finally part of the Navy elite.

In the short time that Mie NAS had been operating, twelve groups had preceded us through the training program. We were the Thirteenth Class. Lieutenant Yamamoto also told us that more than 2,000 *yokaren* were living and training at Mie. *Yokaren* was short for *Yoka Renshusei,* Reserve Trainees. They were teenage volunteers who were being trained as pilots. I thought it a bit strange that future Naval officers and raw recruits like the teenagers—many of them farm boys—were sharing the base. I wondered why such low-ranking types were being trained to fly, when one of my dreams, and, I was sure, the dreams of most of the others who took the exam in May, was to become an aviator. But I told myself that the military must have a good reason, and put it out of my mind. When Lieutenant Yamamoto finished, he left us with the three lieutenants junior grade who were in charge of our barracks.

The junior lieutenants took over, marched us back to the barracks and began our first training exercise—drills on getting into and out of bed. They lined us up in the central hallway of the first floor. One of them yelled "To bed!" We ran, jumped out of our clothes and into bed. At the shout "Reveille," we jumped up, got our clothes on, made our beds, and lined up in the middle of the room. We did it over and over until the junior lieutenants were satisfied that we could get up and assembled in thirty seconds, and get ourselves into bed, again in thirty seconds. This was our first introduction to Navy discipline.

The next few days were spent on physical and mental aptitude tests. The results determined our assignments. The vision and balance tests were especially rigorous. I was proud that I could read even the tiniest items on the eye chart and walk a straight line after being spun about in a barbershop-style chair. We were also set to work adding sums. On the monitor's signal, we opened test books, to find them filled with nothing but rows and columns of numbers. We were told to begin by adding each of the horizontal rows, and then the totals of each row on the page, and then the total of each page as we went along through the book. They kept us at it for about three minutes. Time was obviously of the essence.

We were also instructed in Navy etiquette. I'm sure everyone was as thrilled as I was to learn that we were considered officers—officially something between petty officer and ensign. Like all Naval officers, we were expected to behave as gentlemen. We were to be in neatly pressed uniforms at all times we were not wearing our work suits. When not sitting down, we were to stand erect. We could sit only on chairs, sofas, and benches—never on the edges of objects not made for sitting. And we were to carry only briefcases or suitcases. Never the traditional *furoshiki*. We always had to salute any senior officer we encountered and return the salutes of junior officers.

And we learned the Navy's famous "five-minutes before" rule. "Five-minutes before Reveille" blaring from the PA system was the first thing we heard every morning, at five minutes to six. It woke us all up, but we were forbidden to move until we heard "Reveille." The junior lieutenants stood observing us to make sure we stayed in our bunks, perfectly still, but poised to jump up and put on our work clothes as soon as the second announcement came. The "five-minutes before" gave us time to get ready to jump to meet the thirty-second deadline, time to think about the day ahead, time to push thoughts of home out of our heads, time to prepare for the future.

After a week, one of the junior lieutenants said, "Good, you're down to twenty-eight seconds." We were dressed, our beds were made, we were lined up. On his order we ran to the parade ground, joined the other divisions, saluted the Commander, bowed toward the east, the rising sun, Tokyo, and the residence of the Emperor, and went through the morning calisthenics regime. Then back to the barracks for breakfast, which we ate very quickly. No one had to tell us that was part of our training for combat.

CLASSES began at eight. Four fifty-minute sessions in the morning: maritime navigation, aerodynamics, astronomy, and Morse code. At the end of the first week, we were thrilled when the aeronautics instructor took us to a hanger to study various aircraft and their engines up close. We were outdoors every afternoon, our studies practical and very intense: gunnery, sailing, rowing, and hands-on navigation. There were also lots of organized sports and many raucous, hard-fought baseball games, or *yakyu* as we had learned to call it, the foreign term *besuboru* banished along with so many of the other phrases of everyday life before the war. After dinner at six, we had two more classes, finishing up at nine.

This was our routine six days a week. Even though we had Sundays free, we weren't allowed off the base. We still had no uniforms, and Naval cadets could not be seen in public in work suits. Finally, after three

Sundays had passed, we got our uniforms and our government-issued daggers. Oh, we looked smart! The insignia on both sides of the front collar of the navy blue uniform had a golden stripe, indicating our status as officers. The daggers had gold-trimmed hafts and sheaths, but the blades were so dull that they couldn't even peel apples. We didn't care; they looked impressive, and we were sure we did too.

THE next Sunday we were finally allowed out. We walked the three kilometers to the station. I joined a group taking a train north to Tsu, the opposite direction from Matsuzaka, which I had seen with Father. Our principal goal was food. The Navy fed us well, but we were yearning for a change from the monotony of the mess hall. We found a restaurant, and I ate two huge helpings of noodles for lunch. Afterwards we strolled down the main street window shopping and turned into some of the side streets, trying to restore our fading memories of civilian life. Children pointed and said, "Look, Navy officers!" A group of boys gathered around us admiring our daggers.

We were due back at the NAS at six. On our way back to Tsu Station, we passed a photographer's studio. On a whim, we went in to have our pictures taken. I still have the group photo, as well as a single shot of just me in my uniform, looking stern, proud, and unbearably young. I suspect that some of the other photos taken that day sat for many years on family altar shelves. I wonder what became of them when the heartbroken mothers finally died themselves. Old faded sepia, lives now completely unremembered....

AT the end of November, Mie NAS held a "Family Day" and allowed visitors on the base for four hours. I was surprised to find Father in the crowd at the gate. His tired face lit up when he saw me. I led him to the grassy area that surrounded the parade ground. We sat and talked and talked. Mother was about to be released from her duties at Zentsuji. The neighbors were all well. Life in Matsuyama sounded fine, but very, very far away. At noontime, Father began unpacking the knapsack he had brought with him. Four wooden boxes wrapped neatly in newspaper emerged. He opened the first two, which were full of rice, way too much for the two of us. The third had home-cooked fish and vegetables. He lifted the last box and slowly removed the lid—fried chicken. My favorite!

With a smile he said he had cooked it late Saturday afternoon before he took the overnight ferry and then the train to get to Mie just in time to meet me. Just as I was admiring the chicken, my friend Kobayashi walked by. No one from his family had made it all the way from Tokyo. I called him over, and he joined Father and me in our feast. With the three of us, none of the food went to waste. Kobayashi heard the story of the fried chicken as he had his first taste of this treat. He ate with his fingers as we told him he must to really enjoy it, then licked his fingers and joked about what a well-traveled meal he was enjoying.

After our lunch, Kobayashi and I walked Father to the station. As the train pulled away, I thought, with pleasure, that I *had* seen Father again. I doubted I would be lucky enough to have another chance. Kobayashi walked next to me back to the base in silence.

ROUTINE resumed. Kobayashi still joked about the fried chicken, asked about my parents, and told me about his mother and sister, but I knew that for him, just as for me, civilian life was becoming harder and harder to remember. Matsuyama was fading, fading and I grew more certain with each passing week that I had seen my last Seto Inland Sea sunset.

Our briefings were giving us a better idea of military operations. Listening to them, we began to understand how dire things must really be at the front, and realized how the bad news was cloaked in special euphemisms. For example, troop "transfer" meant defeat and retreat. We all knew in our bones that Japan's dominance of Asia was drawing to an end, and that the fate that awaited us, the fate of a glorious battle death that many of us had dreamed and hoped for, would, in fact, be nothing but a waste. But what still came out of our mouths was, "Wait till we get there. We'll take care of it!" It was just that our hearts flopped about as we said it.

At the end of January, Division Commander Lieutenant Yamamoto assembled us in the hallway of our barracks. After a little more than four months, our basic training was coming to an end; he had orders for each of us. Mine read "Flight training at Izumi Naval Air Corps." I had no idea where Izumi was, but I didn't care. I was to be trained as a pilot.

CHAPTER 9

SAM

Izumi, 1944

WE ARRIVED LATE, after marching, one hundred strong, from the train station. Lieutenant Senior Grade Takeuchi appeared as we ate a special dinner in the barracks. He was tall, lanky, and didn't seem tough, but I believed him when he said, "When I'm finished training you, no one will be able to tell the difference between you reserve cadets and regular Navy." He announced that formal orientation would begin first thing in the morning. There was only enough time for a quick bath before lights out.

And now that we were assembled in the sunshine, the Lieutenant began by explaining where we were. "You've probably noticed how warm it is for early February," he said, and went on to explain that Izumi Naval Air Corps was not only one of the newest in the nation but also the southern-most base in Kyushu. "The prevailing winds," he told us, "are from the north, so the runway was built on a north-south axis." I could hear planes landing and taking off as he spoke. *Finally, I'm on an airbase.*

"As you may know, Kagoshima Prefecture is famous for its beautiful women, rugged mountains, volcanoes both dormant and active, outlandishly oversized radishes, and the good nature of its people. The locals are fond of us, have been generous to our young flight cadets like you, and especially kind to the *yokaren*. And there's another thing the people of Izumi are fond of: cranes."

I thought, what craziness is this, *cranes?* But Lieutenant Takeuchi went on to explain, "Thousands of cranes migrate annually from Siberia's Lake Baikal and the Amur River regions, via China and Korea. They nest in this area from October to February. Most of them are *kurozuru*, common cranes, or *manazuru*, white-naped cranes, but there are also

many other species. All of them are treasured by the local people, who are quite proud they come here every year. There are still almost a thousand of them here now. They are likely to be gone by the end of the month, but be careful when you're flying. We don't want to harm these exquisite creatures, these symbols of our country."

And then his voice changed and his whole demeanor shifted. He didn't seem to be focused on us anymore or even aware of what he was saying. *"Yu no hara ni / naku ashitazu wa / a ga gotoku / imo ni koure ya / toki wakazu naku. Near these hot springs / cranes are crying in a field / and I wonder if like myself / they long for love / and weep unmindful of time."*

He changed again and was back with us. "Time," he said. "Cadets, time is passing and is calling you to come along with it. We start flight training tomorrow. Be ready." His official demeanor couldn't hide his sincerity, his passion, or his kind nature; he reminded me of Yamamura-sensei.

We spent the afternoon learning our way around the base. After a good meal that evening, we were sorting ourselves and our belongings in the barracks, before getting ready for bed, when talk turned from the promised thrill of learning to fly to Lieutenant Takeuchi's odd speech.

"What," said Saito, a country boy from Yamaguchi, "was that talk about the cranes? Did I really hear him say something about cranes crying and then something about crying himself for love? I couldn't understand that old literary language. What the heck is going on with the Lieutenant?"

A number of others joined Saito in laughing, but as the laughter faded, a cadet I didn't know said, "Actually he was quoting the *Manyoshu,* you know, *The Thousand Leaves.* Lieutenant Takeuchi is very well educated. He was a Kyodai student and a literature major. He was reciting a poem by Otomo Tabito that was written about thirteen hundred years ago. After Otomo had served at court for many years, the Emperor sent him here to Kyushu as Governor General. Maybe the Lieutenant wanted to illustrate how, like Otomo, all of us from all parts of the country can learn to appreciate the cranes as the Izumi locals do."

"You're way over my head, Iwanami," said Saito. "They really stuffed your head full of weird stuff at Todai."

Iwanami laughed good-naturedly with Saito and his buddies and then said, "Well, here's some more for you from the *Manyoshu.* This one was written about a century later by Monobe Akimochi, who served the

Emperor as a border guard: *Kashikoki ya / mikoto kagafuri / asu yuri ya / kae ga muta nemu / imu nashi no shite. We have received / our Imperial Orders / and from tomorrow / we will sleep among the reeds / while our wives remain behind.* As the Lieutenant said, we have our orders. From tomorrow we start learning to fly. And once we know how to fly, I'm sure there will be new orders."

That was the end of the laughter. We finished stowing our gear in silence. I'm sure I wasn't the only one who thought I was too young to even have a wife. As I lay in my bunk, I thought of Yamamura-sensei and the birds in the fields at Ishii Village. My thoughts then drifted to Principal Tomihisa and my first day at Bancho, and then I found myself remembering a Raymond Weill class excursion. I was running, running through a wide field on the Marin headlands. A stiff wind carried the tang of the ocean to mix with the sharp smell of the mélange of grasses. I was careening downhill so fast I felt like I would take off and fly into the beautifully blue water before me, the vast and pitilessly calm Pacific.

I heard those around me falling into sleep, and one of the last things my memory presented me before I joined them was a *haiku* that Basho wrote when he visited the far north town of Takadachi five centuries after a famous battle there: *Natsukusa ya / tsuwamono-domo ga / yume no ato. Summer grasses / where soldiers / once dreamed.* Iwanami, the tall, bright scion of a prestigious family and an honors graduate of Japan's best university, perished on a mission less than a year later.

I can't remember now what I dreamed that night, and I find myself now wondering if poetry was what Iwanami held in his mind and his heart when he took off from the Philippines for his mission. In the little bit of reading that I've done to spur my memories for this memoir, I learned that eighty percent of all those who perished as Navy special attack aviators were university student officers, like myself and Iwanami. When student deferments ended about the time I arrived at Mie, the military was flooded with even more students. In a matter of days in December 1943, more than 5,000 students were drafted, with 500 of them from Todai alone.

THE next morning, after a hearty breakfast, we assembled at the eastern edge of the airfield at eight. We were suited up and eager to get started, having practiced putting on our flight uniforms the night before. We weren't wearing full winter uniforms, but we had been shown them—

fur-lined pants and jackets wired with their own electrical heating systems—a triumph of both form and function. The supply sergeant had even shown us the electrically heated socks that we would use for cold weather missions.

With the usual Navy attention to detail, we had practiced and practiced. The brown pants first over our underwear. Large pockets above each knee. I was still wondering what flight equipment would go in those pockets—maybe maps? Beautiful brown leather boots, fleece lined. Next, the matching brown jacket, and over the jacket, the brown life vest, covered with pockets full of kapok. The life vests were worn at all times with the flight suit. The fur collar of the jacket flipped down over the vest. Our parachutes went on our backs, with the ties looped through the life vests. The life vests also had a clip for carrying oxygen masks. Last was the leather helmet. A beautiful piece of craftsmanship. Fur-lined ear flaps. Snaps to secure our goggles and oxygen masks. We were issued goggles, but not oxygen masks—not yet.

We stood in formation in the bright morning sun, the breeze on our faces. We know we looked good, but were nervous because we were about to begin learning what we needed to make the image a reality. To become pilots.

Lieutenant Takeuchi split us into groups of ten. We were told to sit on the grass, cross-legged, and listen. One non-com instructor was assigned to each group. He went over the gears and the instruments. Again and again. I forced myself to concentrate. We had learned all of this at Mie. Finally, two by two, the instructor took us out on the tarmac to a plane. He pointed to each of the gears, each instrument, and each gauge. The bi-wing planes, Model 93 Intermediate Trainers, had cloth-covered wooden frames. On the tarmac, they sat back on their tail wheels at steep angles, perched high over their landing gears. Their big engines were in front of two open cockpits, one behind the other. The non-com explained that the trainee would sit in the front, with the instructor in the rear. He pointed out the voice tube and how the throttles, the control sticks, and the steering sticks in the two cockpits were linked together, to allow the instructors to correct the mistakes of the trainees.

"YOU can't see hardly anything, can you?" came the voice through the tube.

"No, Sir."

"Crank the seat forward." I struggled with gravity, pulling uphill, and only managed to shift it a bit.

"But be careful not to go too far. Your feet still have to be able to push the steering stick the full length, left and right. That's probably better, isn't it?"

"Yes, Sir."

"I know you still can't see much over the engine cowling. That's because our nose is up and our tail is down. Let's get going and see if we can change that."

The ground crew finished cranking the propellers and shouted "Inertia all right." That was the cue for the pilot to yell, "Switch on," as he turned the ignition key. The pilot. *That's me!*

The engine was running. We were ready to go.

"Taxi?" I asked.

"Taxi," came the answer.

"Chocks away," I shouted to the ground crew. We were off down the runway.

"Streamer," I heard through the tube. The instructor was reminding me to check the wind. The red-and-white windsock indicated north wind. We were aimed toward the south end of the runway. No, not we. My hands were clutching the rims of the cockpit, where they were supposed to be for the first flight. I was forbidden to touch anything. My job was simply to observe everything happening in the cockpit.

As we taxied down the runway, panic seized me. I wondered if the instructor was incompetent, or insane. He swung the plane to the left and then to the right. What was he doing? How would we ever get off the ground? *Calm down and think, calm down and think. He's swinging the plane so we can see where we're going, since we still can't see over the engine.* We swooshed our way to the south end of the runway and slowly turned north to face the wind. "Check the runway," he ordered.

The flagman a few hundred yards in front of us put away his red flag and held up a white one. When he signaled by swinging it down, I yelled, "Takeoff!"

I watched the throttle move slowly, slowly, and then a little faster until it was fully forward. The tail rose, the plane leveled out. Now I could see everything. And we were in the air. I was flying. *Flying!*

The control stick moved back a bit, and we nosed up, at about a thirty-degree angle. The throttle also moved back. From takeoff to climbing speed, I told myself. When we had gone about 1,000 meters north, the control stick and the steering stick showed that we were going to turn right. The instructor turned us ninety degrees, due east. By then we had reached the takeoff and landing practice altitude of 300 meters. After we traveled 500 meters east, we again turned ninety degrees to the right, and headed south, parallel to the runway. I was reciting these details to myself, knowing I would have to be able to report and describe them accurately, but I was besotted by the view, by the scenery.

The Izumi Plain lay below us, bisected by the airfield, which was now to the west. Several flocks of cranes were scattered about below, feeding in the fields. We were a little closer to mountains to the east, and I could see Mt. Shibi, the tallest in the range. The ocean bays of the Yatsushiro Sea lay to the west. How beautiful it all was. Islands scattered in the sea. I thought of the innumerable islands of the Inland Sea and my ferry trips to and from Matsuyama. And remembered standing at the top of the Castle grounds with Michiko, gazing out at the floating islands of Seto.

Another ninety-degree turn, a slight throttle down. The instructor began a gentle descent. As the runway came clearly into view, we made another right turn to face it squarely. The throttle moved further back. As we neared the ground, the instructor called out, "Thirty meters, twenty-five meters, twenty meters, fifteen meters...." At five meters, he pulled the throttle and the control stick all the way back for a perfect three-point landing. I knew I would have to learn a lot to match this perfection and meet the Navy's standards. And I knew that I'd have to learn more about the wind—about its velocity and direction—in order to be able to be a good pilot.

But at the moment I climbed out of the plane, the wind was just the part of nature that had lifted me and carried me aloft, part of the beautiful package of green mountains and blue water, of shimmering islands and towering peaks. I'm sure I didn't completely suppress my exultant grin—or my shaking legs—as I stood at the side of the plane—the wonderful, wonderful plane—saluted the instructor, and said "Thank you, Sir!"

TWO weeks into our training, when we were anticipating our solo flights, Lieutenant Takeuchi assembled the entire division. There had been another mishap. It was minor, but it was the third that week. We knew he couldn't tolerate such sloppiness. "Rows one, three, and five, about face," came the shouted order. I was happy when I realized that I didn't know the cadet I was now facing.

"Legs apart!" and then the pause, just enough time for us to think about what was coming.

"Go."

I took a step forward, my head high, my right arm raised, and put all my strength into the punch. It landed hard on the cadet, just as his landed on my left cheek. The Lieutenant had keen eyes. "Tanaka, Yamashita, Ogonogi, and Minoda, and those you are paired with, stay where you are. All others, two steps back. Hup!"

I was glad I had learned the rules the last time and didn't have to go through it again, under the Lieutenant's close scrutiny. My left cheek, like those of all my buddies, was hardened by months of this discipline.

AS the days of training went on, our grips on the controls became firmer and firmer, but we never resisted the movements of the instructor. Then came that wonderful day when right after takeoff I heard, "Okay, Student Imagawa, you're on your own," through the tube. It took me a second or two to realize that the instructor's hands and feet were off the controls. I began to sweat but kept on doing exactly as we had trained. My turns were smooth. The descent seemed to go well. "Five meters," I yelled, and pulled the throttle and control stick back, but just a bit too fast. The plane glided about a meter off the ground for about three seconds and then thumped to a landing. I was lucky that it wasn't bad enough to damage the landing gear.

After three days of this, I had my first solo. Once I was in the air, I was overwhelmed with the joy of flying and the power in my hands. I was in full control, not only of one airplane: I controlled the entire world! The scenery below was especially beautiful. I wanted to ease the plane into a roll or a loop, but didn't know how, so I brought the plane in for landing, with as much nonchalance as I could muster. The landing was perfect. I wasn't surprised—it was part of the absolute and powerful purity of the experience.

A few days later, after all of us completed solo flights, we began advanced intermediate night training—loops, slow rolls, quick rolls, pursuits, and dodging pursuits. Nose diving from 1,500 meters and pulling up at 500 meters was fun. The hardest was formation flying. The Model 93 had a maximum speed of only seventy-five knots, so if you fell behind it was hard to catch up. But we were flying every day. The more we flew, the more we loved it.

THIS time because it was just our squad, the remedy was "Navy spirit injection." We had had four less-than-perfect landings, and Utsumi had ripped his uniform. "Take position," shouted the Lieutenant. All too familiar with this from our days in Mie, we bent over, pushed our butts out behind us and held our arms straight out in front of us. The Navy Spirit Injection Stick was four feet long. Lieutenant Takeuchi moved down the line, whacking each of us as hard as he could on the bottom. When the injection was accomplished, each of us, in turn, despite the effort involved, stood up straight, saluted, and said, "Thank you!" We made sure we were loud, and sincere.

TO our regret, we weren't in the air all the time. Once we had our basic skills under control, only one squad at a time trained. The others worked on Morse code, aircraft engine maintenance, athletics, and rifle and bayonet training. Life at Izumi had settled into a routine.

VERY early in the morning of the first Sunday of April, Lieutenant Takeuchi marched into our barracks and announced that we were going sailing. As we jumped to attention, he laughed at our surprise, "Well, you *are* naval officers, aren't you? We're going to sea."

The ship was a small workhorse minesweeper, but it was painted battleship gray and flew the magnificent rising sun battle emblem, with its bold, defiant beams radiating to the borders of the flag. The smell of the paint reminded me of the Japanese fleet visit to San Francisco.

We sailed from Izumi across the Ariake Bay to Amakusa. Lieutenant Takeuchi announced that we would have a short shore leave and that he had arranged for a quick tour around the small town. The Lieutenant walked at the front of the group, with the guide, a tall, thin elderly woman with a toothy smile and sun-dark skin. Although she looked like a farmer's wife, her manner of speaking reminded me of Hoshino-sensei, my history and jurisprudence teacher. Could it have been only three years ago that I sat in his classroom? Before the war began, I was shocked when he made sarcastic comments about "you-know-who" taking over. "You-know-who," General Tojo, had been Prime Minister for two and a half years now, and the war against the United States was more than two years old. And I was a naval cadet and a pilot, part of a great and glorious historic adventure.

As we climbed the hill to the Castle, the old lady told us about Amakusa. "In the early eighteenth century, many of the local farmers converted to Christianity. With the new religion, the Jesuit missionaries also taught the farmers a taste for self-determination. When the cruel persecutions of the Tokugawa Shogun culminated in an outright ban of Christianity, the local farmers rebelled, seizing this castle and the one at Shimabara. There were long, bitter sieges during the winter of 1737–38, and the rebels were eventually defeated in fierce, bloody assaults by the Tokugawa troops. The few rebels who weren't killed in the battles were only able to save their families and keep their heads if they smashed statues of the Virgin Mary and stamped on crosses. Christianity was officially obliterated, and the area came under the direct control of the Shogun. In 1739, the Tokugawas ejected all Portuguese and Spanish from the country. Only the Dutch and the Chinese were able to continue to trade, and the Dutch were restricted to the island of Dejima in Nagasaki Bay."

The exhibits in the small museum on the ground floor of the Castle were touching because they were somewhat ridiculous. "Imagawa, take a look at this," called Utsumi, who was joking around with Kobayashi. He was pointing at the neatly labeled "Christian scissors" in a display case.

I smiled but didn't reply. With the guide's words still in my head, I drifted from thinking about foreign religions to foreign influences, and then the interplay of words took me across languages and cultures: *Amakusa, Amakusa*…Heavenly Grass, Grass of Heaven, Grass Heaven, what's the translation, what's the best way to say it in English? And what about *Amanogawa*? It's poetic, I thought, that the Japanese for Milky Way was River of Heaven, Heavenly River. And *Amanohashidate,* Bridge of Heaven, Heavenly Bridge, one of Japan's three most famous views, the sandbar with the beautiful pine woods where, supposedly, the Japanese gods had conceived the islands of our country—the story I had heard my second week at Bancho. Now I was mixing not just English and Japanese, but Shinto and Christianity. Why had English popped into my head? It wasn't part of my life any more. In fact, it was the enemy. The fact that I had spent so much time around Christianity had no relevance to my life now. But here I was in the area that sparked Japan's isolation for almost 150 years, learning that much of what happened had been triggered by ideas that came with Christianity, with foreign religions and foreign ideas.

Ridiculous but not really harmful, I had always thought as I sang "Rock of Ages" with the Grahams, enjoying the music, thinking everything else was silly. While Utsumi and Kobayshi laughed, I thought of Mrs. Graham sitting at her dining room table in Matsuyama, cutting out a pattern for a new dress for Jane, while Morgan and I played with tin soldiers on the floor at her feet. "Christian scissors" at work in Japan two hundred years after the bloody battles of Shimabara and Amakusa.

My musings about religion and foreign influences had faded by the time we got back to the dock. Before we sailed, the staff from a local restaurant delivered a delicious picnic lunch. We feasted on the fish for which the area was famous, fresh vegetables from local farms, and mounds of perfectly sticky rice balls, some sprinkled with black sesames and others wrapped in sheets of seaweed. We cruised back to Izumi in the fading light. I stood with my friends, feeling completely alive and content, the breeze on my face, my senses full of the briny, mollusky smell of the sea, watching the yellow, pink, and then red of the sky as the sun sank. Lieutenant Takeuchi, who had been so tough on us for so long, stood with me, Utsumi, and Kobayashi for much of the return trip. He too seemed content just to be there. His only comment was, "A good day."

As we headed back to our barracks in the dark, I wondered if I would ever again experience the rising joy of a journey across water, and thought of all the wonderful ones I had made, even in my short life: the ship pulling away from San Francisco Bay, and then across the majesty of the wide Pacific, and my many ferry trips across the serenely beautiful Inland Sea with its islands floating and shining in the sun.

WE knew that our time in Izumi was limited. As we awaited our orders, we looked forward to our next assignments and took pride in the inevitability of our fates. But the mood of our elders, including the senior officers, was rather elegiac. The town wasn't big enough for an officers' club, but, as Lieutenant Takeuchi told us, the local people were very kind. I'm

sure now that their affection had a great deal to do with their awareness of
our fate. Even though they lived with the privations the war had brought,
they were willing to share what little they had with us.

THE Sunday after our sailing excursion, local families invited the cadets on home visits. Kobayashi and I teamed up. It took us twenty-five
minutes to walk to the home of "our" family. When we arrived, everyone
was waiting for us: Mr. and Mrs. Tanaka; Reiko, the oldest daughter;
two younger girls; a baby boy; and a maid. Kobayashi and I grinned at
each other: lucky, lucky, lucky. Reiko was the prettiest girl in Izumi, no
question about it.

> After a delicious dinner, only Kobayashi, Mr. Tanaka, and I remained
at the table. I leaned back on the *tatami* and thought, this *is* a warm and
wonderful place. The lovely Reiko brought another container of *shochu*.

> "Thank you, my dear. That will be all for tonight," said Mr. Tanaka.
I thought of my father, and his love of alcohol, as Mr. Tanaka filled my
glass again. The local liquor was strong. It had a big, broad taste, like the
oily local fish, like the white radishes as big as watermelons, and like the
pungent purple potatoes.

THE next Sunday Reiko sat with Kobayashi and me at dinner and responded to our questions. I wondered then and I wondered over the next
few weeks whether she liked me or Kobayashi better. But it didn't really
matter. We were short-timers. Short-timers in Izumi, short-timers in this
life. That second Sunday, by the time Mr. Tanaka and I had finished
the third container, I stopped thinking about Reiko and realized I had
learned to love *shochu*. Kyushu really was quite wonderful. I only made
it back to the barracks because Mr. Tanaka took me on his bicycle. My
sober-sided friend Kobayashi trotted alongside.

I was delighted when a letter from Mother arrived at the end of April
announcing that she was setting out to visit me. She had been released
from her nursing service in Zentsuji in March and was back home in
Matsuyama. She wanted to see me before I was transferred somewhere
far away, and she was coming by herself because Father had seen me since
I had left Matsuyama.

> She traveled from Matsuyama across the Inland Sea to Oita by ferry,

and by train to Izumi. I was shocked to see how thin she was. I was used to her being rather plump, and remembered Father's loyal jokes about the unattractiveness of skinny women. Mother said that everything was scarce, especially food. She also brought the news that she and Father were moving back to the family home in Ishii Village because our Yanai-machi house in the city was going to be torn down to create a fire break. The city was expecting bombings. I was horrified. I had never imagined that the war would reach Matsuyama.

Mother must have noticed my distress, but clearly didn't want to talk about it. She reached in her bag and pulled out an old *furoshiki* that I could remember her carrying on shopping trips in Japantown when I was small. "Isamu dear, I have something wonderful for you."

"Yes, Mother?"

She untied the *furoshiki*. It fell open, revealing a delicate white silk cloth with bright red stitches: a beautiful *senninbari*.

"I saw that Shizuyama girl, Michiko, on the corner by the train station. She was asking passersby. I stopped to talk to her since you knew her at Bancho. Well, was I surprised when I learned that she was making it for you. How nice of her. I had her bring it round as soon as she was finished. It turned out quite well, didn't it?"

I took the long silk scarf and ran my fingers over the stitches. I thought of Michiko making the stitches and pictured her standing alone near the station asking others to take a stitch for her. I had wondered why I hadn't heard from her. My last letter from her had arrived shortly after we began training in Izumi. Michiko had written it in late January, and it had been forwarded to me from Mie. I had had no answer to the letters I had written her about learning to fly, about our trip to Amakusa, about where I thought I might be going next, about how I thought I might never see her again.

"It's really quite unfortunate about her parents."

"What?"

"Oh, Isamu, I thought you were in touch with her. After the way she cried when I found her on the street with the *senninbari*. Both her brothers were killed in action, and now her parents are gone as well. Evidently her mother had tuberculosis for quite some time. I had no idea. What a danger for everyone who associated with them. It's quite dreadful when you think about all the people in and out of that shop. The mother died in mid-February, and then within a week, the father had a heart attack. When she brought this to me, she said she was on her way to Kure with a group of her classmates to work at the Arsenal. I guess that little shop will be sold—if anyone will buy it."

IN the afternoon we went to visit the Tanakas. I still have the photo. Mother sits smiling with Mrs. Tanaka. Kobayashi and I stand with Mr. Tanaka. Reiko, lovely Reiko, is in the corner. So young. We had a feast that evening. It was our last night in Izumi. Our orders had come through. I was assigned to Wonson, in South Korea, for further flight training. I wasn't sure, but I thought it meant the Zero. But those of us assigned to Wonson were ordered to go first to Oita, on the opposite side of Kyushu.

I got Mother on the train with us when we left for Oita. She chatted cheerfully during the four-hour journey and joked with my friends. I thought it was our last, precious time together, but Mother was focused on a different future from the one I knew awaited me. She had her eyes on a bride for me. I dismissed it all as ridiculous, as wishful thinking. But, of course, I didn't say any of that. No mother wants her son insisting that he will soon be dead. I listened dutifully to what she had to say as I went with her to the ferry slip at Oita and waved as she set out for Shikoku, for the home I was sure I'd never see again.

BUT THANKS to another of fate's surprises, less than two months later I was sitting on the *tatami* at home again. And Mother was talking. She was completely focused. She wanted it so much. I couldn't, I didn't want anything, so I said yes. What did it matter? I would be dead soon. But she would be happy now.

"Yes, Mother. I agree."

THE afternoon heat shimmered outside the Ishii Village house. After only a short time in Oita, my orders for Wonson had come through. I had leave for three days before we sailed for Korea—just long enough for me to make a trip to Matsuyama.

The bustle and excitement of my surprise arrival had passed. But I wasn't going to get the relaxation I was looking forward to. Mother had business for us to attend to. There was no breeze, and the sound of the cicadas and the sharp summer smells of the fields filled the house.

"It's a splendid match. You'll be a fine couple. The Katayamas are a very good family. Their roots here in Ishii are as deep as those of the Imagawas. Kayoko-san's grandfather was a close associate of your grandfather when he was mayor of Ishii Village. The doctors of their family and the mayors of our family have known each other and worked together for generations."

"Congratulations," said Father.

"I'll have to leave the details to you," I said.

"That's fine, my dear, but I do want you to see her again on this visit. After that I can take care of all the formalities. It's unfortunate, but for the sake of the country we have to accept that it may be impossible for you to be present for the official engagement ceremony."

"I don't have much time, Mother."

Ignoring what I was saying, as I expected she would, she sailed on. "We'll find the time while you're here. Even though you probably don't want to admit it, I'm sure you remember her well. If I can arrange everything, we could even have a ceremony and sign the register the next time you get leave."

SHE had started earlier that year, mentioning Kayoko in every letter. Now that she was back home in Matsuyama, she was thinking about the Imagawa family position there and my proper future. And as much as I had tried to tune it out, she had brought it up over and over again when she visited Izumi. She kept saying that she was sure I had the same good impression of Kayoko that she had and reminded me of the visit we had paid to her family two years earlier when she was home on leave from Zentsuji. At that time, Mother was consulting with Dr. Katayama about nursing techniques he was pioneering at Matsuyama Hospital, but I should have known better: she had been much too insistent that Father and I accompany her.

I had only fragmentary memories of that visit: the hot sun in Yanai-machi, the long trolley ride. Mother in her best *kimono*, clucking at Father as we were getting ready to leave, "Don't be so slow. Help me tie this *obi*. We can't be late."

I did remember that Kayoko, who was almost three years older than

I, was a terrible *koto* player. Like most proper young ladies, she had no education beyond elementary school and had spent the years since she left school helping her mother and studying flower arranging and *koto*, so she had been at it for quite a while. Her mother insisted on the recital after the medical business was concluded. As Kayoko knelt before the instrument and moved her hands across its strings, her father's face wore one of those patient, indulgent parental looks. I kept my face under control by thinking about Yamamura-sensei and what his reaction would have been. Mother's letters always mentioned Kayoko's beauty, but I could only remember a narrow face and long, lank hair.

"Fine, now that's settled. Your father has been saving our ration for three months, so we have enough *sake* for all of us, and I'm going to start the fried chicken now. We'll have a feast. We have lots to celebrate."

THE next morning, I asked Mother for my old college clothes, but she insisted that I appear in public only in my uniform. I set off for the city to visit my old teachers. For a Navy officer, riding a bicycle was prohibited, so I had to walk all the way. I visited both Bancho and Matsuchu and saw a number of my old teachers. I know they wanted me to be safe and well, but all they could manage to say were the conventional exhortations to do my best for the Emperor and the country. But what I saw in their faces was the deep and sure knowledge that was mine too—the time left to me was very short. I regretted that Yamamura-sensei was not at Matsuchu that day; I had especially wanted to see him.

On the long walk back to Ishii Village in the midday heat, I consoled myself with the thought that my death would mean the survival of my family and all the good people I had seen that day.

Mother was waiting. We were going out again right away. I was to wear my uniform again. She had been making plans, and as she bustled about, she laid out her vision of the future. I would be serving in the Navy for many years to come. I would come home on leave again soon, and there would be time for the marriage ceremony. And then Kayoko would be a Naval officer's wife. Still chattering, she rushed me out the door, and off we went to Kayoko's aunt's house, where my fiancée and I were to meet again.

When we arrived, the four of us sat in Aunt Furusawa's tiny parlor, which was crowded with examples of her craft work. I certainly didn't know what to say; no one else seemed to either. I concentrated on the *sashiko* cover on the table, letting my eyes drift in and out of focus and letting first the squares and then the diamonds in the pattern float into prominence. I wondered if Aunt Furusawa helped girls and women work on the *senninbari* they made for their loved ones.

Thinking of the *senninbari* offered an escape route, and I removed myself from the situation I was in by thinking about Michiko.

Mother commented on how hot it was for mid-June. With that the older women launched into a conversation about how the rainy season should begin soon. Neither Kayoko nor I had anything at all to say. We sat and listened to Mother and Aunt Furusawa. Their conversation had drifted to textiles. Suddenly they stood and then disappeared upstairs to look at some special samples of *iyo kasuri* that Aunt Furusawa had bought at a local temple festival.

My fiancée and I sat in silence. When I couldn't bear it any longer, I said, "Your name is Kayoko, isn't it?"

"Yes."

"When did you first hear about me?"

No answer. I tried again.

"Did you do well in school? Did you enjoy it?"

Again no answer.

"Do you know what a Zero fighter is?"

"No."

"Do you have a hobby?" Again, she looked down at the table. No answer. I gave up on the conversation. We sat again in silence. I looked at her closely. She kept her eyes cast down. After a long time, she looked up, caught my eye and quickly turned away again. The minutes ticked by. I wondered how much more of this I'd have to endure.

Kayoko was visibly working herself up to something—she first seemed to brace herself, then wriggled in her place and finally whispered, "May I serve you some tea?"

"Oh yes, please. By all means," I responded, surprised that she could produce a sentence on her own.

She went to the kitchen, and I relaxed for a few moments as I listened to the kettle rattle and then whistle. The ladies upstairs must have heard it too. They came downstairs chatting about the humble beauties of the local folk arts. The group reformed when Kayoko brought the tea cups and pot in from the kitchen. She served us with grace; it was obvious she had studied tea ceremony. The atmosphere relaxed a bit. Conversation turned to mutual acquaintances and Ishii Village characters. Kayoko giggled, but again didn't have anything to say. I was bored silly and glad when we finally escaped.

Mother continued to chat about Ishii Village and Kayoko as we walked home. I thought, she's a nice enough girl, I'm sure. Typical, a nice typical, reserved, well-mannered Japanese girl. But not my type. I wanted someone curious, frank, and humorous. Michiko was like that, and flexible as well. But my stubborn mother had made up her mind about who was appropriate for me. *But none of Mother's plans mattered. Michiko was gone. I'd be gone soon, and I wasn't coming home alive.*

When we got home, Mother asked directly what I thought of Kayoko. I kept my thoughts to myself.

MOTHER, Father, and I had another feast that night but only one drink each: I had an early train the next morning. I successfully steered the conversation clear of Kayoko by talking about the Zero and what a great honor it was that I was going to learn to fly such a magnificent aircraft. I didn't sleep well that night and thought about Michiko as I lay awake. I was probably anxious about the journeys ahead of me, and worried that I would never see Michiko again, much less have a chance to bid her farewell before my final journey.

CHAPTER 10

SAM

Oita, Japan and Wonson, Korea, 1944

IT WASN'T UNTIL we arrived at Oita that we learned why our posting to Korea was delayed. The winter there had been especially harsh and the runway at Wonson needed extensive repairs. We would have to stay at Oita for at least a month and would start our fighter training there.

We were now at the northeastern corner of Kyushu, on the shore of the Inland Sea. Shikoku was to the east. Oita Naval Air Corps (NAC), the airfield we were assigned to, was only a short distance from Beppu, Japan's most famous seaside hot spring. We were thrilled that we were going to become fighter pilots, and we were excited to be close to the fabled resort; we found its honky-tonk reputation alluring.

But we were deflated when we learned that there were no Zeros at Oita. Our training would start on Model 96 fighters. Since our days at Mie we had been talking about the Zero: a sleek, powerful, maneuverable engineering marvel. And now we were going to work with an outdated plane that had had its heyday in the 1930s on the China front. Like the Model 93s we used at Izumi, the Model 96 was a sturdy plane with a big engine up front, a tail wheel, and non-retractable landing gear. The most obvious difference was that the Model 96 was a single-wing plane. Well, we told each other, looking at the clunkers, we have to make do—it's all part of our contribution to the war effort. And we'll learn fighter techniques.

Oita NAC was a busy place. Hundreds of *yokaren* were in basic flight training, and the runway was being lengthened to accommodate the fighters that arrived with us. An army of construction workers, aided by high school and middle school students, worked long shifts.

Our training repeated the process from Izumi: hands off first; hands

lightly on the controls; flying with the instructor in the rear seat; soloing. But the speeds were much faster and the rates of ascent and descent
much steeper. It was more dangerous, and discipline was tighter. Navy
Spirit "injections" were frequent. But the discipline didn't assure safety.
In just one week, I saw one of the ground crew killed when he walked
into a propeller, and watched as another plane cartwheeled on landing.
The flames flashed immediately—brilliant and cruel. It was quite some
time before the fire crew could even approach the plane. The NAC Commander, a remote and severe character, stood as the firefighters did their
work. Watching him, I realized that it would be his job to write to the
cadet's parents.

We had three or four Sundays free while we were at Oita. We were
far from the mountains and the plains of Izumi, and its small-town atmosphere. Cranes were definitely not the biggest thing here. Beppu was
a seaside city, but nature was remote—no one seemed to think about the
beach. The local people were all in business and the local business was
pleasure.

Beppu called. Several hotels had been singled out for our patronage.
The Navy designation entitled the hotels to extra food and liquor rations,
and we ate and drank to our hearts' content. We soaked in the warm
waters.

By the end of the second Sunday, we were a bit bored: we wanted
more than just eating, drinking, and relaxing in the warm waters. Someone mentioned *geisha*. As the conversation continued, I realized I wasn't
the only one confused. I knew that *geisha* were high-class entertainers,
specialists in traditional Japanese instruments, art song, and classical
dance, and I knew that the word *geisha* literally meant "arts person" or
artiste. But with the altered circumstances of the war years, the term had
been adopted by women at all levels of the "water trade," from the traditional *geisha artistes*, whose performances were no doubt beyond our
tastes as well as our wallets, to the lowest level "entertainers," who provided nothing more than sex.

Not having even the remotest idea of how to find these *geisha*, we
asked the hotel manager for advice. He was happy to oblige, and we soon
found ourselves at a tea house where the women were all too well ac-
quainted with Naval officers. They knew all the Navy songs and joined us
in spirited renditions. Once everyone was drunk, we and the girls joined

in an off-key but robust chorus of the Navy's Battleship March: *Defending or attacking, like a floating fortress of steel…so reliable.* I loved the singing, just as I had when I was singing hymns in English, but I didn't have the skills to join in when my colleagues from the big cities spun the girls around the room in foxtrots.

When the party wound down, we paired off and went to bed. It was my first experience with sex. The physical act itself was pure delight, but that experience taught me that with sex comes a cascade of emotional reactions and connections.

After we finished, "my girl"—whose name I cannot for the life of me remember—sat with me and talked for quite some time. It slowly dawned on me that she was an indentured servant, not an employee, and had virtually no personal freedom. She had to have special permission to leave the premises, and was only allowed out for short periods of time. She was checked weekly for venereal disease, and she had absolutely no say in when she had to work or how many customers she had to entertain. Evidently, a number of her "customers" were quite unpleasant and some of them downright abusive. I resolved then and there to stay away from the sex-for-money business. And in the years since the war I've wondered why so many of my countrymen expend so much energy denying that the "comfort women" system existed in Japan and in the lands we conquered.

On June 1, we were all promoted and officially made officers. I was now Ensign Imagawa. It was also the first day for summer uniforms. We were all delighted with our shining cherry blossom pins and our new epaulets with one gold stripe. We knew we looked sharp. We were also told that the repair work at Wonson was finally finished. We could expect our orders any day.

But first, the stern Commander told us, "All of you brave new officers will have three days leave. You can leave tomorrow as early as you like. Pick up your travel vouchers at the gate. Enjoy your time with your families." I realize now that this was a form of compassionate leave. There would be a death in each of our families, and those deaths were likely to be far away from home. But we tamped down those thoughts as we raced off in our crisp, bright uniforms, with our new cherry blossoms, our glittering convictions, and our dreams of glory.

I got home to the Ishii Village house by early afternoon. It felt so good to sit on the *tatami*. Of course, there had been a *tatami* at the Tanakas when I was in Izumi, but this was special, this was home. Here I could relax. I looked forward to the rest of that day and another full day with my parents.

My fears that Mother's ambitions to advance my match with Kayoko would occupy my one precious day at home proved unfounded. At breakfast the next morning she announced that she was satisfied that her negotiations with the Katayamas were almost finished; all that remained were the details on when and where the marriage would take place. She bemoaned the fact that I had appeared without notice and that no visit could be undertaken because Kayoko's mother was sick. "If only we had known you would be here," she said. "But no worries, I'll have everything arranged and will write to you with all the information I know you'll be anxious to receive."

So I was able to enjoy my day at home, cherishing what I was sure were my last hours with Mother and Father, and put all thoughts of the Katayamas and Kayoko out of my head. Dinner with my parents in the quiet of the farmhouse was to be savored—I did just that, and then slept well, safe at home.

THE next morning at Takahama Port, my head was filled with memories of the year before. But this time Father was not with me. And now I knew this would really be the last time, that there would be no more reprieves. Matsuyama faded away; the ferry went through the Inland Sea and down the east coast of Kyushu to Beppu.

Less than a week later, we headed out from Oita for Shimonoseki, where we boarded the Kampu Ferry for Korea. As I stepped aboard, I thought about the 12th century battle fought nearby at Dan-no-Ura, the battle that brought to an end the power and influence of the Taira clan and set the stage for the rise of the Minamotos, and Japan's first military government. Thoughts of the Taira often led to thoughts of cherry blossoms and transience. Basho's *samazama* haiku that Professor Takahashi taught us floated quickly into my consciousness, but I found myself focusing on the victorious Minamotos. I was trying to work out some sort of link between their Kamakura government of long ago and the government that had led us into the grand but perilous adventure in which we were now engaged as the ferry pulled away.

After we cleared the straits between Kyushu and Honshu, we were out on the open sea. I remembered our pleasant cruise at Amakusa just two months earlier, but now things were different. The Americans had taken Guadalcanal and the Marshall Islands, and air raids had started on the major cities; it was dangerous to be so exposed. But we reached Pusan safely and then took a long train ride north to Seoul. After a layover in Seoul, we headed farther north and finally reached Wonson, which is on the eastern coast, facing the Japan Sea, in what is now North Korea.

Early the next morning we finally got to see what had been our obsession since we first started training as aviators: the Zeros. They were magnificent. As we headed for our first morning assembly, most of us had big grins on our faces—we were finally going to fly the Zero! And the Zero did not disappoint. It was the pinnacle of aviation engineering. Its engine power of about 1,000 horsepower was about twice that of the clunky Model 96s we had trained on at Oita. It was sleek and responsive, and the pilots had excellent views from the cockpits.

But the weight of history was pressing on us and we soon learned how precious time was. The situation at the front was worsening. Island after island was falling, Japan was losing pilots, cherry blossoms falling and scattering. As soon as we had a feel for the Zero, our instructors began formation and dog-fight training. And we worked, intensely, on night flights and target shooting. The accident rate was even higher than at Oita. I especially remember the horror of a mid-air collision. And since the base was short on fuel, each of us was able to train for at most half an hour a day. I checked this memory last year; the official records show that Mie's Thirteenth Class had an average of only seventy hours flight training, a mere tenth of the number of hours of flying experience Japanese Navy pilots had before Pearl Harbor.

Sundays were again a day for diversion. We took a bus to town. One time, a group of us decided to go to the local beach. We swam a bit, but spent most of our time eating and drinking at a small restaurant. One of the waitresses seemed to take a special liking to me. She was very pretty and very young—only about seventeen, I think. I took myself back to the same place—alone—the next week. I ate. I drank. We flirted. She disappeared. I was surprised when she reappeared in a few minutes and announced that her boss had given her the rest of the day off so she could take me home to meet her family.

Her family was quite large. We all sat in the living room sipping tea and chatting about life in the Navy. Her mother and father talked about how some Japanese officers got drunk and rowdy when they were on leave. After about an hour, I realized that everyone else had drifted off. The girl and I were alone in the living room—the entire house was suddenly empty. This was now, without question, a seduction scene—or an entrapment. I'm still not sure how I got out of there—when I broke away she was fondling me, making her intentions quite clear. I hurried back to the base, burning with desire, anger, and shame. In my heart, I realized that this confused and confusing episode was part of what a number of my colleagues had talked about: the deep fury and loathing that sat just beneath the surface when the Korean people dealt with their Japanese occupiers. But that day and for a long time afterward I resolutely told myself another story—that I had been smart to avoid an unwise romantic entanglement since I wouldn't be in Korea long.

The next Sunday, I made sure I went in the opposite direction. About ten minutes away from the base, I thought I saw a stable from the bus window. Curious, I got off at the next stop and walked back. Sure enough, there was a stable, with a beautiful white horse. I stood in admiration and didn't hear the person who materialized beside me until he began to speak. When he got a good look at me, he was startled to see a Naval officer, but recovered enough to introduce himself as Mr. Kim and ask if I was interested in horses. I explained that I had been the president of the riding club at my college. Mr. Kim told me with pride that his horse was a Russian Cossack—he was a magnificent animal, taller and slimmer than the average Japanese horse. As I expressed my thanks to Mr. Kim for giving me the pleasure of visiting his stable and prepared to leave, he asked if I had any plans for the evening. When he learned that my only obligation was to be back at the barracks by ten, he invited me for dinner. So I got back on the bus, entertained myself in town, and returned for dinner at six.

Mr. Kim and his wife served me a full course meal on beautiful silver dinnerware. I love spicy, hot food, and that dinner met the bill. We had a free, wide-ranging discussion. The Kims brought up the issue of Korean-Japanese relations. Not all Koreans, they told me, automatically hated Japanese. There was always some good in people, and person-to-person, there was always a lot to be learned; they believed in the benefits of cross-national exchanges. I hadn't heard anyone express such sentiments since the last time I had spoken with Yamamura-sensei. I accepted their hospitality gratefully. I ate and drank my fill of the peppery dishes and the delicious cold beer, expressed my thanks, and bid them a good night.

As I took the bus back to the barracks, I tried to make sense of the last two Sundays. Other than realizing that Mr. Kim reminded me of a mixture of Professor Hoshino and Minister Graham, I just couldn't figure it out. I sat on the bus humming one of the hymns we had sung in the Grahams' parlor after dinner on Sundays. But when I hurried through the gate just before my curfew, my speculations evaporated, and all my focus was once again and only on the Zero, the beautiful Zero.

CHAPTER 11

SAM

Tokyo, 1944–1945

IN EARLY OCTOBER, we finished the last of our training at Wonson. I still have the commemorative photo taken in front of the hangars to mark our "graduation." Our orders would be notice of how long we would survive. Okinawa or further south meant very little time, perhaps only weeks, before a mission.

My orders read Tokyo Detachment of Kasumigaura Naval Air Corps. I had never heard of it. When I inquired, I learned that it was a small training facility for *yokaren*, the teenage recruits. Farm boys one month; mission-ready pilots the next. They were sent off with even less air time than Mie's Thirteenth Class.

The Tokyo Detachment was located at Haneda, a commercial airport and the home base of Japan Airlines. It wasn't at all what I expected; I would be an aviation instructor and would therefore survive for a while. Utsumi, Yamamoto, and Watanabe, who had been with me since Mie, were assigned to Tokyo too. And so was Kawazaki, who had joined us at Wonson. Most of the others, including my good friend Kobayashi, were sent to the front lines.

Once we arrived back in Japan at Shimonoseki, we had until 5 P.M. the next day to report to Tokyo. Yamamoto, who was from Tokyo, was delighted. He and the others rushed for the trains, sweeping me along with them. Kawazaki was going to stop at home in Nagoya, and Watanabe in Shizuoka, both on the way to Tokyo. Utsumi, who was from Sendai, far to the north of the capital, decided to visit an uncle in Tokyo. I was at loose ends; there wasn't enough time for me to make it to Matsuyama for a visit. And then I thought of Michiko, at Kure Naval Arsenal near Hiroshima.

I was the first to get off the train. I remembered working at the

Arsenal during my last spring break at Kosho. Hiroshima Station was bustling with sailors. I walked especially tall through it, a Naval officer with cherry blossoms shining on my lapel. The local train to Kure was full of other Naval officers, and as we traveled south past the huge shipyards, I could see the beautiful green hills, the sweeping blue bay, and nestling between them, Hiroshima's busy downtown, spread out on the delta formed by the city's rivers.

At the Arsenal's gate, I explained why I was there. The guard responded that it was the middle of the work day, and even volunteers, like Michiko, were not permitted visitors. But then he gave me a big grin, nodded at my insignia and said, "But the Naval Arsenal will be happy to accommodate one of its own," as he reached for the phone to call the factory floor.

I was seated in the Visitors' Room when she came in. She was wearing *mompe* pantaloons like a farmer's wife and smelled of gunpowder. When she saw me, a huge smile replaced the puzzled look on her face, "Imagawa-san, I couldn't imagine who it was. They just told me to report here to meet someone. What a wonderful surprise." As she sat down, she untied her headscarf and shook her hair loose. "Oh, that feels good." She was pale and thin, but seeing the beautiful balanced oval of her face and her warm eyes lifted my heart.

"I'm glad I had a chance to see you today. I thought I had lost you. The Navy has moved me around so much, and now I'm on my way to Tokyo—as an aviation instructor, can you believe it?"

"You've only been in the Navy a year and you're already an officer? Congratulations."

"Only an Ensign," I said, struggling to keep the pride out of my voice.

But there were more important things to talk about. "Michiko, I heard about your brothers. I'm so sorry. I remember marching in the parades to the station when they left. And then your mother and father. My deepest condolences."

She nodded, but didn't speak, her eyes filling.

"And I wanted to thank you for the *senninbari*. It means a lot to me. It's done a great job of keeping me safe so far, and I'm counting on it to keep doing that job. I have it here in my bag. I'll keep it and my memories of you with me always."

She was trying not to cry, so I kept talking, telling her about Izumi, the cranes, the *shochu*, and learning to fly, and about Wonson and the thrill of mastering the Zero. As Michiko recovered, she told me a bit about her life at Kure. She talked about her friend Keiko, who, she said, understood her and kept her laughing. We visited for about an hour, remembering our happy times in Matsuyama. I was sad to have to say goodbye. As I sat on the train back to Hiroshima, I thought of how lucky we were to have had that hour, some final precious moments together. I was sure she felt the same way.

AFTER a trip through the foggy capital city, I met up with Utsumi, Yamamoto, Watanabe, and Kawazaki at the gate to the Tokyo Detachment, which was wedged into a small area hugging Tokyo Bay. We were directed to one of a number of shabby wooden buildings. In the Commander's office, we found a small, gray old man behind a modest desk. Despite his insignia, I found it hard to believe that he was our leader. He didn't have the dignity I expected of a Naval officer. He looked like a kindly grandpa, but when he spoke, his voice was strong and assured. The office was too small for all of us to sit, so Commander Fujimura took us to the junior officers' Gun Room. He told us that there were two hundred *yokaren* at the Detachment, which he expected to soon be upgraded to a Naval Air Center. We were to train them on the Intermediate 93 trainers—the plane I had learned on in Izumi. When he finished explaining our duties, Commander Fujimura told us about himself. In his younger days, he had commanded a destroyer that collided with another destroyer during training maneuvers. And that, he thought, was the end of his career. He retired as a Lieutenant Commander. He had been recalled to service earlier in the year due to the Navy's manpower shortages. He cheerfully explained that as a "real" sailor he knew nothing about flying, and left all responsibility for all flight operations to Shimizu, his Lieutenant Commander. It was time to eat by the time we finished.

Our opinion of the Tokyo Detachment improved at dinner. We were among the group of about twenty eligible to eat in the Officers' Mess. Gone was the cafeteria-style dining hall of our other postings; we were seated in a real dining room. Rather than metal bowls and plates, we used real chinaware. And, best of all, instead of mass-produced meals, our food was cooked in a special, separate kitchen, and a group of seamen, under the supervision of an NCO, served the dinner. The first night the five of us sat with the Commander. Our opinion of the Detachment improved even further when he delivered a final piece of news: each of us would be assigned one of the seamen to assist with our personal needs. My valet, Seaman Hashimoto, was one of those serving dinner, and we were introduced then and there. Hashimoto was rather effeminate, and I learned that in civilian life he was the choreographer and director of a traditional Japanese *odori* dance troupe before he was drafted, but what impressed me most was his age. Commander Fujimura was old enough to be my grandfather, and Hashimoto was surely old enough to be my father. What strange situations military service put us in.

After dinner, Lieutenant Commander Shimizu called a meeting for the five of us who were new to the Tokyo Detachment. He was about forty, a sharp Naval Academy graduate. A former dive-bomber, he had been assigned to Tokyo after being injured in a crash landing. We were impressed with his military bearing, his obvious competence, and his high level of knowledge about the war situation. He introduced us to four Senior Grade Lieutenants: two were regular Naval officers, but the other two were college-graduate reserve officers like us. Lieutenant Suga would lead my group—Squad 2.

The briefing ran until nine. The five of us were still sitting in the dining room when Seaman Hashimoto appeared and asked if we would like *sake* or wine. A pleasant surprise. We all preferred *sake*, and we got it. We also had the privilege of ignoring lights out if we wanted, but decided that it would be best to take heed. Hard work awaited us in the morning.

Our first full day in Tokyo began with the traditional "five-minutes before," reveille at six, and the routine of morning assembly, which, because there was no parade ground, took place on the airfield apron. Standing at the head of the rows and facing the men was another new experience for us. It felt important and I thought about how serious my responsibilities were. After the assembly, we went back to the of-ficers' quarters and found our seamen making our beds and cleaning our rooms. Things were really going to be different here! When we went to the dining room, we had a choice of Japanese style or Western style breakfast.

Training the cadets was scheduled to start at eight, but the five of us were told to assemble at seven-thirty. Each of us was to take a plane up so we could regain a feel for the Model 93. When I got in the front cockpit, I was shocked at the difference from the Zero. I put it in full throttle, but wondered if it would really get off the ground. But by the time I had tax-ied to the end of the runway, I was ready, and then up and aloft. Away I went, to the south, remembering my first takeoff from Izumi. But by the time I had climbed and turned to the left over Tokyo Bay, I was present only in the moment, flying again. I headed toward the Boso Peninsula and then made another left turn, to the north. The saw-ridges of Mt. Nokogiri on the Peninsula were on my right. Tokyo spread out to my left. I was astonished at how vast it was and then surprised again: when I turned left once more, straight on toward the city, I could see Mt. Fuji. I hadn't realized how close Fuji was to Tokyo. It was massive—and gor-geous. I thought about the last time I had seen it—through the train win-dow in 1932, on the way to Matsuyama with Mother when I first arrived in Japan. Twelve years ago. How I had changed, how times had changed, I thought as I made the last turn and descended toward the runway. A perfect three-point landing. I was ready to go. Ready for the cadets.

I parked the plane and reported to Lieutenant Suga. He introduced me to the four NCOs who would work with my squad. They all had combat experience, and I was confident that we would do a good job with the cadets. Utsumi, Yamamoto, Watanabe, Kawazaki, and I lined up as the cadets came running in formation from their barracks. Lieu-tenant Suga introduced us. He said, "These are Zero fighter pilots. They are full of Navy spirit. Learn well from them." It was clear we were ex-pected to be tough on the cadets. Lieutenant Suga gave the order for us to begin.

My first cadet was nervous. I had never been in the rear cockpit seat, but gave him much the same talk I had heard myself just ten months before in Izumi. But things had changed; the training schedule was ac-celerated. He was to put his hands and feet on the controls even on this first flight. Once we were in the air, I let him take control. He over-reacted, and the plane banked to the right. He made the same mistake twice more, and when we approached the runway to land, he gripped the controls so tightly that I had difficulty pulling the nose up in time. Needless to say, when we climbed out of the plane, he got a good whack on the cheek.

The next cadet did much better. He had some trouble maintaining altitude, tending to dip a bit. I pulled the plane back up a few times, but his sense of balance improved by the end of the flight. The full day's work involved eight or nine cadets. Because we were deep into autumn, the days were getting shorter, and we had to stop at four-thirty.

ON November 1, we were training as usual. It was a bright, warm day, an unusual bonus of later summer-like weather. Just before noon, when I had begun wondering what we would have for lunch, a huge plane appeared, flying north far above us. Its silvery body was beautiful against the clear blue sky. As the trainers landed, the Lieutenants kept them on the ground. Those with binoculars reported that the mysterious plane was flying at about 10,000 meters. About five minutes after the plane had passed out of sight, sirens sounded and the PA announced the same thing over and over: "Enemy aircraft raiding Tokyo!"

We were stunned. An enemy aircraft flying right over our heads? We stood around, not knowing what to do. About twenty minutes later, the plane reappeared, this time a bit further to the east, but flying in the opposite direction—going south—back where it came from. There was no sign of bombing. It was just as beautiful the second time we saw it. We watched it in awe. Once the plane was gone, we couldn't get it out of our thoughts.

It was only later that the rumors were confirmed. It was a B-29 Superfortress, a much more powerful bomber than what the Allies had deployed in Europe. The more I thought about it, the more confused I was—my awe yielded to fear, and even dread—but I resolutely banished those emotions. *Spirit is what we need.*

That night the B-29 was the only topic of conversation in the Gun Room. The consensus was that the plane was on a reconnaissance mission, and that bombing of Tokyo would begin soon. *Bombing! Tokyo! We had to prepare!*

Training continued. Three weeks passed with no air raids. Some of the cadets were close to soloing. And then one day, we heard the siren again. We grounded the planes and ushered the cadets to the shelters. Other than moving them into the hangars, we had no procedure for protecting or concealing the planes, so we waited and worried. Nothing happened. The Communications Officer arrived with the news that an area west of Tokyo was being bombed. Then we heard planes, a large number,

flying east. They were much too far away for us to see them clearly, but by
the sound of their engines we decided they were B-29s again. We learned
later that an aircraft plant was bombed that day.

In late November, regular nighttime raids of Tokyo started—most
of them in residential areas. By late December, it hit home for us at the
Detachment. Incendiary bombs fell all around us. One landed on the
roof of the shelter, which had a thick dirt cover. As the dirt fell around
us, we realized how lucky we were that there wasn't a concrete roof to
collapse on us. When we emerged, there were flames all around us. There
was nothing we could do but wait for the fire crew to arrive with extin-
guishers.

Early the next morning, the Commander ordered me to take a patrol
out to the residential area nearby. Much of it was burnt to the ground,
and we saw a number of incinerated bodies lying in the streets. We also
saw a few people who were just standing in the rubble dazed. We stopped
to talk to one man and learned that his home was gone. He kept saying
that he was happy that his family had evacuated to another part of the
city, that they were safe. It was clear that he was in shock and had no idea
what to do. I went back to the Commander and suggested that he send
food and arrange for shelter for our neighbors. He sent off a few cables;
once he had secured permission, he ordered Lieutenant Shimizu to help
our neighbors. We loaded up food to distribute and assigned cadets to
use Detachment trucks to transport the civilians anywhere they wanted
to go within the city limits. Evidently there was no space for them at the
Detachment. That was the day we felt the war had come to mainland
Japan.

Late in the afternoon of December 1, I was summoned to Commander Fujimura's office. As I entered his office I wondered why he
wanted to see me and tried to think if there was something I had done
wrong. As I stood in front of him and bowed, I was astonished to hear
him say, "Congratulations." I didn't understand and worried more about
what I had done wrong.

"May I ask what this is about, Sir?"

"I offered my congratulations because as of this date you are promoted to Lieutenant Junior Grade," he said.

I was so surprised that I said the first thing that came into my head.
"What about my classmates, Sir?" We had all been promoted to Ensign

together the previous July, and I assumed that all our promotions would be on a lockstep basis.

"No, it's just you. Here," he said handing me two small silver cherry blossom pins, "these are to add to the emblems on your collar."

Back in my quarters, Seaman Hashimoto did a careful, professional tailoring job: he cut the emblems off my collar, pushed the new silver cherry blossoms through them and sewed them back on. It would have taken me hours, but Hashimoto finished in about half an hour. I slipped my jacket on again and admired the gleam of the silver blossoms in the mirror, two of them on each side of my collar.

At dinner time, I strolled into the dining room as nonchalantly as I could manage. Most of the other junior officers were already there. No one noticed anything until I took my seat at the table. Kawazaki, sitting across from me said, "Hey, Imagawa, are you sure you're wearing your own jacket?" When all heads swiveled in my direction, I explained. There was some joking about how I shouldn't pull rank on them. I truly couldn't figure out why I was promoted, and I don't think any of my colleagues could either. I did find out later that about ten percent of those whom I started with at Mie were promoted that day; I was the only one at the Tokyo Detachment.

With my promotion, I was appointed Deck Officer, which, I learned, meant I was responsible for morale. We had a three-day break to celebrate the New Year holiday. As Deck Officer, I was at the front gate to welcome the professional comics, dancers, and singers who came to entertain us. Several of them greeted Hashimoto as old friends. The cadets loved the performance, and the other officers and I enjoyed it too, of course. Losing ourselves in laughter was a rare treat.

Now that I was Deck Officer, Seaman Second Class Ito was an even greater asset to me than Hashimoto. Ito was a well-known *samurai* actor. Like Hashimoto, he had been drafted and considered himself lucky to be stationed in Tokyo. I often sent him to movie distributors to borrow films. The distributors were happy to supply them and refused to accept payment. The cadets loved *samurai* films, and all of the first ones we watched featured Ito. There was always a great cheer when he appeared on the screen.

One day when Ito returned to the Detachment, he told me that we had seen most of the *samurai* films available, but the distributors had

American films we could borrow. I was surprised, thinking they had all been locked away or destroyed. They were absolutely forbidden in movie theaters. The other officers wanted to see them, and I was curious. I told Ito to bring some back the next time. They had Japanese subtitles, so the cadets enjoyed them—but not as much as the *samurai* films, of course. I sat transfixed in the dark, watching the elegant, long-limbed actresses, and listening to the language of my childhood. Many winter and early spring mornings were foggy. When there wasn't enough visibility to fly, we organized activities to keep the cadets busy. Volleyball was the most popular. We also organized group singing. We had the cadets form circles, with one ring around another. I loved watching the inner ring march in one direction, and the outer ring the other way. The cadets sang as they marched, and the sounds of their voices crossed each other, mingled, and made a wonderful whole. Every one of these group sings concluded with the naval aviators' version of the popular song *Doki no Sakura*: *We are cherry blossoms that bloomed on the same day. Although we are not blood relatives we cannot be separated. We will scatter and fall together for our country. Although we will die elsewhere, we will meet and bloom again as cherry blossoms in the spring tree tops of Yasukuni Shrine.* Music was always sheer joy for me, and I loved watching the cadets march and listening to them sing. Listening to the lyrics and the layers of harmony of the song made me remember the cherry blossoms at Matsuyama Castle. I didn't allow myself to think much about Yasukuni Shrine and these teenagers— and myself—dying far from home.

As it got warmer, we let the cadets wade in the Bay on some of the foggy mornings, digging for clams. The area was off-limits to civilians, so the catch was quite plentiful. And when the cadets were successful, the officers were the beneficiaries; because they had no way to cook the clams they caught, the cadets gave them all to us, and we grilled them on a *hibachi* in our Gun Room. Needless to say, a great deal of *sake* went down with those clams. Our bellies were full, and one evening I realized that I had come to quite enjoy the shabby place called the Tokyo Detachment.

FEBRUARY 11 is the day Japanese celebrate the origins of the country, the old story I had learned at Bancho about the god and goddess dipping their spears into the sea at Amanohashidate and shaking off droplets that became the islands of Japan. During the war, the holiday was called

Empire Day, and the glory of the Japan's Asian Empire was the focus of the celebration. It was still dark at our morning assembly that day. We knew there would be no training because of the holiday, but had no idea how special the day would be until Commander Fujimura finished his holiday address, and then went on, solemnly, to say that he had received a special communication. The Naval General Staff Office had ordered him to form a Special Attack Unit at the Tokyo Detachment. By then we all knew what that meant. Special Attack units had been operating since the fall, first from the Philippines and then from Okinawa and Kyushu.

Commander Fujimura never mentioned the death—the suicide—that was involved. Instead he said, "The time has come for you to serve your country in the best way possible. But the Special Attack Unit of this Detachment will be formed with volunteers only. You need not volunteer if you are married or if you are the first or only son of your family. Think carefully. I will ask those of you who want to volunteer to take one step forward."

There was absolute silence. Time stretched and warped during his pause of a few seconds. "Volunteers, one step forward!"

There was a loud thud. Virtually everyone stepped forward—together. Cadets and instructors alike. I was among them. I gave no thought, no consideration to the fact that I was the first and only son of the Imagawa family. In fact, I don't think I thought about anything at all. At the command, my body moved automatically. To volunteer to die for the country was the only thing to do. I was not afraid, and afterwards I had absolutely no regrets.

"I commend you for your courageous decision, but I see that we have too many volunteers for the small number of aircraft available to us. The squadron commanders will take down the names of the volunteers, and later the senior officers will select the pilots and navigators needed for the Unit."

We were given the news in the Gun Room. Lieutenant Commander Shimizu was appointed the training commander for the Special Attack Unit, which would consist of two squadrons. Each squadron would have three squads of four planes each. I was to lead the second squadron and was also the leader for my group's first squad. With twenty-four planes assigned to the Special Attack Unit, there would be only about a dozen planes left for regular flight training.

Special Attack Unit training began the next day to prepare us to fly those flimsy bi-wing trainers into the territory of enemy fighters. If we allowed ourselves to think about it, we would have felt helpless at such a prospect, but we were determined to succeed in our missions. We put everything we had into our training.

We concentrated on formation flying. The squad leader took off first and had to gain altitude while keeping speed down to give the others time to catch up. At first the formations were quite loose, but with practice they got tighter and tighter, until the four pilots could make out each other's facial expressions. We cruised at 2,000 meters to specific points, such as Odawara to the south and Choshi to the east, before turning around to return to the airfield.

On March 1, 1945, the Detachment became the Tokyo Naval Air Corps (NAC) under the command of the Eleventh Combined Air Force. But it was a change in name only. Everything remained the same. By then we were ready to begin night flight training. Taking off for our missions in the dark would help us evade enemy fighters and give us a chance to make it to our targets. The idea was that we would dive into the targets at dawn.

MARCH 9 was a lovely spring-like day—a first taste of real warmth. That afternoon we again witnessed a single B-29 flying high above the city. The afternoon was windy and the sky clear. By evening, even though the winds had risen, we decided it was warm enough to show the evening movie outside. We were enjoying Olivia de Havilland in *Robin Hood* when the air raid siren sounded. We ran toward the planes still on the tarmac, moved them into the hangars, and then scrambled into the shelters. The B-29s roared in overhead. It sounded like there were hundreds, in large formations. They flew from the southwest to the northeast, dropping bombs—most of them incendiary bombs—along the way. It sounded to us like the central and northern parts of the city were taking the hardest hits. Fires began almost immediately; they were so huge that we heard and felt them in the shelter. When we emerged it looked like the entire city was in flames. We scanned the sky, looking for the enemy planes. When the cloud cover parted, the underbellies of the huge silvery aircraft glowed red, reflecting the sea of fire below. The B-29s remained beautiful, sailing high above the destruction.

The all clear sounded just before dawn. After our morning assembly, Commander Fujimura took me aside and ordered me to fly around the city and report back with an assessment of the damage. He was particularly concerned about the Imperial Palace. Following orders, I flew to the Palace first and was relieved to see that the large green oasis in the middle of the city was untouched. But when I turned northeast, the picture changed dramatically. The central, northern, and eastern portions of the city, the oldest and most traditional parts—Tokyo's old *shitamachi*—spread on either side of the Sumida River, were flattened, burned to nothing. Where there had been miles and miles of factories and the small wooden houses of the working classes, only the shells of a few concrete buildings remained.

The winds had tossed burning embers and debris into the air and whipped the fires from the incendiary bombs into a storm that had devoured the flimsy dwellings along with their occupants, who had heeded the government's instructions to avoid the few public shelters and stay near their homes to defend them. Fires were still burning and I could make out the smoldering skeleton of Kokugikan, the national *sumo* wrestling hall. I descended to look for the nearby Asakusa Kannon Temple, which had been a refuge for the people of that neighborhood during the great Tokyo fire that followed the earthquake of 1923. I couldn't find any trace of that grand structure and was shocked that at the lower altitude, the heat from the ground reached up to my plane.

It was hard to grasp what I was witnessing. Tokyo, the heart of the nation, the vast ocean of the metropolis that I had encountered as a ten-year-old, was devastated. Much of one of the world's great cities was gone. The B-29s had done their job with startling and ruthless efficiency. America's might had obliterated much of the capital and many of its citizens. How much longer could this be endured?

After an hour, I returned to the Detachment and reported to Commander Fujimura. He was happy to hear that the radio reports he was receiving about damage to the Palace were wrong. I learned after the war that two hundred B-29s took part in the raid and dropped 25,000 bombs; at least 80,000, and perhaps more than 100,000, died in that raid.

WITHIN a month, spring really arrived. The Detachment had one—and only one—cherry tree. It stood in front of the Officers' Quarters.

Young and spindly, it produced only a few blossoms. As I stood gazing at them at their peak, the old *haiku* we had learned from Professor Taka-hashi came to mind, *Samazama no / koto omoidasu / sakura kana*, and I thought how I was lucky to see those flowers, the last cherries I would ever see. Every spring since, I have remembered that scrawny cherry tree. *Samazama no koto.*

The now-regular visits of the B-29s were bad enough, but the fighters and dive-bombers were worse—along with the realization that they were launched from aircraft carriers cruising off the coast. When those raids started, Utsumi remarked in the Gun Room one night, "If we added up all the American aircraft carriers that Imperial Headquarters has an-nounced we have sunk, there wouldn't be a single one left to fly those damn fighters from!" My good friend and colleague was known for his wit and outspoken frankness, and I usually enjoyed bantering with him. This time, however, I couldn't think of what to say, but I did begin to wonder...even more than I had on my own.

During one of the raids, four fighters swept down on our airfield. The only target they managed to destroy was one of Japan Airline's DC-3s, which was, of course, a U.S.-manufactured commercial plane. Or so we thought, until we were told that one of our sailors had been strafed while on an errand just outside our walls. A group of us went out to investigate and discovered that he had been blown into the waters of the Bay. We hauled him out and took the corpse back to the base. It was the most mutilated body I had ever seen.

By mid-April, our Special Attack Unit had begun instrument flight training. The navigator and the pilot had to work together to make sure we would be able to reach our targets in the dark. We trained during the day, with the navigator in the rear seat of the cockpit, covered with a dark cloth to blot out his view. It was his job to work with the instruments and call out guidance to the pilot. On one training run, with a cadet as the navigator, we were headed for Katori Naval Base, northeast of Tokyo. It was such a long mission that we had to land and refuel for the trip back to Tokyo. As I had a cup of tea while I waited, I noticed that an officer in a flight uniform was eyeing me. When I looked up, he came over and said, "Are you Imagawa from Matsuyama?"

When I said yes, he introduced himself. "I'm Norimasa Hayashi from Tokumura, on the opposite side of Matsuyama from where your family lives. My sister Nobue is married to your cousin Yukio Otani. I remember seeing you at the wedding about five years ago, but I don't think we were ever introduced."

He was a dive-bomber. It was a great pleasure to see a friendly face from home. Time was short. We shook hands and wished each other well, before I headed back to my plane and the waiting cadet. We were back at home base in an hour and a half. By the end of the year, I had learned that Norimasa carried out his mission on August 9, just days before the end of the war. My cousin's wife is mourning him to this day.

In mid-May rumors began to circulate that the Tokyo NAC would be relocated. Evacuation had seemed inevitable for a while: B-29 incendiary carpet bombing was a nightly affair, and the planes from American carriers were strafing and bombing almost daily, making training impossible. There were even rumors of submarines lurking in Tokyo Bay. One morning in the last week of May, Commander Fujimura announced that the Tokyo NAC was moving outside the city and would be absorbed by the Kasumigaura Naval Air Corps on June 1. The Commander was retiring and would return to civilian life. As he stood before all of us, he said, with genuine sorrow, "I am saddened that I will not be with you when you depart on your last missions."

ON June 1, I flew one of the planes to Kasumigaura. The navigators and the pilots who didn't have planes took the train. The ground crew had the big job of moving everything else and getting it all accomplished in three days.

Kasumigaura is the name of Japan's second-largest lake, which is located about thirty miles northeast of Tokyo. The Japanese Navy built its first airbase on a plateau south of the lake in 1922. By 1945, it was known as the "Eagle's Nest," and thousands of pilots, both officers and NCOs, had been trained there. Many had already gone to their missions. We joined the several Kasumigaura squadrons that were training, beginning the day after we arrived, and we soon settled into a new routine.

A few days into July, we heard the air raid siren and moved the planes to secure concrete hangars. Because we were so far inland, we were confident we were safe, and sat on the grass at the edge of the tarmac, talking. Suddenly, a group of five or six carrier-based fighters flew in very low from the west, headed straight for the airfield. There was nothing we could do but fall flat on our stomachs. The bullets swept alongside where I was lying—in perfectly straight rows. A flick of the pilot's wrist or a slip of his foot and he would have gotten all of us. As the fighters flew away eastward and we thought it was safe to get up, one of them dropped what we thought was a bomb. We hit the ground again and covered our ears. We waited and waited, but no explosion. Finally, we went to explore. It was an auxiliary fuel tank, not a bomb. Its smell gave us one more piece of information: the enemy was still using the real thing. We had long since switched to gasoline mixed with alcohol produced from sweet potatoes. As we were inspecting the fuel tank, we heard desperate shouts from the woods around the airfield and realized that a group of cadets who had taken cover there had been hit. The raid left us with losses at Kasumigaura and at the neighboring Tsuchiura Naval Air Corps. The next day, there was a joint funeral service. There wasn't enough space for the thirty coffins to be set out properly, so they were stacked up, with blood from a few of them seeping down to stain those below. The Commander of Tsuchiura spoke about avenging the dead cadets by defeating the enemy. I doubt that any of us had much conviction that that was possible.

I WILL always remember July 29, and am sure many others hold similar memories. As we ate that evening, we heard the B-29s passing overhead. They were headed north for the city of Mito. We couldn't hear the raid, but we could see the city in the distance as it dissolved into flame. We watched until about midnight, with the usual mixture of awe, dread, and frustrated anger. We finally went to bed, but shortly thereafter the PA blared, "All hands, prepare for Operation Ketsu." We couldn't believe our ears. Ketsu was the code-word for the mobilization of the entire military against enemy invasion of the mainland. With the others, I ran to the conference room of the underground base headquarters, questions racing through my head. As we crowded into the room, Commander Wada began to speak. An enemy fleet had been spotted off the coast of the Boso Peninsula. From the large number of vessels involved, Naval intelligence judged it to be an invasion force. All Army and Navy bases in the area were to participate in a dawn attack. "Even those of you flying slower planes will be able to reach your targets in about half an hour. Return to your quarters and get your belongings in order. Report back at 0300."

Walking back, I said to myself, this is what you've been training for, what you've waited for. This is it. But by the time I reached my room, I was a welter of emotions. Was I scared? Maybe. After dawn, no more cherry trees to see, no more parents to care for, no more friends to chat with, no more....

I pulled open my drawer and took out my letters from Mother and Father and Michiko. I had read them so often that I knew many passages by heart. We would all be valiant, but might not be able to prevent an invasion. Enemy invaders shouldn't be able to get their hands on these. No one should think that a Naval Officer was such a sissy, saving all his letters, as if they were precious jewels. But I couldn't bring myself to destroy them; instead I put them in my cloth shoe sack, tied it, and wrote "Burn" on it. I straightened up the room and dressed in my flight uniform, wrapping Michiko's *senninbari* around my throat before putting on my jacket. I gave a salute—perhaps a farewell—to no one and nothing in particular before I left the room.

Walking back to the base headquarters, I found myself utterly calm. The night was black, the sky full of glittering stars. There was still a red glow in the sky to the north. I thought of Mother, Father, and Michiko. *Samazama no koto omoidasu.* So much to remember. And only this time now and this place here to do that remembering. As I neared the headquarters, I joined others streaming back, everyone fully suited up. I made myself focus on my mission to crush the enemy, to protect the homeland. *I'll hit the biggest transport ship I can find. I'll take as many invaders' lives as I can. And I have to get my squad to the targets before Lieutenant Yamauchi gets his there. We have to outdo the Naval Academy graduates.* By the time I entered the building for our final briefing, fear had vanished. I felt not a speck of regret; I was feeling only excitement.

We were assigned our planes and told the takeoff order would be conveyed by phone because planes were scattered all over the base in secured concrete hangars. I had to walk clear to the other side of the airfield to reach my plane. There was a tremendous amount of activity all around me. As I passed an elderly officer addressing a group of seamen, I heard him say, "Go out to nearby farm houses and confiscate all the foodstuffs you can find—rice, vegetables, chickens, anything." Things were grim. Now I understood why civilians had been trained to fight the enemy with plows, hoes, and bamboo spears. But what would they do for food? Would the military feed them?

When I arrived at my plane, the navigator was already there, supervising the preparatory work. A large bomb, about 500 pounds, was fitted to the fuselage. The gas tanks were filled halfway—that was all we needed to reach our targets. *But what if it's cloudy and we can't find our targets?* And just as quickly as I had that thought, I realized that I wasn't supposed to be thinking like that at this point.

The phone rang. The order for takeoff already?

No, all pilots and navigators were to return to headquarters immediately. No explanation. We hurried back to learn that the operation was called off. Even the top brass did not know why. A few days later we learned that the red alert had been called when radar showed so many blips that the intelligence analysts decided that an invasion was imminent. Only after the operation had begun did the experts realize that the radar was picking up tin foil dropped off Boso Peninsula by the B-29s on their way home to their Tinian and Saipan bases after the Mito bombing. A false alarm.

Every year since then, even now, many years later, July 29 brings back memories, vivid and intense. *Samazama no koto....*

WE had left Tokyo for Kasumigaura, but it soon became clear that even this far outside the city there was no safety. There were no more direct attacks on the base, but air raids continued every night, and the other bases nearby were attacked. Early in August, we received orders that the entire training unit would be moved to Chitose Air Base in Hokkaido, on the northernmost island. This time I would be the senior officer in the group on the move, so I had to travel with the cadets by train. We began our trip on my twenty-third birthday, August 14.

————

Gen looked up when he finished. His grandmother was sitting still, her needlework neglected in her lap. She said, "Thank you, my dear," but then fell silent.

After sitting with her for a few moments, Gen said, "Gran?" softly. When there was no response, he got up and went to his room.

Michiko was thinking about the last days of the war and travel by train.

CHAPTER 12

MICHIKO

Haruyama, 1945

"MICHIKO," KEIKO SAID, tugging at her sleeve, "Haruyama is next. We have to start working our way out."

"Mmm," was all Michiko managed in response. Crammed in all the way from Kyoto, she had been napping on her feet.

The train lurched around a curve, brushing against the bare branches of the trees crowding up against the tracks. Keiko fell into her friend. After a pause, the train started to climb again. "Oh, this is going to be hard," Keiko said as she turned away from Michiko and began to move forward.

Michiko followed; they worked their way up the aisle of the train, pushing past others who were standing, and climbing over those who were collapsed and asleep on the floor.

"Close it! It's cold," came a chorus of shouted complaints when they opened the door. Three of the people crammed between the cars rushed past them into the warmth of the car. The mountain air brought Michiko fully awake. Swaying over the couplings, she inhaled deeply. *It was only yesterday that I decided to do this. It's a real leap off Kiyomizudera, but it has to be better than Matsuyama.*

AT noon the day before Michiko had stood in the cafeteria looking at the notice just posted on the bulletin board. The Director had told them to expect official word within a week, but there it was already: the Arsenal was closing. Behind her, the slow, thick hometown accents of the Matsuyama girls floated above the general hum of conversation. They were talking about how to manage the trip home: fretting that it would be impossible to get on trains from Kure, and concluding that, if they had to, they could just walk to Hiroshima's port. "I want to get home, but I'm worried. Will we be safe out on the open water?" said Se-chan.

As she listened, the only thought that came to Michiko was *Why go back?* There was nothing for her in Matsuyama. Keiko was right. Her friend had been saying for more than a month that she expected they would be sent home. The ten hour days on the production line, the nights of falling exhausted into the bunks in the dormitory, damp from the bath, but still dirty because there wasn't enough hot water for everyone, were over. In the fall, the shifts had been reduced to eight hours. After the bleak and cheerless New Year holiday, the shifts had officially been six hours, but most days the girls were sent back to the dorm an hour or two after they reported to the factory floor. The work had dwindled away to nothing, although the smell of cordite remained. Keiko said she hated having that sharp smell overwhelm her when she was hungry. And now it was clear that the Arsenal had no more materials, nothing at all to give the girls to work with.

Michiko didn't notice that Keiko had come and was standing next to her until she heard her friend say, "I knew it. The Navy has no reason to feed us 'volunteers' if we're not working.

"*A security measure. Kure Arsenal closing, but full production continuing at all other facilities around the country,*'" she went on, mimicking the Director's tone in his special speech after dinner the night before as he mouthed the bureaucratic euphemisms. "Hah! Ridiculous."

"Come on. Let's eat while we can," she said, giving Michiko a shove toward the cafeteria line. "Interesting that the bosses are nowhere to be seen today, isn't it?" she said as she snatched bowls of soup and plates of pickles and put them on her tray and the one she had handed Michiko.

"No one here today but us and the poor staff. I wonder if they've all scattered," she went on, lapsing into the Director's pompous voice again.

The cafeteria worker serving the main courses laughed out loud and said, "You can be sure they've skedaddled. Them's the types to take care of theirselves and leave us here with nothing but a mess." She winked at Michiko as she reached to place an extra plate of fish on her tray. "You share that with your friend now, Missy," she said, her face crinkled into wrinkles around full dark eyes.

Keiko and Michiko sat down near the Matsuyama group. Se-chan turned her head; the Matsuyama girls drew closer together and dropped their voices to whispers. This was the way it had been since Keiko first did her impersonation of the Director; Michiko had laughed but the rest of the Matsuyama group had been shocked, and had distanced themselves as best they could. Keiko was a troublemaker; it just wouldn't do to associate with her.

Keiko gave Michiko a big smile as she called down the table, "Hey, Se-chan, how are you today? How soon are you all going to leave? Won't it be good to get out of this place and go home?"

When she got no answer, Keiko turned back to Michiko. "What a bunch of empty-headed bumpkins. They did just as the Director told them; they pretended that the blackouts and all those trips to the air raid shelter never involved any real danger, while we sat here in a tinderbox surrounded by munitions. And now that the precious Director is nowhere to be found and they're on their own, they're suddenly worried about the ferry being bombed." She looked at the group again and waved at one of the girls, who had flashed a quick look over her shoulder. Sighing, she said, "Actually, none of this stuff about the old hometown is sounding good, is it?"

Michiko smiled, but couldn't think of what to say. She drifted back to her parent's shop on *Okaido,* leaving Keiko behind and letting the Matsuyama accents fade into the background.

"Michiko," Keiko said, "stop daydreaming and pay attention. It's what I've been telling you since the New Year—you should come home with me. It'll be fine. Matsuyama's too far, the trip will be too dangerous, and when you get there, what will you do, where will you live, *how* will you live with the memories and the sorrow?"

Keiko's words snapped Michiko back to the Arsenal's cafeteria, to the chipped gray paint of the walls, the worn wooden tables, the smell of steamed barley and cheap *miso,* and the clattering noises from the kitchen. She blinked, cleared her eyes, and focused on the dust motes drifting in one of the streams of light from the high windows. "All right," she said. "Shall we go tomorrow morning?"

THEY left before dawn. Kure station was empty and looked abandoned in the gray beginning of the winter day. "It'll take all day if we have to walk all the way," said Keiko.

"But there's nothing else to do," said Michiko, and they set off for Hiroshima, staying parallel to the train line.

As it grew lighter, they realized that they were walking through fields of rubble and past skeletons of vast factories. When it was light enough to see well, they stopped for breakfast, eating part of what they had taken from the pantry.

When she finished eating Keiko stood, squared her shoulders, held her hand out for her friend, and said, "All those air raid drills, all those trips to the shelters. I guess we were lucky that they didn't let us off the Arsenal's grounds. We were living in happy ignorance, weren't we?" Waving her hand at the desolate landscape all around them, she said, "Now we can see how lucky we are to be alive at all. How many people were lost here? How many more before it's over? It really is time to get away from the coast, out of the city. We'll be safe in the mountains."

After two hours of walking they were able to squeeze onto a train at a tiny station from which it took only a half hour to Hiroshima station. The train from Hiroshima was crowded, and the smaller one they switched to at Kyoto was even more crowded and much slower as it climbed the mountains northeast of the ancient capital. At least the press of bodies—everyone wrapped in layers of patched and mismatched winter clothes—had made it warm.

IT was almost dark when the train pulled into the tiny station in Haruyama. Keiko and Michiko stumbled to the platform and stood a moment to catch their breaths, their legs unsteady. The train slowly started up again. The station employee on duty turned to Keiko and greeted her by name.

"Kawamura-san," said the short, stocky man with a big smile on his round face. "We didn't know you were coming home."

"Ogawa-san," Keiko said, the relief of finally being off the train evident in her voice, "it's so good to be home. Thank you. This is my friend Michiko. Michiko Shizuyama. She's come to stay with us."

Keiko led her friend through the village, and the two young women climbed a sloping path to an old house tucked below a hill. Even though it was really too cold to be outdoors, and there was only the last wash of light in the sky, a woman was sitting on the huge, flat stone that served as the doorstep for the house. She jumped up and ran to Keiko.

"Mama, they sent us home, and I brought my friend Michiko. I wrote you about her."

Keiko's mother pulled her daughter into a tight hug, laughed, and then began crying. Somehow, Michiko wasn't sure how, she too ended up in the warm embrace of the older woman. When they separated, Keiko's mother said, "I knew something was drawing me outside. I knew I was waiting for something."

Michiko tried to express her gratitude, but she only got as far as saying "Kawamura-san, I'm so worried about imposing on you."

Keiko's mother said, "No, Michiko, that's much too formal. You're here with us now. You're part of our family. You're one of my daughters as long as you're with us. Maybe 'Auntie Kazue' will do, but I'm definitely not 'Kawamura-san' to you."

"Yes, Kazue Obasan," said Michiko, trying it out.

"Well, that's settled," laughed Keiko and then shouted with joy as her younger twin sisters and little brother spilled out of the house and danced around the three women.

"Big sister is home! Big sister is home."

The girls giggled and climbed into their sister's arms as the boy jumped up at her side, "What did you bring us?"

"Come, all of you. We must introduce Michiko to Granny," said Kazue Obasan. Everyone trooped into the house. Granny was standing on the wooden floor just above the *genkan*.

"So Keiko's back," she said.

"Yes, Granny, and I've brought my friend Michiko Shizuyama with me. She's going to stay with us." Granny nodded and narrowed her eyes as she inspected Michiko, but she didn't say a word before turning and walking toward the large room with soft *tatami* straw mats in the center of the house.

Michiko was still smiling and bowing at Granny's back when she heard Keiko start to lie. "No, Mama, we ate a big breakfast and then had meals on the trains. These are for everyone else," she said as she took dried fish and barley from her satchel. Michiko emptied the food she had in her *furoshiki* and pulled out the three apples she had stashed in her pockets. She smiled as she handed them over to Kazue Obasan. Looking at her friend's face, Michiko knew that Keiko too was remembering their raid on the Arsenal's scant pantry. "What are they going to do if they catch us?" Keiko had whispered. "Force us to work day and night making munitions?"

Kazue Obasan, who was looking closely at her daughter, laughed, and Michiko laughed too. Then, with a hint of sorrow overlaying her amusement, Kazue Obasan said, "You two are too much, and all this wonderful food is too much. Thank you." *She understands everything, and she's at peace.*

THEY all sat in the *tatami* room around the family's *kotatsu*. They were bundled against the cold, and everyone huddled together under the quilts spread on top of the table, with their feet dangling over the embers of the fire in the sunken hearth. Keiko's little sisters snuggled in between the two young women, Kazue Obasan sat beside Keiko, and Granny kept the boy at her side. Kazue Obasan served *hojicha* roasted tea, a rare treat, and promised the children the food from Kure for dinner the next day. "You've already had your dinner. After we finish our tea, you have to go to bed. I want to catch up with Keiko and get to know her friend."

When Kazue Obasan asked Michiko and her daughter what time they had started from Kure in the morning, Granny interrupted. "What I want to know is what you did wrong."

"Granny," said Kazue Obasan.

"No," she said, "the two of them. I want to know what they did wrong. Why were they dismissed?"

"Granny, nothing," said Keiko, "the Arsenal closed. Production is shifting to other areas."

"If you hadn't done something wrong you would have been transferred to one of those other facilities. Supporting the war effort is what you young people should be doing. That's your job now, and it's your duty."

"Granny, they just sent us home. We didn't do anything wrong. Michiko and I were always in the group awarded bonus points for productivity. That's why we brought all this food. They told us they have nothing for us to do and told us to go."

"My Masao did his duty," Granny said, looking across the room at the portrait on the mini Buddhist altar atop a cabinet. "Your father was a hero. You should follow his example. I know your brother will," she said, pulling her grandson closer to her but keeping her eyes focused on the altar. "You're going to be an army officer too, aren't you, sweetie?"

The little boy leaned into his grandmother and smiled. He was old enough to know that no answer was necessary. Kazue Obasan poured more tea. The old woman continued, "Your father's a hero. You should be honoring him!"

When Kazue Obasan started to get up, Granny waved her hand in annoyance, upsetting her tea cup. "Not you!" she snapped. "Let his daughter show her respect. She should have done that as soon as she set foot in this house. Let her explain to him why she's not doing what she should."

Keiko got up and crossed the room to the altar while her mother went to the kitchen to get a towel. Keiko was bowing her head to the portrait of her father as her mother bowed over the dark table to mop up the tea that had settled into the crevices of the old wood. Keiko lit a stick of incense, struck the small bell that sat next to the photograph and whispered, "Papa, I'm home. We miss you so much."

KEIKO and Michiko took the job of sorting the bedding. As they hauled the *futon* from the closet and arranged them in the room where they would sleep with the children, Michiko said, "Keiko, now that I've met Kazue Obasan, I understand where you got your big heart."

"My Mama is the best," said Keiko, as she knelt to push a mattress into place against the wall. "And," she continued, turning her head in Michiko's direction, but not meeting her eye, "don't take Granny too seriously. She's the classic mother-in-law when it comes to how she treats Mama. Granny's lived in Haruyama her whole life. Mama grew up in Yokohama and met Papa in Tokyo when he was a student at the Imperial War College. So Mama will always be an outsider, and with Papa gone...."

"It's so hard to imagine what it must be like for your mother."

"Yes," said Keiko, "your parents were lucky in a way."

Michiko thought of the day her father died, how she had been sitting with him in the tiny room behind the shop talking about the seventh-day memorial service that was scheduled for her mother the next day. He was smiling and laughing for the first time in that awful week because Michiko had reminded him of the time her brothers had persuaded their mother that they wanted to learn how to bake. "Oh, they were such scamps," he said. "They just wanted her to make those fancy French cream puff pastries."

"I helped Mom clean up the kitchen afterwards," said Michiko. "She knew exactly what they were up to. She laughed about it the whole time we were washing the pans."

"Oh, how delicious those pastries always were—but maybe that time more than any of the others." Her father was still laughing when his face contorted. He was gasping for breath as he fell out of the chair. By the time Michiko had run around the table, he was unconscious. And dead before the ambulance crew got him to the hospital.

KEIKO, still kneeling by the mattress, pivoted herself with her hands, turned all the way around and looked Michiko full in the face. Just her glance said it all.

How lucky I am to have a friend who doesn't mouth platitudes. And now I have Kazue Obasan too. Keiko was right. I will be safe here.

"Poor Granny," Keiko said as she turned away to shake a cover out over the mattress. "Don't worry. She'll come around—after all we represent two more ration cards. It's been years since she's had as much rice as she wants, which certainly hasn't been good for her disposition."

With the *futon* arranged, Keiko put the few extra clothes the two of them had brought into the chest of drawers. The only things Michiko had left were her photos and letters. She spread the photos out—one of her parents, one of her brothers, and a formal portrait of the whole family. The letters—from her brothers home to the family and from Sam to her—were stacked by her right hand. Keiko moved next to her and they looked at the photos together. She nodded when Michiko said, "Enough, it's time to put them away."

Michiko stacked the letters on top of the photos and wrapped them in the *furoshiki*, remembering the day her mother had stitched its *sashiko* pattern. Keiko took it from her and slipped it in the bottom drawer, under the clothes.

"You'll know where this is," she said, before standing and sliding the door open. "Mama, we're ready. Time for the girls to go to bed."

AS it grew warmer, Keiko and Michiko worked in the garden and were extravagantly proud of each shoot they coaxed from the rough soil. They talked endlessly of how delicious their turnips and pumpkins would be come the harvest. The children were set the task of gathering the twigs and dried leaves the household needed for fuel. Everyone but Granny went foraging for wild greens. Keiko and Michiko often climbed high up the mountains. Most days there was precious little to be found. But there was always talk at dinner time of the berries they would find in the summer, the nuts in the fall.

IN April, the nation was mobilized for a new patriotic effort. All citizens were ordered to gather pine roots so their resin could be distilled into aviation fuel. The job of filling the family quota fell to Keiko and Michiko. On the first day of this new endeavor, they set off very early. They tied their hair in scarves and wore the baggy *mompe* trousers that had been their uniform at the Arsenal.

They climbed higher and higher, digging the roots as they went and filling the baskets they had tied to their backs. Keiko joked that at least they didn't have to worry about their hands—years of making munitions had made them tough. "We look like we've been manual laborers our whole lives. I can't even imagine anymore what it would be like to wear a *kimono* or a nice dress and have my hair done and my hands smooth and really clean. I hate these *mompe,* and I'm sick and tired of having to be patriotic all the time. Patriotism now is just like the cloth for these ugly *mompe.* Remember how cloth used to be so nicely made, so pretty to look at when you went to the fabric shop, so nice to the touch?"

Michiko nodded, remembering a Bancho Elementary School class trip to the *iyo kasuri* workshop that produced the traditional Matsuyama splashed-pattern textiles. As she said "Yes" to her friend, she remembered how she had come home and announced to her mother that she wanted to be an *iyo kasuri* weaver when she grew up.

"Michiko, my dear, yes they make beautiful things, but those ladies work long hours and make very little money."

"But Mom!"

"The ladies who work with the dye never really get the color off their hands or out from under their nails. And the ladies who work on the looms sit at them for at least ten hours a day."

"I liked the clackety-clack. I liked watching the pattern form."

"Oh Michiko, many of those ladies lose their hearing after years of the clackety-clack," said her mother. "But, yes, what comes out of those looms is beautiful, in the best way—subdued and quiet. And I think I know how you—even now—can make something like that, make some beauty of your own. Then you can decide when you're all grown up if you still want to learn how to weave. Once you learn this, you'll have it forever. If you decide you want to be a teacher or a nurse or even a house-wife, you'll still have this."

She walked to the cabinet where the family kept its clothing, knelt, and pulled open the bottom drawer. "This is from an old jacket of your grandfather's," she said, unfolding wrapping paper and spreading out a piece of indigo blue cloth. "You can see it's the same blue as the *iyo kasuri*. Let's see what we can do with it. I think we may be able to make a runner for the dining room table."

Starting the next afternoon, her mother began to show her how to make the running stitch *sashiko* embroidery pattern, working a number of stitches at once. The white stitches on the dark indigo ground made the same contrasting color scheme as the *iyo kasuri;* what was missing in the complexity of the weave was made up for by the texture of the stitches atop the cloth.

"Michiko, darling," her mother said, "see how the stitches make a pattern of stacked boxes? It's lovely. You're doing good work. Your dad will be so surprised when he sees this new piece of your work on the table."

Her mother was right. She remembered her father's lavish praise when the runner was finished and laid in the middle of the table for the first time. He ran his fingers over the stitches and smiled at her as he said, "Michiko, you did a great job."

She squirmed with the pleasure of the compliment and ignored her brothers, who were saying, "Dad, enough about Michiko's sewing proj-ect. We're hungry. Let's eat!"

Her father looked again at the stitches and then at his wife. "A love-ly job. So beautiful," he said slowly and gently before he picked up his soup bowl and chopsticks, cleared his throat, and said in his loud official Dad voice, "*Now* we eat." The boys laughed, picked up their bowls, and elbowed each other out of the way reaching for the pickles. Michiko watched her mother and father. They were still looking at each other, ignoring the racket around them. Slowly her mother picked up her soup bowl and chopsticks. Michiko watched her parents decide together that

it was again time to pay attention to their children. Her father sipped his
soup. Her mother looked away and smiled at the boys; the moment was
gone.

"NOW," Keiko said, "we have ugly patched *mompe* made of cloth mixed
with scrap paper and twigs. They're as dirty and ugly and ill-fitting and
uncomfortable as all this endless patriotism. "

"And I just hate seeing Mama dressed in these damn *mompe* too. She's
re-sewn all her clothes into outfits for the kids. I remember how beautiful she was when I was young. She shimmered when she was dressed up.
My sisters will never have that memory. But now with 'Extravagance the
Enemy,' I guess I'm lucky to have my extravagant memories, unless the
kempeitai decide they're dangerous too."

They lapsed into silence, concentrating on climbing, listening to
their breath and the sounds of the forest.

AHEAD on the steep path, Keiko called out, "Ah, Michiko, you'll love
this when you catch up and see the view. It's so romantic. You should be
here with Sam, not with me."

Michiko was happy to hear Keiko mention Sam. Just as she had told
only Keiko the details of the deaths of her parents, it was only Keiko she
had confided in after Sam's visit to the Arsenal in October. The Matsuyama girls had hounded her for details, but Michiko knew that to them
she was an object of curiosity—and perhaps a bit of pity—and most of
all, a topic for gossip. Only Keiko knew what hopes she held on to and
how futile she was sure they were. Even if both she and Sam survived the
war, there would be no place for an "us" in Matsuyama. And for Sam,
the only son of his proud mother, it would have to be Matsuyama, and
the utmost respectability. No place for the orphaned child of sweet shop
owners.

Michiko no longer saw her surroundings as she trudged upward.
She was back in Matsuyama again, on *Okaido*, headed to the Prefectural
Girls' School at the end of the main shopping street. She was trailing
behind a gaggle of her classmates, who were eyeing the Matsuchu schoolboys headed in the opposite direction. The girls moved in a cascade of
giggles and whispered comments. Michiko didn't care that she couldn't
hear what they were saying—she was busy sneaking glances at Sam. He

was marching forward in his new elite Matsuchu uniform, back straight, chin thrust forward, pretending to ignore everyone around him. But she knew he was actually busy looking at her and hoping she was happy to be the object of his attention. She smiled as she had on *Okaido,* happy with her delicious secret, and smiled again when she thought of the pleasure of sharing her secret with Keiko.

As Michiko got closer to the peak, Keiko continued, "But your Sam is probably sitting at some airfield waiting for what the Navy has persuaded him is his chance for glory. But it looks now like even that can't happen until we gather enough pine roots to make the fuel for his plane. How stupid, stupid, stupid everything about this war is!"

And then she was there with her friend and with the lake. Biwa spread out below them, sparkling in the bright spring sunshine. Michiko felt that she and Keiko were one with the pine forest; it embraced them from behind and spread below them down to the water. They even smelled like the forest, with the roots piled in their baskets and the resin staining their hands and clothes. Keiko turned, smiled, and they fell into each other's arms. They hugged and laughed, at the glorious blue lake, at the deep green pines, at themselves, and at their joy. They laughed in the presence of the sheer beauty of their surroundings.

Michiko thought fleetingly of the Inland Sea and the poem after poem about its calm beauty. She remembered climbing to the top of the Matsuyama Castle grounds and looking at the sun sliding down the sky and gilding the glimmering waters. She remembered Sam's arm around her waist and his words in her ear, "We have to start so we'll get you home before dark. Remember me, Michiko, please. Remember this day." But she had never felt exactly this way, not even then; now she understood, for the first time, what beauty was for. All the sorrow, the pain, and the loneliness of the last years had fled. She was transfixed, transformed, exalted. And grateful. Grateful for Keiko, for the day, the place, the moment.

When she was ready to speak, she said, in her best mock formal matter, "Keiko, I'm so glad you brought me with you to your village. I feel at home with you and in this place. And you have arranged such a grand sightseeing excursion for me. My most sincere and humble gratitude is yours."

They were still laughing as they started back down the mountain.

They carried the view of the lake, the smell of the pine, and the warmth
of the sunshine with them, even as the shadows fell. They had remembered that they were alive and young. When they reached the clearing
atop the hill behind the cluster of village houses, they came upon a
young man. He too had a basket, but it hung loose and empty on his
back. Still full of high spirits, they laughed and told him the better roots
were farther up and that there wasn't much time left before it got dark.
His reply was only a quiet, "Thank you," but his smile was gentle, and
his eyes showed his amusement. He stood aside as they continued toward the village. When they were far enough past that he couldn't hear,
Michiko said, "Keiko, who's that, and why is someone our age not in the
military?"

"I have no idea. I've never seen him before." When they turned and
looked back, he was limping slowly in the opposite direction. He disappeared into the woods.

When they got back to the house, Kazue Obasan was happy to see
them, and Granny was quite pleased with their haul of pine roots, "We'll
do well with the town association officials because you've collected so
many. How helpful for the war effort."

"Yes, Granny," Keiko said. "I'm going to make us some tea. I'm sure
you'd like some, and Michiko and I need to revive ourselves. We did a
lot of climbing today." Michiko nodded and smiled at Granny and then
followed Keiko to the kitchen.

"I hate that they're everywhere, even inside our own house," Keiko
whispered when they were out of earshot.

She was back to talking about the thought police. They had lived
with the influence of the *kempeitai* at the Arsenal, but Keiko was right,
freed from the military they now had be careful about the *tokko,* the
Home Ministry's Special Higher Police force, which had grown more
vigilant as the fortunes of war turned against Japan. Keiko told Michiko
what she had learned from her mother: they *were* everywhere, even in this
tiny town. Those most active locally were Ogawa-san, the Assistant Station Manager, Nishizawa-san, the Mayor's haughty needle-nosed sister,
and Abe-san, the proprietor of the local general store.

Abe-san's stock of farm equipment and electrical goods—radios and
phonographs—was long gone. His jobs now were collecting scrap and
patching and re-patching the goods he had sold his neighbors years be-

fore. Abe-san talked about how the repair work was his patriotic duty, his contribution to the war effort, but Keiko had learned from her mother that his real work, carried out with great gusto, was watching, listening, and reporting. "He and his dark shop always scared me when I was a child," she had told Michiko, "and I always hated Nishizawa-san. She's so bossy and mean and loves to lord it over everyone. But Ogawa-san would always smile and salute, and he looks so good in his uniform, with his hat, his white gloves, and his flag tucked under his arm. Remember how he was there the night we arrived from Kure? It was the same when I was a kid. I loved to see his happy face when we reached home after a trip to the city. How can all this have happened to us?"

There was no doubt about it—the influence of the thought police was everywhere, listening and judging every word, every breath, searching for every thought that tried to stay hidden. They were as strong a presence as Granny; they brought the ugliness of the war into each household, into each life in the village.

Keiko poured the hot water, "Well at least we have our memory of today. But no more complaining about *mompe* or anything else, and certainly no comments about the obviously desperate straits of a military that sends civilians out to collect roots to be distilled as fuel for its aircraft. Time to agree with Granny."

Kazue Obasan joined them when they brought the tea back to the table and asked, "Did you see young Miyazawa?"

"We saw a guy our age, Mama, and Michiko couldn't believe I didn't know who he was. She's convinced that here in the country, everyone knows everyone else."

"Well, I guess he's officially a *sokaijin*, an evacuee from the city. Actually, I guess our dear Michiko is one herself. Anyway, he's a nephew of the Miyazawas. He's just arrived from Osaka. His name is Shotaro."

"Polio," Granny said, "when he was a child. He's an only son. And both his parents are gone."

"He's the son of Mr. Miyazawa's younger brother, who was a department head and professor at the university hospital. Shotaro-san finished college last year. Since the medical school closed, he couldn't continue his studies. His dad arranged for him to work in the hospital, and that's where he was, on a night shift, when the B-29s obliterated their whole neighborhood. He brought his uncle some things from his dad's office:

a few books, one photograph from his parents' wedding. That's all that's left of his family. Oh, my dear Keiko, my dear Michiko, we're lucky we still have each other."

Granny turned her head.

SHOTARO came to call the next day. Keiko and Michiko were sitting outside under the eaves of the house. They were tired from the excursion the day before; there had been only rice and barley gruel for breakfast and nothing for lunch. The three children sat next to them, too listless to play. The twins were talking to each other in their private made-up language, and the boy, hungry and cranky, had woken up from a nap and was whining. Shotaro limped up the path. He was unbearably thin in baggy clothes that were probably his uncle's. Keiko and Michiko got to their feet, and as he approached he said, "Hello, again. I'm Miyazawa. My aunt and uncle asked me to come to visit."

Keiko and Michiko led him into the cool, dark house. Keiko escorted him to the *tatami* room to meet Granny. Michiko went to the kitchen with Kazue Obasan. Michiko held the tea pot as the older woman lifted the lid and inspected the washed-out leaves they had been using for three days. "Since we have company, let's see what we can do," she said, reaching for the tea canister. "At least a few new leaves," she said, tipping a quarter teaspoonful of fresh tea into the pot. She took the pot from Michiko, poured in hot water, and placed it on a tray. Handing the tray to Michiko, she said, "I've got the extra cups. Let's see how Granny and Keiko are entertaining our new neighbor."

They arranged the tea on the low table in the *tatami* room. Kazue Obasan nodded to Keiko. "Oh, it smells so good, fresh and green like summer," Keiko said, as she poured the thin green liquid, first for Shotaro and then for Granny.

As Michiko knelt to join the group around the table, she noticed that Shotaro's leg was folded awkwardly under him. *I wonder how much it's hurting him to sit here.*

Shotaro said thank you to Keiko and took a sip of his tea. He then turned to the old woman and said, "My auntie especially wanted me to see you, Granny."

"How kind of her to think of me. How lucky you are to have such a good aunt."

"Yes, she's very kind, and she's good to everyone and everything, even her hen." And with that Shotaro pulled a bandana out of his pocket, untied it and placed an egg on the table.

It sat pale and gleaming against the worn deep brown of the mahogany. "Auntie wanted you to have this, Granny. She says you have to keep your health up. She said that these gorgeous young ladies are strong and healthy and that you need to be able to hold your own with them." Michiko gave the requisite giggle at Shotaro's rhetorical flourish and hoped it hid her greedy fascination: the egg was beautiful.

Shotaro put his tea cup down and turned his attention from Granny to bow in the direction of Keiko and Michiko. "Of course, ladies, I'm only quoting Auntie word for word. I'd never say anything so forward myself." Granny snorted, everyone else smiled, and Michiko feasted her eyes on Shotaro's sharp features and dark deep-set eyes. *He's an orphan too.*

"Please tell your aunt," said Granny, "that I'm grateful and honored that she's been so kind to remember a tired, sick, old woman. I'm really not worth wasting anything on." But she didn't even incline her head in thanks, Michiko noted, and sat looking straight at Shotaro as Kazue Obasan urged more tea on him. He refused with a smile and stood to take his leave. He bowed deeply to Granny and Kazue Obasan and nodded at Keiko and Michiko. Kazue Obasan, Keiko, and Michiko walked him to the door to see him off.

They were still standing in the entryway when Granny, who had remained seated at the table, took the egg in her left hand and told her daughter-in-law, "Call the children." With her right hand, she pulled a hairpin from her bun, pricked a hole in the bottom of the egg, held it to her mouth and began to suck. When the children came in, she gave it to the boy and told him, "Have some and then give it to your sisters."

He took it and tried to do as his grandmother said, but when he tipped his head back and held the egg up, his little hands gripped too hard and the shell broke apart. What was left inside the egg was now on his face. Granny picked up the pieces and handed them to the girls, who held them delicately and sucked off what they could. Granny pulled the boy to her and wiped the egg from his nose, his cheeks, and his chin with her index finger, which she then put in his mouth for him to suck. She did this several times. After she made a last pass over the boy's face, she put her finger in her own mouth and sat sucking on it, eyes closed, self-contained in her pleasure.

SUMMER arrived and wore on, one clear hot day after another. Everything slowed down. The harvest was small, and the few turnips and pumpkins that ripened were stretched over many meals. Kazue Obasan, Keiko, and Michiko gave most of their food to the children. Impervious, Granny endured the hunger and the heat. She now occupied the large, cool *tatami* room as her exclusive domain, and others were admitted only at her whim. They were all allowed into Granny's room for Shotaro's next two visits on errands for his aunt, but after that only the visitor was admitted. He never stayed long, but would always stop to talk to Keiko and Michiko before climbing up the hill to take the shortcut home.

Keiko and Michiko spent most of their days sitting outdoors under the eaves, trying to keep cool in the shade. In the first part of the summer, they had laughed that they were too skinny to sit on the rough, pebbly ground, that they were so delicate they should be seated on Granny's sweet cool *tatami*. Shotaro's "gorgeous young ladies" became their stock phrase, and Keiko worked out a perfect imitation of his Osaka accent. Michiko laughed with Keiko; never certain when he would appear again, she liked having a reason to talk about him.

By July, they rarely chose to speak. The hunger took everything: desire, personality, memory. Michiko knew she wanted to survive, but could no longer remember why.

KEIKO was the first to fall ill. Then the two little girls. They lay in the dark narrow room to the side of the *tatami* room. Michiko and Kazue Obasan kept wet compresses on their heads and held them up to give them sips of tea and rice gruel. There was no medicine. There was nothing they could do but bear witnesses to the power of the dengue and the suffering it inflicted.

In the middle of the third day of Keiko's illness, Michiko began to feel sick herself; by the end of the day, she was lost. The next morning, there was only fever and pain. She was in the dark room, she was outside under the eaves. She lay in the shade, she lay in the sun. She was the pebbles. She was gravel. She was dust. She was the space between the dust.

Time came back, and she realized Shotaro was in the next room, talking with Granny. She turned her head and saw the face of her dear friend. Keiko lay next to her, utterly pale, filmed in sweat, eyes unfocused. At that moment, listening to Shotaro's voice and looking at Keiko, she knew her friend's fate, and her own: Keiko would be gone and she would grieve for the rest of her life.

Michiko was restless all night; in the small hours of the morning, she felt the fever begin to lose its grip. By morning, it was clear that Keiko would not live through the day. Michiko spent the morning lying on her side, looking at her friend and drifting in and out of sleep, and in and out of consciousness. Her thoughts of her friend's smile, her quick wit, and her passion melted into dreams of the dirt and the smell of Kure, which were followed by dreams of the playground at Bancho Elementary School.

Michiko awoke when Kazue Obasan got up to leave the sickroom to serve Granny her lunch. Michiko lay on her back, listening to them talking in the next room. She couldn't make out the words; she just heard the conciliatory tone that Kazue Obasan always used with Granny. She was happy when Kazue Obasan came back to the sickroom; she belonged with her daughters.

After lunch Granny began to grumble, loud enough to be heard in the sickroom. As the painful minutes of the afternoon slipped past, Granny was growing more and more agitated. Slowly her words penetrated, and Michiko began to understand what she was saying. With understanding came fear; she was terrified, for herself and for Kazue Obasan, but she couldn't move. There was nothing she could do but listen with horror as Granny blamed the two of them for everything that was happening.

Granny never moved from her place at the low table in the *tatami* room, but her anger and her menace filled the whole house. "No, I said, no," she grumbled. "I didn't want a stranger in my house. Another mouth to feed. Someone taking food out of my mouth."

And then louder, "No, no, no, I said. Send her away. But does she listen? *No.* All she ever does is defy me. She took my son from me. She's the reason I'm alone. All she does is deny me and defy me." The ranting grew louder and louder, and soon Granny's shouting blocked out all other sound. Kazue Obasan looked at Michiko, shaking her head, and smiling. Michiko thought *I will never again see someone who is so burdened smile like that.* She shifted her gaze to look at Keiko, wanting to talk to her, but her friend was beyond hearing.

I must remember my dear Keiko's face, she thought as she drifted away from the noise and back into the embrace of the illness. She awoke at about three. Granny was back to just grumbling. Michiko looked at Keiko and knew the end was near.

She watched Kazue Obasan hold her daughter's hand and stroke her face. As Keiko's breath grew slower and more difficult, her mother kept whispering, "My darling, I love you. I'm with you. I love you."

When Keiko was gone, Kazue Obasan let out a cry of grief, but caught herself and turned to the little sisters, lying next to Keiko. Michiko looked at them and saw that they too had the vacant look she had seen on Keiko's face the day before.

When Granny heard Kazue Obasan's cry, the grumbling again became outright screaming. "Is she dead? Have you taken my son's daughter from me? Why did you do this? Why did you keep this stranger here? Why, why, why do you do nothing but defy me? Will my son's other children be next? I'm keeping my grandson here with me. Away from you. I won't let you near him!"

Silent tears streamed down Kazue Obasan's face as she reached out for Michiko. She grasped her right hand and said, "Michiko, you know I love you, and you know Keiko loved you. I've been lucky to have two grown daughters during this terrible year." She held her gaze steady on Michiko and kept Michiko's hand in hers as the screaming continued. Michiko thought of her own mother and the different kinds of pain her last few years had brought her. The sharp stab of pain she felt for Kazue Obasan surprised her; she thought her heart was too bruised and damaged for anything more.

Michiko felt the older woman tighten her grip when they heard Granny rise from the table in the next room and order the little boy to stay put. She felt her shudder when the dull thump of angry footsteps told them that Granny was crossing the *tatami* room. Kazue Obasan kept her eyes steady on Michiko. Granny stormed into the sickroom, still screaming, and started to pull Michiko up from the floor. Kazue Obasan tried to hold on to her, but Granny ripped Michiko away, pulling her by her left arm and dragging her from the room.

Everything went dark. She must have lost consciousness. Her awareness of where she was and what was happening returned when she landed on the stone step at the front of the house. She fell hard on her right arm and her hip, and she felt her ankle rip open on the sharp edge of the stone. She heard the door slam and the heavy stamping steps retreating.

She was grateful that the noise was muffled. Too weak to get up, she gathered herself around her wounded arm and laid her cheek on the stone. *Think about how cool it is, how good it feels. Don't think about anything else.* But unconsciousness did not come to release her again, and she was aware of everything, everything she had lost.

When Granny finally stopped screaming, Michiko could hear Kazue Obasan talking to the little girls, quietly begging them to live. She imagined that Granny had gone back to the *tatami* room and was sitting with the little boy at her side.

MICHIKO was still there when Shotaro arrived. He took her hand and asked what had happened. When Michiko couldn't speak, he went inside, not even bothering to announce himself. He was back quickly. He picked Michiko up and carried her off.

SHOTARO was by her side when she awoke the next morning. When she struggled to get up, he held her down gently and said, "No, no, stay put. You're safe. Starting from today, I am taking care of you." His eyes were full of concern, his attention fully on her. Knowing that what he said was true, she slipped back into the illness and into sleep. The fever came again and held her in its grip.

He was by her side every time she awoke. She came to understand that she was in the shed behind his aunt and uncle's house. When she was well enough to ask how long she had been there, Shotaro said, "Three days so far. It's the last day of July."

The next day she asked if his aunt and uncle minded that they had a guest, and he said, "Don't worry. I'm taking care of you. You're *my* guest. And from tomorrow you start eating."

During the heat of the next day, as she lay in the cool, dark shed, she was aware for the first time that the old wood was still dank with the smell of the yams and potatoes that had been stored there in happier days. She moved her right arm slowly; it was neatly and expertly bandaged. She looked at it with surprise and saw bruising that extended far beyond the edge of the bandage. She reached her arm out and was running her fingers over the nubs and ridges of the wall when she heard Shotaro open the door.

"I thought you'd be better today. I'm glad I was right." She turned toward the doorway, eager to see his face. The sunlight hurt her eyes, but as he closed the door and moved next to her in the tiny space, she tried to smile, wondering if her muscles were working.

"It's so good to see you smiling." Leaning close, he said, "Yes, you are better, and it is time for you to eat." He had tea and scraps of food.

Day by day she slowly healed and improved. She was able to sit, to stand, and to walk short distances. He was always there, even when she didn't know she needed him. She loved the warmth in his voice, in his eyes. He was the reason she was alive, her antidote to loss and sorrow. He was her world.

The first time she was strong enough to leave the shed, they stood in a soft evening twilight. He began to tell her the news of the last few weeks. "Early every evening, after I was sure you were asleep, I came out here. In the last fading light, the planes would pass overhead. They were like flocks of birds—so many you couldn't count them. Usually they were so high I couldn't hear them, and watching them pass in pure silence was somehow even more dreadful than hearing the roar of engines. Sometimes one of them would catch a ray of the last light in the sky and gleam, soft and silvery, before passing on, into the dark and towards the cities. Those moments were so quietly beautiful they'd take my breath away. How can I think that? I'd say to myself. They're bombers on their way to their fearsome work. Watching them every evening made me so, so sad. I'd stand here wondering how I could bear any more of this. How I can live the rest of my life remembering just what I have to remember now?

"It rained after the bombing in Osaka, so the fires didn't last, and I was able to go home the next morning. All I found was a sodden pile of rubble where our house had been. It was like that for about a ten-square block area. I wouldn't have known where I was but for the empty burned space that had been the bamboo grove that stood behind our garden. My parents loved to sit there in the evening and listen to the cicadas and the trees knocking against each other." He paused, and Michiko thought he was finished, but he added, "I'd heard about the stench of charred flesh from the other hospital workers. I was spared that," before he fell silent.

Michiko did not know how to respond. She was overwhelmed with emotion, with the power and the pain of memory—his, and her own. All she could do was murmur his name. Only after she had said, "Shotaro," did she realize how intimate they were and how far in the past all proprieties and formalities were.

"But you, Michiko, are why I know I can bear this and how I'll be able to bear what is to come. We can do it together."

"Yes," she whispered.

"You know you can't trust most of what you hear, but Nishizawa-san has been quiet, and her brother the mayor is too busy writing reports to Tokyo to answer anyone's questions. I think the rumors are true that there have been fire bombings, assaults so intense that whole cities have burned. I think only Kyoto has been spared. It is much worse than those isolated raids like the one that killed my mom and dad. Osaka, and Nagoya and even Tokyo are flattened. The official radio reports of 'light damage to property and only a few reported casualties' are garbage."

Suddenly cold, Michiko shivered and swallowed a sob. He pulled her close to him, and said, "Don't be afraid. It has to be over soon. We'll start anew, the two of us. You'll be with me always." Starting that night, he slept next to her in the shed.

A few days later, he told her he had heard stories about some strange new bomb that had completely obliterated Hiroshima and said there were rumors that Nagasaki had met the same fate. The next morning when he returned from an early-morning foray searching for food, he said, "Michiko, today's the fifteenth of August. Do you think you're strong enough to walk awhile? It's important."

As he led her slowly toward the center of the village, he explained about the broadcast. The mayor had set up a radio on a chair outside his front door. They stood in the crowd of villagers. Not caring what anyone thought, they leaned against each other listening to the unimaginable, to the strange thin high voice exhorting them to *endure the unendurable and bear the unbearable.*

They were the first to leave. Many of the older people were still kneeling or bowing low before the radio; most of the villagers were just standing still in shock. For those able to move beyond shock there was fear as they tried to understand what had happened to them, what had happened to Japan, and what the future would bring. Shotaro took Michiko's arm, and they walked through the village. Rather than turning onto the path to his aunt and uncle's house, Shotaro steered her up the hill behind the shed. They picked over the rough terrain together. Michiko stumbled at the top of the climb, and he was reaching to help her when he stumbled himself and leaned on her to take the weight off his bad leg. They reached the crest of the hill in each other's arms. Michiko looked up to realize they were in the clearing where she and Keiko had first seen Shotaro; at that same moment, she saw Kazue Obasan and the graves.

The midday sun fell mercilessly on the clearing. There was no mystery, no atmosphere, nothing but the scars of the turned earth. Michiko felt Shotaro's embrace tighten. Kazue Obasan and her son were on the other side of the clearing, heading toward the Kawamura home. Kazue Obasan glanced back at the noise and then turned, bowed, and stood motionless looking at them. When Michiko, choking on a cry, started toward her, she shook her head almost imperceptibly. The little boy too had turned. He stood next to Kazue Obasan, staring, his face flat and blind with malice. Kazue Obasan reached for his hand and pulled him gently onward on the path.

"No," said Shotaro, "she can't stop. You know she can't stop. She has to go back. Let her go in peace." He put both his arms around Michiko and pulled her close. She buried herself in him, closing out the sun, the heat, the loss. When she was steady, he said, "Darling, we have to go. Come with me to see my aunt and uncle."

Still holding her in his arms, he turned her around so they faced back toward his aunt and uncle's house. "Come with me to say goodbye. Then we have to get ready. We're leaving for Osaka tomorrow."

Michiko opened her eyes, reached for his hand and started forward. As they went down the hill, a small breeze they couldn't feel stirred the tree tops; she heard the bamboos behind the clearing knock against each other.

CHAPTER 13

SAM

Chitose, 1945

"IT'S NOT TRUE. Say it again and I'll hit you. "

The army sergeant looked at me directly for a moment before he turned his eyes aside and lowered his head. "Go ahead, but it's still true. Look around."

I couldn't find any words. I turned away, but had to steady myself before I walked back across the platform to the train and the waiting cadets. They had slept on the ferry, tired from roughhousing all day through the long train journey, but I had sat up, troubled by the tough crossing from Aomori, rumors that the straits were mined, and thoughts of enemy bombers. At Sapporo I had marched them quickly to the waiting train that would take us to Chitose and ordered them to stay in their seats. I had gone back to the platform to find out what was happening, why Sapporo Station, which should have been bustling, felt so dead.

It's not true, I thought. It can't be true. *The Emperor can't have spoken on the radio. Unconditional surrender is impossible.*

When I got back to the train, I said nothing, not even to Utsumi. We started up soon enough. During the trip through the Hokkaido countryside, I sat silent, thinking. *They have vast resources; but we have spirit, we will never surrender. They even seem to have a new special bomb, but the reports are that damage in Hiroshima and Nagasaki was minimal. We have our people, our strength, our courage. Like these three hundred young men we'll shape into warriors.*

IT was dark when we arrived in Chitose. After we loaded the baggage on trucks and organized the cadets in formation, we marched them to the base. I was relieved that the sentries at the gate gave a perfectly normal salute. Business as usual.

We dismissed the cadets in front of their barracks. Utsumi, Morita, and I headed for the Officers' Mess. Opening the door and stepping inside, we knew the war was over. The officers, in their uniforms, sat silently at the tables, their heads bowed. I hesitated, but brought myself to do my duty. "Lieutenant Junior Grade Imagawa, arriving from Kasumigaura Naval Air Corps. Three officers and three hundred cadets, Sir." The commanding officer acknowledged my report with only his eyes. The others didn't even seem to notice us.

The next morning, the Commander called all the officers together and told us that he had no orders, no idea what we should do or how we should do it. He left us on our own to decide.

When the Commander left, we agreed easily and unanimously—we would keep training. We took the cadets up for drills. And in the air, swooping and banking over the deep northern forests, we forgot. We soared on spirit. But the third morning, the mechanics were lounging around when we arrived at the hangers. "Get the planes ready!" I yelled, angry at their lack of discipline.

"We can't. The carburetors have been taken away."

"By whom? To where?"

"The chief mechanic. We don't know where, Sir."

When we found the Commander he told us that he had orders that all flights had to cease, but that was all he knew. We would probably be demobilized in a few weeks, and all he could tell us was that we had to keep order. Again, how was up to us. We had to figure out how to keep the cadets occupied.

Utsumi and I sat up that night talking. "We can't have them play volleyball all day and sing all night," I said.

"Well, we could read to them."

"So now we're kindergarten teachers," I exclaimed.

"No, no, we could read something wonderful, strong, something with, I don't know, *hope.*"

"Utsumi, what am I going to do with you?"

"What about *Musashi Miyamoto*?"

"Utsumi, what am I going to do with you, you *genius?*" The seventeenth-century *samurai* tale had been retold in an immensely popular novel by Eiji Yoshikawa and had also been a radio serial. Everyone knew the story and loved its sweeping historical themes. "Not only is it perfect, it's *long*. It will keep us busy for quite a while. It's settled. Reading in the morning, baseball and volleyball in the afternoon, and reading again after dinner."

The cadets loved the story. As a youth, Musashi, a wild loner, alienated everyone in his hometown except the beautiful Otsu. He grew even wilder and more rash after his attempt to be a *samurai* and his defeat at the Battle of Sekigahara. A Buddhist monk, Takuan, proved to be Musashi's salvation. In one of the story's most famous chapters, Takuan caught Musashi, tied him up and hung him from a tree. Somehow the experience of being suspended in the tree until Takuan decided to release him opened the door to self-awareness for the angry young man. Under the monk's tutelage, Musashi studied martial arts, learning self-control, discipline, and true courage. He ultimately achieved great fame as a swordsman.

As Utsumi and I worked through the complex tale, we discovered that we were hams. The cadets enjoyed our acting as we assumed the roles of lords and ladies, warriors and merchants, villagers and farmers. The sports competitions went well too. And we still kept up our earlier tradition of singing, but now we did it at night after we had finished our reading aloud sessions. At the end of many of our evenings I thought about my Sundays at the Grahams—the layers of sounds and the harmonies of the naval hymns really did give me a church-like feeling. I felt that these times were precious and sacred in a way that had nothing to do with religion.

Without the harsh discipline of training, we all had fun, and Utsumi and I realized we appreciated the cadets as individuals—very young and very vulnerable individuals—something we had never allowed ourselves to do during the relentless training process. We found ourselves looking forward to our reading sessions and our conversations with the young cadets. After a week or so, we asked permission for something that would never have occurred to us before the end of the war. We were pleasantly surprised when Commander Fujita agreed. "Yes, Imagawa, you and Utsumi can take beer from the Officers' Mess to the cadets in their barracks in the evenings. Alcohol is the last thing we want to turn over to the Americans when they arrive. Just be sure to go easy, and keep the cadets in line. Remember, they're still under-age."

Commander Fujita summoned all the officers early the morning of

September 5. "Orders have arrived," he said. "Demobilization will begin in two days. You will all go home. There's a lot to be done before then. Get your men and start immediately."

We destroyed everything—Navy fashion, with discipline and in a completely orderly fashion. We collected weapons, ammunition, equipment, uniforms, bedding, training manuals, records, reports, and even extra bales of rice and crocks of *miso,* and lit huge bonfires.

Utsumi and I were in charge of dismantling the planes; we supervised the mechanics and our cadets. When they finished, the stacks of the parts were satisfyingly neat, but inspecting them, I mourned for the beautiful planes that had taken us aloft. But as I thought that, I realized that the cadets—so young, and so eager just three weeks ago to fly those planes to their deaths—would not have to be mourned. They would go home to their families.

WHEN we finished with the planes, I returned to my quarters. I didn't care anymore that I was supposed to burn all "classified" photos. I was packing my memories from Mie, Izumi, Wonson, and Tokyo when the summons came from Commander Fujita. I went without concern or curiosity to his office.

"Imagawa, you've been promoted. As of September first, you are Lieutenant Senior Grade. Congratulations."

As I tried to recover from my confusion, he pinned on the new cherry blossom pins. I was thrilled when he addressed me by my new rank.

"Lieutenant Senior Grade, be sure that you get your charges home safe, and take the initiative I've seen you demonstrate into the next phase of your life. We need inventiveness—and great courage—for the difficult tasks that lie ahead for Japan."

"Yes, Sir. Commander, thank you for this honor and for the honor of serving under you."

WHEN we left the next day, I had my severance pay in my pocket—fatter because of my new rank—and twenty cadets in my charge. We marched to the station, where a train waited. The Hokkaido woods sped by, and when we reached the ferry it was still early in the day. This time the crossing was easy, the straits calm. But Aomori Station was chaos. Civilians and soldiers milled about. The stationmaster was under siege. I used my best powers of persuasion, but my three cherry blossoms didn't make much of an impression. Finally, I wangled the information that a "special" would leave at midnight; it would link up at Akita with an Osaka-bound express. I dismissed the cadets, without any doubt that they would obey the order to be back by eleven-thirty P.M.

They were fully assembled exactly on time, and with our naval discipline, we managed to get on the train and get seats. All that five-minutes-before training was still paying dividends. Exhausted from the long day, we slept long and well. When we awoke in the morning, we found the aisles crammed with soldiers—the officers and enlisted men indistinguishable since they had stripped themselves of their insignia—and discovered that we had gone only two stations south on the route along the Japan Sea coast. We didn't reach Akita until noon, and from there on the train was even more crowded. The journey ground on, slowly, slowly, slowly. Several times when I awoke, I found that the train was marooned on a siding. We were hungry, and the few stations where *bento* box lunches were available were the scenes of mad scrambles.

It took three days to reach Osaka. The entire journey was a series of farewells. I was proud of the young cadets I had gotten to know and, as each left the group, was happy knowing that he would soon be home with his family. When the train finally pulled into Osaka Station, only six of my charges were left. We regrouped and changed trains. When we reached Okayama, the group was down to three. We changed trains there again, and at Uno caught the ferry across the Inland Sea, headed for Shikoku. I exulted in the sky and the island-dotted sea. *I was on my way home!* I'm sure the cadets felt the same way. One was from Takamatsu, so we parted ways at the ferry terminal, and the last cadet, Ishimitsu, and I took the next train. We reached Kita-Iyo, outside Matsuyama, on the fourth day after we left Chitose. Cadet Ishimitsu was headed farther down the line. He carried my wicker trunk to the platform. We shook hands, saluted, and parted ways.

I ALLOWED myself to feel only the exhaustion of the journey as I walked to our Ishii Village country home. No one was on the road; the late summer sun slanted on the familiar rice paddies and fields and the orchard behind the house. My steps, one after another, crunching on the country paths, were the only sounds I heard.

I took off my hat and shoes and stepped up into the dim front room. Mother and Father looked up.

I bowed. "I'm back. I'm sorry I—"

"I know you're disappointed that we didn't win, but we are so happy you're home safe," said Father. "Come sit with us."

Mother said, "We have been so proud of you, and now we have you back."

Father was the first to cry. My parents sat across from each other. I stood rooted at the edge of the *genkan,* unable to cross the room to join them.

CHAPTER 14

SAM

Matsuyama, 1945–1948

"LOLLIPOP," I REPEATED, too shocked to do anything but comply with the order, not really processing how casually it had been delivered. *What am I supposed to do? Two weeks ago, I was Lieutenant Senior Grade Imagawa of the Imperial Japanese Navy. And here I am standing in front of an American officer—a superior officer.*

"Fine," said the Colonel, "report for work tomorrow morning at eight A.M." He turned around to talk to the sergeant who was standing behind him holding papers.

As I began to sputter, "But," Yamamura-sensei elbowed me. "Yes, Sir," I said as my teacher turned and led me back into the hallway.

"Let's go," said Yamamura-sensei. "We'll stop at my house before I take you home."

Sensei had shown up late that morning on his motorcycle, as positive as ever. I heard the engine sputtering and grinding long before I could see who it was. I went and stood outside the house, wondering if it could be him and was very pleased when he rolled up.

"Imagawa, welcome back! I'm so glad you're home alive. I asked around in Yanai-machi, and some of your neighbors there said your family was out here at Ishii again. I'm lucky today to have enough fuel to come out here."

"Welcome, *Sensei*," said Mother, who had come to the entrance from the kitchen, "it is wonderful to see you again. It's certainly been quite some time, hasn't it?"

"Ah, Mrs. Imagawa, you're fortunate to have your son back," said Yamamura-sensei.

Where was talk of the war, talk of Japan's failure, and talk of how I was back only because I somehow hadn't been able to do my duty? Why weren't my elders and those near and dear to me saying anything about what had kept me awake at night and fretting through the beautiful autumn days?

"When I heard you were here, Mrs. Imagawa, I of course wanted to see Isamu," he said, "but I must also confess that I thought that coming out here would give me a chance to ask if you or your neighbors have any extra food. It's quite difficult finding much in the city. My wife has been doing a tremendous job making do, but...."

"Oh, *Sensei*," said Mother, "I'm afraid we don't have anything to spare ourselves, but let me go ask some of the neighbors." As she ran off, she called over her shoulder, "Isamu, don't forget your manners. Ask *Sensei* in and make him comfortable. I'll be back as soon as I can."

Yamamura-sensei and I did just that, sitting at the table, drinking tea. We hadn't seen each other for two years. He had news of my Matsuchu classmates. I heard with sorrow the names of my classmates who were dead: Suzuki, Mitsui, Yanagibachi, as well as Sakuragi, who was the bugler in the class behind mine.

"Yes," he said, "there has been much too much death, Isamu, and we are going to have to live with this sorrow for the rest of our lives. For the young ones like you who were lucky enough to survive, there's a great deal of work to be done to assure a different future."

I was wondering how to say that the future was the one thing I couldn't imagine when we heard the door open and Mother's wooden sandals clattering in the *genkan*. She rushed into the room where we were sitting, her face flushed, and her apron filled with wrinkled sweet potatoes.

"Our neighbor, Farmer Morita had these extras, *Sensei*," she said. "I brought as many as I could carry for you. It's not much, but...."

"Mrs. Imagawa, that's not at all the case. It's sheer delight to see such abundance. I'm sure that my wife can feed the family for weeks. My deepest thanks."

As Mother knelt and began wrapping the sweet potatoes in a *furoshiki,* Yamamura-sensei said, "Mrs. Imagawa, can I impose on your further and borrow Isamu for the afternoon?"

"Of course, *Sensei*," said Mother. "If there's anything he can do to help you, please—"

"Well, I'd like him to come into the city with me. He can hold the sweet potatoes. I want to be sure to get this precious cargo back in good order. And I'll take him to Yanai-machi. He hasn't seen the changes in the neighborhood."

Mother insisted that Yamamura-sensei stay for lunch. She had prepared my lunch and hers when she packed Father's lunch box early in the morning. I'm not sure how she stretched what she had for the two of us, but we had a good lunch. Yamamura-sensei told Mother stories about his Matsuchu music students. It was fascinating to hear the familiar stories from the teacher's point of view.

"Well, Mrs. Imagawa, I'm sure you never suspected how much behind-the-scenes comedy there was as we prepared for those glorious parades of the troops to the station," he said, as he finished the last of his rice.

"I still remember the first parade we saw when we arrived home from San Francisco," said Mother, "and how proud I was the first time Isamu marched as a musician in one himself."

"And I will always remember how heavy my heart was last year when we accompanied the last group to the station. I thought of how many of my students I had seen off. Of course, we didn't know at the time that it was the last group, but everything did get smaller and smaller and harder and harder, didn't it?"

Mother smiled and bowed. *Sensei* suddenly became his energetic self again. Jumping up, he said, "Well, off we go. I'll get him back before nightfall, Mrs. Imagawa. Thank you again for your hospitality and for these wonderful sweet potatoes."

I had been on *Sensei's* old scooter years before, but his new motorcycle was bigger and much older; the fifteen-minute ride into the city on the rackety bike was harrowing. While I was wondering if the sweet potatoes and I would survive, I was also steeling myself for the sad sight of the wide street and the empty space where the Yanai-machi house had stood. I had thought about it often in the last year and remembered staring at the dull gray of the Japan Sea on the long train trip from the north, wondering what home would be like with Yanai-machi obliterated.

When Yamamura-sensei stopped and I stepped off the motorcycle, it was worse, much worse than I had imagined. The house was gone; the street was unnaturally wide—about three or four times what it had been, and the new ugly street slashed diagonally through the neighborhood. It wasn't just our house that was gone—all our neighbors' houses were gone too. My eleven years there had vanished without a trace. The past was gone, the future still unimaginable.

"Had enough of this?" asked Yamamura-sensei. "Let's go. I have one more place I need to take you."

Rather than heading for his house, he turned the bike and headed in the opposite direction. "Where are we going?" I asked.

"You'll see," he yelled over his shoulder. I soon concluded that we were headed for Bancho Elementary School, but he stopped in front of the Ehime Prefectural Library building opposite the school and down the street from the house where the Grahams had lived.

With his usual confident walk, *Sensei* started toward the Library. "*Sensei*," I called, wondering if he didn't see the big sign in English and Japanese that now hung above the entrance, HEADQUARTERS, ADVANCE PARTY, 24TH INFANTRY.

"Come on, come on, don't dawdle, Isamu," he called. "They won't hurt you."

He was my teacher. I had to do as he said.

Once we were inside, Yamamura-sensei headed straight for the first room with an open door. I was scrambling to keep up with him. There was a uniformed American sitting behind the desk.

"Good afternoon, Colonel," said Yamamura-sensei in his lovely, precise English. "This young man was born in San Francisco and can speak English. His name is Isamu Imagawa."

The officer looked from Yamamura-sensei to me. I stumbled sideways and took a step back. The scrutiny was excruciating. Time stretched as he sized me up. I was shocked when all he did was tell me to repeat the English word for a treat I remembered from San Francisco.

❀ ❀ ❀

I ENTERED the building with great trepidation. There was no *Sensei* to push me along. Only my sense of duty, my obligation of obedience. But I was obeying reluctantly. Why should I work for people I had fought against only a month before? What could Yamamura-sensei possibly have been thinking?

My fear was almost immediately replaced with surprise and then, eventually, with curiosity about what my future could hold.

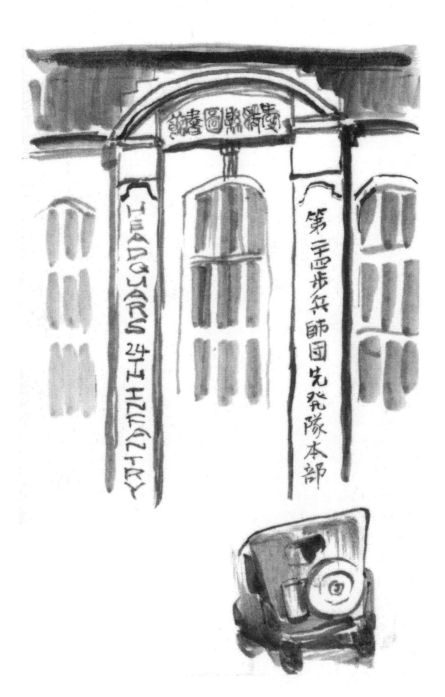

And it was that morning that my future began. Those who survived the *kamikaze* corps and wrote their memoirs all focused on their wartime experiences—as well they should. The Great Pacific War, as it is called in Japanese, was the defining event for those my age—on both sides of the Pacific as well as in Europe. We came of age with our military service and what we experienced during the war shaped our characters for the rest of our lives, even if most of us rarely, if ever, talked about it. But for me, my dual background, my roots in both my Mother and Father Countries, and my English language abilities also changed and shaped my life after the war. I had joy and sorrow, satisfaction and disappointment, struggle and triumph, with the good always outweighing the bad. To complete my story I have to and want to write about my life after the war—the life that began that day—a life that gave me the chance to do some good, and, even though this is a rather grandiose sentiment that I'd never express aloud, a chance to promote international understanding and peace. It has also been a life I've shared with my beloved wife. It is a story I want to write. I've known for almost two decades that I should tell my story. And now I'm finally fulfilling that promise to myself.

It was in Ohio that I first decided I had to put pen to paper.

I THINK there was so much press fuss because the student reporter's article about the "*Kamikaze* Professor" was published in December 1978 just a few weeks after the news of the mass suicide in Guyana. I don't know who was more surprised, me or the young girl my colleague Lloyd had sent over from the journalism school for a practice interview. With the camera crews and the wire service reports, we both had our full fifteen minutes. Interesting, and even a bit entertaining.

Memories of the war were already sketchy then, so now in 1994, almost another twenty years later, I'm glad I'm putting the whole story of "the American *Kamikaze*" down on paper. Americans have never had any clue about these kinds of things, and now, having been back in Japan for so many years, I see knowledge of the war fading away here. The young people are now like the Americans I taught for twenty years. It's not just a matter of knowing more about computers and *anime* than abacuses and *shamisen*. They don't understand how we let ourselves be led into a ruinous and doomed misadventure, nor do they remember or mourn the dead or regret the folly that took so many young lives.

My dearest Akiko thinks that I don't realize it, but I know time is short. I keep up my part of our charade by demanding the second glass of scotch and pestering her for fried chicken as if I didn't know what the doctors think—and what I'm sure they've told her. One of the sweet secrets of a long-married couple: what we pretend we don't know. Like how relieved she is that we ended up here in this small city with the beautiful castle rather than "home" in Matsuyama. I still can't help myself—sometimes I still talk about it—all those places of my childhood still call me, just as the even earlier places in San Francisco's Japantown still call too.

I started writing in English because the Mother Country tongue comes easier, especially because I started at the beginning, with San Francisco. Next year the Father Country will take over and I'll translate into Japanese.

I haven't done any serious research—it's been enough to look through my own materials and leaf through a few books over the last months. I'm sure I'll misremember some of the details and horrify any historian who may read my memoir. But I have my photographs—from San Francisco, from Matsuyama, and even the ones from the bases at Mie, Izumi, Wonson, Haneda, and Chitose that we were supposed to burn. The pictures have helped me remember so much that what I've forgotten won't matter.

I only have one goal. It is my hope that my story will help others realize that what they strongly believe in at one point in life, even to the point that they're willing to sacrifice their lives for it, may ring completely hollow in later life. No disagreements, no differences of opinion—political, economic, social, religious, or otherwise—are worth the sacrifice of human life, including one's own. If this message gets through, I will have succeeded. Writing my story will be worth it.

THE COLONEL was in the center hallway outside his office and saw me as soon as I came through the front entrance. He was obviously on his way somewhere, but stopped and said, "Good morning, Mr. Imagawa." Turning back to his office, he called, "Sergeant, take this gentleman to the Translation Section and introduce him to Lieutenant Elmenhall." Turning again and looking at me, he said, "Good luck. Do well," and went off down the hall.

The sergeant I had seen the day before came into the hall and said, "Come with me." I climbed the steps behind him. *Gentleman? The enemy is referring to me as a gentleman? How can that be?*

The sergeant led me into a high-ceilinged room, where I saw a tall man with sandy hair, a sprinkling of freckles, and greenish-blue eyes. At first glance he reminded me of Morgan, and I realized that I hadn't thought of my friend for years. Had he lived to have post-war experiences as strange as what I was experiencing that morning?

"Sir, here's the new translator," said the sergeant, saluting before he turned to go back downstairs. The tall fellow looked me over and smiled.

"I understand you've passed the Colonel's famous English proficiency test," he said. "So you can obviously manage my name. I'm Lieutenant Gregory Elmenhall, and I run this section."

"Yes, Sir," I said. The office was reassuring. It looked orderly and the four Japanese working at the desks looked fine. *Okay. This tall American is going to be my boss.*

With great kindness Lieutenant Elmenhall explained that I was to join four others and work at translating Japanese newspaper articles into English. Lieutenant Elmenhall told me we would sometimes have to work as interpreters as well. The others were American-born *nisei* just like me, but I had never met any of them before. The two I remember best were the Sawada twins—Carol and Louise.

The Americans were serious about their work, but very casual in their interactions. Almost immediately I was Sam again to everyone. After the first week, I lost both my impulse to salute and my horror that I was inclined to salute *Americans, the enemy.* Every so often I still bristled inwardly at taking orders from an enlisted man younger than myself, but slowly, slowly I recovered a civilian mentality.

I came to realize that the Americans were the people I remembered from my childhood, not the devilish barbarians that had been the staples of the wartime propaganda. All that rhetoric, all that ugliness, had vanished like spring snow. It disappeared, of course, because of the Occupation. But it wasn't just me—my colleagues had come to terms with the Americans, and slowly, and sometimes in small bursts of joy, people began to relax. But there were long-term effects of the rhetoric of the war—we weren't left with memories of beautiful spring snow. No, even as we began to rediscover joy, we Japanese were left with shame and confusion and having to live with the knowledge that we had wholeheartedly participated in the folly of the war.

I plunged into the work. It was good to have something to do, and I enjoyed it a great deal. Like the others, I found the official documents troublesome. We often pored over our dictionaries. I was shocked at how rusty my English had become. For the two years I was in the military, I neither spoke nor read a word of English. And my command of English had always been colloquial, the language of a kid in San Francisco. I did a lot of studying in my hours away from the office, teaching myself the terminology for civil engineering, plant pathology, and medicine. It took a while, but eventually I mastered the bureaucratic jargon and was happy to learn a bit of substance in a number of different areas.

In October, the entire 24th Infantry moved into Matsuyama. Its nickname, the Taro Leaf Division, was a tribute to its home base of Hawaii. The U.S. soldiers camped on the grounds of the former Matsuyama Naval Air Base, set up checkpoints, and dispatched patrols all over Shikoku Island. All the activity caused a fair amount of local consternation, but it didn't take long for everyone to reach the same conclusion that Yamamura-sensei had known, instinctively, was correct and that I had come to in my month of working for the Occupation—they were not going to do us any harm.

Like Yamamura-sensei, Father came to this conclusion early. After my trip to the city with *Sensei*, he brought me back to Ishii and dropped me off with a cheery wave to Mother and shouted, "Thanks again for the sweet potatoes. My wife loved them when we dropped them off. Isamu has some interesting news for you."

When Father arrived home from work, Mother and I were anxiously discussing the afternoon's events. After he listened to the lollipop story, Father laughed, and said, "Son, I think it'll be fine. You'll be a natural. And you need to stop moping around the house. Time to move forward."

I watched Mother swallow her worries and decide to agree with Father. The next thing she said was, "A bit of chicken and some sweet potatoes," in response to Father's inquiry about dinner.

He laughed again, "Ah, the infamous trouble-making sweet potatoes. I'm looking forward to an interesting chat with Yamamura-sensei the next time I see him. I think, Isamu, that I should thank him. I know you don't think that's appropriate, but I have a little bet with myself that you will eventually." Turning to Mother, he said, "Let's have a taste of those sweet potatoes, and I do believe we still have a bit of *shochu* in the back of the kitchen cupboard, dear. Let's drink a toast to our son's new work."

LATE ONE night I arrived home after interpreting during a meeting of the civic officials in Tobe with the Division representative; the trip from the far suburb had taken much longer than I expected. I found Mother and Father laughing at the table, waiting for me before starting dinner. They looked lighthearted and younger than they had in a long while. "Isamu, come listen to the funny story your father has to tell you."

"Yes, my son the translator should be proud of me," said Father as he made space for me at the table. "I got home early from work today and decided to do a little weeding in the vegetable garden. And from there I went to see Farmer Morita. I was walking back along the road. I still had my hoe with me—but mind you, *no sweet potatoes*," he laughed. "I must have looked the complete country bumpkin. I went past an American soldier—Isamu, he was no more than eighteen—a baby compared even to you—who was standing sentry at the checkpoint. I did the polite Japanese thing and smiled.

"When the soldier saw, me he said—in English of course—*'Hi there, old man. How are you today?'*

"*'Well, I'm just fine thank you,'* I replied. *'How are you?'*

"*'Did you just speak English?'* he said. I don't think he could believe his ears. I guess English-speaking old Japanese farmers weren't what this kid was expecting. So I stopped and explained why I knew English. He was from Pennsylvania, and San Francisco is, I think, as unimaginable to him as I'm sure Matsuyama was just a few weeks ago. It was a pleasant chat. I wish you could have been there."

NOT only were they not going to do us any harm, they were determined to improve things. A few weeks after all the excitement of the full occupation—and after the patrols had become nominal at best, small teams of U.S. Army personnel moved into the capital cities of all four of Shikoku's prefectures.

The Ehime Prefecture Military Government Team (MGT) was stationed in Matsuyama. The MGT took over civil administration from the Division, and the translators were reassigned to the team. And soon thereafter the entire Division moved off Shikoku and set up operations in Okayama. The teams were then the only military presence. In each prefecture, the teams were divided into four administrative functions: a Civil Information and Education Section (CI&E), an Economic and Labor Section, a Legal and Government Section, and a Medical and Social Section. I was assigned to the CI&E Section, and with the new assignment, I moved to an office on the fourth floor of the Prefectural Library building. I found it ironic that CI&E was occupying this space.

The large room where we were working had been a ceremonial space, and it was there that the Prefectural Governor had bowed to the Imperial portraits before and after he read official decrees, including the one that supplemented the Emperor's speech and formally ended the war. The portraits were still there. Looking at them the first day I worked in that room, I remembered my first experience with Japanese official ceremonies and remembered how alien and fascinating it all had been to the out-of-place little American gentlemen with his neat suit and long hair.

All of us translators started our new assignments with considerably more confidence than we had had in our first days working for the Division. And at this time my life began to shift—inexorably, I now realize—toward English. I was using my English every day. Of course, everyone in Ishii Village knew where I was working and what I was doing. And now everyone remembered that Mother and Father had lived in San Francisco, that I was born there, and that I still spoke English.

First two, then four of the Ishii Village children knocked on our door and asked about English lessons. Soon I lost track of how many had asked, and I was teaching free classes two nights a week. Mother joked about her son following in Yamamura-sensei's footsteps, and Father sometimes poked his head in and helped me demonstrate simple phrases. The children sometimes brought little offerings—vegetables, some rice or barley, a piece of cloth, some charcoal. Mother and Father would make sure that they sorted these things out, and redistributed any extras we had to neighbors with too many mouths to feed.

My new job at CI&E was to travel as a translator-interpreter throughout the prefecture with Captain Roger Rudolph. Our job was to make sure that local schools were complying with the educational directives from General Headquarters (GHQ) in Tokyo that were promulgated through the Ministry of Education. The specifics of this mandate included checking to be sure that the new textbooks were in use and that there were no remnants of the old imperialistic, militaristic slant that had dominated education during the war.

CI&E also had the duty of checking to be sure that no weapons were stored in the schools or hidden on their grounds—it had been common in the last months of the war to bury caches of weapons for use during the final battle the government expected on the homeland. The plan was to distribute them to all civilians when the fateful day arrived. All weapons should have been surrendered to the Americans during the first days of the occupation, but rumors circulated about caches that were still hidden. Given how peaceful everything had quickly become, I found it hard to take this seriously, but it was still, officially, part of the job.

Captain Rudolph and I got along well, and I became quite fond of Roger, as I believe he did of me. We started with the schools in Matsuyama, which were all relatively large. We then progressed to the suburbs, like Tobe. Finally all that was left were the schools in the remote villages at the far reaches of the prefecture. We went by jeep. Captain Rudolph drove and I was the passenger. In the out-of-the-way places, the small fishing villages or the farming towns way up in the mountain valleys, our arrival invariably caused a great stir. Captain Rudolph's large body, big round eyes and—as we say in Japanese—his "high" nose, made him scary to the folks in these isolated places. Many of them had never actually seen any foreigners, but he fit the image of the "foreign devil" they had been told about endlessly during the war.

Not surprisingly, we often got lost on these excursions. On several occasions, we would see villagers far ahead on the road and were relieved that there would be someone to ask for directions. But by the time the jeep reached the place where we had seen them, they would have disappeared, scampering into hiding, like children playing hide and seek. After this happened a few times, we figured out how to deal with it. Roger would drop me off and drive on ahead. I would stand in the road and wait until the villagers felt safe enough to come out of hiding. Once they were convinced that we were there only to visit the school, they were happy to give directions.

Our reception at the schools was an entirely different matter. Usually the children ran out of their classrooms as soon as the jeep pulled up. They kids were full of curiosity and somehow convinced that this big funny-looking foreigner would have treats. As they surrounded the jeep, the teachers stood sheepishly in the background. Our usual drill was to send everyone back to the classrooms. Captain Rudolph would meet with the principal in his office and then tour the school, being introduced to each teacher, asking the questions, and making the inspections he was there for in the most casual way imaginable. We virtually never found anything out of line. At the end of his tour, he would ask the teachers to assemble the students in the playground. By now, the teachers were able to reassert control, and they lined the students up neatly. And this was where Captain Rudolph always had the most fun. He did indeed have treats, usually candy and sometimes small notepads or supplies of pencils. Discipline was destroyed again as he distributed the candy to the children, who were usually literally jumping with joy. The teachers were always especially grateful for the supplies, and they would be bowing deeply as we left, as the children ran alongside the jeep, begging for even more candy, and yelling a chorus of "Hallo! Good-bye!" or whatever other tiny scraps of English they knew.

Only one of our excursions had no lighthearted elements at all. CI&E received an anonymous letter saying that army rifles were buried in the sandbox in the playground of a junior high school in the suburbs. Captain Rudolph and I went to the school to investigate. The principal met us at the entrance, pale as a ghost. He had clearly ordered that the students be kept indoors and seemed to know exactly why we were there; when we asked him to have the school custodian dig up the sandbox, he began trembling. "But, Sir," he said, "there were some rifles there, and they might still be there. The neighborhood association folks came the week the war ended. They didn't really ask. They just buried the box. But they were just wooden dummy rifles. They were used when they held the training sessions for all the civilians in this area here in this playground."

"Well, let's see," said Captain Rudolph. "Please call the custodian."

The principal was still agitated, but he walked off and came back with the custodian, who had a shovel over his shoulder. As the custodian went to work digging, the principal stood by the side of the sandbox. He nervously pushed his hair back from his forehead, and then reached in his pocket. He must have been looking for a handkerchief, but didn't seen to have one. He finally used his hands to wipe the perspiration from his forehead. When he finished, he didn't seem to know what to do with his hands, and eventually starting wringing them. I had never seen anyone do that—I learned that day that people actually do that under stress; it's not just a dramatic detail added to stories. Every time Captain Rudolph said something to me in English, the principal looked even more anxious. I really wanted to say something to him, but there was nothing for me to translate, and I knew that anything I'd say would be improper interference.

The custodian grunted when his shovel thudded against something. Captain Rudolph and I helped him push off the last of the sand from the top of the box and wrestle it out. We lifted it out of the sandbox and stepped back as Roger leaned over and opened the latch. The principal stood behind him, still wringing his hands. About twenty wooden rifles were shoved every which way into the box. Roger and I upended the box and dumped them—just to make sure they were all just dummies. As we bent over them, Captain Rudolph looked over his shoulder at the principal. "Well, Sir, you were absolutely correct. Thanks for letting us take a look." Even before I could translate, the principal was sagging with relief.

He hung his head as he apologized and thanked Captain Rudolph for being so understanding. As he spoke, the custodian started quickly dumping the wooden rifles back into the box. He finished as Captain Rudolph and I were walking back to the jeep. My last memory of this episode was hearing the custodian ask the principal, "So what should I do with these damn things now? Bury them again?"

I GOT married on December 14, just four months after the war ended. The bride? Kayoko, of course; the wedding was the culmination of the *omiai* meeting the year before. Mother started pushing the arrangements to their final, unavoidable conclusion the week after I arrived home.

I had the day off from work. Mother, Father, and I walked to Ishii Station, took the train to Matsuyama City Station, where we changed trains and headed to a small town called Gunchu out in the far suburbs on the other side of the city. As I walked through Matsuyama City Station with my parents, all of us dressed in the best outfits we could patch together from our sparse wardrobes, I imagined myself slipping away. I thought about how quickly I could be at the office, doing my interesting work in English. Somehow, Mother and Father wouldn't notice and wouldn't care.

Mother chose Gunchu for the wedding because that was where

her younger brother, a successful doctor, lived. His house was large, the rooms spacious. When we arrived the Shinto priest was already there, waiting rather impatiently. The wedding began almost immediately. The bride entered, in full traditional Japanese wedding dress. Looking at her, all I could think was that she was not my type at all. The ceremony was soon over, and the priest, with his cash envelope from my uncle discreetly pocketed, was on his way. The twenty or so guests—all close relatives of my family and Kayoko's—sat in the spacious *tatami* room chatting. I sat with them, but had nothing to say.

Kayoko went off with her mother to change. When she reappeared, she was wearing an obviously high quality Western-style dress. As she walked back into the room, I thought this outfit's no improvement. She absolutely is not my type. The entire wedding party then walked to a local inn for dinner. It was a feast—the best food I had had in years. After dinner, everyone left, but Kayoko and I stayed the night at the inn. The next morning, I awoke, and lay still as she slept. I tried to think, to reason myself into accepting my marriage to the woman beside me, but I couldn't get very far because I was overwhelmed by the knowledge deep in my being that Kayoko was not my type.

The two of us took the train trip back to Ishii Village. I provided the only conversation, announcing the travel directions, "We'll stay on this train for six stops."…"The next stop will be Matsuyama City Station. We'll change trains there."…"Now we're at Ishii Station. It will only take ten minutes to walk home."

It was with great relief that I crossed the threshold into our Ishii Village house and called, "Mother, we're back," and with even greater relief that I left for work as soon as we all finished the lunch that Mother had prepared.

Only Mother had talked during lunch, chattering on and on about how well everyone looked at the wedding, how nicely everyone had managed to dress, how kind her brother had been to lend his house for the ceremony, when would be the best time to go to Ishii Town Hall to record the wedding in our family register, how nice the plates and bowls were that the inn used in the place settings for our lunch, how delicious the food had been, how our lunch was so poor in comparison, but at least we had some delicious local sweet potatoes from our neighbor and tenant farmer Morita. "Have Isamu tell you why sweet potatoes are such a big joke in this household," she said to Kayoko. "And of course he'll tell

you all about that dear man Yamamura-sensei, the teacher at Matsuchu."
Kayoko gave her usual response: *Nothing!*

Finally, even Mother seemed to give up and said, "Kayoko, dear, let's
clear these lunch dishes and get them washed. I want to make sure you
know how the kitchen is laid out and where everything is stored." I made
my escape.

When I got to the Prefectural Library, a peaceful early afternoon
quiet filled the wide entrance corridor, and I didn't meet anyone as I
climbed the wide stairs to the fourth floor. I savored being truly by myself
for a few moments and inhaled the kerosene fumes from the heaters and
the familiar wintertime wet wool smell. The kettle was bubbling on the
top of the heater when I walked into our big work space on the fourth
floor. Carol and Louise were eating their lunches at their desks. Everyone
else had disappeared. "You missed everyone, and so did we," said Louise.
"When we got back late from going with the Colonel to see that visiting
general off at the station, everyone else was gone. There was a last-minute
translation job at the Regiment. I think the schedules were confused because everyone was busy thinking about the general."

"Congratulations," said Carol. "Welcome back."

"Yes," said Louise, "we're very happy for you."

"I guess," I said, hoping I didn't sound as ungrateful as I felt, and
added, *"Thanks a lot, actually,"* in English, because we all liked using the
easy, casual phrases of our childhood. I then switched back, into work
mode, "Is there anything for me to do?"

Carol laughed and said, "The Captain has a big report on his desk
from the Education Ministry. He said he wanted it summarized and that
whoever had the most free time should start the project. Isn't that you,
Sam?"

"Yes, today that's me, most assuredly," I said, as I picked up the report. This dull work would be fine for the afternoon. The first afternoon
that my mother and my wife, *my wife,* were at home, getting to know
each other. I turned to the statistics on textbook inventory.

CAPTAIN Rudolph left the next week. "If I'm lucky, I'll catch the right
flights that will get me home to Seattle by Christmas Eve. My first order of business after hugging my mom and dad is proposing to Evelyn.
I hope she'll still have me. I hope to have the same sort of happiness
in front of me that you have now that you're married, Sam. All the

best of luck to you," he said. "I wish you well in everything that lies before you."

I had heard a lot of stories about Evelyn, a grade school teacher, as we drove around looking for those country schools. I imagined the tinsel shining on a Christmas tree in the living room of his parents' home and pictured Roger and Evelyn sitting with his parents, opening presents, and admiring the ring shining on her finger. I wondered if he thought it was odd that I had never spoken to him about Kayoko. *My wife.*

"I'm so grateful for all you've taught me. I wish you a safe trip and a long and happy life with Evelyn. Take care of yourself, Roger."

By this point, although I was a little surprised at myself for using his first name to his face, I wasn't at all surprised at my impulse to do so. I was comfortable with the Americans, happy to be speaking English so much, my mother tongue, as I was now thinking of it, and taking pleasure and a sense of accomplishment from my work. I had begun reading everything I could get my hands on about language teaching.

Roger's successor was John Bolunkly, a civilian on temporary assignment. I did the same job with him, but his style was even more casual than Roger's. After a few months, he was replaced by Bill Scott, another civilian. Bill was a little less than a year younger than I was. He had majored in psychology and joined the Navy immediately upon graduation. The Navy sent him to its language program in Boulder. His Japanese was already fluent when he arrived in Matsuyama, and got better with each passing day. So my job was much easier—except when it was harder. Because Bill wanted what he said in public officially to be flawless, he still had me translate. Occasionally, after I finished, he would look at me, give me his special wry smile, and say, as quickly as he could so no one else would understand, "Hey, Sam, that's not what I said."

I spent a fair amount of time studying up on the educational terminology we worked with every day. And I continued to read as much as I could on language training. Bill was very helpful. He shared everything he had learned from the Navy, made sure I knew about everything published by the Occupation on language education, and lent me all of his books. I still have some books on language pedagogy that he had his sister send us from Berkeley, where she was studying. Working with Bill, I was sure that I had found my life's work. Teaching language was, for me, challenging and thrilling. Watching my students realize that they were not just memorizing dull formulas and phrases, but acquiring and mastering

190 ·   A THOUSAND STITCHES

the skills to actually communicate with other humans, was a great joy. Giving them the confidence to do well was my challenge.

With Bill, I also worked on the comprehensive reorganization of the Japanese education system. The work we began that year, under the direction of General HQ in Tokyo, became part of the complete reform of the system that went into effect in 1948. Japan adopted an American-style system of six years elementary school, three years junior high school, and three years high school, followed by four years of higher education. New school buildings were built all over the country; textbooks were completely rewritten. English became an elective starting at the junior high level. It was a time of change, creativity, and a certain amount of turmoil. I loved it.

IT was about the time that Bill arrived that things changed at home. I arrived home from work one night and was surprised to find Mother was waiting in the *genkan*. She took my arm and walked me up and down the road in front of the house. "Isamu, darling," she said, "I have the most wonderful news."

The whole situation had me unsettled. Mother's obvious excitement was making me apprehensive. "Yes," I said hesitantly.

"It's Kayoko. She's pregnant. It's such wonderful news for our family."

I was searching for the appropriate response when she continued, "I guessed. She wasn't ready to tell you—or anyone—and she is very nervous and worried, but it's such wonderful news. Everything will be fine. She'll start feeling better soon, and then she'll look forward to the baby as much as I'm looking forward to being a grandmother."

By the time we walked back into the house, I realized that Mother was right. I was thrilled at the prospect of a son. Mother and Father joined in my excitement, but Kayoko was adamant. When we were alone she stubbornly insisted that she wanted an abortion. "There's not enough room in this Ishii house," she said. "How am I supposed to raise a child here? There are only two rooms plus that antiquated kitchen. I won't do it."

THE topic was still under unpleasant discussion when I got an urgent call at work one afternoon. Mother was calling from an obstetrician's office downtown, and told me that Kayoko had had a miscarriage. Mother found her bleeding and in great pain that morning. Mother's nursing skills and her resourcefulness were both on display that day. She took care of Kayoko and wangled a ride into town from the only neighbor who owned a car. When Mother brought her home, Kayoko was even quieter than usual. I sometimes wondered what went on in her head, but there was no way for me to know or to figure out what had really happened. Her only topic of conversation was the impossibility of our living conditions; it was all she ever talked to me about.

Events far beyond our control were pushing us in directions we could never have anticipated. Land reform was Kayoko's unexpected salvation. The new Agriculture Reform Laws required absentee landlords to surrender their lands to the new agricultural cooperatives, so Father was forced to sell the lands he owned to the Ishii Village tenants. The proceeds were just enough to finance a new house in town. It was our final farewell to Ishii. For many years I would mourn the loss of the old house with the thatched roof, the soft, warm *tatami*, the vegetable garden, the fields, and the stream. My life was to be in cities, but memories of the sweet country ways of Ishii were always with me.

Father and I went to see my friend Maki, who was in the construction business. We arranged for a new Yanai-machi house to be built. Maki assured us that our plot there, where reconstruction was now allowed, could accommodate a two-story house. He went to work, and about six months later we all moved into our new home. There were four *tatami* rooms, a dining room, a study, a bath, and a large kitchen where the two housewives could work together.

But part of Ishii came with us to the city. The children I had been teaching were not going to be deterred just because I was moving away. Nor were they deterred when I told them I had to start charging. They were willing to travel almost a half-hour by bike into the city for their lessons, and they were willing to pay. So my evening classes after my days at Ehime MGT continued, two sessions an evening, three evenings a week. The extra income was good as we pieced together a new life in the city. I had no idea at the time that this was probably the real beginning of my career, the beginning of work I would do for half a century.

Bill Scott went home early in the summer of 1947. He had been accepted in a graduate program at the University of Michigan. As summer turned to fall, it made me smile to think of him crossing the campus kicking the autumn leaves, carrying his books, back to being a student. I knew he would be happy and successful. I wondered if he found anyone in Michigan to speak Japanese to.

Bill's replacement was Captain Shirley Schneider. Captain Schneider was much older than I and a rather stern personality. When I learned that she had been a high school principal in Saint Louis before she joined the army, I was not surprised. It was the first time I had ever had a woman boss, and they were rare enough even in the U.S. military, but I found working for her and following her orders easy. She was an expert school administrator and made great contributions to education in Ehime and neighboring prefectures. The improvements she put into effect earned her my respect, and the respect, even though it was sometimes grudging, of all the local Japanese officials.

Once we had moved to Yanai-machi, things settled down at home. Kayoko seemed happier, but never said anything, one way or the other, to me. She and Mother grew even closer. I missed my own closeness to Mother, but I was so busy with work and with my nighttime teaching that I didn't have much time to dwell on it. About this time, I found a book by Dr. Charles C. Fries of the University of Michigan entitled *The Teaching and Learning of English as a Foreign Language*. I was enthralled. Dr. Fries' book supported many of the ideas I was developing on my own with my Ishii students. Persuading my students that learning English was the key to communication across cultures was easy to do at that point; watching the light in their eyes when one of my explanations made sense, when one of our drills gave them the confidence to speak to the Americans, was a great thrill for me, and Dr. Fries' book made me, I believe, a better teacher. On the evenings when the students and I were working in the study, Mother or Kayoko would come in halfway through the lesson with a tray, a big tea kettle, and a supply of cups. Mother would say, in English, "Good evening, everyone," and would sometimes add "*Gambatte*" in Japanese, and "Good luck with your studies," in English. Kayoko would just put the kettle and the tea cups down on the table, smile slightly, and leave. She never asked a single question about English, about teaching, about my interests. And her attitude made it clear that she had no interest in studying herself.

Captain Schneider and I continued our work, and I had no idea of doing anything else. It was still interesting, and I was learning a great deal about education. However, one day early in 1948, officials of a school called Nitta Gakuen in the Matsuyama suburbs approached me. They were working on establishing a new institution to be called Matsuyama Junior College of Foreign Languages and invited me to join the faculty and teach English. I was flattered and interested in the job, but I told the officials that I couldn't leave my job with MGT. They pressed. Finally, although I was sure the answer would be no, I promised to ask the U.S. military if they would let me take on the teaching as a second job. To my surprise, the answer was yes. Their theory was that the classroom work would make me a better translator-interpreter for educational matters. With this endorsement and with the confidence I took from Dr. Fries's book, I began my work. My students at the Junior College were quite enthusiastic. My class was their first opportunity to learn spoken English. As I ran my students through drills and guided them through conversations, I often thought of Suzuki-sensei from Matsuchu and how thoroughly I had disgraced myself by embarrassing him. I looked back with the sympathy I had been too young and too naïve to have at the time.

CHAPTER 15

MICHIKO

Osaka, 1945–1946

AS THEY WALKED away from Osaka Station, Michiko told herself that she would just forget what the two-day trip had been like. What was important was that Shotaro had been with her, had stood behind her, propping her up when she needed it, letting her lean back on him when exhaustion overwhelmed her.

And now, after an hour of walking, they were approaching the neighborhood where Shotaro had lived. They had bought cups of tea from a vendor outside the station, and had eaten the last of the rice balls Shotaro's aunt had packed for them. The sun wasn't yet fully in the sky, but the heat and the humidity were pressing down on them.

About ten minutes earlier, Shotaro had said, "It won't be long." They trudged along in the heat, Michiko wondering how hard it was for him to walk such a great distance, but knowing that if she asked his only answer would be to assure her that he was fine and say that his real worry was that she was doing too much, because he knew she was still so weak from her illness.

The ten-block-square area of rubble had expanded, but they didn't fully realize that until they reached their goal. "Oh," he said. They stood and looked at where the Miyazawa home had been.

"Right there," he said, "on the left edge." He was pointing at a fenced compound. Inside there were a few rickety newly constructed buildings—really shacks made of scrap wood—but the fence looked quite serious. A sign announcing "Keep Out" in large stern characters leaned sideways against the entranceway. In smaller letters it referred to the *kempeitai*. Even though the sign was valuable—in just the walk from the station they had learned that anything still intact was valuable—no one

had touched it. It was under the nose of the loutish men loitering at the
gate. A few of them were young, with greased slick hair, but most of them
were tough-looking, thick-bodied middle-aged men, about a dozen in
all. Three of them sported sunglasses, and lurid tattoos were visible on the
forearms of the one wearing a short-sleeved shirt.

"Well," said Shotaro, "at least it's clear that we won't be staying here
anytime soon. The *kempeitai* may be gone, but gangsters—no, we're not
going to tangle with them. I wonder what the Americans will make of
them."

Michiko stood in the hot sun, trying not to cry for him and for his
family. She grew fearful when one of the thugs walked over to where they
were standing. Feeling Shotaro ease his stance, letting his arms fall loose
at his sides, she willed herself to relax.

"Hey, buddy, whatcha looking at?"

"We just stopped to try to get our bearings. We're looking for Tozawa
University Hospital."

"For that you're gonna have to have eyes that can see to the Western
Paradise." The gangster laughed. "It got it just about a week before we
began *enduring*," he said, with sarcastic emphasis on the last word. He
flashed a yellowed, leering smile.

"But it was that way?" Shotaro asked, pointing beyond the far side
of the compound.

"Sure was."

"Thanks," said Shotaro, taking Michiko's hand and starting off again,
in the direction he had pointed.

"You be careful now," the gangster called out behind them. There
seemed to be some real solicitude mixed with what was, no doubt, his
usual tone of sarcasm and menace.

Michiko forced herself to match Shotaro's confidence as they walked
away, but it wasn't until they had gone a full two city blocks that she
spoke. "Shotaro, is there anything you can do? Your family's property is
inside that fence."

"I think that for now, we just keep walking. We have to find our own
future." As he said this he stepped to the side of the road and picked up a
twisted scrap of metal about two feet in length. He poked at the ground
with the twist of metal and tried it as a cane—but it was too short. "Let's
go look at where the hospital was and then decide what we'll do next," he

said, taking her arm and slipping the scrap through his belt so it sat on his hip like a shortened *samurai* sword.

In another ten minutes they reached the site of the hospital. Part of the entrance, with its name engraved over the gate, still stood, and about ten feet of the front wall was still intact—the bombing was still recent enough that scavengers hadn't carried off all the bricks. Although the hospital site was on its way to becoming just another part of the rubble plain that stretched in every direction, there was still evidence of what had been there—a smashed and twisted refrigerator for specimens, and the remnants of a sunken auditorium. When Michiko asked, Shotaro told her that it was the autopsy amphitheater and said, "Death used to be special. We dealt with it with reverence and with science. We never should have had to grow so used to it."

They were walking around the perimeter of the ruined hospital when they heard someone calling, "Miyazawa-san, Young Master Miyazawa!" They turned to see a tiny old woman running toward them, her brown berry face crinkled into a wide smile.

"O-Hana?" said Shotaro.

"Yes, it is you, isn't it?" said the old woman, her *geta* clomping on the broken pavement.

When she caught up with them, she reached up to Shotaro. "I'm an old lady, so I have no need for decorum any longer," she said to Michiko, as she hugged him.

With O-Hana's arms still wrapped around him, Shotaro looked over the old woman's head at Michiko and shrugged, his eyes lively with amusement and affection. "O-Hana, may I present my fiancée, Michiko Shizuyama?" he said. The old woman waved an arm at Michiko but didn't let go of Shotaro.

"O-Hana has worked at the hospital as long as I can remember," he said to Michiko. "I met her the very first time my dad brought me here."

"Always the best, always the best," O-Hana said as she stepped back and looked up at Shotaro. "Dr. Miyazawa and Young Master Miyazawa. I'm very pleased to meet you, Miss. I can see that you know how special he is."

"O-Hana, what happened here?"

"Well, it finally happened to us too. I guess we were too lucky for too long. The hospital was just about the only thing left standing in this neighborhood, and those monkey American boys in those big shiny airplanes were good—real good—they rained some of their bombs right on us here at the hospital.

"Come, come with me," she said. "I want you to meet Shun. He was always busy off with his business, but now that the hospital's gone, he's making sure we stick together." She ran ahead of them and started climbing over the rubble, calling "Shun, Shun, dearest, where are you?"

As Shotaro and Michiko hurried to keep up with her, Shotaro explained that O-Hana had been the custodian at the hospital, and told her about the time he came with his father to the hospital when he was about ten. O-Hana had chased behind them when they left, with a cartoon book that Shotaro had left behind. "Young Master, don't forget your book. It's no good for the likes of me who can't read," she had said as she handed it over.

As they walked away, Dr. Miyazawa, in response to his son's puzzled questions, had said that yes, O-Hana was illiterate, but he emphasized how big-hearted she was, telling his son he was sure he could see that himself. He also said she was a dedicated worker, someone who put her heart and soul into the hospital, the welfare of the staff, and what she could do for the care of the patients.

Michiko and Shotaro watched as O-Hana disappeared inside a small mountain of rubble. As they got closer to where they had last seen her, she reappeared, emerging from what appeared to be the mouth of a cave. "Come out, Shun," she said. "Young Master Miyazawa has returned and he has a beautiful bride with him."

"I'm here," said the old man who appeared behind her. He wasn't much taller than O-Hana, but was stocky and tough-looking next to his skinny wife. To Shotaro he said, "I'm pleased to meet you, having heard about you since you were a little boy." Turning to Michiko, he said, with great formality, "I am pleased to make your acquaintance."

"I'm Michiko," she said, bowing. "I'm grateful for your kind consideration of both of us."

"Come, come, sit down," said O-Hana, moving pieces of the rubble to arrange seating for Michiko and Shotaro. Once she had everyone settled, she ducked back inside the cave and reappeared holding a dented canteen. "*Mugicha* is just what we need in heat like this," she said, tipping some of the liquid into battered cups and handing them around.

As they sat and sipped the cool barley tea, Shotaro told the old couple about his aunt and uncle, the trip from Haruyama, and their encounter with the gangsters. O-Hana and Shun were shocked but not surprised. They talked about how dangerous everything was and how they wouldn't go out after dark. They explained that they were using the cave to conceal what they had found scavenging. As they talked, Michiko realized that Shun knew everything there was to know about scavenging and possessed the skills that in just one day she and Shotaro had learned were now crucial to survival. All the years O-Hana had worked at the hospital, she and Shun had lived together in the tiny custodian's room on the ground floor of the hospital. Shun had gone out during the day, working as a collector of scrap metal. "We were lucky, that the doctors thought so well of O-Hana that we had such a nice, safe place to live," he said.

O-Hana explained that after the hospital was bombed, Dr. Ashikaga, who had taken Shotaro's father's job as head of the internal medicine department, decided, once the surviving patients were transferred to other hospitals, that he would go to Hiroshima to volunteer. Shun looked at Michiko and Shotaro and asked what they knew.

"Not much really," said Shotaro. "We only know what we heard in the speech—that and rumors, of course."

"Well, there are all sorts of rumors, and even a bit of information on the radio now," said Shun. "But I think the doctors know more about what really happened. I was with Dr. Ashikaga at his house when he got a call from a colleague in Okayama who had spent a week in Hiroshima. Dr. Ashikaga said he just had to go. His colleague told him that the center of the city was completely obliterated and that those who died were the lucky ones. People were burned and injured beyond what we can imagine. Dr. Ashikaga didn't spend much time thinking about it. He packed up and left—the day before...." He hesitated, finally concluding with "the broadcast."

O-Hana took up the story. "After the raid when your dear father and mother were taken, Dr. Ashikaga sent his wife and daughters to the country, to her family in Shiga. He didn't want his house left empty while he was in Hiroshima, so he asked us to stay there. And now you'll stay there with us."

Shotaro hesitated for just a moment, but rather than the usual refusals that etiquette demanded, he merely said, "O-Hana, Shun, thank you. We would be delighted."

"Wonderful," said Shun. "And now that that's settled, Shotaro, I hope I can persuade you to help me with my scrap business. I'm getting too old to manage all by myself."

As Shotaro was nodding, trying to decide how to answer, O-Hana said, "Shun, give them time to get settled. Then we'll talk about business."

Shun laughed. "Yes, we should wait, but," he said as he reached toward Shotaro, "let me see that piece you have tucked in your belt. It's chrome. You have a good eye. I can get you a good price for that."

ALL four of them went together to the Ashikaga residence, Shotaro helping Shun carry four more pieces of scrap metal that materialized from the old man's underground hiding place.

Dr. Ashikaga's fine house, another ten minutes past the hospital, sat behind a tall wall. The thick, dark rhododendrons in the garden were an inviting green, but they were wilting in the heat.

O-Hana unlocked the entrance gate. They walked through the garden to an old carriage house. Shun said, "The doctor wanted us to stay in the house, but my stubborn wife insists on staying here."

"But now," said O-Hana, "that Shotaro and Michiko are here, they'll stay in the house, so there'll be no chance that anyone will think it's abandoned. And Shun," she said, turning to her husband, "I'm not stubborn.... Not stubborn. I just knew they were coming," she concluded with a triumphant laugh.

After Shun and Shotaro added the scrap to a neat stack against the wall of the carriage house, O-Hana led them into the kitchen at the back of the main house. She took the lid off a large wooden bucket and spooned rice into four bowls, added pickles and some dried fish.

When they finished dinner, O-Hana and Shun went back to the carriage house. Michiko and Shotaro walked through the house, through the lovely rooms of a family that had managed to hold on to most of its possessions. Shotaro lingered in Dr. Ashikaga's study, running his fingers over the medical texts. They found a room upstairs that they decided was a guest room and spread out the *futons* that were stored in the closet.

After breakfast the next morning, Shun announced that the first order of business was a trip to the ward office to inquire about the status of the Miyazawa property. They all set out together. Again, even though it was early, the heat was oppressive. It took more than a half-hour to reach the ward office.

There was one clerk behind the public inquiry desk. Michiko, while waiting for her eyes to adjust, felt her knees buckle. Suddenly, all the exhaustion of the last week overwhelmed her. O-Hana was at her side before she realized she needed help, leading her to the bench along the wall. The clerk looked them over, but rather than acknowledging them, turned back and bent his head over the newspaper spread out over his desk. After they helped O-Hana settle Michiko, Shun and Shotaro walked to the counter and waited. The clerk took a last drag on the cigarette in the ash tray on the desk and finally looked up again. "Yes," he said.

"I would like to get a copy of the deed to my family's property. It was bombed early in the year, and I've just now returned from the country."

"And you?" the clerk sneered at Shun.

"Just here to help out my friend," said the old man companionably.

"Give me the address," the clerk said languidly, turning again to Shotaro.

Shotaro wrote it on the piece of paper the clerk pushed across the counter.

"I'll get the book," he said, and disappeared into the rows of shelves behind the desk. Much more quickly than they expected, he was back.

"It's gone," he said, pleased to deliver bad news.

"Gone?" said Shun.

"The whole book is missing. There's a note that it was requisitioned by City Hall in April. It never came back."

"Damn," said Shun. "Let's go."

Shotaro bowed to the clerk, who shrugged, watching Shun walk through the door, and turned back to his desk with another smirk.

When the others caught up with the old man, Shotaro said, "Thank you, Shun. I'm sorry this was a waste of time. I'll try City Hall later when I have time."

"No, there's no point," said the old man. "City Hall was hit last month. There's nothing left. Who knows if the records are really gone, but they might as well be. The unsavory types always survive and flourish. I don't think there's anything you can do now about the property."

Shotaro limped alongside Shun, O-Hana and Michiko walking behind them.

"O-Hana and I will help you, and you and Michiko will help us.

We'll survive together. We'll work extra hard so those people can't hurt you again."

THE next day, O-Hana took Michiko and Shotaro out with her. They made the rounds of the open-air markets. In just the few days since the war had ended, they were taking on the trappings of permanency. Michiko and Shotaro were surprised at how many people O-Hana knew. She introduced them to everyone, smiling with pride each time. As they walked back, O-Hana said she was especially glad they had met Nishida-san, a cheerful woman who was selling foodstuffs. She had gotten to know Nishida-san after the hospital was bombed and had taken a great liking to her. O-Hana considered the day a success. She had deftly traded two pairs of shoes and an old padded cotton jacket for a large bunch of beets and a whole kilo of rice. O-Hana had added those ingredients to others she was storing at the Ashikagas. For dinner, she produced green vegetables and even bits of pork. It was a feast.

When they finished, O-Hana looked over at her husband for as-surance and then turned to Michiko and Shotaro. "My dears," she said, "my Shun and I have a proposition for you. Neither of us is getting any younger, and we'll all have to work if we want to eat. Could we persuade you two to help us? Michiko, will you help me? We could be in charge of our daily provisions if Shotaro helps my Shun. Everyone's a scrap man now, so he needs an edge to stay in the business and prosper. Shotaro would be a much better assistant than his old wife. What about it?"

Michiko felt Shotaro beside her take a deep breath. He put down his bowl and chopsticks, pushed his chair back, and stood up before bowing deeply to Shun and O-Hana. "If you would be so kind as to let me help and if you would teach me what to do, I would do my very best and be eternally grateful," he said.

Michiko joined him bowing and said, "And I would too, of course."

"Sit down, sit down," said Shun as he gave Shotaro a big smile and reached across the table to slap him on the back. "Good, now I have a partner."

Michiko was watching O-Hana beam at Shotaro and her hus-band. Then O-Hana turned to look at her, winked, and said "So, we're all set."

The next morning, true to his word, Shun collected Shotaro and off they went. By the end of a week, Shotaro had met all the dealers with

whom Shun traded, and his good eye had grown much more sophisticated. Shotaro learned who could be trusted and who couldn't; who was
powerful and who was dangerous. It was clear that the gangsters who had
set up shop on the site of the Miyazawa home were no anomaly. They,
more than anyone else, had what it took to succeed in the new world
Japan's defeat had hurled them all into.

As the heat abated and autumn approached, they established routines. Shun and Shotaro were up early and out collecting. O-Hana and
Michiko packed them the lunches they ate on the run. They made the
rounds of the wholesalers in the afternoon and collected more on their
way home, making sure they were back before dark.

Michiko and O-Hana went out every day. They almost always had
enough money or something to trade and thus were assured that they
had enough to eat. Michiko and O-Hana found that they spent more
and more time with Nishida-san, who often had good produce for
sale. They were surprised when Nishida-san was selling candy one day.
When Michiko asked, she said she had made it herself the night before.
A discussion about Michiko's parents' shop followed. Within the week,
Michiko was helping Nishida-san make candy every morning, while O-
Hana minded Nishida-san's stall at what was by then a sprawling black
market. Michiko and Nishida-san joined her in the afternoon. The candy
was so popular it usually sold out in an hour or two.

One day in October, Nishida-san told them that she would be away
for a day or so. She was going to her hometown in Mie Prefecture to see
what more she could get to sell in the city. When she came back, she had
lots of new produce and told them that she was planning to go to the
country every two weeks.

When it was time for the next trip, she took Michiko with her. But
for the presence of cheerful, confident Nishida-san, Michiko felt she
would have been overwhelmed, as she was in Haruyama, by the suspi-
cious locals and the claustrophobic provincialism of the country town.
But Nishida-san had her roots in Mie, and her shrewd, impersonal bargaining style and no-nonsense attitude served her well with the country
people, who complained ceaselessly and dramatically about the poor harvest. Michiko stuck close to Nishida-san, anxious and smiling. But, she
realized when they staggered off the crowded train back in Osaka, she was
learning how to bargain.

Autumn closed in, and winter approached. Late one November afternoon, they all arrived back at the Ashikaga residence at the same time, O-Hana and Michiko proud that they had extra rice with them and proud too that they could report that they had managed, with Nishida-san's help, to get a supply of kerosene for the heaters. They would be prepared for the cold weather. Shun and Shotaro were tired. They bragged about how much they had collected and sold that day and listened as the women described their triumphs. Shun said he was especially pleased about the kerosene and then, with a flourish, produced an apple from his pocket. He laughed when he saw the surprise on Shotaro's face and the pleasure on his wife's and Michiko's. "You didn't notice, did you, Young Master?" he said.

"No," said Shotaro. "Where...? How did you...?"

"Oh, I'll keep that my secret," said the old man. "But we'll all enjoy it now." He pulled out his pocket knife and deftly peeled and sliced the apple, distributing the pieces. Michiko bit into the piece he handed her and tasted autumn, crisp and cool. She saw the same pleasure on Shotaro's face and thought, not for the first time since they arrived in Osaka, how lucky they were. They had each other, and together they would have a future.

The next day, Michiko and O-Hana arrived home about an hour after Shun and Shotaro. Shotaro told them that Shun was sleeping and explained why. As they worked, Shun had complained that he was tired. They finished early, and on the way back from the wholesaler where they sold everything they had collected, the old man grew short of breath. "Shotaro," the old man had said, "I believe I have to rest." He stumbled and then sat on the low wall at the edge of a property about two blocks from the Ashikaga home. Shotaro sat down by the old man and was alarmed to see how pale he was.

"Shun, does it hurt?"

"Just a bit, my young friend."

"On your side, down your left arm?"

"Yes, just a bit. It feels like I've fallen under a big package."

After Shun had sat for about ten minutes, he fell asleep.

Shotaro knelt in front of the wall, reached behind himself, and pulled the old man onto his back. He was outside the gate at the Ashikagas before Shun woke up.

"Put me down Shotaro," he said, indignantly. "What are you doing carrying me?"

"We're home now," Shotaro said, setting Shun down. "I want you to lie down and rest. And stop arguing with me."

"Fine, fine," said the old man. He leaned heavily against Shotaro until they reached the carriage house. He allowed Shotaro to ease him onto the bed he and O-Hana had built along one wall. Shotaro left him there and returned in a few minutes with the kerosene heater from the kitchen. Shun protested only feebly as Shotaro lit the heater.

O-HANA rushed to her husband's his side and Shotaro walked Michiko to the kitchen in the main house, talking to her while she prepared their dinner.

"I'm certain he's had a heart attack," said Shotaro. "There's not much I can do for him other than make him rest."

O-Hana took her dinner and Shun's back to the carriage house and fed her husband there. After dinner, Shotaro and O-Hana talked for a long while. When they crawled into their *futon* upstairs, Shotaro told Michiko that O-Hana had told him where another of his father's former colleagues was living. "I'll go first thing in the morning to see Dr. Hagiwara."

The next morning, Shotaro was up and out before dawn and brought the doctor back with him in the first light. Dr. Hagiwara was well over seventy and was dressed in an immaculate suit that had been fashionable twenty years earlier. He examined Shun and ordered him, over the old man's strenuous objections, to stay put for at least a week. After he finished, Dr. Hagiwara walked Shotaro out to the garden. "Yes, you're right. He's had a heart attack. It could have been worse, much worse, but he'll have to rest completely and then when he wants to work again, you have to be sure that he doesn't take up his old work again. It's simply too strenuous." He handed Shotaro a supply of medicine packets. "See that he has one each morning and one when he's ready for bed. Let him sleep as much as he wants."

Shotaro went back to Shun's bedside, and Dr. Hagiwara went to the kitchen, where O-Hana and Michiko were waiting. He accepted a cup of tea from O-Hana and said, "My dear O-Hana, your Shun is quite ill. He needs to rest and can't work so hard anymore. I've told young Miyazawa all of this and how to care for him. I'm glad you have these young people here with you. Otherwise, I'd worry about you and Shun. Still no word from Dr. Ashikaga?"

"No," said O-Hana. "Thank you for all your efforts on behalf of Shun. We'll be careful. And when we hear from Dr. Ashikaga, we'll let him know you were asking for him."

When Shun recovered enough to be up and about, the four had a meeting over dinner. Michiko and Shotaro reported on what they had decided, and even though they protested, the older couple agreed to reallocate the tasks of their little family. O-Hana would go collecting with Shotaro. Shun would go to the market in the morning while Michiko and Nishida-san made candy, and then stay there in the afternoon when they joined him there. "Your job will be to look tough so no one bothers the women," said Shotaro. "And you can put all of your bargaining skills to good use too, my friend."

THE letter from Hiroshima arrived in mid-December. Shotaro read it for Shun and O-Hana. Dr. Ashikaga said he planned to travel to Shiga to celebrate the New Year holiday with his wife and her parents. He would then bring his wife and daughters home to Osaka. The university hospital was on the Occupation's priority rebuilding list and he was coming back to supervise. He made it clear that he and his wife wanted Shun and O-Hana to stay at his home until the hospital was rebuilt.

The next afternoon, Shun was grinning when Michiko and Nishida-san arrived at the market. When Michiko asked why, he said, "I have news. But I want to tell you and Shotaro together. So you'll just have to wait." Nishida-san sent Michiko on an errand—she had forgotten the turnips she had promised one of her customers. Michiko made the trip to Nishida-san's house to retrieve them.

When Michiko arrived back at the market, breathless, Nishida-san too was grinning. She was now in on Shun's secret, but she too refused to tell Michiko anything. "You'll hear soon enough," she said.

That evening, O-Hana had dinner ready by the time Shun and Michiko arrived back at the Ashikagas. Shotaro, who had worked alone that afternoon, came in a few minutes later and joined the group around the kitchen table once he had washed up.

"I have an announcement," said Shun. He got up from the table, walked to the cupboard, and pulled out the Ashikagas' set of *sake* cups. "I don't think the good doctor would mind," he said, walking back to the table, where he set out the cups. As he eased himself back into his seat, he pulled a small bottle of *sake* out of his pocket and put it on the table with the cups. "We have something to celebrate. O-Hana met Hashimoto-san yesterday. Then he came to see me at the market. You don't know him, but he owned a medical supply company. The company used to have a warehouse and assembly facility not far from here. Like the hospital, Hashimoto-san's business is gone. However, the dorm where his workers lived is still there. And it will have some empty rooms as of the end of the month. One of them is yours, dear Michiko and Shotaro. You'll have your own place."

Michiko looked at Shotaro and then at the old couple—their weathered faces shining with happiness at being able to offer such a magnificent gift. "We can't thank you enough," she said, standing and bowing to Shun and O-Hana. Shotaro joined her, and took his hand in hers as they finished bowing.

"Fine, it's settled. Enough formal stuff. Let's drink. To youth and to new beginnings," said Shun.

Starting the next day, Shun or O-Hana, or sometimes both of them, produced something for the new household every evening: a cooking pot, soap, quilts. There was a great deal of laughter the night both of them showed up with fancy chopsticks. "See, even without consulting, we knew you needed these—and needed two pairs," said O-Hana.

AS the New Year holiday approached, it grew bitter cold. Shun had Shotaro sit with him and examine the simple accounts he kept for the scrap business. He then announced they could slow down and get ready for the holiday. He and O-Hana said they would stay home and work to make the house ready for the Ashikagas.

Shotaro decided he would search for some scrap on his own, knowing that the old couple wouldn't let him help with the menial household jobs they considered theirs alone. Michiko left for another trip to Mie with Nishida-san.

She didn't arrive home until dawn the next day, after a cold, crowded overnight train trip. She entered the house and searched for Shotaro, and when she didn't find him, walked into the back yard, calling "O-Hana. Where are you?" When she finally reached the doorway of the carriage house, she saw Shun asleep on the bed. Shotaro was sitting at his side, holding his hand. "My darling," he said, quietly. "It's another funeral.

This time we have to plan it." She sat down beside him and he told her the story, careful not to disturb the old man.

SHOTARO had not had a successful day, and he tired quickly in the cold. He trailed back to the Ashikagas' with the few pieces of scrap he had found. As he approached, he could see a group in front of the gate. He quickened his pace, his anxiety growing as he drew closer. When he reached the entrance, he was filled with dread—many in the group were police officers. It took him a while to talk his way past the officials. By the time he reached the carriage house, he had heard most of the story. Dr. Hagiwara was in the carriage house with Shun, who was again lying on the bed—this time without the determination he displayed after his heart attack. "I didn't help. I didn't protect her," he was moaning.

"They've just taken her away," said Dr. Hagiwara when he saw Shotaro in the doorway. "This is a bad business."

When he went home, Dr. Hagiwara left behind some sleeping potions. Shotaro sat with the old man, who kept mumbling through his story. "She was outside sweeping the road and picking up the litter. Cheerful as always when she went out. She was joking about Christmas and tried to sing me a Christmas carol. I told her I couldn't stand any more of her singing. She was still laughing as she went through the gate with her broom."

"Shun, quiet now," said Shotaro. "You need your rest." But the old man kept talking. He had heard a loud bang. He rushed out to find O-Hana lying unconscious in the road, the left side of her body bloody and bruised. The police appeared quickly and carried her into the carriage house. One of the first police officers on the scene fetched Dr. Hagiwara. Despite the doctor's efforts, O-Hana never regained consciousness. The police had asked Shun the same questions over and over, but all he could tell them was what he repeated to Shotaro. "There was a huge shiny car pulling away. It was bright yellow and its chrome glinted in the sunlight. Along the sides, it had a black and red dragon decoration, like a tattoo."

Shun refused the food Shotaro offered, but finally drank some tea. It was long into the night before he fell asleep.

TWO days later, on a cold gray afternoon, they helped Shun home and then back to his bed after the funeral service. He placed the container

with O-Hana's ashes carefully on the one shelf in the tiny room and
let Michiko pull the quilts up to his chin. Shotaro carried the kerosene
heater from the kitchen into the carriage house. Once he had it going,
he went to the kitchen to help Michiko make dinner. Shun sat up to eat
the rice and vegetables they brought for him, but couldn't manage more
than one or two spoonfuls. When he lay down, they piled quilts on him
again, knowing the fuel in the heater would soon run out. The days since
O-Hana's death had diminished him—he now seemed no more substan-
tial than his tiny wife. He refused to let them stay, shooing them away
to their room in the house. As Michiko leaned over him one last time
to make sure he was comfortable, he took her hand and said, "She was
everything, my heart and soul. You have the same thing. Be good to the
Young Master."

"WE shouldn't be surprised," she said to Shotaro the next morning when
they found Shun dead in his bed. "He couldn't live without her."

"A bad business, a very bad business," Dr. Hagiwara repeated when
he returned again with Shotaro. "And the police won't do anything about
the gangsters. Just promise me you'll be careful and stay out of their
way."

"We will. We will," Shotaro replied.

Michiko walked to the market to tell Nishida-san she wouldn't be
available to help for a few more days. She and Shotaro made more sad arrangements, attended yet another sad service and arranged for interment
and a marker for both of the old people. *We were orphans when we met
and now, together, we're orphans all over again.* It was a cold, lonely day;
there was plenty of time to think.

When they returned from the cemetery, they began a top-to-bottom
cleaning of the Ashikaga residence and the carriage house. Shotaro took
all of the scrap stacked in the yard to the dealer with whom he had the
best relationship. They arranged all of their meager belongings in the
kitchen and on New Year's Eve they made several trips, carrying them to
their new home in Hashimoto-san's former dormitory.

Three days after the New Year, the Ashikagas returned. Dr. Ashikaga
was surprised but happy to see Shotaro waiting at the gate when he pulled
up in a rare taxi with his wife and daughters, and then overwhelmed
when he heard about Shun and O-Hana. "I suppose I shouldn't be able

to care at all anymore," he said. "There's been too much death. Too much. And there will only be more."

ON their way back from the public bath to their new home, Shotaro said, "The ward office isn't someplace I want to go to again, but it's time for us to do it. I want to update my family register. It's time for us to be husband and wife officially."

Michiko thought of O-Hana and Shun, and shuddered with sudden, piercing sorrow when she remembered the last thing the old man had said to her. *How could anything be dearer to her than Shotaro, but what if she lost him?*

Feeling her tremble beside her, he put his arm around her. "Darling, you're not going to say no, are you?"

"No, my dear, but can we afford another day off?"

"Yes, with what Shun taught me and what he left us, I know I can be successful carrying on the business. I know we'll be secure. We are starting this New Year well, thanks to him and O-Hana."

They climbed the stairs to their room, spread one of O-Hana's quilts over the dirty, dingy *tatami*, and spread out their *futon*.

The hair at the nape of her neck still damp from the bath, Michiko snuggled into the *futon* and into warmth. She let the exhaustion of the day and the week claim her. She began to drift toward the sweet oblivion of sleep. Almost there, she started to roll to her side, pulling herself up to the top of the arc of the turn, and then, feeling safe, fully aware of her youth, and certain, despite the pain and illness of the year past, of her good health, she relaxed and let gravity do the rest of the job. She felt Shotaro's left arm beneath her, and felt his right arm encircling her as he curled around her. "Remember, my darling, the ward office tomorrow," was the last thing she heard before she left herself go and melted away.

CHAPTER 16

SAM

Matsuyama, 1948–1963

THE OCCUPATION LASTED until 1951, but by 1949, the Americans had decided to dissolve the military government teams in each of the prefectures on Shikoku. That spring it was announced that only one team would remain, and it would be in Takamatsu, not Matsuyama. Captain Schneider was being transferred to army headquarters in Washington, D.C. Our group of translator-interpreters, which had worked together for four years, was about to break up. Like my colleagues, I was apprehensive about where I would find work. But soon after the official announcement, Colonel Scranton, the Ehime MGT commanding officer, summoned me to his office. I was dumbfounded when he announced that he had arranged for me to be hired by the Ehime Prefectural Board of Education as its first English Teacher Consultant.

It was a wonderful job. I worked hard during the day, taught my classes at night, and spent whatever time I could find studying more about language teaching. And I also thought a lot about my life so far. Even though I was only twenty-seven, I felt that I had experienced a great deal. I wondered how I could have thought and functioned as I did during the war. Now I was clear about who I was. I was an educator. Peace was ultimately what I was working for, but I think that even then, with all the effort I had put into trying to sort out what had happened to me during the war, I would not have quite put it that way. But I did know that I was extremely fortunate to have work that involved both Japanese and Americans, to be helping both sides, and to have arrived at a point where my everyday life reconciled my skills from my Mother Country and Mother tongue and my Father Country and its language. And I knew that I was fortunate to have had my post-war experiences and be doing work I loved because my home life was getting no better, no better at all.

I officially held my job with the Prefectural Board of Education for six years, but I was on leave of absence for two of those six years. More about the leave of absence in a bit.

As the Prefecture's English Language Consultant, I observed that most of those teaching English in the secondary schools were woefully ill-equipped for their jobs. Suzuki-sensei, I realized, had not been an anomaly. Tragically, high school teachers were not educated in spoken English, and they had virtually no opportunity to practice. Hence, both their abilities to speak and their abilities to understand spoken English were extremely limited.

After one year in my new post, I decided to start a special program for the vacation period before the start of the academic year in April. I commandeered an old school building that had been standing empty since the educational reforms were put into place two years earlier. And I pressed virtually every native speaker I knew into volunteer service. We managed to gather a group of about a dozen educators and military personnel. They came from all over western Japan. We called the program "in-service" training and circulated materials to all teachers in Ehime, making it clear that if they came, they were to expect housing in the same unheated school where the class would be held. We even told them to bring their own blankets. We only had enough funds to purchase *tatami* mats to spread over the wooden floors of the classrooms at night. Teachers as well as students would have to curl up in their own blankets. The program was strictly on a volunteer basis, and our brochures made it clear that the one rule absolutely enforced during the two-week intensive program was that only English could be spoken. Japanese was completely banned.

I was astonished when a hundred teachers registered. The program, the first of its kind in Japan, was a spectacular and unexpected success. The teachers were enthusiastic and made great strides. They found the experience of working on their listening and speaking skills extremely rewarding. I particularly loved watching them gain confidence day by day.

After that first year, the prefectural officials endorsed the program as an annual event; they were delighted when word of the program spread and officials of other prefectures asked to borrow me as an advisor. I traveled to Hiroshima, to Sendai, and to Kyushu to help officials there set up similar programs. Those were happy days professionally.

Late in 1950, I read an announcement that competitive exams would be held to choose scholarship recipients for a one-year study program in the United States. It seized my imagination. I didn't talk about it much at home, but Father and I discussed it one weekend during a fishing excursion. They were now rare occasions for us, but I still treasured those peaceful times. He said he understood my enthusiasm, and talked about how he would like to see the States again. Kayoko wasn't mentioned, and he didn't speak about Mother. We both knew she was not likely to be pleased. "Isamu," he said, "you're quieter about it now than you were then, but I remember this kind of enthusiasm when you were determined to pass the Navy's entrance exam."

I pulled my line out of the water, saw, as I suspected, that the bait was gone, added some more, and recast as I thought of how to respond.

"Well, Father, I'm a different person now."

"Yes, I know, son," he replied. "I've been proud of everything you've accomplished since the day Yamamura-sensei took you to the office of the Occupation. You've built a career to be proud of, and this would be an opportunity to secure your future in that career. I'm sure you'll succeed."

Late in the year, I traveled to Tokyo to take the exam. It didn't seem that difficult to me, but the throngs of applicants—thousands I thought—made me doubt that I would be chosen. An oral interview followed the written exam. On the trip home I told myself not to get my hopes up too high. My welcome home was a week-long dose of the silent treatment from Mother and Kayoko. I went back to work and tried to forget about seeing San Francisco again.

About a month later, I was summoned to the office of the Prefectural Education Director. There was a phone call from the States for me. When I picked up the phone, I was astonished to hear Shirley Schneider's voice. She had retired from the army after reaching the rank of major and was now working at the Institute for International Education in Washington. She told me she happened to notice my name when the list of scholarship applicants had come across her desk,

"Now, Isamu," she said, "if you pass, what university would you like to go to? Scholarship recipients are not given the option of choosing their schools, but if I know what you're thinking about, I may be able to help."

Without hesitation, I said, "University of Michigan," and explained how much I admired Dr. Fries' work and what an honor it would be to study with him.

"Well, Sam, there are no guarantees, and you do have to pass. But I can't imagine that you found the exam all that difficult. I'll do what I can. I was delighted to see your name on the list. I spent all day yesterday remembering the good times I had in Matsuyama."

IN June, official word arrived that I had been awarded a scholarship. And I was going to attend the University of Michigan after an orientation at Yale. I was supposed to report to the GARIOA (Grant in Aid and Relief in Occupied Areas) office in Tokyo on July 9. A month of frantic activity commenced. My superiors at the Prefectural Board of Education gave their permission reluctantly, and only after a week of negotiations. Leaving in the middle of the school year was highly irregular. When I announced my news at home, there was no acknowledgement, except Father's quick smile of pride, that my achievement was valued. During my last weeks in Matsuyama, Kayoko spoke to me rarely, and when she did her tone was either surly or sarcastic. I began to yearn for my release and started telling myself that the time in the U.S. would be good. I would miss Kayoko, and missing her I would learn to appreciate her. My feelings would change.

I went to Tokyo alone, reported to the GARIOA office, listened to the orientations, and reported to the dock in Yokohama on the morning of July 13 with a great sense of excitement. It was almost twenty years since the journey that had brought me to Yokohama. Twenty years since the only home I had known was relegated to memory and Matsuyama became my world. The ship was a troop transport, crammed with GIs on their way home from battle in Korea and all of the 470 GARIOA scholarship students. We slept in bunks in three tiers and had little to do during the long days. It took us eleven days to reach San Francisco. Everyone was on deck when we sailed under Golden Gate Bridge, which had not yet been built when Mother and I had left for Japan. Father talked about how he had seen the towers when he left the year after us—but only the towers; construction had been just beginning when he left. When the white houses and streets of San Francisco came into view, I was close to tears. My home town. What a journey my life had been.

The ship docked in Oakland, where we spent a few days in dorms on the campus of Mills College. One day the group went on a bus tour of San Francisco. I found myself pointing out landmarks.

I also went on an excursion with Mr. Nishikage, a friend of Father's, who had been in San Francisco all this time, except for when he, like all *issei* and *nisei,* was interned during the war. Mr. Nishikage kindly drove me around to all the places I wanted to see: our old house on Cedar Street, the beach, Cliff House, North Beach, Fisherman's Wharf, and Chinatown. Mr. Nishikage also took me home to meet his family. That was the day I saw my first television.

After a few days, the entire GARIOA group was put on a special train for the East Coast. The trip to New York took five days, and small groups of students got off in Denver, Chicago, and Pittsburgh. After we arrived in New York, the five of us who were scheduled for orientation at Yale changed trains and headed for New Haven. We stayed in dorms with students from all over the world. My roommate was Finnish. Our orientation lasted three weeks. The days were filled with lectures on American history, geography, architecture, and popular culture. On the weekends, local families took us in for home stays. I spent my weekends with the Weber family in Westport. I still remember their warm hospitality and many kindnesses.

When the program at Yale ended, I had a week before I had to be in Ann Arbor for my first classes there. I went to New York and saw all the sights and then went to Washington, where I stayed with Major Schneider, who insisted that I call her Shirley. I tried, with mixed success. She took time off from work. The first day we went sightseeing. The second day we stayed home and watched the signing of the U.S.-Japan formal peace treaty on television. Here I am, I thought, sitting in the capital of the country where I was born, my Mother Country—the country I considered my enemy for many years, the country I fought against—and I'm alive, well, safe, and prospering. As I watched Prime Minister Yoshida sign the treaty in San Francisco, I thought about all those who were gone—Kobayashi and Hayashi among the hundreds of thousands—and was grateful that I was not among them. Grateful for my new life.

When I arrived in Ann Arbor, my first order of business was to introduce myself to Dr. Fries, who kindly agreed to be my advisor. I followed his suggestion and enrolled as a regular student so I could earn academic credit. I loaded up about twice the number of courses most students took and buckled down to study. At the end of the year, I was grateful that I had been earning credits. Dr. Fries suggested that I stay for another year and finally get a bachelor's degree, but there were complications. The scholarship couldn't be extended for another year, even though the GARIOA program would pay for my return passage to Japan if I managed to find a way to finance another year. Again, I was lucky. Dr. Robert Brown, a full professor who had sought me out earlier in the year for assistance with Japanese-to-English translations, had just received a grant and employed me as his research assistant. In addition to taking summer classes, I picked tomatoes and other crops on the farms outside the town. I was very proud when I received my B.A. in June 1953 and immediately set out for Japan. I wondered what awaited me at the Prefectural Board of Education and at home.

The trip was quite comfortable—on a commercial liner. When we docked at Yokohama, I smelled Japan again—a mixture of *takuan* pickles and soy sauce—and realized that I had gotten used to the Campbell's soup smell that surrounded me and reminded me of my childhood when I had arrived back in San Francisco after my years away.

I sent a telegram from Tokyo, and Father was at the pier in Matsuyama. I got off the ferry, intoxicated, all over again, with the beauty of the Seto Inland Sea. "It's wonderful to have you home," he said. "We have sea bream for dinner. We're celebrating." He arranged for my trunk to be delivered and suggested that we walk home. "It'll give you a chance to stretch your legs, and it'll give me a chance to hear everything. Start with San Francisco. When we get home, there won't be time for all the details I want to hear."

Dinner was delicious but conversation was strained. My feelings for Kayoko had not changed for the better; in fact they were slightly worse. Mother had no interest in stories from the States and only wanted to know about my plans for my future in Matsuyama. She mentioned grandchildren several times during dinner. I tried not to think about the child my wife had wanted to dispose of.

The next morning, I went to the office and thanked my colleagues for tolerating my two-year absence. I learned that the in-service program had grown so large that a summer session had been added. I had a month to get everything ready. I was happy to jump into work, to do my part to support my colleagues who had filled in for me, and to have an alternative to the chilly atmosphere at home.

The in-service session was a great success. We took over an old country retreat in a mountain town called Kuma, and two hundred students and twenty teachers had a wonderful summer adventure. The program continued for years, with the spring session in Matsuyama and the summer session in the mountains at Kuma. The programs were always exhilarating for everyone involved. The group photos show smiling teachers—and teachers of teachers. Everyone came away with a great sense of accomplishment.

In 1955, I was invited to join the faculty of Ehime University. I was happy to do so and became an assistant professor in the English Department of the College of Education. About a month after I started and was still settling in, Dr. Robert Brown, the professor I had assisted at the University of Michigan, called from Tokyo. He had just arrived there to head the Asia Foundation and invited me to come to work for him. When I explained that I had just started a new job and couldn't leave Matsuyama, his response was "Okay, if you can't come to us, we'll come to you," and went on to say that the Foundation was willing to fund any project I considered beneficial for education in Japan. I did go to Tokyo to discuss this with him and his staff. Starting from that summer, the physical conditions of the in-service program improved immensely thanks to Foundation funding. We all still slept on *tatami* mats on the floor, but the food improved, we were able to paint and patch the old buildings in Kuma, and we could afford heating for the spring program.

I also undertook regular missions on behalf of the Foundation to schools all around Japan, to give advice on curriculum innovations and suggestions on how to operate an effective in-service teacher training program. In the spring of 1957, one of those trips took me to the University of the Ryukyus in Okinawa, where I helped the school set up its first language laboratory. The University had an advisory committee of educators from Ohio State University and from secondary schools around the state. They were interested in my work and stopped in Matsuyama on their way back to Tokyo on their trip home that summer. They observed both the Kuma in-service session and the special English Language Training Center I had established at the University. The Center was, I believed, the logical next step after the in-service spring and summer sessions. It allowed junior and senior high school English teachers who were able to get a three-month leave of absence to focus exclusively on new pedagogical methods and on sharpening their own language skills.

My professional life was full of challenges and successes. But my life with Kayoko was no better. *I can't live my entire life like this,* I told myself. After the New Year holiday in 1960, I finally suggested divorce.

Kayoko was horrified. "No, never," was her one and only response. Mother agreed with her, and Father too, by his silence. When I insisted, a huge family council took place. All the aunts and uncles got together to discuss the situation. The result: no divorce.

I rented a small apartment. I lived alone and found that the life of a rebel was quite lonely. The only visitors to my apartment were my private students. Some of my colleagues at the university were understanding, and a few of them even went in a delegation to Kayoko to try to persuade her to agree to a divorce. They were unsuccessful. All they would tell me was that they had spoken with Mother as well as with Kayoko.

By the end of the year, despite my loneliness, my resolve had grown. Kayoko couldn't be the center of the rest of my life. Mother made it clear, via messages delivered by Father, that my presence was expected for the New Year holiday. The week before Christmas, I ran into Yamamura-sensei on *Okaido.* We stood and chatted for quite a while, and by the end of our conversation I had agreed to attend the Christmas Eve service at Reverend Graham's old church, where *Sensei's* wife was a congregant.

It was dark and raining that evening, and I was almost late. I slipped into the last pew as the service began. The church was full and smelled of wet wool. The others passed a hymnal down the row and smiled as they shifted to make room. I enjoyed singing some of the hymns I remembered from Sundays in the Grahams' parlor and found the familiar gospel story about the birth in the manger touching. The high point, however, was during the communion, when I sat in the pew and listened to Yamamura-sensei's flute solo. I knew he believed no more than I did, but was convinced that he too found the experience peaceful, satisfying, and quite comforting. As I listened, I realized, once again, what a talented musician he was, and thought about how lucky I was to have him in my life.

When the service finished, *Sensei* appeared at my elbow and said, "My wife sent me to make sure you join the reception in the church hall."

We climbed up the steps to a wide room with a skylight. The ladies of the congregation had arranged tables around the edges of the room. Warm punch and sweet treats awaited us. It was very western-style and reminded me of post-lecture wine and cheese parties in Ann

Arbor. Yamamura-sensei and I were met by an officious elderly gentleman, Morishita-san, who was clearly a pillar of the church community;
he congratulated *Sensei* on his performance and made a vague, incom-
prehensible comment about looking for the Christmas star through the
skylight. As he moved away, Mrs. Yamamura appeared at the top of the
steps and walked toward us. "My dear, you were wonderful," she said to
her husband. "And I'm so happy you persuaded Imagawa-sensei to join
us. Thank you." Her broad smile was a Christmas present for both of us.

   Sensei announced that he would get us all drinks, and Mrs. Yamamura smiled her thanks, turning all attention to me as her husband started
off across the room.

   "Isamu, I'm glad we have a minute to ourselves," she said. "And I'm
going to be direct, because I think you'll want to hear what I have to say.
I see that you met Morishita-san. His wife, who grew up next door to
the Shizuyamas, told me that she ran into Michiko in Osaka last month.
Since none of us had heard anything since the end of the war, and because I know how close the two of you once were, I thought you'd want
to know. She had a little boy about five with her. She told Mrs. Morishita
that she met her husband in the country when she was evacuated from
Kure before the end of the war."

THE rain had stopped. I walked home through the quiet misty streets,
the cloying taste of the punch still in my mouth, thinking about Michiko.
I wished her every happiness, but couldn't help wondering how many
others in Matsuyama knew. Sometimes I felt that my hometown was one
giant conspiracy to keep me tied to the unhappiness of my personal situation. Perhaps even Mother had heard the news about Michiko. But, of
course, she'd never breathe a word to me.

   By the time I reached my apartment, I decided that it would be
best to stop fretting about what Matsuyama thought about me. I knew I
should be very grateful for the genuinely kind affection of the Yamamu-
ras. I unlocked the door, slipped off my shoes, got out the whiskey bottle,
and poured myself a drink before I even turned on the heater. I'd manage
the holidays, I promised myself as I took the first sip.

THE New Year brought a wonderful and welcome surprise. In February, I was invited to Ohio to establish an intensive English program at
the university to train foreign students and prepare them for the rigors

of English language instruction in the regular undergraduate and graduate programs. I decided to accept the offer and spent much of my time thinking about how I would be in the Midwest by the end of the year.

And I thought a lot about Akiko Sato. She was the new secretary in the English Language Training Center. She had arrived the year before. After she was there about a week, she came into my office to ask me a question about her work. It was the first time we had spoken in private; it was immediately and overwhelmingly thrilling for me. As she said, "*Sensei*, I wanted to check with you about paying these invoices," I was seized with the sudden and absolute knowledge that she could change my life. I know she felt something too, because she never again came into my office alone.

Akiko's job with the English Department was her first after she finished her own degree in English literature. She had come to Matsuyama to attend the university. Although she had a large family in her home town of Ukawa in the mountains of Ehime, she was alone in the city. Each day that followed I grew more and more aware of her. She was pretty, cheerful, and full of bright, open interest in language, literature, and teaching. When we returned to school after the holiday, I finally allowed myself to acknowledge that I was smitten. I determined to take action.

I realized that seeing her face when I came through the door was absolutely the best thing in my day. It was hard for me to concentrate in the office. My colleagues noticed too. "Sam," said Mori-sensei, a perceptive young teacher who had come to Matsuyama after studying in the States for three years, "you'd be a lucky guy to get a girl like her, but...." He was, of course, referring to the Kayoko situation. I held my tongue until the summer, and just before I told everyone that I was going to take the position in Ohio the next year and asked for a leave of absence, I spoke to Akiko late on a Friday afternoon when the rest of the staff had left.

When I finished speaking, I felt that I had handed her my heart. I was convinced she thought the same thing; she reached out toward me, cupping her hands, holding me in her gaze. Tears filled her eyes but she kept her focus on me and leaned forward as they began to spill. "Oh, *Sensei*, oh, Isamu," she finally said. "What are we to do? How can I answer?"

I wanted to take her in my arms, but with her words, she looked away, folded her hands in her lap, looked down at them, and said the words that thrilled and crushed me at the same time, "You are so precious to me. But, but...I have to think. I have to think what to do." She shook her head and never lifted her gaze. I sat in agony. Here was a woman I loved, a woman I wanted to spend my life with. There was nothing I could offer her. She was right. She had to think what to do. She got up quietly and left. I spent the weekend alone with my books and my work, replaying our conversation over and over in my head. As I recalled her tears, the strength of the connection between us, and her look of absolute resignation as she turned away, I pictured Father turning away from me outside the gate to Mie and starting back to the train station.

So I wasn't really surprised when Akiko was not at her desk on Monday morning. After everyone was settled, the chief administrative assistant came to see me with a letter in his hand. "*Sensei*," he said, "Akiko has resigned, and she's left already. Her letter says that her sister, who teaches school in Tokyo, has had an accident and broken her leg. Akiko has gone to help her. I doubt that she'll be back before the end of the year. I'm very sorry to lose her. She was a good worker, a good colleague, and a wonderfully cheerful person to have here everyday." His words were kind; he knew exactly how I felt. I was grateful for his discretion.

"Yes, we will all miss her," I said, and turned to my work.

THE year in Ohio flew by. Establishing a program at a major U.S. university presented a challenge I was eager to test myself against. Working with students from all over the world was a new experience, one that yielded its own difficulties and its own rewards. I learned how to manage a classroom with Scandinavians, Latin Americans, and Arabs, as well as with Asians. My colleagues were kind, but loneliness was a constant companion. I wrote to Akiko every week. After I arrived in Ohio, Mori-san had kindly sent me her address in Tokyo. I suspect that he had it sooner but waited until I had left Japan because he knew she didn't want to see me. I poured my heart out and told her about every new experience, every challenge, every triumph, and every failure. I also wrote about my childhood memories of San Francisco, and what I now thought about my early experiences in both of my countries. In these letters, I did the most thorough job I could of trying to figure out how I ended up eager to give my life for the cruel, false phantom of patriotism and loyalty the war had led us into. I wrote about my new experiences and my ideas for language training and promoting cross-cultural understanding. And how astonishing it was that I was alive to write about such things and how lucky I was to have work that made use of all my experiences.

It didn't matter that she didn't answer. In the spring, when the end of my time in Ohio was in sight, I wrote about the cherry trees blooming on campus and how they reminded me of the evening in Tokyo we suited up for attack. I told her how I had left my papers to be burned, what I was allowing myself to think then, and what I thought about all of it with more than a decade's distance and perspective. Two weeks later a postcard arrived with a picture of the cherry blossoms at Yasukuni Shrine in their full glory. The only message was Basho's: *Samazama no / koto omoidasu / sakura kana.* I stood on my doorstep holding the postcard. *Why did I have to meet this woman, this woman who strikes the perfect right note in everything she does with me, even when she withholds herself from me because I'm not free to be with her?*

In my last month, three letters from Mother and one from Father arrived. Mother wrote about how everyone missed me, especially Kayoko, and how important it was to the family to have me back home in Matsuyama. Kayoko, she wrote, was willing to try again. When Father's letter arrived—supporting Mother of course—it was clear that I had no choice. I wrote back to Father, told him I agreed, and sent details on my itinerary.

He met me again at Matsuyama Port on a bright June day. Sunlight spilled from a blue sky and danced on the water as the ferry pulled into the dock. I told myself that I was happy to be home, and that sunshine and the beautiful day were part of a new beginning. Seeing Father's dear face was a joy, but realizing that both he and Mother had aged visibly diminished my happiness and made me all that much more resolute to try to make everything work.

I THREW myself into my work at Ehime University, but found everything just a bit too small. Mori-san, who had filled in while I was away, had done a great job. At home, things were strained, and, to me, unreal at first. They improved to polite and perfunctory. Kayoko and Mother had no interest in hearing anything about Ohio. For the first few weeks, Father talked about San Francisco, where I had stopped on my way home, and made me talk about the flight, since this was the first time I had traveled across the Pacific by air, peppering me with questions and asking my opinions as a pilot. But after a few dinners where Mother's only contribution had been, "Oh, is that so?" and Kayoko's had been complete silence, Father dropped it.

I took on private students again, and on the few nights when I wasn't using the study for classes, I sat in there planning lessons, sketching out new materials for classes and for the in-service program—and writing more letters to Akiko.

At the end of October, Kayoko announced that she was pregnant again. She told Mother first, and Father and I found out at dinner one night. Mother was glowing with excitement; she talked about continuing the family line and about the history of our two families in Matsuyama and in Ishii. Kayoko looked rather pale and said nothing, but seemed thoroughly pleased with herself. Father leaned back at the table and said, "Ah, now that's news. Congratulations to you two. How lucky we will be to be grandparents." When he raised his glass to toast Kayoko, she smiled at him; her eyes then glanced past mine and she turned to smile at Mother, who was sitting beside her. It was clear that there would be no talk of abortion this time. I thought about a son, about my son's future, about our future in Matsuyama. *This would be it.*

Kayoko was sick most of the time, and Mother fussed over her, nursing her with tenderness and care. By the end of the year, her color had improved; she began eating and started to help Mother in the kitchen again. Mother made the New Year celebration especially festive. The house was decorated, and we were doing well enough to buy presents for family, friends, and colleagues and to have a delicious feast for the holiday. I had a nice break from work, but even in the midst of the festivities and even as I told myself that things would be fine, the certainty that *this would be it* wormed its way into my consciousness. I smiled and joined the family activities, but felt flat and unconnected.

I spent my free days during the holiday reading the latest Graham Greene novel, which had arrived in a package along with an Amish quilt and handmade chocolates from my boss in Ohio, Jim Knowlton, who had been promoted to full professor and appointed director of the university's international center. Father liked the chocolates; Mother, who was famous for her sweet tooth, did too, even though she pronounced them too sweet. Kayoko tried one, swallowed only part of it, and said, "Not for me. I can't imagine ever getting used to foreign food."

Mother and Kayoko examined the quilt. "Look at how regular these stitches are," said Mother.

"Yes," said Kayoko, "but don't you think the pattern is rather loud?"

"I think it may be a traditional American pattern," said Mother. "Didn't Sam say something about it being a pattern of some religious group? Let's take it when we pay our New Year's call on Aunt Furusawa. She can tell us all about it."

When they were off in Ishii Village the next day visiting Aunt Furusawa and the other neighbors there, I wrote Jim and thanked him for the package. I made sure to also thank Jane, his wife. I didn't have much of an idea about the details, but imagined that she had spent long hours working on the quilt. I remembered a similar one in the Knowlton's guest bedroom, where I had stayed for a few days after my lease came to an end and I was making my final arrangements to leave for San Francisco and catch my flight to Tokyo.

"My grandmother made it," Jane had told me. "Every stitch in it was put there with love for her family. I think of her every time I come in this room."

I emphasized how impressed all the women in my family were with the beautiful pattern and the skilled details of the construction of the quilt and how they had told me to send special thanks to her for such a generous present.

Jim wrote back toward the end of January telling me that the program wasn't going well without me and offering me a full-time job as director. I had to write back and say no, but his answer was, "Just keep it in mind. We need you. We'd love to welcome all three of you after the baby is born. Remember, the new school year doesn't start until September."

THE crisis came in late March, during the break between school years. I was in my office at the university, getting ready for the opening ceremony of the in-service session, scheduled for that evening, when the phone rang. Father said, "Isamu, go to the hospital immediately. I'm on my way there now. Your mother is already there with Kayoko. It seems she's in labor."

"But it's too soon!"

"Go, go now," Father said. "I'll see you there."

IT was long after midnight when the three of us arrived home. My son had been born and lived for less than an hour. His mother had lived for about an hour after that, but her hemorrhaging was so severe the doctors could not save her.

When we came through the door, Mother ordered me and Father to sit down and said she'd make tea. We heard her crying in the kitchen. As she knelt to join us at the low table and began to pour the tea she said, "Calling Kayoko's parents tonight was the hardest thing I've ever had to do. What a loss for our family."

Father pushed his tea cup aside, got up, and went to the cabinet where he kept his scotch. "What we all need is a real drink," he said. He poured for all of us and said, as he lifted his glass to his lips, "There are no words for this." We sipped in silence, until Mother, who was still crying quietly, got up and went to bed. When she left the room, Father's only comment was "Son, you need another." He filled my glass. I drank again, and we sat together, drinking without talking, until the sun came up.

I'm not sure how the next month went by, but it did. All I can remember of the funeral, which was held on a chilly, rainy morning, were wet, warm sympathies of friends and family. As I gazed at my family, I thought, these are the same aunts and uncles who had ruled that there could be no divorce. After the funeral, there was the in-service session and planning for the new school year.

I MADE up my mind just before the school year was scheduled to begin. I wrote to Jim and sent the letter special delivery. He wired back. I made an announcement at the university the next day. My colleagues were surprised, but supportive. Mori-san clapped me on the back and said it might well be the best thing. He made me promise to write and to consider coming back to work in the summer in-service program.

Mother was shocked. "No, you can't. Not now," she said.

Father said nothing, but searched my face with the intensity I remembered from Mie. Finally he asked, "When?"

"Actually, tomorrow, I think," I said. "I need to go."

"No," said Mother, "you have to wait for the forty-ninth-day ceremony."

"No, Mother, I can't."

I had to go to Tokyo before I left for Ohio. I went to pack.

CHAPTER 17

MICHIKO

Matsuyama, 1965

MICHIKO STACKED THE lacquer boxes of special New Year's foods and straightened the pile of greeting cards the postman had delivered earlier that morning. She knew that Shotaro would look carefully through them, so many from his employees and those whose businesses supplied his company. He and Tetsutaro were in the park a block away, flying the boy's new kite; it would be a while before they returned. The night before they had agreed with Tetsutaro that at ten he was old enough to stay up to greet the New Year, but he had fallen asleep in his father's lap long before the midnight ringing of the temple bell. When the last of the 108 tolls had faded away, Shotaro had carried the boy to bed.

Shotaro started the New Year by making sure they were up in time for the sunrise. They had stood behind their house, Shotaro's arms around her, his hands and hers together clasping their son in front of her. The sky brightened and the sun rose lighting a scrim of clouds on the horizon navy and gold, violet and mauve. "It will be a good year," said Shotaro, hugging her closer.

MICHIKO made a cup of tea and went to sit in the *tatami* room. The house was warm and the neighborhood had the special silence of the holiday. She looked at the pine and bamboo in the garden where Shotaro loved to putter and thought about the year ahead with the same calm and confidence she had felt watching the sunrise. She thought about how her husband's grit and tenacity had kept her safe for twenty years.

THEY brought the cold with them into the room and stories about how the kite had almost gotten away but finally had flown high and true.

Shotaro went with Tetsutaro to help him store the kite away. When he came back, she poured tea for him, and as he sat down he said, "He's reading his new book, but he'll be asleep in ten minutes. He ran himself ragged in the park. I'm glad to have you to myself for a few minutes. I want to tell you about the plans of Miyazawa Industries for this year. It's time for another plant, and my managers tell me that the best prospective location is Iyoshi. I'll have to go there and visit soon. I want you to come."

"But, Shikoku, Matsuyama—"

"Michiko, my dear, you know I hate traveling by myself. I'd rather be home with you and Tetsutaro. What if I make them wait until spring break so we can take the boy too?"

"Well...."

"Fine, it's set."

THEY didn't tell Tetsutaro until just before his school term ended. Shotaro came home with the full itinerary, the train tickets, and the brochure for the hotel in Matsuyama. Tetsutaro jumped about, yelling, "We're going traveling, traveling on the *Shinkansen!*"

"Quiet, Tetchan," said Michiko.

"Stop," growled his father. "We're going in the opposite direction, so we won't be on the bullet train." Tetsutaro stopped jumping and asked, "Where's Matsuyama?"

"Stop your foolishness. What are they teaching you in that school? Go get the atlas and we'll see where Matsuyama is."

When the impromptu lesson was finished and Tetsutaro was balanced on a step stool tipping the big book back on the shelf, Shotaro said, "The next time I go to Tokyo, maybe I'll take you on the *Shinkansen*. But now it's time for bed."

SHOTARO had his driver pick them up early. Osaka Station was crowded and Michiko waited with their bags in a coffee shop near the entrance to the platforms while Shotaro took Tetchan to the shops at the other end of the concourse.

When Tetsutaro reappeared at Michiko's side, she was sitting with coffee and cake untouched in front of her, looking across the street at an old country granny, bent over under the weight of the huge box tied to

her back, moving slowly through the city bustle. As she turned to hug her son, Shotaro limped up behind the boy, his smile the same sweet treat it had been that first day in the pine forest.

"Mama, look at my model *Shinkansen*. And we got all these *mikan* and the *sembei* you like."

"It is a fine train, don't you agree, my dear?" said Shotaro to his wife, even though his eyes had followed hers; he too was watching the granny.

"Yes, my dears, it is a fine train. And thank you for remembering my favorite snack. We're going to have lots of treats: we'll see beautiful scenery and have good things to eat."

TETCHAN was asleep by the time the express train was just three stops from Osaka. They had to wake him, and he was still groggy when they arrived at the ferry.

"Papa, where are we?"

"It's the Seto Inland Sea. We're going to Shikoku."

"It's not the ocean?"

"You used to be sure Lake Biwa was the ocean. Remember?"

"No, I don't remember, Mama. Everyone knows that Lake Biwa is Japan's largest lake. Is Papa kidding?"

"No, darling. Look at the beautiful islands. Look at the boats."

"Yes, Mama, it is beautiful. I'm glad we're going to Shikoku so I can see where you lived when you were a kid."

THEY had enough time in Takamatsu to take a taxi to the Castle and walk around. The cherries were in bloom. "What do you think, a farmers' cooperative?" Shotaro asked as they stepped off the path for a group of beaming old folks. As they passed, a gust of wind loosened some of the petals and blew them across the group. Michiko watched one old man stop walking and stepping behind his wife to brush petals from her collar and flick them from her hair. As soon as he finished, a second gust landed even more on her. When the wind died down, he smiled, put his hand on her shoulder, and leaned forward to say something to her. She shook her head and they laughed together. He stepped back to her side and they moved forward with the rest of their group, both smiling and both with their jackets and hair sprinkled with petals.

And, as they settled in on the train for Matsuyama, he said, "Country people. Country trains. Old equipment. Old ways. Slow. But we'll get there. And we'll probably enjoy it more. Today we experienced a great luxury—time to appreciate the *sakura*."

THEY ate their *mikan*, Michiko peeling. Shotaro grumbled at Tetchan's questions about his mom's hometown. "You'll see. You'll see. You'll see everything."

When the conductor entered the car, Shotaro gave his son the tickets. "Assistant Conductor Nakahara," according to the tag pinned to his tunic, was no more than twice Tetchan's age. He took the tickets from the boy, made a great show of examining them, and finally said, "Well, Sir, I see you've traveled a long way. Are you from Osaka?"

"Yes!"

"And you're going all the way to Matsuyama?"

"Yes. Are you going to punch our tickets? Are you from Matsuyama? My mom is from Matsuyama."

"No, I live in Sendai now, but I'm from Ohara, outside Kyoto. But this is my favorite route. I love the trip along the water to Matsuyama."

"Look at this." Tetchan pulled his new prize possession out of his knapsack. "My dad got me this *Shinkansen*."

"The *Shinkansen* is the best. And Miyazawa-san, here are your tickets, with my punch. See it looks like a fish. I think maybe it's a Seto Inland Sea fish."

"Wow. Cool. Mom, look."

THREE officials of Ehime Prefecture and the Mayor of Iyoshi met them at Matsuyama Station. As the limo took them to the Grand Castle View Hotel, the local officials were full of the plans they had made for Shotaro. He listened politely and said, "Thank you very much for your kindness. We are most grateful that you came out of your way to pick us up. But we are tired from our long journey and need to rest tonight. What time do you want me to be ready in the morning? I am very much looking forward to touring the factory site."

Michiko thought, how wonderful that we'll have the evening to ourselves.

The locals bowed them into the hotel, and once the registration form was completed, the hotel staff bowed the Miyazawas into the elevator.

As they ate a quiet dinner in a corner of the hotel dining room, Shotaro explained his responsibilities to Tetchan. "I have to take a little trip to another town with those men tomorrow. So you will go with Mom to the Castle. It's famous because it's a dark wood one. A powerful ruler named Lord Matsudaira lived there. It's so high on a hill you have to take a ropeway to the top. After you see where the lord lived, I think you should walk back down the hill. It's a job I can't do. Your mom needs to see all these places again. I have to work, and even if I didn't, I wouldn't enjoy climbing that big hill. Can I depend on you, Tetsutaro?"

"Yes, Papa. I'll take care of Mama."

"How do you know all this about Matsuyama and the Castle?" Michiko asked her husband.

"Since my wife never talks about her home town, I've had to read up on it." Shotaro pulled a small travel guide out of his pocket and handed it to Tetsutaro. "You keep this, son, and check to see if Mom still remembers all the important details about her hometown."

AS they walked down the hill from the Castle, Tetsutaro said, "Mama, it was even better than Papa said. We could see everything. The mountains were so tall."

"Yes, Lord Matsudaira sat at the top of a world that was all his. I had forgotten how wonderful the view is and how the mountains and the Inland Sea cradle the city. And seeing the collection boxes made me remember all the *haiku* our teachers made us memorize. And of course we wrote our own and put them in the boxes. *Kiri ki naru / ichi ugoku ya / kageboshi, A human shadow / hovers in these foggy streets / a cloud of yellow.* That's about the most famous Matsuyama *haiku* poet."

"Mama, I don't like that one so much. Too many clouds and shadows."

"Yes, my dear, it does feel sad, doesn't it? Soseki the novelist and poet was in foggy London when he heard about the death of his friend, Shiki. He was cold and lonely in a foreign land, thinking of Matsuyama and Shiki, so far away. But here are some others. These are much older. This poet's name was Basho. He lived about two hundred years before Shiki and Soseki, and he traveled all over Japan. Here's one where he was looking out at water, the rough waters of the Japan Sea, not at all like the calm Seto waters: *Araumiya / Sado ni yokotau / ama-no- kawa. The wild sea / and the Milky Way / next to Sado Island.*"

"Yes, Mama, I like the water. The sea and the river of heaven, the Milky Way."

"Very good Tetchan. And listen to this one: *Samazama no / koto omoidasu / sakura kana. So many things / are brought to mind by / cherry blossoms.* Remember those old farmers we saw yesterday looking at the cherries at Takamatsu Castle? How happy they were to walk in the sunlight and enjoy the beautiful blooms. But I think they were also smiling because they were remembering the other times they had seen *sakura.*"

"Mama, they were really old. They probably remember lots and lots of other times, don't you think?"

"Yes, darling, and you, Dad, and I were lucky yesterday to be together when we saw those blossoms, and today you and I have seen another castle and more beautiful blooms."

Michiko hoped that, in his old age, her son's memories would include not only this day, but also yesterday and the creased faces of the old farmers smiling under the blooming trees, remembering the many other times they had seen the blossoms. When Tetsutaro stumbled, she took his hand and said "It's been a long day, hasn't it, darling? Here's a taxi. We'll be back at the hotel soon."

"MICHIKO? Michiko-san? Michiko Shizuyama? Is that really you? It's Masako. Masako Mikawa. Used to be Sugano."

"It's Miyazawa now, not Shizuyama. Yes, Masako, it's me. How are you?"

"I'm fine. I'm here to meet my husband. He's here with a visiting manufacturer from Osaka.... Oh, Michiko. Is that Miyazawa-san your husband?"

"Yes, Masako," she said, feeling sorry for Masako's embarrassment. Poor thing, no longer the queen of the Prefectural Girls' High School, lording it over Michiko and all the other not-so-well-off girls. "Mikawa-san, I think I met your husband last night. He's with the Prefectural government, isn't he?"

"Yes, he's the head of his division now."

Michiko realized there was no escape. "Shall we sit down and have some tea?"

"Oh Miyazawa-san, that would be so wonderful. I'm not sure how much longer my husband, our husbands, will be. Oh, and is this your son?"

"Tetchan, say hello to Mikawa-san."

"Pleased to meet you, Ma'am."

"Tetchan, Mrs. Mikawa and I went to school together, and we haven't seen each other for more than twenty years. She and I are going to sit here in the lobby and talk. I want you to go out in the garden and wait for us. You'll be able to see us, and we'll see you through the window. You have your book about Lord Matsudaira and the Castle, don't you? Good."

As soon as they sat down, Masako started, "What a lovely boy. I have three children myself. My oldest girl is in our old high school now. My second, the first boy, is at Matsuchu, and so is our second boy. They aren't even two years apart. Well, of course, the name isn't Matsuchu any more—officially. But we all still call it that here. We know it's the most prestigious school in Shikoku. My husband is pleased that our boys are doing so well. He's already talking about Kyodai or Todai for them, but I'm not sure I want them that far away."

"How proud you must be."

"Yes, thank you. Have you been past the old school? How about Matsuchu? Everything's changed so much. My kids don't believe it when my husband and I tell them stories about the old days. Oh, Michiko-san, do you remember how we would walk to school on *Okaido* while the Matsuchu boys were going the other way? We'd even stop in your parents' sweet shop sometimes. Oh, that was so much fun. My husband was a Matsuchu boy himself."

"I'm sorry I don't remember him from then."

"Ah, those were the days, weren't they? There were so many handsome guys. Furuyama-san works with my husband. And Kawada-san is a doctor. He has a big clinic near Dogo-Onsen. And...." She paused to think, and said, "Oh, Michiko, I'm sure you remember Imagawa-san, don't you?"

"Yes," Michiko said carefully, "he married Kayoko Katayama, didn't he? How are they?"

"Oh, Michiko-san, you don't know? Well, how would you, living in Osaka.... It's such a story."

"Mmm."

"Well, you know they married soon after the end of the war. Yamamura-sensei, from Matsuchu, got Imagawa-san a job with the Occupation Army. He spent a lot of time traveling around with those Americans checking on the schools. Poor Kayoko was alone. She stayed with her mom and with Mrs. Imagawa out in Ishii Village because both families had lost their houses in the city. I heard she had two miscarriages. He never seemed to care. Maybe he was so cold and selfish"—and here she dropped her voice—"from his Special Attack Corps experience. Or maybe all that time with the foreigners. Speaking English all the time. Then he began teaching at the university and there was a lot of talk about him and a young secretary. She was more than ten years younger. From some small town up in the mountains. Everyone said he was really chasing her. Well, she—her name was Akiko Sato—she just suddenly disappeared.

"Then the Americans got him a scholarship, and he went away for two years. Just sailed off. Kayoko was sick—everyone said it was a miscarriage—just before he left to study in the States.

"When he came back, he had some fancy American degree and went back to the university to teach. Poor Kayoko didn't look any happier, but she was soon pregnant again.

"And then, and this is the really sad part, Kayoko died in childbirth, and the baby didn't survive. It was at the end of the school year. He left for America again without even staying for the forty-ninth-day services for his wife. The Katayamas never spoke to his mother again. A tough situation for such a proud lady. And to make it worse, everyone thinks that Akiko is with him in the States. We're sure he'll never come home again.

"Ah, Michiko-san, here they are. Our husbands." Masako hurried across the lobby and made the most extravagant bows possible, while gushing, "Ah, Miyazawa-san, I'm Mikawa. I was lucky enough to meet your wife here in the hotel. We were schoolgirls together. It's such an honor to meet you. I hope your day was a good one."

Shotaro said, "How pleasant to meet you, Mrs. Mikawa. Your husband and his colleagues showed me so much. It was a great day."

Michiko stood next to Shotaro and bowed as Mikawa and his colleagues, with Masako in tow, made their exit.

As they smiled, Shotaro asked, "Where's our boy?"

"Safe. In the garden."

"Let's call him. I need a bath and dinner and my wife and my son. Tomorrow we can go home."

CHAPTER 18

GENTARO

Izumi, 2000

THE WOMAN BEHIND the kiosk was trying to maintain her dignity but wanted to make the sale. Her quick glance at Michiko indicated that she found her young male customer as entertaining as he was unusual. Gen pretended he didn't see the glance the old ladies exchanged.

"Look, Gran, there's a sand sauna Kitty," said Gen. "I know we got the purple potato sake-drinking Kitty and the giant radish Kitty yesterday, but I think I have to get this one too."

"It's certainly as ridiculous as the purple one," said Michiko.

"Oh, and there's a *bonton ame* phone charm too. I can't leave without that. "

"But it won't mean anything to Lynn."

"No, Gran, the Hello Kitty ones are for her. I'm keeping the *bonton ame* one for myself. I remember Dad mentioning *bonton ame* and saying how he discovered it on a trip to Shikoku with you and Gramps. And now I've discovered it with you."

"Sort of a silly family tradition," said Michiko, trying to sound grumpy.

Gen ignored her and told the sales clerk that he wanted all the knick-knack charms he had selected. She thanked Gen and smiled again at Michiko as she wrapped them. They crossed the station concourse, headed for the bus terminal, and joined the queue.

THEY had arrived in Ibusuki early the day before and had had a chance to revel in the odd mix of the resort's attractions—the sand saunas, the hot spring baths, the gardens around the pink hotel buildings, and the art museum tucked away in a corner of the grounds. By the time they had exhausted themselves with all of that, there was only an hour before dinner. Michiko was seated at the table in their *tatami* room and reviewing the dinner menu and the hotel flyer listing the evening's events. She commented that the exotic Hawaii-themed show of the 1960s was evidently history, and Gen responded cheerfully that the neat path with palm trees that led to the beach was like Hawaii. He leaned over and gave his grandmother a big hug and sloppy kiss, and promised to be back soon from a run to the beach. When he left, Michiko moved to the balcony and sat. She saw her grandson emerge from under the hotel's entranceway and head for the beach. She watched him head along the curved path, and leaned back, relaxing in the sunshine as he disappeared out of sight around a bend. She awoke when she heard the key in the door to the room.

"Gran, I've already been to the bath and have cleaned up. It's almost time for dinner. Are you ready?"

THE dining room was Japanese Christmas season excess incarnate. "At least it's *cheerfully* vulgar," said Michiko as the maître d' walked them to their table. A dozen white Christmas trees were situated throughout the room, shining under spotlights. Each was decorated with different-colored balls. Gen entertained himself by reciting all the colors for his grandmother: red, green, navy blue, aqua, baby blue, silver, gold, purple, fuchsia, rose, baby pink, and early summer rice-paddy green.

"They've certainly covered all the bases," Michiko said.

"Gran, stop grumping. I know you secretly love this stuff as much as you love Hello Kitty," he said, knowing he would make her laugh.

"Yes," she said, obliging him with a laugh. "I feel the same way about all of it. It's all ridiculous. Now what's for dinner?"

As they worked through the courses, Michiko commented that the meal, like everything else they had encountered that day, was too much.

"Well, Gran, at least our stomachs will be full for our trip tomorrow. I don't think we'll find such fancy stuff where we're going."

"I'm sure you're right, my dear," she said.

THE trip to Chiran was accomplished in stages, with two bus changes, and other stops at scenic spots. The first stop was at Lake Ikeda, Kyushu's largest body of water. Its beautiful, clear blue waters reflected the graceful lines of Mt. Kaimon, which dominated the landscape. The bus labored up and down the hills that rose from the coast, and all the passengers snapped pictures of the mountain as the changes in altitude provided varied views of the "Mount Fuji of Kyushu."

At Chiran, Gen escorted his grandmother to the museum dedicated to peace and to the sacrifices of the *kamikaze* pilots. He suspected she found it all too sentimental, but she made no comments.

The museum was a warren of small, irregularly-connected rooms, and Gen had been in a room with the photos on the wall for quite some time before he looked up from the display cases and took in how much was crammed in the room. The walls were covered with rows and rows of portraits. He was mesmerized, walking slowly and looking at one face after another. After the first dozen or so, he got beyond the faded sepia and the stern looks, and was aware—no, overwhelmed—by the one blinding fact of all of the portraits. They were young—his age or even younger. Finally, he noticed that but for one elderly gentleman he was alone. The old man was in his seventies. His hands were clasped behind his back, his gray jacket lay open, unzipped, and his face was impassive as he stooped over an exhibit of a manned torpedo horribly named the Cherry Blossom, inspecting it closely. *He's my Gran's age. How have any of them survived with the sorrows their hearts hold?*

Thinking of his grandmother made him realize he had lingered much too long. He retraced his steps through the welter of rooms but didn't find her until he emerged from the museum. She was sitting on a bench across from a memorial stone with just the word "Firefly" carved on it. Michiko was watching ladies her age, one after another, move to stand in front of the stone and pose for photos. Two ladies were switching places and exchanging cameras as Gen walked up to his grandmother.

"Gran, sorry. I got carried away," he said. "Do you want me to take your picture?" he asked, looking at the ladies.

"Do you know what this 'Firefly' stuff is about?" she asked.

"No," he said.

"Well," she said, "there's a sentimental story about Tomiya, an inn here in Chiran patronized by the special attack pilots. One of them, Saburo Miyakawa, was drinking at the inn on the night before his mission. He promised the owner and her daughter that he would return the next night as a firefly. And sure enough, the next night, when he was mere ashes somewhere far to the south, a firefly appeared at Tomiya. Those two ladies just finishing with their photos told me that the story is being filmed and will be released as a movie next year."

"Well, Gran, why don't you let me take your photo?"

Her slight hesitation made Gen think that perhaps she didn't think it was such a good idea, but Michiko smiled at him, and moved to stand next to the stone, nodding to the two chatting ladies, who were gathering their belongings and moving off. Michiko smiled at her grandson as he raised the camera, but her face was grave when he clicked the shutter.

When he finished, Michiko announced that she was tired and suggested that they take the next bus back rather than touring the *samurai* houses that were Chiran's other tourist attraction. They sat in companionable silence as the bus retraced the route they had taken that morning; the mountains were gilded by the dying light.

THEY ordered dinner in their room and relaxed away from the crowds in the dining room. Early the next morning they visited the hot spring baths as soon as they opened, had breakfast in their room, checked out, and set off for Izumi.

When the train arrived in Izumi, Gen sensed that his grandmother was finally truly interested. The only way to get around was to hire a taxi, and the elderly driver took them from one to another of the obscure memorial stones associated with the former Naval Air Station and the special attack pilots who had been trained there. The memorials were shabby, but still tended: a glass jar with wilted flowers at one; a bottle of whiskey with an inch of liquid at the base of another; and, at the last they visited, sake cups with crusted rims where the liquid had evaporated. Izumi was a country town. Its connection with the special attack forces was part of its history, but not a tourist attraction. The real focus in Izumi was the birds.

When the taxi driver finished showing them all the memorial stones, he told them about the Bird Center and the Bird Museum. He also offered to take them to a shrine dedicated to special attack aviators or to Fumoto, the area of town with old *samurai* residences. Gen was surprised when his grandmother chose Fumoto, and the taxi driver was pleased by the unexpected extra fare.

They passed the shrine as they headed away from Izumi's small downtown. When Gen saw the concrete statue of a naval aviator decked out in his flight suit astride a thirty-foot-tall arch dominating the neighborhood around it, he wondered if he had been wrong about Izumi. When he turned to his grandmother, he saw her squint just a tiny bit. He thought she was going to say something, but she didn't.

Gen held his grandmother's arm as they walked the quiet streets of Fumoto and toured the one old mansion that was open to the public. "We're just building anticipation for the birds, you know," she said as they walked back to the taxi. "I suspect you've never seen anything like this."

"You're right, Gran."

"Good, I was too tired for the *samurai* houses in Chiran but pleased that we didn't skip them today." She smiled at the taxi driver, who bowed low and helped her into his vehicle. When they were settled in the car, he began to talk about the Bird Center and Bird Museum again. Michiko finally got him to admit that the Bird Center was closer to where the birds actually were, and off they went. When they arrived the parking lot was surprisingly empty and they went into the Center. Soon, however, a bus tour group flooded in.

"I've seen enough. Time to go," said Michiko.

"Look," said Gen, as they emerged from the building and walked away from the parking lot, passing a sign that said "12,980."

"Amazing," said Michiko as a broad field came into sight. "So many of them." The field was full, covered, as far as the eye could see. Huge, beautiful, stately, colorful cranes covered the center of the field. Thousands upon thousands.

"*Sembazuru* times ten and then plus," said Gen. When his grandmother turned and looked at him smiling, he said, "Sorry, couldn't help it. Bet you didn't know I was literary. I wonder how they arrive at such an exact number."

"I'm sure that's the job of one of the learned scientists at the Center, but we can't really care, can we, Gen-chan, when there's such beauty to behold?" She stepped up to one of the platforms that lined the field and looked at the cranes through binoculars. "Take a look," she said to him after staring for quite a while.

As Gen was looking, an older woman walked up and started chatting with Michiko. Gen listened long enough to realize that she was with one

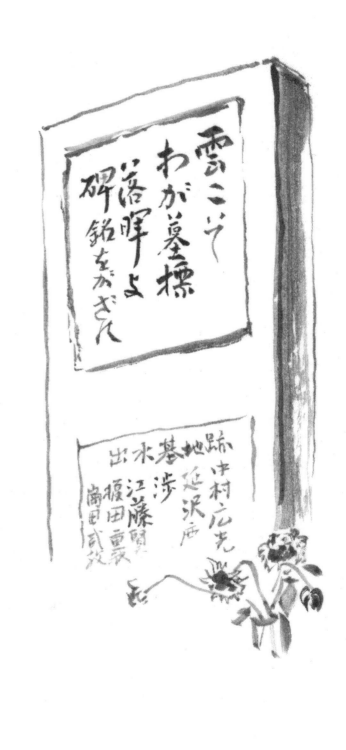

of the bus groups and that members of the group were beginning to drift out of the Center. Gran is being polite, he told himself, knowing that she would find something she had in common with this lady, and that he was free to drift off. He climbed down from the platform, excused himself, told his grandmother he was going to stretch his legs, and walked about the length of a city block along the fence.

He was beyond the group from the bus and standing alone. He had a good view of the birds across the field. He noticed that a few had moved a bit away from the huge group. He could see the crane closest to him clearly, but it had its head down, searching the ground for food. On an impulse, trying to get its attention, he took his keys from his pocket and began shaking them, and then hitting them gently against the closest fence pole. The crane he had his eye on looked up and then came toward him, lifting and bending its long legs one at a time, moving slowly and placing its feet deliberately. Obviously curious, it kept high-stepping gracefully, closer and closer to Gen and the fence that was vibrating with the noise he was making. *Come here, my beauty, come here. I want to have a better look at you.*

The crane didn't stop until it was only about two feet from the fence. It stood sideways, looking at Gen with its small shining black eye. It moved its long neck, looked at him straight on, then moved back, still observing him. At first, Gen held his breath, but as both he and the bird relaxed, Gen relished all the beautiful details. He knew that, in English, this bird, the *tanchozuru,* was simply called a "Japanese crane." It was larger than most of the others Gen could see, and its markings were bright, beautiful, and quite dramatic.

As the bird kept watching him, Gen took in the silver-dollar sized bumpy red patch above its eyes that looked like the surface of an ink pad, the white above that at the top of its nape, and the black that curled down its beautiful neck like a graceful swirl of *sumi* ink from a calligraphy brush. The feathers of its plump body were dazzling white. Even in the weak winter sunlight they were gleaming. The white feathers grew larger toward the end of the bird's body and presented a breathtaking contrast to the long black feathers at its rear.

As the bird drew nearer, two things happened. Some of the group from the tour bus noticed what Gen was doing, and several of the old men began to walk toward Gen and what he was thinking of as *his crane.*

And another crane noticed. As the second bird detached himself from the group, Gen realized that it was even larger than the one standing before him. *It's her mate, coming to protect her from the ojiisans—and from me.*

When the male reached his mate, the two birds stood facing Gen. He stopped hitting his keys against the fence, and the *ojiisans* stopped walking, took out their cameras, and began snapping the magnificent birds. The male took a few steps forward, flapping his wings and then a few steps back, positioning himself next to his mate. The two of them stood looking calmly at Gen, until in silent and imperceptible agreement, they turned together and walked slowly back to the small group. Shortly thereafter, that small group, just a few beats behind the majority of the large group at the center of the field, ran for a few steps and took off, pointing and pulling themselves up into the air and wheeling out to the Yatsushiro Sea.

Gen walked back to where his grandmother stood, now by herself. "Let's walk in the other direction," she said. He walked with her for about ten minutes. They stood at the fence, again away from the crowd, enjoying the solitude and the views of the birds.

"They're so beautiful, Gen. I'm glad you came here with me. So many of them here. And they've come so far. No wonder the people of Izumi are so proud of them. It makes me think of the lieutenant Sam wrote about." After a few more moments, she took his arm and said, "I suppose we should start back."

The taxi driver smiled when they returned to the parking lot. "To the station?" he asked.

"Yes, please," said Michiko.

But when they were almost back to the station, and again passing the shrine, Gen leaned forward and asked the driver to stop at the first of the memorial stones they had visited. "Come with me, Gran," he said.

Michiko got out of the taxi without asking any questions and walked with Gen to the memorial. Gen looked again at the jar on the ledge in front of the stone, the flowers it contained drooping over its sides, and squatted down to read the inscription. "I want to leave something, Gran. It's silly, but it's all I have," he said reaching in his pocket and pulling out the giant radish Hello Kitty charm. "Lynn will understand when I tell her."

"Thank you, Gen."

"*Samazama,* Gran," he said, as he stood up and took her arm. Walking her back to the taxi he thought about Lynn. And about what he had learned about his grandmother's memories; he thought about Sam's memories—Sam, who had loved being dressed like the cold crude concrete flight jock; he thought about the memories of the old man shuffling quietly about the crowded, pokey little rooms of the museum. And he thought about the Pacific stretching east from Japan and west from California. *We've already made some of our own memories, and I know there will be lots more.*

"Now to the station, please," he said to the driver.

CHAPTER 19

GENTARO

Kamakura, 2000

GEN WAS UPSTAIRS in his room at his desk. His review books were in three neat stacks, put away for the day.

"Don't forget to thank your Gran," Lynn said. "The jacket is beautiful. I love the pattern the stitches make. Yuko told me it's called *sashiko*. And I've finally figured out how to attach those ridiculous Hello Kitty things to my cell phone. *So* sophisticated," she laughed.

"Merry Christmas, Lynn. Wish I were there."

"Gen-chan, I wish you were here too, but we'll see each other soon. Love you," she said before she hung up.

TETSUTARO called from downstairs, reminding Gen and his mom that they should leave in ten minutes.

"Yes, dear. I'm just finishing," his mom answered.

"I'm ready to go, Dad. I'm just going to call Dave and Yuko to say Merry Christmas," Gen called, as he dialed again.

"Dave, Merry Christmas. I miss you all."

"Gen, we miss you. My mom was complaining this afternoon that with you gone, no one wants to help her bake. Hold on a sec, while I go get Yuko. She's upstairs still wrapping some presents. It took us a long time to get the kids to bed. They're so excited, I doubt they'll sleep much tonight."

"My dear Gen. How are you?" said Yuko when she picked up the phone. "And how are your mom and dad? What are you doing to celebrate Christmas?"

"Going to a year-end party at the hospital. My dad's getting an award."

"How was Kyushu?

"Great. Loved the time with my Gran. Learned a lot."

"The studying?"

"I've been resolute and I'm ready. I could take the exams today. So next month will be fine."

"Lynn?"

"Just talked to her. I'll be there in March with my mom and dad, so we'll see you all then, and I'll come back again in the summer. Lynn will come back with me then. I have to take her to Nara to meet my Gran."

"Merry Christmas, dear Gen, and *Akemashite* in advance. I know the New Year will bring you success and much happiness."

CHAPTER 20

AKIKO

Himeji, 2000

THE TABLE WAS set, this time for seven. Akiko finished reading the Christmas cards from Katherine, Pauline, and friends in Ohio and stacked them on top of her bookcase next to Sam's picture. *Two years.*

A postcard was propped up against the metal bowl in front of the picture. As soon as she had pulled it out of her mailbox the week before, even before she turned it over and saw just the word *samazama* as its message, she had known it was from Michiko. The picture—thousands upon thousands of cranes—displayed Izumi's splendor and pride.

She lit a stick of incense, and struck the side of the bowl with the tiny hammer that sat at its side. "My darling, thinking of you," she said. After a few moments of perfect stillness, she turned and walked into her husband's study. She sat at the desk and looked out the window at the Castle in the distance. The light was fading from the sky and the White Heron would soon be glowing.

The day they came to look at the condo, Sam had come in here while she was still chatting with the real estate agent in the living room. When he stepped back to join them, he said, "Akiko, go look." She had walked in and been delighted with the light and the view. He turned when he heard her come back. Her eyes met his and they agreed. "We like it," he said, turning back to the agent. "Can we get started on the paperwork?"

It had been all they knew it would be at that moment. Lovely, and spacious, these rooms had been their refuge. A new home as happy as their house in Ohio and their apartment in San Francisco. He had loved his work, just as he had ever since the first days after the war, his experiences deepening and strengthening with every passing year, with each new class, with each batch of bright young students.

She sat at his desk, where in the last year, she had found herself often. She was happy among his things, the souvenirs of his years of work, and had stacked her books on his desk. Her haiku group wouldn't meet until long after the New Year holiday, but she sat to read, leafing through her favorite volumes of poetry. After all her adventures with Sam, she had returned to the magic and comforts of literature, the magic that had inspired her in Ukawa, promising a wider world she was eager to rush out to meet, and the comfort she had drawn on the lonely nights in Tokyo when she was convinced that, even though she had taken the first steps into that wider world, she would have to continue the journey without the one for her—the person who would complete her.

She had been finding her inspiration in her books as well as in her walks around her neighborhood and the garden of the Castle. Her haiku group had visited Mount Shoshazan and Engyoji Temple in the autumn when the foliage had been spectacular, before the winds stripped the trees and brought the cold. Many of the poems she was drawn to were old, old friends and too personal for haiku, but she read on, knowing that the beauty of their words could uncoil at any time; they gave not just immediate pleasure, but insight and inspiration that could come at any time—a new way of looking and seeing, the source of ideas and sometimes even the very words she would shape into haiku. *Yes, it's all here,* she thought.

All through the autumn, she thought, *as the winds blew, I thought about managing the nights alone. When the leaves turned brilliant red, and were then touched by frost and fell, I thought of all the years ahead of me, and how in all that time I will not forget you—ever. And now it is winter again, and the night is cold. There's no sleet tonight, but there was two years ago. And, my darling, like that cold night of wet snow, tonight, without the pillow of your arms, again I shall have to sleep alone. But tonight, like every night, and like the bright days when I sit here, I know that you will return in memories. Even though you have traveled into death's dateless night, all I have to do is think on thee. With that, my losses are restored and my sorrows ended. My sweet, sweet love remembered.*

Akiko's thoughts of love and loneliness borrowed phrases from some of her favorite poems in the *Manyoshu,* the eighth-century anthology of

Japanese poetry, and from William Shakespeare's sonnets. These words by a few of Akiko's favorite poets seemed to capture her mood and give her strength.

THE knock at the door that she was expecting came.

She rose from the desk and called, "Welcome," as she started through the living room. The incense was still burning, and she stopped to strike the bell one more time. "I'm coming, big sister" she added, but paused to listen to the last of the bell tone. She whispered to her husband, "I've set out the ornaments again, my darling."

"*MERI kurisumasu*. It's as cold as the North Pole," called Junko from the *genkan*. Akiko could hear her put her packages down and begin to struggle out of her boots. "The first order of business is getting some tea made. I need to warm up so I can enjoy the good party I know Sam wants us to have. I wonder if the Professor will get completely slogged again."

Fortified by her time with the books and the poetry, Akiko walked to the hallway. As she remembered again holding his hand in the hospital and the trip home alone on that cold night, she thought about the journey of life, realizing with wonder and gratitude, that even though stitched together on a foundation of sorrow, loss, and tragedy, it could be happy and long. There had been great adventures on her journey, and joy in her companion as long as grace had granted her him. Now, she knew, her happiness endured in memories, sustaining her for what was to come. She stepped forward and reached out to help her sister, smiling.

Notes About Japanese

Names

When both names are used, Japanese names are presented Western style, with personal names first and family names second.

Orthography and Transliteration

Many Japanese words have long vowels. Various conventions are used to indicate them, with macrons being the most typical. However, that convention is abandoned for very common words such as Tōkyō and Ōsaka, which are typically written merely as Tokyo and Osaka. This text takes the same liberties with all Japanese words with long vowels, and numerous personal and place names, most notably the names of the men of the Miyazawa family: Shōtarō, Tetsutarō, and Gentarō, appear in the text without any indication of their long vowels. Other personal names (some real, some imaginary, and some mythical) that have lost their macrons in the text include Ōtomo (Tabito, Yakamochi, and Fumimochi) Natsume Sōseki, Kūkai, Matsuo Bashō, Akiko Satō, Saburō Miyakawa, Masao Katō, Amaterasu Ōmikami. Names of places and institutions (some real and some imaginary) that have suffered the same fate include: Hōryūji Temple, Hokkaidō, Honshū, Kyūshū, the Ryūkyūs, Chūō University, Kyōdai (Kyoto University), Tōdai (Tokyo University), Keiō (University), Tōzawa (University Hospital), Ōkaidō. The Manyōshū, Japan's great eighth century compilation of famous poems, is another victim, and is referred to in the text simply as the Manyoshu. Other words that are missing long vowels in the text include shōchū, Shintō, *tokkō*, Itō, *Dōki no Sakura, tokkō, Ōaka-gera.*

The sound written with "n" in Japanese is pronounced "m" before bilabials such as b and p. Thus, the Tokyo neighborhood, "Shinbashi" is often rendered in English as *Shimbashi* (as it is typically pronounced). In this work, words with this combination are therefore transliterated using an "m" rather than "n." Hence, *kempeitai* rather than kenpeitai, and *mompe* rather than monpe.

A Note About Aircraft

This story uses the Japanese names for aircraft. The Model 93 Intermediate Trainer (Kugisho Navy Type 93 Intermediate Trainer (K5Y)), the Model 96 fighter (Mitsubishi Navy Type 96 Carrier Fighter (A5M)), and the Zero (Mitsubishi Navy Type 0 Carrier Fighter (A6M)), were, respectively, code-named "Willow," "Claude," and "Zeke" by the Allies.

Glossary

Akemashite (omedeto gozaimasu) New Year greeting

Anime Japanese animated film entertainments

Ao-gera Japanese green woodpecker

Banzai Literally, "ten thousand years"; hooray

Bento Lunch box in which various small dishes are packed in individual compartments

Bizen Much-prized pottery from the Okayama-Himeji area of Japan, usually brown and unglazed

Bonton ame Old-fashioned chewy citrus candy of Kyushu; chewy squares wrapped in clear edible wrappers that dissolve on the tongue

Botan yuki Large snowflakes; literally, "peony snow"

Botchan Title of famous novel by Natsume Soseki; literally, "young master" or "greenhorn"

-chan A suffix used after a first name; a term of affection used with the names of children and very close friends

Chankoro Derogatory term for "Chinese"

Daruma Roly-poly dolls; Japanese color in one of their blank eyes when they make a wish, and then the other when the wish comes true

Dōki no Sakura Japanese song about cherry blossoms that bloom at the same time/on the same day; popular in the last years of the war in several versions, including one used by the Japanese Imperial Navy

Edo Old name for Tokyo; the period when the *Shoguns* were the real rulers of Japan (1603–1867) is referred to as the Edo Era.

Furoshiki Traditional cloth used to wrap and carry parcels

Futon Traditional Japanese bedding; mattresses spread on the floor

Gaijin Japanese for "foreigner"

Gambatte "Good Luck"; "Do your best!"

Geisha Artistes; female entertainers who specialize in traditional Japanese music and dance

Genkan Entryway to Japanese homes; at a lower level than the interior flooring

Genmaicha Japanese green tea combined with popped rice

Geta Wooden sandals

Haiku Japanese verse form that traditionally includes a seasonal reference and consists of seventeen syllables arranged in three lines of five, seven, and five syllables

Hibachi Japanese grill

Hoanden Enshrinement Hall

Hojicha Roasted tea

Hōryūji Famous Buddhist temple in Nara

Issei First-generation Japanese-American(s)

Iyo kasuri Indigo splashed pattern textile of Ehime Prefecture

Judo Japanese martial art

Kaki kueba First two words (and first line) of a famous *haiku* poem that all Japanese schoolchildren learn

Kakkō Common cuckoo

Kamikaze Literally, "divine wind." In the 13th century, two attempts by the Mongolians to invade Japan failed, thanks to storms of typhoon magnitude. The Japanese never forgot this myth, which reinforced the belief that the Shinto gods protected Japan. During the last part of World War II, the term *kamikaze* was applied to members of the Japanese Special Attack Forces, Japanese fighter pilots trained to make suicide attacks on Allied ships.

Kempeitai Wartime military secret police; "thought" police

Kendo Japanese martial art

Kimigayo The Japanese national anthem

Kiyomizudera Famous Kyoto Buddhist temple with a broad veranda over a valley

Kimono Traditional Japanese women's dress

Ko-gera Japanese pygmy woodpecker

kokeshi Cylindrical wooden dolls from the northern parts of Japan

komadori Japanese robin

Kosho Matsuyama Commercial College

Kotatsu A low table covered with quilts and a tabletop; situated above a fireplace or constructed with a heat source attached to the bottom of the table

Koto Japanese transverse harp

Kozara Small plate(s)

Kurozuro Common cranes

Kyōdai Kyōto University nickname (Kyōto + Daigaku)

Manazuru White-napped cranes

Manyōshu First anthology of Japanese poetry; compiled in the 7th–8th century

Meboso mushikui Arctic warbler

Meiji Name of the Japanese era from 1868–1912

Mikan Japanese mandarin oranges; sometimes marked in the U.S. as "Satsuma" oranges

Miso Soybean paste; staple of Japanese cuisine

Momotaro Literally "peach boy"; a fairy tale that every Japanese knows

Mompe Pants made of simple fabric, typically worn by farmwives

Mugicha Barley tea

Ne-san Literally, "Big (older) sister"

Nihon katta, Rosha maketa "Japan won; Russia lost"

Nisei Second-generation Japanese-American(s)

Ōaka-gera White-backed woodpecker

Obasan Literally "aunt"; used as an honorific title (in lieu of a family name) for an adult woman

Obi Belt for a woman's *kimono*

Ochazuke Japanese snack: green tea poured over rice to make a porridge

Odori Traditional Japanese dance

Ojiisan Literally "grandfather"; used as an honorific title (in lieu of a family name) for older men

Ohayo gozaimasu Good morning

Ōkaidō Literally, "Big Shopping Street"; Matsuyama's principal commercial street

Okusan Honorific term for "wife"

Omiai Meeting in advance of an arranged marriage

Omiyage A souvenir; a hostess gift

Ronin Literally, "masterless *samurai*"; used to describe students who take time off from school to prepare for entrance exams for the next educational level

Saikeirei Deepest bow

Sake Japanese rice wine

Sakura Cherry blossoms

Samazama First word of a Bashō *haiku*

Samurai Japanese warrior

-san Honorific title used in lieu of Mr., Mrs., or Ms. Appended to family names as a suffix

Sashiko Japanese traditional craft stitch

Sembazuru Literally, "A Thousand Cranes"; title of the 1952 novel by Yasunari Kawabata, winner of the 1968 Nobel Prize for Literature

Sembei Japanese rice crackers

Senninbari "Thousand stitch belt;" scarf-like white cloths hand-stitched with red crosses, typically made for men serving in the Japanese military by their wives, sweethearts, or female relatives. In order to have stitches made by a "thousand" different hands, those making *senninbari* for their loved ones asked friends, neighbors, and even strangers in public places to add stitches.

Sensei Literally, "teacher." Honorary title for teachers, doctors, etc. Can replace the honorific *"san"* as the suffix used with family names

Seto no Hanayome Literally "Seto Bride." *Seto Naikai* is Japan's Seto Inland Sea, between the main island of Honshu and Shikoku, the smallest of Japan's four main islands.

Shamisen Three-stringed musical instrument; somewhat similar in sound to a banjo

Shinkansen Literally, "New trunk line"; Japan's bullet train

Shiso Perilla; beefsteak plant leaf

Shitamachi Tōkyō's traditional "downtown"; Asakusa and other neighborhoods in the eastern, older part of the city, near the Sumida River

Shōchū Alcoholic drink made from potatoes

Showa Name of the Japanese era from 1925–1989; name of the reign of Emperor Hirohito

Soba Japanese buckwheat noodles

Sokaijin Evacuee from the city to the countryside

Sukiyaki Japanese beef stew dish prepared at the table fondue-style

Sumo Japanese wrestling

Sumi Black calligraphy ink made from charcoal

Suribachi Mortar

Surikogi Pestle

Sushi Raw fish and/or vegetables served atop canapés of rice or wrapped in rice and seaweed rolls that are then sliced into individual pieces

Takuan Japanese pickle made from *daikon* white radish; typically yellow in color

Tanchōzuru Japanese crane

Tatami Woven straw mats used for flooring

Tenno Heika Banzai "Long Live the Emperor"

Tōdai Tokyo University nickname (Tōkyo + Daigaku)

Tokkō Wartime civilian secret police; "thought" police

Tokonoma Alcove in a traditional Japanese room, typically used to display a hanging scroll and a flower arrangement

Tsubame Swallow

Tsutusdori Oriental cuckoo

Umeboshi Picked plum

Yakyu Baseball game, a term that replaced the foreign word *besuboru* during the war

Yasukuni Tokyo Shinto Shrine famous for its cherry blossoms; place where those killed in service to Japan are enshrined. In that respect, comparable to Arlington Cemetery, but controversial, especially with Japan's neighbors because individuals adjudged war criminals after World War II are among those enshrined there

Yokaren Japanese naval recruits—often teenage farm boys—trained as aviators for suicide missions

Yuzu Japanese citrus

Bibliography

Suggestions for further reading

Axell, Albert & Hideaki Kase (2002). *Kamikaze: Japan's Suicide Gods.*
  London: Pearson Education.
Batty, David (2004). *Japan at War in Color.* London: Carlton Books.
Blyth, R.H. (1963). *A History of Haiku* (Volumes One and Two). Tokyo:
  Hokuseido.
Brines, Russell (1944). *Until They Eat Stones.* New York: Lippincott.
Briscoe, Susan (2005). *The Ultimate Sashiko Sourcebook.* Devon, UK:
  David & Charles.
Cook, Haruko Taya & Theodore F. Cook (1992). *Japan at War: An Oral
  History.* New York: New Press.
Crew, Quentin (1962). *Japan: Portrait of Paradox.* New York: Thomas
  Nelson & Sons.
Dower, John W. (1993). *Japan in War & Peace: Selected Essays.* New York:
  New Press.
Dower, John W. (1999). *Embracing Defeat: Japan in the Wake of World
  War II.* New York: Norton/New Press.
Frédéric, Louis (Kathe Roth trans.) (2002). *Japan: Encyclopedia.* Cam-
  bridge: Harvard University Press.
Guillain, Robert (William Byron, trans.) (1981). *I Saw Tokyo Burning.*
  Garden City: Doubleday.
Havens, Thomas R. H. (1978). *Valley of Darkness: The Japanese People
  and World War Two.* New York: Norton.
Ienaga, Saburo (1978). *The Pacific War, 1931–1945.* New York: Pantheon
  Books.
Imamura, Shigeo. (2001). *Shig: The True Story of an American Kamikaze.*
  Baltimore: American Literary Press.
Jansen, Marius B. (2000). *The Making of Modern Japan.* Cambridge:
  Belknap Press/Harvard.

Kuwahara, Yasuo & Gordon T. Allred (2007). *Kamikaze: A Japanese pilot's Own Spectacular Story of the Famous Suicide Squadrons.* Clearfield, UT: American Legacy Media.

Mikesh, Robert C. (1993). *Japanese Aircraft Code Names & Designations.* Atglen, PA: Schiffer Military/Aviation History.

Mikesh, Robert C. (1994). *Zero: Combat & Development History of Japan's Legendary Mitsubishi A6M Zero Fighter.* Osceola, WI: Motorbooks International.

Ohnuki-Tierney, Emiko (2002). *Kamikaze, Cherry Blossoms, and Nationalisms: The Militarization of Aesthetics in Japanese History.* Chicago: The University of Chicago Press.

Ohnuki-Tierney, Emiko (2006). *Kamikaze Diaries: Reflections of Japanese Student Soldiers.* Chicago: The University of Chicago Press.

Peter, Carolyn (2006). *A Letter from Japan: The Photographs of John Swope.* Los Angeles: The UCLA Grunwald Center for the Graphic Arts and the Armand Hammer Museum of Art and Cultural Center.

Reichhold, Jane (2008). *Basho: The Complete Haiku.* Tokyo: Kodansha International.

Saito, Takafumi & William R. Nelson (2006). *102 Haiku in Translation: The Heart of Basho, Buson and Issa.* North Charleston: BookSurge.

Senoh, Kappa (2002). *A Boy Called H: A Childhood in Wartime Japan.* Tokyo: Kodansha International.

Sheftall, M.G. (2005). *Blossoms in the Wind: Human Legacies of the Kamikaze.* New York: New American Library.

Spector, Ronald H. (1955). *Eagle Against the Sun: The American War With Japan.* New York: The Free Press.

Skulski, Janusz (2004). *The Battleship Yamato: Anatomy of the Ship.* Annapolis: The Naval Institute Press.

Terasaki, Gwen (1954). *Bridge to the Sun.* Chapel Hill: The University of North Carolina Press.

Ueda, Makoto (1992). *Basho and his Interpreters: Selected Hokku with Commentary.* Stanford: Stanford University Press.

Warner, Dennis & Peggy Warner, with Seno, Sadao (1982). *The Sacred Warriors: Japan's Suicide Legions.* New York: Van Nostrand Reinhold.

Wild Bird Society of Japan & Shinji Takano (1982). *A Field Guide to the Birds of Japan.* Tokyo: Kodansha International.

Wright, Harold (1979). *Ten Thousand Leaves. Love Poems from the* Manyoshu. *Translated from the Japanese by Harold Wright.* Woodstock, NY: The Overlook Press.

Yamashita, Samuel Hideo (2005). *Leaves from an Autumn of Emergencies: Selections from the Wartime Diaries of Ordinary Japanese.* Honolulu: The University of Hawai'i Press.

Yoshikawa, Eiji (Charles S. Terry, trans; Edwin O. Reischauer, forward) (1981). *Musashi.* Tokyo: Kodansha International. (Original work published 1935–1939).

Yoshimura, Akira (Vincent Murphy, trans.) (1999). *Battleship Musashi: The Making and Sinking of the World's Biggest Battleship.* Tokyo: Kodansha International.

Acknowledgements

WHEN I was a graduate student who had never known anything but Philadelphia, Professor Shigeo Imamura and his wife, Isako, opened the world for me. They have been an important part of my life ever since then. *A Thousand Stitches* started with Isako and her determination that her husband's memoir have the effect he intended—to serve as a testament of peace.

Almost thirty years after I first met Isako, I was part of a group that scattered her husband's ashes in San Francisco Bay on an overcast summer morning. After the ceremony and a celebratory lunch, we gathered in a hotel in Japantown. Isako showed us pictures from her life with her husband and from his time as an aviator and a member of the Special Attack Force—the *kamikaze* corps—of the Imperial Japanese Navy. Isako also showed us a manuscript Shig had written in his last years, and asked me and Johnnie Hafernik and Stephanie Vandrick to help get her husband's memoir published. Thus, what we quickly came to call the "Shig Project" was born.

Ten years later, the Shig Project is a success. Professor Imamura's memoir has been published in English (*Shig: The True Story of an American Kamikaze*, Baltimore: American Literary Press). The first edition in 2001 was followed by another in 2009. Thanks to the passion and dedication of Ken Oshima, a translation of the memoir was published in Japan in 2003 (Tokyo: Soshisha). Professor Imamura's book and his work were honored at a special event at the University of San Francisco in November 2001. Many of Shig's former colleagues and friends reminisced, and Professor Uldis Kruze set the memoir in its historical context. The book and Professor Imamura's life are featured on a website that displays the amazing photographs used to illustrate the memoir. I recommend the website to those interested in more background: www.shigproject.com. Finally, thanks to Mrs. Imamura's generosity, endowed fellowships at the University of San Francisco and Michigan State University honor her husband's life's work as a cross-cultural educator. The fellowships support graduate students affiliated with USF's Center for the Pacific Rim and MSU's English Language Center, and give others interested in Shig's life and work one more way to honor him and continue his life's work.

For those of us who worked on the memoir, the best, and most wonderfully astonishing aspect of the Shig Project has been the places it has led us and the people we have encountered. All of our experiences have been positive. Our horizons have expanded; we have learned so much; we have met scores of kind and interesting people, far many more than those mentioned here, and each of them has been supportive and helpful. My thanks to all of them.

One day not too long after the event in San Francisco, Isako told me about how one of her friends had suggested that the story—Shig's and hers—needed another version, one that included the romance her typically-Japanese-style-reticent husband had omitted. I agreed and was honored when Isako agreed that I could try my hand at turning the memoir into a novel—just before I was overwhelmed with *what have I gotten myself into?* But, like all of the journeys the Shig Project has taken me on, this too has been a joy.

I have many, many to thank. Some are others of Shig's protégés: Johnnie Johnson Hafernik, Charles J. Quinn, Michael Raleigh, and Stephanie Vandrick. Shig and Isako made deep impressions on all of them, and they have carried Professor Imamura lesson's forward through distinguished academic and publishing careers of their own. Special thanks to Charlie Quinn for his assistance with literary Japanese and translations. The assistance all these old friends offered has made me grateful, all over again, for the bonds we formed many years ago as graduate students. Others who have helped never met Professor Imamura, but were touched by his story and the message he was so passionate to deliver. They provided invaluable assistance in the earlier stages of the Shig Project and have given me generous support as I worked to turn the story into a novel. They all have my deepest gratitude and affection: Eiji Kanno, Fumiko Kanno, Etsuko Kawasaki, Mamoru Kabori, and Ryoichi Miura.

The love, patience, and encouragement of Johnnie Johnson Hafernik, Mary O'Keefe, and Michael W. Dolan have enriched my life and supported and sustained me as I've worked on this latest version of Shig and Isako's story. Stacey Bredhoff, Janice Fitzgerald, Nina Johns, Marianne Klugheit, Monica Petersson, and Polly Rich have provided the same support I have been privileged to have for decades. My thanks too to Katherine Andrus, Anders Bengtsson, Charles F. Donley, John Hafernik, Don Hainbach, Michael Feldman, Colin Flynn, Carlos Grau-Tanner, Leslie Lugo, Mark MacKeigan, Nancy Malan, Mike Muller, Carl Nelson, Marilena Perrella, Bruce Rabinovitz, Amy Sloan, Joanne Szafran, Antoinette Tatta, and Carlos Tornero. Special thanks to Sen Huang and to Robert E. Bristow and all of his capable, caring colleagues.

Finally, my thanks to other members of the Washington, D.C. area writing community and other friends who, along with Isako, generously read drafts and offered constructive criticisms along with their support: Kathy Anderson, Alana Black, Frances Holmes, Mark Klugheit, Nandini Lal, Ann McLaughlin, Junko Mukoyama, Ilse Munro, Bernadette Pedagno, Judith Penski, Cathleen Peterson, Lynn Purple, Dan Ryan, David Schmidt, Briana Spencer, Madeline Tedesco, Mark Toner, Natasha Tynes, and James Yagley. All errors are mine.